To Catch a Killer

Emma Kavanagh was born in Wales in 1978 and currently lives in South Wales with her husband and two young sons. She trained as a psychologist and, after leaving university, started her own business as a psychology consultant, specialising in human performance in extreme situations. For seven years she provided training and consultation for police forces and NATO and military personnel throughout the UK and Europe.

For more information, tweet Emma @EmmaLK

To Catch a Killer

Emma Kavanagh

ORION

First published in Great Britain 2019 by Orion Books,
an imprint of The Orion Publishing Group Ltd
Carmelite House, 50 Victoria Embankment
London EC4Y 0DZ

An Hachette UK Company

1 3 5 7 9 10 8 6 4 2

A CIP catalogue record for this book is
available from the British Library.

ISBN 978 1 4091 7498 1

Typeset by Deltatype Ltd, Birkenhead, Merseyside

Printed in Great Britain by Clays Ltd, Elcograf S.p.A.

www.orionbooks.co.uk

For Camilla

Prologue

When I think about that day, when I think about her, it is her hands that I remember the most. Long, patrician fingers, the nails shaped into a smooth arc, filed with a care that, even to this day, baffles me. The muted pink of them so perfectly applied, the blood that had worked its way into the creases of her fingers, ghoulish and macabre besides the effortless glamour. I remember the way her fingers clutched mine, those perfect nails raking at my palm as if I represented the final rung on a falling ladder, and that by holding on to me she could hold on to a rapidly disappearing life. Perhaps that was true. Perhaps that was precisely what I was to her.

I think about that a lot, you know. About what else I could have done.

Had I realised then what I was dealing with, had I understood just how it would go, could things have been different?

There was so much blood. Her throat had been sliced open, the wound a sick mimicry of a smile. The blood spilled out of her in a relentless cascade. And that was without the rest of it, without the battery of puncture wounds that had pierced her torso, and her arms.

I

It had begun like any other day. But then, don't they all? The moment before your world changes is just a moment like any other, only becoming notable in the aftermath. It was cold, but the kind of skittish cold that April brings, with the faintest suggestion of warmth lurking just over the horizon. The sun still sat low as if it were considering beating a hasty retreat, not fully committed to the day ahead yet. I knew the feeling well. I hadn't been sleeping. Or, rather, I had, but in bursts and starts so that when the time came to wake it would always feel as if I hadn't slept at all.

I picked up my pace, my trainers padding against the tarmac. The wind blew, a huff of cigarette smoke sweeping into my face, causing my eyes to prick, my throat to contract; and my gaze found the smoker, a young man, early twenties maybe, narrow arms protruding from beneath a thin T-shirt, leaning against the front wall of a youth hostel. Our eyes met, his gaze roaming approvingly across me. To be fair, he was on my good side. I winked at him, a show of bravado, glorying in his ignorance of what was hidden.

This isn't important. Or, rather, it is, because it explains everything. Rampant insomnia and a resolutely hurried step, pushed faster by unknowing stares. That was it, that was why I was there within ninety seconds of the call coming in. Why it was me and not somebody else. Why we sit here today.

I had set out to work early, reframing my insomnia as enthusiasm for life and the day ahead; had decided against the Northern line, telling myself that the walk

2

would do me more good, even with the chill in the air, that the still empty streets would revive me so that once I got to the police station I would have the energy to spend yet one more day being Detective Sergeant Alice Parr. London in the mornings can do that, you know, the potency of it.

The silence before the storm.

Only it turned out that that silence was too loud. The sound of my feet, their beat upon the pavement, the abiding groan of traffic, edging in on me, swamping me. And so I turned my airwave radio on so that I could feel the weight of it, hear the thrum of life through it, DS Parr, reporting for duty.

I remember the moment the call came over the radio – stabbing reported in Brunswick Square Gardens, just off Hunter Street. It took me a moment to translate the words into a reality, to orient myself. Woburn Place. Two minutes away. I started to run.

I remember taking a hard left, my jacket flapping uselessly, the wind whipping at my face, and – I blush to remember this now – feeling that surge of adrenaline, it bubbling up in me so that a distant and deeply unprofessional part of me wanted to laugh.

I didn't. I've been doing this long enough.

I rounded the corner onto Brunswick Square, seeing up ahead an old woman. She appeared to be dancing. Of course, that made little sense, but my first awareness of her was of a dark figure pirouetting, silhouetted against the wrought-iron fence of the park, a golden retriever on a lead being co-opted as a reluctant partner.

Then she saw me, and the pirouetting stopped and she began to wave. Not like a 'Hi, how are you?' wave, but instead a 'Help me, I'm drowning!' one.

'You police?' She dropped the lead, gripping my hands, the dog exhaling a tremendous sigh and settling back onto its haunches, apparently just grateful that the motion had stopped.

'Yes. Where ...'

'In the fields. Through there. The ambulance man is trying to save her. Oh, but there's so much blood ...'

I pulled my hands away, taking off in the direction of the treeline. 'Stay there,' I yelled back over my shoulder. 'I'll be back.'

I pressed the radio. 'DS Alice Parr on scene at Brunswick Square Gardens. Paramedic on scene. Going to need uniform to establish a cordon.'

There must have been a reply, but I don't remember what it was.

I remember the tree roots, remember darting and weaving through them, willing myself not to trip. I remember the puddled shadows, the sudden sense that this was twilight rather than dawn. I remember my heartbeat climbing, my mind focusing so that all of the extraneous crap was forgotten. Then, just beneath the shadow of a spreading tree, a narrow, low-heeled pump, its pale blue leather spattered with dark blood. And just beyond that another.

Then stockinged feet. A spreading pool of blood. A paramedic working feverishly.

I thought that she was dead. Whether it was the

4

blood, or whether it was the simple fact that I was there and, frankly, by the time that I get there most of my victims are dead. Sometimes I wonder, what would have happened if that was true? If I had arrived to find Jane Doe, deceased, instead of Jane Doe, fighting for her life, would the case have meant less to me? Would I have worked as hard, gone so far? Would I be here today?

I'd like to tell you it wouldn't have made a difference, but I have an uncomfortable suspicion that I would be lying.

The paramedic turned to look at me, a quick scan, enough to pick out the 'police' that oozed through the pores of me. 'Help me,' he said, shortly.

It was then that I realised that her throat had been slashed. That her torso, her midriff, had been stabbed, again and again. I processed the movement of her, the bucking, the twisting, the way her eyes rolled back in her head, wild with terror. Those perfect fingers, clawing at the paramedic's hands, at the compress he attempted to hold over the wound at her throat. The foaming flecks of red at the corner of her mouth as she fought to catch a breath.

Oh my god.

I dropped to my knees beside her head, pulled her hands into mine, to stop her struggling, so that the paramedic could try and save her life. 'It'll be okay. You're going to be okay.' Her gaze snapping to me, fingers raking at the palm of my hand as she clung to me. Another scrape across my skin. Diamond rings. She's married. Her mouth opening, a rush of air. 'I'm Alice,' I said, my voice absurdly calm. 'What's your name?'

Nothing but air and bubbles and blood.

'She can't speak,' muttered the paramedic. 'Bastard has nearly taken her head off her shoulders. Where the hell is that ambulance?'

I freed one hand, toggling the radio. 'Victim's throat has been cut. We need the ambulance here now.'

'Acknowledged. Ambulance is two minutes out.'

Then she twisted again, knocking the compress from her throat, the blood spurting out, the warmth of it hitting my jacket, the tumbledown blonde hair that splayed out beneath her.

'Shit. Hold her.'

I grabbed her hands again, cursing myself. 'Hey, hey, come on. Work with us now. It's okay. The ambulance is on its way, and this nice man ...'

'Christian,' he muttered. 'She needs to lay still. We have to stem the blood flow.'

'Right, yes, this is Christian, and we're both going to take care of you. Now, I need you to stay as still as you can, okay?'

She quieted, her gaze locked on mine, eyes wide as if she could somehow telegraph her thoughts to me. I stared at her, at eyes the colour of moss, flecks of hazelnut that spiralled out from the sinkhole pupils. Something twisted in my gut. 'You're going to be okay,' I said. I was aware, even at the time, that the words came out as a prayer.

The sound of footsteps running across the neat

6

trimmed grass to our backs, and I twisted, praying for an ambulance crew. Instead, our newest DC, looking little more than a child in a suit.

'Harry!' I flung the word out. 'Get a cordon set up.'

The fresh-from-the-packet detective hovered for a moment, or an hour, staring at me and at her and at the blood.

'Harry! Now!'

Then a second beat of footsteps, a flash of purple, a fleck of dark hair. DC Poppy Stone pulled up short, surveying the scene, her gaze locking on mine, a grimace. This is bad.

'Harry, push the crowd back,' Poppy barked, all East End and proud of it.

At the time, I thought that 'crowd' was a rather hyperbolic way of describing an old Jamaican woman and her dog. Yet when I twisted and looked beyond them, through the open park gates, I could just make out that a throng of people had gathered, all watching unashamedly, more than you would think possible for the early hour.

Poppy drew closer, carefully selecting her path about the scene so as not to disturb evidence. Leaned in, muttered, 'Ambulance is pulling in.'

The paramedic twisted in position, squinting back towards the road, as if the promise of backup was more than he could hope for, would not believe it until he saw it with his own eyes. Then, 'Thank god.'

Two paramedics hurried into view.

'We need the gurney, guys!' called Christian. 'I'm

sorry, Alice, but would you mind giving us some room?'

'Yes, of course, I ...'

The victim – no, the woman – had begun to cling harder to me, her manicured nails threatening to puncture the dry skin on my palm. I looked down at her, probably to say something inane and resolutely useless, but her gaze had locked on mine, her mouth moving, blood bubbling up from beneath the compress at her throat as her muscles strained with effort.

'No,' I said, 'it's okay. You need to lie still.'

But her mouth was still moving and her fingers had begun to claw at my wrist, pulling me closer. I glanced over my shoulder, could see the paramedics moving along the path at a run, the backboard between them. Leaned into her quickly so that my cheek brushed hers. Now, intermingled with the metallic tang of blood, I could smell her perfume, could pick out jasmine. The smell would cling to me for days after, and still when I smell it I think of her.

She exhaled, a rush of warmth passing by my good cheek. Was there a shape to it, a word buried in the breath? Maybe I wanted so badly for her to speak that I heard meaning in what was only air.

'I'm sorry,' said the incoming female paramedic. 'We really need to do this. Can you give us some room?'

So, of course, I moved, right? Because I was in the way and because they were trying to save her life and because I wasn't insane.

Only her fingers were still wrapped tight around my wrist and there were tears now working their way down her cheeks, slipping into the blood that slid from the gaping wound at her neck. So I ducked in, one last time, her exhalation stroking my cheek. And from in amongst it I could discern a word.

Sometimes it seems that there are moments, segments of life, upon which everything hangs itself, altering beyond recognition all that comes after. And that, there, the pressure on my cheek, the feel of her breath grazing my skin, when I look back on it, when I think to where it all began, it is that moment that I think of.

Before I could think, I was being physically moved aside, her hands sliding from mine, her eyes closing, the tears rolling fast, as if she had finally figured out what the rest of us already knew. Her time was almost up.

I stepped back, cradling my palms, lifted upwards, feeling them strangely empty.

'You okay?' murmured Poppy. 'You look pale.' She scanned me, up and down, at the blood that had soaked through my jacket, my trousers, my hands stained with the fingermarks of Jane Doe. 'Let me amend that. Dude, you look like shit.'

I nodded, not fully trusting myself to speak. I see them when they're dead. When this bit is over. I watched the woman being loaded onto the gurney. Death is kinder than this.

'You get a name?' Poppy asked.

I shook my head. 'No,' I murmured. 'Not yet.' My mind was racing ahead of me – to the search of her belongings, the credit card or driver's licence that would inevitably hide within them. 'But we will.'

I had no idea then just how little I knew.

Poppy nodded slowly. 'Jane Doe, then.'

A breath of wind brushed by me, chilling my bloody damp clothes, and I shivered, forcing myself to look away from the paramedics, the woman all but lost between them. Looked back to her shoes, closer to the trees, the spray of blood across them. That was the attack site. That was where Jane Doe's world spun entirely beyond her control, where the attack pushed her backwards, flinging body from shoes, driving her down, through the trees, onto the green beyond.

I looked back at the ground, the grass stained where she had lain, tried to remember how it had looked. What shape had her body been in? Had she fallen there in the course of the attack? Had she crawled? Had the paramedic moved her when he began his treatment?

'Why here?' I said to Poppy, keeping my voice low. 'It's close to the road. Anyone could be walking by. There's barely any cover.'

Poppy pursed her lips. 'Maybe it was spontaneous. Saw her walking, took the opportunity.'

She was going to continue, there was more she had to say, but a flurry of movement stilled her. What had been an orderly if hurried loading of our Jane Doe onto the trolley had become a mass of activity, of chest compressions and breaths, of voices raised to an urgent pitch. I moved closer, looked to the woman's hands, where they hung limp at her side.

'Come on,' I muttered, uselessly.

The two new paramedics, the nameless ones, were

with her, more hands than seemed possible between them. A spurt of blood. A shout, 'Hold it!' A pause that seemed to stretch into forever. Then, from one or the other of them, 'Okay, we've got her, let's go.'

I let out a breath I hadn't known I was holding, felt my hands begin to shake. Only that couldn't be true, could it? Because I'm a professional and this is what I do.

Christian, the blood that coated me coating him too, broke away from the pack, jogged towards me with a long-limbed lope. 'They're taking her in.' His gaze caught mine, grim. 'It's bad.'

'I'll send someone with them,' I said. 'To get a statement.'

He paused, glanced back towards the all but lifeless body of Jane Doe, to the other paramedics with their steady, determined rote of activity, then back at me, his look sympathetic now. 'You can try,' he said, softly. 'You never know, eh?'

I turned to watch him as he jogged back towards her, the sunlight making his blood-drenched clothes shimmer, and I remembered the weight of her face against mine, the movement of her lips and that single murmured word.

Wolf.

Part One

Part One

Chapter 1

The doors of the ambulance hung wide open, waiting. Not for us. For Jane Doe. If you looked at her and only her, you would think that the world had stopped, was holding its breath for her as she clung on to the last embers of life. She – whoever she was – had closed her eyes. Although that suggested some agency, as if it was a choice she had made, rather than the forceful emptiness of a system beginning its slow shutdown. I watched her, searching for a movement of the chest in amongst the jostling of the gurney, of the paramedics as they leaned into her, words short and expeditious. Was that it? Was that a breath, air struggling its way into her collapsing lungs? Or was it merely an illusion, my brain translating stillness into life. I thought of the word she had whispered. Wolf.

The paramedics slowed, stopped, a collective deep breath, then hoisted the gurney and the woman upon it into the waiting ambulance. A burst of sound broke the silence, an out-of-place laugh, and I swung my gaze upwards, irritation bubbling. The blocky building, the international halls of residence, had been sleeping before. But the commotion must have woken them, window after window now stuffed with faces. A girl with vio-let-streaked hair hung from a third-floor window, her back to us, a mobile phone held up high as she tilted her head for just the right effect for the death selfie.

I made a low noise in the back of my throat.

'Shall I go with her?' I hadn't noticed Harry at my elbow, and the suddenness of his voice sent my heart racing. 'In the ambulance?'

I glanced back up at the gathered students, then turned to him, forcing myself into motion. 'Sure.' I thought of what Christian said, 'I don't think you're going to get much from her at this point,' I allowed, 'but just in case. Make sure they package up the clothing properly, yeah?'

'Sure thing, Sarge.'

I watched him march towards the ambulance, swing-ing his way in as one door closed and vanishing into the tumult beyond. A quick swirl of sirens and then the vehicle shifted, easing its way through the police cordon, the waiting crowd beyond. In the distance, I could just make out the roof of a news van, its satellite dish alien in the quiet street. A cameraman had elbowed his way through to the cordon, black eye of the camera's lens trained, first on the ambulance, and then, once it departed with a blast of siren, he turned, twisting so that the camera lens rested on the open park gates, and on me.

I turned my back on it all, walking into the muted greenness, to where Poppy stood scowling beside the park map.

'What a way to start the day, eh?' Poppy shook her head. Thirty-five years old and yet still looking closer to seventeen, Poppy Stone came up to my shoulder, a teenage-boy frame, elfin features, her dark hair shaped into a pixie cut – the entire thing designed apparently to make her look smaller, safer, than she really was. I've known Poppy forever, or, if not forever, since first joining the Met, which is tantamount to the same thing. Her four-year-old son, Charlie, is my godson. It builds a special kind of closeness, moving from civilian life into police life. They warn you that the police force can be all-encompassing, especially at the beginning, exposing you to a side of life that is hidden from the rest of the world. You can drown in it, if you're not careful. Poppy and I had been keeping each other afloat for ten years now.

'Indeed.' I looked beyond her to the stained grass beneath the old plane tree, the evidence markers standing proud in amongst it. Jane Doe's blood had soaked its way through my shirt, the damp sending shivers of cold through to my skin, and I suppressed a shudder, looking up to the tree beneath which she had fallen, branches of it rustling with the low breeze that swept across the square of the park. It should have been midnight. The amount of life that had forced itself into this small space of time felt suffocating. I turned on my heel, pivoting back towards the street. The girl with the violet hair was hanging from her window now, chattering animatedly with a muscle-bound boy in the room next door. I suppressed the urge to shout at them.

'We're already up on Facebook, aren't we?' I asked, quietly.

Poppy snorted. 'Welcome to the world, baby girl.'

'Shit.' I moved to push my hair back, fingers brushing together, the sudden realisation that they are sticky with blood still. I blew out a breath. 'Okay, so ... this is central London. So there's got to be ...' I inched closer to the road, scanning the building opposite, my face prickling with the sense of being stared at. Then I found it, a neat white bauble tucked right at the building's edge. 'There. CCTV.'

Poppy squinted up. 'Looks like that should take in the park gates.' Her gaze shifted, past the squawking onlookers. 'Another one on the other corner. Hopefully that'll give us some nice coverage.'

I turned in a circle, silent for a moment. 'Well, I'll give him one thing. He really did pick a shitty place to attempt to pull off a murder. The cameras, the windows, broad daylight. He likely would have had more luck in Paddington Station. At least the witnesses would have been in a hurry to make their trains.' I turned to look the way the ambulance had left. 'Why? Why the hell would you go after someone here? This time of day?'

The violet-haired girl was laughing again. I wondered briefly if I could arrest her for something. Breach of the peace. Being obnoxious at the scene of a crime.

'Well,' said Poppy, 'look, at the risk of being cold ...'

'You? Stop it.'

She snorted. 'At the risk of being cold ... even if she does die, this one shouldn't take too long to sort through.'

I glanced back at her. 'You really are all soft and fuzzy, aren't you?'

She shivered. 'Tried soft and fuzzy once. Didn't like it.'

The sun had clambered up, appeared to have given way to the inevitable, committing itself fully to the day to come. I turned my face into the breeze, feeling it scour against the raw skin of my scar and wishing I had coffee.

I squeezed Poppy's elbow in a silent goodbye and spun on my heels, stalking back towards the plane tree, pavement giving way to boggy grass. The scene of the murder remained as I had left it, with only the absence of the victim's body to mark the passage of time. Crime scenes are like paintings. You have to look at them, I mean really look, if you want to truly get into the mind of the creator.

A pool of blood shimmering in sunlight.

A single shoe, tipped upon its side.

It felt to me that I could hear her breathing, sharp, fearful, hear the little oh of surprise when the knife first went in, see her moss-green eyes widen. Did she know? She knew she was in trouble, clearly, would have understood that this day was not going at all how it had been planned. But did she know just how deep she was in? Did she feel the knife entering her, leaving, entering again? I found myself offering up a brief, hypocritical prayer that it all happened too fast, that her brain simply could not keep up with the blow that followed blow.

I inched forward, along the trail of blood, to the

abandoned shoe. Could see her stumbling backwards, her blonde hair flying out, her arms reaching, as if magically that would be enough to fend off the attacks, one narrow pump, pale blue, falling from her stockinged feet.

The ground was uneven there, the softened earth pushed up into two long trenches that worked their way further from the road.

She had kept struggling. She had kept trying to get away, levering herself on hands and elbows, not wanting to turn away from her attacker, wanting to make him face her. If you're going to kill me, you're going to have to look at me whilst you do it. One metre. Two. Then the final blow. Was that the slice across her throat? I stooped down beside the blood pool, keeping my distance, careful where I put my feet. Surrounding it, there in amongst the dried mud, if you looked really closely you could just about make out blood spatter. A spray of crimson.

'You okay, Al?'

I started, the DI's voice breaking into my reverie. 'God, Guv!' I stood, feeling a creak in my knees. 'You should be a ninja.'

He grinned, hands on his hips. He was always smiling, DI Noah Solway. Never seemed to find him when he wasn't happy. I asked him about that once, some ha-ha conversation, like 'so what's the secret to happiness, then'. And he'd gotten quiet and serious and soft and said find someone you love to spend your life with, have a bunch of kids – he had three, a fourth on the way – and do what makes you feel whole. It probably won't surprise you to learn that Noah was known as the Dalai Lama.

'CSIs are incoming.' He motioned back towards the gate, a figure ghostly in white marching towards us. 'Any ID on the victim?'

'No. Not yet. Harry's gone with her to the hospital, but …' It seemed that the words caught there. I cleared my throat. 'It's not looking great,' I finished.

'Robbery, you think?'

I shrugged. 'We haven't found a handbag. No wallet, phone, that we could see. It's possible that her attacker made off with those things. But she had some pretty serious wedding rings on. Seems like one hell of a missed opportunity.' I looked back to the flattened grass, the blood. 'Guv, she said something to me. Or, at least, I think she did. Before they took her, she said … I think she said "wolf".'

He frowned. 'Wolf? Like, as in a name?'

I shook my head. 'I don't know. Maybe.'

Noah pursed his lips, raising his airwave to them. 'I'll get someone looking into it.' He hesitated, looking back towards the crowd. 'What about witnesses? Anyone see the attack?'

'Old lady walking her dog. She was the one who called it in.' I glanced back towards the crowd. 'Actually, I should go see her, get a quick statement so she can get out of here.'

The DI hesitated, looking me up and down. 'You … ah … you need to get … um … cleaned up first?'

I looked down at myself, at the mud on my legs and the blood on my shirt and my hands. 'What? I came in like this. I'm calling this look urban chic.' I grinned. 'I'll go, Guv. Let me just touch base with the witness first, yeah?'

Noah nodded, doubtful. 'Just … maybe stand upwind, yeah?'

The street beyond the park had changed now. The ambulance gone, inconvenient victim removed from site, the whole scene had taken on a carnival atmosphere, of laughter and bubbling conversation. Someone, somewhere within the halls of residence, was cooking bacon, the heady smell of it winding its way through the lingering scent of blood. I studied the crowd. Are you here? Have you hung around, looking to see the effects of your knife work? A narrow young man, his face angry with the puckered sores of acne. A middle-aged man, solid build, scowling, his head shaking in perpetual motion. A woman, her hand over her mouth, eyes wide with fear, or with faux fear. Hard to tell. Is it you? Or you? Or you? Three, four, five mobile phones, all held up, all watching me. Their owners' faces locked in grim determination, like they were the journalists of old and this was their Watergate.

I could pick out the actual journalists by their expressions, livid with determination; counted two, three, one cameraman, a photographer skirting around the edges, trying to find himself the best angle.

As I moved towards the cordon, a hand thrust itself out from within the melee, a small blonde woman gripping a microphone tight in her fist. 'Detective! Who is the victim?'

I brushed the microphone aside, flung over my shoulder at her, 'We're still in the process of identifying her.'

In the process. A much nicer way of saying 'Not a bloody clue.'

The Jamaican woman had moved herself to beneath the shade of the building, was walking in a small, tight circle, towards the pavement's edge, a sharp right at the kerb, around again. The golden retriever sat, his back pressed up against the wall, and watched her with liquid eyes. Every so often he would sigh.

'Excuse me, you're the lady who called 999, yes?'

The woman stopped mid-circuit, her grip on the lead tightening, and turned to study me with a frown. 'You that police lady who was here first?' She marched right up to me, stood so that her toes pressed up against mine, smelling of burnt caramel, the early morning sunshine shining off her skin, shimmying with the shifting of her weight, left foot to right and then back again. 'I mean, awful. Terrible. To think that you can go out your own front door and some monster ... well, it just don't bear thinking about.' She shook her head heavily, her gaze finally resting on me, and then the moment, the inevitable motion of her eyes coming to rest on the uneven puckered scarring that laced the left side of my face, my lacklustre hair not enough to hide it. Her mouth opened, the words approaching with the inevitability of a steam train on tracks. 'Oh, love, what happened to you? My goodness ...'

23

There was never a satisfactory answer, that much I had already learned, there were no words I could offer which would seem adequate to explain my appearance. The golden retriever sank lower, his weighty stomach grazing against the roughened ground, his gaze forlorn. He glanced up at me – she's always like this, you get used to her.

'An accident,' I said. 'And it just goes to show, you should never play with matches.' I gave a quick laugh, painful in its falsity. Shit. I really did need to figure out a better line.

She reached out a narrow hand, gripping tight to my arm. 'I'm gonna remember you in my prayers, you hear?'

I shook her hand off, a reflex as if her touch had stung my skin. 'So,' I said, my voice impressively even, 'I'm sorry, it's Mrs ...'

'Clarke. Edwina Clarke. Do you know who she is? That lady as got stabbed? Poor angel. I want to pray for her too.'

'I ... no, not yet. We're still working on it. So, can you tell me what you saw, Mrs Clarke?'

She shrugged, the red wool coat shifting in the breeze. 'I was walking Billy. He's gettin' on now, but we have to keep ourselves going, don't we, Bill? No point sitting about waiting for death.'

Billy shifted his wide heft from side to side and farted loudly. He had the good grace to look embarrassed.

'I was goin' to Brunswick Square Gardens. We always do. And I saw something laying there, and I thought,

24

well, don't you know, I didn't know what it was, but then, it moved and … I tell you, I thought as I was goin' to drop down dead right there. This man, he was laying on top of this girl, and I thought, well,' she patted my arm again, eyes meaningfully wide, 'you can imagine what it was I thought. And then he just springs up like he's been electrocuted and dashes off. And then … then I saw. All that blood. The poor girl.'

My heart had begun to beat faster. Although, in fairness, that might have been from the pungent scent of Billy's releases, carried towards me on the breeze. 'Which way? When he ran, which way did he go?'

The woman stopped for a moment, turned again in a tight circle, frowning heavily, then gestured towards the park. 'That way. Up towards that there school of whatsit … pharmceuticals.'

'Pharmacy.'

'That's the one. I saw him dash right up there. Although I lost sight of him pretty quick.'

North. I made a note. 'What did he look like?'

'Oh, of course, I didn' see him close, no, but big fella.' She held her hands out about her disappearing waist. 'You know, belly on him. He had one of them silly hats on that the lads wear, like, you know, a wool one …'

'A beanie?'

'I don' know, love, but if you say so, I'm not one to argue. And his hair, long it was. You could see it sticking from under his hat.' She shook her head. 'I should have done somethin'. I should have set Billy on him.'

Billy glanced mournfully up at her, his expression unconvinced.

I looked from Billy to Mrs Clarke, struggling to dispel the unlikely image. 'Okay, um, the victim,' I said, 'did you speak to her? Did she say anything to you?'

'No, love,' said the woman triumphantly, resting her thick-fingered hand on my forearm 'I stayed well clear. I watch *CSI*. I know all about them DNA and such, and all that contamination of evidence. No, Billy and I, once we saw what was goin' on here, we kept well back. To preserve the scene,' she added, helpfully. 'I called 999 and talked to a woman – very rude she was, kept telling me to calm down. Calm down! Like there wasn't a dead body lying not ten feet from me. Calm down ... Course, then she turned out not to be dead ...' She shook her head. 'Poor angel.' She looked at me sadly so that it was not clear whether the angel in question was the victim or, rather, me.

'You know, the worst thing ...' she lowered her voice, stepping closer into me again, Billy shifting out of the way with a long-suffering grunt '... somewhere out there, there's a mother, going about her business, no idea that her daughter is lying dead in a park. Awful. Just awful.'

I found myself recoiling, whether from the over-whelming scent of Billy, or from the sudden intimacy that had been forced upon me. Nodding in what I hoped appeared to be a professional way. Because it was the eternal truth, that death was never simply death. It had many fingers, strands that wound its way out from

26

the victim, wrapping themselves around countless other lives. And those lives, where were they? A husband at work? Children in a crèche? All moving through a shattered world protected by their blissful ignorance. In minutes, or in hours, someone – quite possibly me – would come and blow that ignorance apart.

I thanked her, told her that someone would be in touch and then turned, all the while feeling her lingering gaze that could not resist settling on my scar.

She had interrupted him. It seemed that Edwina Clarke, wittingly or not, had saved Jane Doe's life. However brief that salvation should prove to be. I ducked in through the wrought-iron gates and thought of the gaping wound that had torn her throat in two, of the puncture holes, one after another after another, that had covered her torso, and a thought settled over me. That he, whoever he was, had meant to kill her, that he had failed, and that was in large part thanks to Edwina Clarke and the flatulent Billy.

'Glad to see I'm in fashion.'

The words seemed to come from a long way away, and I stared at Christian, the paramedic, his uniform still slick with the same blood that covered me, trying to fit together the movement of his lips with the distant sound of speech.

'Oh, yeah.' I looked down at what remained of my clothing. 'Well, you have to be willing to try something new, I always say. And you've really nailed the smell,' I offered, 'which, personally, I think is the most important bit.'

Christian stood with Poppy, their backs towards the riotous colours of the flower bed. 'You know,' he said, softly, 'some days I wonder what the hell I'm doing bringing kids up in London. My wife's family, they're from Wales. Sometimes I think, yeah, that's what we should do. Pack this all in and head down there. You don't get this in Wales.'

I nodded, privately thinking that you did indeed get attempted murders in Wales.

'How old are your kids?' asked Poppy in the awkward manner of one who hates small talk, her pen poised above her open notepad.

'Four and coming up on two.' He wasn't looking at us, his gaze focused beyond, on the unspooling crime scene tape, the puddle of blood. He was attractive, in a slender, clean-cut kind of way, dark hair cropped close to his scalp. 'Days like this ... I don't know, it really makes you think, you know? About the kind of life you want to give them?'

'Amen to that,' muttered Poppy. 'So, sorry, you were saying, you were just finishing your shift?'

'Huh?' Christian pulled his attention back towards her, the slightest shake of his head. 'No, I'd already finished. I'm based out of Brent. I train around here, the martial arts centre on Tavistock Place. I'd parked up ...'

'Where?' I asked.

He glanced around him, orienting himself. 'Ah, up by the Blind Institute? I was just getting my stuff together and I heard the call come in over the radio. I realised I was close. So I grabbed my stuff, ran for it. I got to the gardens ...'

'Which way?' I interrupted. 'Which way did you come in?'

He pointed to the left of us, up towards the School of Pharmacy. 'From the top end. Came on down and could see the victim lying on the ground.' He shook his head. 'What a goddamn mess. She was conscious, as you saw, struggling. No sign of her attacker.'

'And you didn't see anyone on your way in? Witness has indicated he left from the north gate.'

He shook his head. 'Sorry, no.' He sighed, fixing me with a soft look. 'I just need to really warn you ... she's in a bad way. Injuries like that ...' His gaze dropped to the ground. 'I wouldn't get your hopes up.'

You can't afford to get too invested in these things. You can't let yourself go, let yourself wallow in the tragedy of it all. Because the job is tragedy, the job is pain, and if you let it in, if you allow yourself to feel it, then you will drown in it.

'Did you move her at all to treat her?' I asked, my voice iron-hard.

Christian shook his head. 'She was lying on her back. Her hands kept going to her throat, the way they were when you arrived. I don't think she fully understood what had happened to her. She stayed pretty much as I found her.' He folded his arms, plastic gloves crinkling with the movement. 'Honest to god, it doesn't pay to think too much about this shit. You'd never drag yourself out of bed in the morning.'

I wholeheartedly agreed.

He studied me. 'She's lucky you got here when you did.'

I started. 'I ... I didn't do anything, not really.'

'No,' he said, softly, 'but you were a comfort to her. And, at a time like this, that matters.'

I nodded, taking longer than I should to arrange my words. 'I'm going to check in with the DI and then see if I can source a nice hot shower,' I said, gesturing down at my clothing with a grimace.

The paramedic grinned. 'Yeah, I think this style has run its course.'

But I had already stopped paying attention, my feet beginning to move through the dew-wet grass, the flashes of rainbow-bright colours dizzying on the edge of my vision. The attacker, he had run north, up through Brunswick Square Gardens towards the hedge-hooded railings, the wrought-iron gate. He had run fast enough that he had been gone by the time Christian got there. I moved north, in my mind following his path, skirting around the blood, the CSI in his Tyvek suit, his gaze hooked on the blades of grass, on the remnants of Jane Doe left in between them.

If it was me, if I had just murdered someone in broad daylight and gotten interrupted, I would want to hug the treeline, minimise my chances of getting seen, give myself time to think, plan what came next.

Hard tarmac jarred against my soles, the shape of it giving way to soft rainfall-soaked soil. Clambering bushes overhung, creating puddles of shadow and chill.

And in amongst the divots and troughs, a shape, one you could easily overlook were you not searching for it. A partial footprint.

'Guv!' I bellowed.

I stooped down beside it. It was clean, the front portion of a shoe represented in earth, the vague suggestion of a tread pattern within it. It sat within a small cluster of bushes, hidden from the road. I turned on myself, focusing. Then something caught me ... it took me a moment to realise what I had seen, to find it again, but there, about a metre from the print, a patch of grass at odds with the rest of it.

'Is that blood?' Noah was breathing lightly, in spite of having run over. He folded himself down beside me, leaning into the shadows.

'Looks like it.'

I was vaguely aware of the radio beeping, of the DI's voice, calm and commanding, but I wasn't paying attention. Not really. He was here. After he stabbed her, after the interruption and the run, he was here. Why?

Had he slipped, falling so that the only thing that could save him was a blood-drenched hand flung forward onto the ground?

I stood, surveying my surroundings. The tennis courts through the diamond-link fence. The red-brick School of Pharmacy peering through the opposite park gate.

Then my name, dim and distant. I turned, trying to focus on it. The DI had moved now, had walked away from me, following the path, was leaning over, his long body folded at the waist like one of those old-fashioned dunking birds.

'What is it, Guv?'

'Bin,' he called, shortly. He looked up, not at me, but at the approaching CSI. 'Joe, you want to check this out for me?'

The suited Joe nodded briefly, spreading plastic sheeting out across the grass.

It happens this, sometimes across a career, when you see things play out before you as if they have already done them once before. Perhaps it is experience, a decade of policing painting a template for the way these things seem to inevitably go. The CSI leaned into the bin, the movement shaking free a breath of the sweet scent of rotted food. He hesitated, studying for a moment the darkness within. Then it was unfolding, just like it already had in my head, an empty crisp wrapper, a page from *The Times*.

The handbag of Jane Doe.

I released a breath, the spurting adrenaline sinking with the oncoming conclusion. Puzzle solved. Game over.

'Guv?' The CSI's voice came low, Scottish lilt containing a warning.

'What?'

He turned to face us, gloved hands holding up the handbag, pulling it open wide. 'It's empty.'

Chapter 2

'She loves you, yeah, yeah, yeah ...'

A young woman, wafer-thin, hair pulled back into a thousand tiny braids, sat on the bench tucked at the rear of the Piccadilly line platform, singing softly, as if to herself. I glanced sideways at her, wondering if she knew that I could hear her, if she was operating under the belief that her low voice was being tugged away, lost in the murmur of voices, the shuddering rumble of the incoming train. She looked back at me, grinned and began singing louder.

It had been three hours now. And so far our victim had no name. I sighed, tugging at the hem of the spare blouse I kept hung in my locker, and watched the backs of those who stood before me, these ordinary people going about their ordinary days.

I shifted my gaze, beaten back by the relentless cheerfulness of the singing woman, staring at the sign above her head. Next train, five minutes.

The platform was muggy, airless after the wide-open space of Brunswick Square, and yet even that in the end had become suffocating, with its queue of witnesses, one following another. I saw the victim crossing the road by the Brunswick Centre. I saw her walking past the park gate. I saw her. I saw her. It seemed that all of London had seen her, and yet no one knew who she was. What about him? Who? How was that possible? How could so many people have seen her walk by and yet not one of them looked at her attacker. The best we had managed was from a homeless guy, heady with the scent of alcohol and a fetid body odour – yeah, I saw someone walking behind her. A guy. Don't remember what he looked like though.

CCTV. That was the answer. The witness that would not be waylaid by the victim herself. And so I had scoured the halls of residence. Because they had CCTV, the answer to the question sitting right there. Oh, you want to speak to the custodian. No. I don't know his name. Nope. No idea how to get hold of him. I saw that woman though, the one that got stabbed?

The manager of the Brunswick Centre was easier to track down, although hardly more helpful. I'm on my way in from Chertsey, but the M3 is at a standstill. It's going to be a while.

I had sworn, vividly, had turned to Noah. 'This is absurd. Poppy and I will go out to the Westminster CCTV control room while we wait.'

And then, because life really can be a relentless bitch sometimes, a burst water main at High Holborn, spooling water out across the unsuspecting thoroughfare, traffic snarling to a halt, the world conspiring, chaos in cahoots. Fine. I'll take the sodding tube then.

Five minutes. How much further away will you have

gotten in five minutes? Has it happened for you yet? Has the flood of adrenaline begun to ease, reality settling over you in a stunning awareness of what it is you have done? Are you shaking? Are you frightened? Or is it something other? Are you breathing hard, thinking what it is you must do now, where it is you must run?

Poppy leaned over, peering into the darkness of the tunnel as if that way she could hurry the train on. 'You think she knew him?' she asked. 'The guy who stabbed her?'

I shook my head, one word rolling through it, a never-ending loop. Wolf. 'I don't know.' I pulled out my phone, opening my emails one more time and scrolling through the list – the London Wolf-Pack as I had begun to think of it. Who would have known there were so many of them? I studied the names, wondering if I held it in my hand, the answer to this. If it would be that simple, a whispered word, a killer hiding in amongst a pack of wolves, and there's an end to it.

'The guys are running the names down,' said Poppy, reading my mind. 'Let's hope they turn up something.'

The platform began to shudder, the wind to whistle. The singing woman pushed herself up to standing, tugged a cloth bag onto her narrow shoulder and turned, moving further down the thronged platform, deeper into the crowd, until she vanished from sight.

Had the victim understood how things would be for her? When she told herself the story of her demise in those midnight hours when sleep seems to have hidden itself behind a solid wall of dark fantasies, did it involve her loved ones besieged by an unerring sense of the wrongness in the world? Being tugged towards her by some invisible and yet inviolate thread? Or did she understand her own world well enough to know that she could disappear, could be fighting for her life, and still no one would have missed her?

But then, I thought, how many of us turn out to be who we thought ourselves to be?

The train emerged from the darkness of the tunnel, slowing to a shuddering halt, the crowd before me surging towards the open doors. I sighed, a dim awareness of Poppy at my right elbow, and stepped into the knot of people, all elbows and joints, the smell of sweat hanging heavy. Poppy tucked herself in beside me, ducking beneath an outstretched arm. A middle-aged man with a goatee, painfully manicured eyebrows, shifted, studying Poppy appraisingly.

'Where the hell are they?' I muttered. 'The family. Why haven't they been in touch? It's been all over the TV.'

It had gone out on the lunchtime news. The police need your help. And the phones had begun ringing soon after. I saw her. I saw her. Until in the end, it seemed that the entire world had seen her, could one way or another claim some kind of acquaintance with her, even if it was only a passing nod. But not them. Not the people who should have loved her the most.

The middle-aged man shifted his look towards me, eyes narrowing, the beginning of a smile, then the gaze tracking to my scar. He looked away.

36

Poppy shrugged. 'It's been, what, three hours? For a family, that's nothing. It's a morning at work. Likely they have no idea she's missing yet.'

Schrödinger's cat, the box yet unopened, puss both alive and dead.

'Besides,' she said, 'even if they have seen it, London's a big place. Likely they're thinking it couldn't possibly have anything to do with them.'

The man's attention had returned to Poppy, a dog studying a chew toy. She glanced up at him, a slight frown.

'You okay?' she asked, her head dipped to one side, faux coy.

'Yeah ...' A mad scramble of emotions, his face shifting to a smile.

'Good. Do me a favour and bugger off then.'

I turned away, hid a smile.

The journey took too long, useless minutes in which it seemed that time stretched and elongated, making my fingers twitch. And yet, in violation of all expectations, it did in fact end, stifling tube eventually giving way to windswept streets. And then to the Westminster CCTV control room. It appeared as a piece of modern art come to life – a study of twenty-first-century London, screen upon screen upon screen revealing dizzying snatches of city life.

The narrow woman at the controls looked up, offered an effortful smile. 'All right? I'm Steph ...' She held out a limp-wristed hand, clasping mine loosely before releasing it like it had burned. 'You're looking for Brunswick Square, yeah?' She shifted in her chair, moving a cursor between a galaxy of red dots. 'Grab a seat. This'll just take a second.'

I slid into a seat, my gaze lingering on the screens before me, the voyeurism of it all somehow strangely addictive. 'This is better than *EastEnders*.'

Steph gave a grimace that I decided to interpret as a smile.

I cleared my throat. 'Yeah, so, we're looking into an attempted murder. Took place this morning at 7.45 a.m. We have witnesses who say they saw our victim approaching via Hunter Street.'

.The woman pulled a face. 'Let me see ... Okay ...'

The screen changed, an empty street, a red-brick apartment building stretching towards the horizon. A burst of movement as a powder-white cat darted across the road, sending my heart rate spiking. Then, a figure moving onto the screen, walking towards us, a slender figure, a fur collar, soft grey coat.

Jane Doe.

'We've got her,' I muttered.

Poppy silently held out a fist to bump against mine, both our eyes locked on the screen as Jane Doe moved closer. She walked quickly, the glow of her standing proud, her handbag tucked tight beneath her arm, and I leaned in as she rounded the corner onto Brunswick Square, my gaze glued to the woman striding forward with no idea of what was to come.

Where did the attack come from? The houses, still

closed up tight? The stacked-up parked cars? The hovering complex of the Brunswick Centre?

Then came another movement from the top of the screen, and all doubt vanished. A dark figure entering the frame steps wide and fast.

'Wait. Freeze it there.' I leaned in, could feel the slightest of tremors in my fingers. 'It's him. It has to be him.'

He had frozen mid-charge, a thick frame, dull grey parka straining at the spare tyre at his middle, the collar of it pulled up high so that it all but met the tan baseball cap that concealed his face. I studied him.

'God, your gaze just ... it kind of slides off him, doesn't it?'

Was it a design? The muted colours, the nondescript clothing? Or was that simply him, the most average of average Joes.

'No wonder none of the witnesses noticed him,' muttered Poppy. 'I barely notice him and I'm staring right at him.'

'What's that there?' I gestured at the screen, a patch of light beneath the dull of the baseball cap.

Poppy stood, peering. 'It's ... it looks like hair, like he's tucked his hair beneath his collar.'

'I'd say that's blond, wouldn't you?'

Poppy nodded.

'Can you let it play?' I asked Steph. 'Come on, you git. Look up.'

The image came to life again, and I stared at him, willing him to shift, to allow us into the shadow of his cap. He walked fast, long, loping strides, his head bobbing, scanning left to right.

'He's checking,' I muttered. 'He's making sure they're alone.'

Then, as Jane Doe neared the entrance to the park, a sudden burst of speed, walk turning to run, and he was hammering towards her, a cheetah closing upon a gazelle, the gap between them vanishing in a heartbeat. She must have heard the sound. She began to turn, but it was already too late, because there was a hand across her mouth, another shoving her, away from the wide-open street and the watching windows, towards the open park gates.

My breath caught in my throat and I could smell the jasmine of her perfume, feel the pressure of her fingers in mine.

She fought. She fought hard. It gave me some small satisfaction to see that. She twisted, and tore at him, her mouth opening as if to scream, only he was too fast for her and where her open mouth had been, now there was a brick-sized hand, spreadeagled across her face, shoving her backwards.

In the blink of an eye, they were gone, vanished through the gates, hidden by a wall of green.

'Holy shit!' said Poppy.

I stared at the now empty street. 'Yeah.' My mouth opened, closed again. Breathe.

'There's another camera, to the north.' Steph sounded bored, her voice an unbroken monotone. Had she not watched it? Had she not seen? I glanced at her, her lips pursed, shimmying the feed. 'May have picked up something ...'

The image shifted, a swathe of green, a burst of colour at its centre, the flowers in their vivid bloom.

Then, from the very bottom of the screen, came a flutter of movement.

'Wait,' said Poppy. 'What is that?'

I studied it, for long moments unable to make sense of what I was seeing. Then realisation hit. 'That's her. That's Jane Doe.'

It was in fact the top of her head, distant and small, the unsteady sheet of her blonde hair fanned out, stark against the shadowed grass. Another movement, and Jane Doe shifted, edging into camera shot, on her back, facing upwards. I leaned closer, imagining that I could see her face, that in amongst the loosely textured pixels there was a rictus of terror. Willing her attacker to step forward, to lean into camera shot. Then, a flash, a spurt of something that stained her blonde hair black.

'He just cut her throat,' muttered Poppy.

A low noise crept from the technician, a moan almost, but when I shifted my gaze to her, her expression was flat, stoic.

I looked back to the screen, seconds thickening into minutes. Jane Doe lay on the grass, a dark funnel of blood billowing from her throat. It seemed to me that her lips were moving, a constant invocation, as if she was saying a rosary. But perhaps that was just me, my imagination filling in what the camera's reach could not. I leaned forward, my elbows rested on my knees, my fingers folded so tight together they hurt, and watched the woman losing her grip on life. Then came another movement, a shape that masked her from view. The paramedic leaning over her.

I leaned back. 'Why didn't we see the attacker's exit? Mrs Clarke, the witness, she said he ran to the north.'

Poppy studied the screen, reached up, her finger tracing the edges of it. 'He's hugged the fence line, managed to stay just beyond the camera's frame.'

I grunted, watched the screen. Wait for it. Wait. Then another movement. Me. I watched myself, hovering over her, more useless than I remember being. My hands sat in my lap, feeling strangely empty. I glanced down at them, expecting to see blood.

'We have him on CCTV,' said Poppy, quietly. 'We have the attack. We'll release it to the media. Stupid bastard picked the wrong victim in the wrong place.'

I sat there for a moment, the edge of a thought pressing on me. I had seen something. What was that? 'I'm sorry,' I said, 'can we back up a bit. To the close-up of the victim right before the attack?'

'Sure.' The screen shifted, and there she was again, vivid in life.

I leaned closer. What was it? What had I seen? 'Look at that.'

'What?' asked Poppy.

'Her handbag. See the shape of it? How full it looks. See? It looks like there's something sticking out the top.'

'Looks like an envelope. Or a ... I don't know, a folder, maybe?'

42

I studied the screen, bit my lip. 'He took it. He tried to kill her and he took whatever that was.' I looked at Poppy. 'So, now the question is, did he attack her and steal whatever that is to throw us off the scent? Or ...'

'Or was the whole attack about whatever is in that envelope?'

Chapter 3

'Police have released CCTV footage of a brutal attack that took place in Brunswick Square Gardens in Holborn this morning, in which a woman suffered life-threatening wounds. They are appealing for the public's help in identifying both the victim and her attacker ...'

My quick steps slowed, stopped, and I allowed myself a moment before pivoting towards the television in the hospital's empty day room. There she was again, Jane Doe, walking proud and tall as she had been such a short time ago. There he was again. Whoever he was. I watched it, one more time, him fly at her, a blitz attack that was done before it had begun.

I rubbed at my scar.

I hated that smell, the one that seemed to work its way into the very walls of hospitals, skin sloughing antiseptic, jagged-edged fear. A nurse passed by the day room, her gaze flicking at me, at my scar, a momentary smile. I returned it, effortfully, then returned my gaze to the television, to the image of Jane Doe as she had been. To the image of him.

I'm coming to get you, you son of a bitch.

I turned on my heel, heading back into the corridor

of St Thomas' Hospital, footsteps echoing hollowly against linoleum. It was quiet here, visiting time not yet begun. Just bed after bed, patients lying in a collage of pyjamas, their faces a symphony of resignation. I felt a prickle across my shoulders, turned my face so that I was focusing dead ahead, not looking left or right.

I thought of Jane Doe, of that footage. What had he taken from her? Was it something worth her dying for?

And once he had taken it, where the hell had he gone? We had spent an hour, a little more perhaps, checking the surrounding streets, comfortable in the premise that a thickset blood-soaked man would not be hard to find, and yet there was nothing. He had, it seemed, simply vanished, disappearing into thin air.

'Could he have made it over the fence? Into Coram's Fields?' I pondered to Poppy earlier on the train ride back – me to the station to collect the car to head out to the hospital, her to join up with the Outside Action Team, to help out with the hunt. 'The gates were open. If he'd gotten over that fence, he could have waited until the street busied, slipped out amongst a crowd.'

She had frowned. 'It's a pretty high fence ... We'll mention it to Noah, get a search going there.' She shrugged. 'Maybe he can fly.'

And that was what we were left with. The power of flight versus the power of invisibility. Talk about an embarrassment of riches.

I took a hard turn into room 313. Empty, with all the character that one would expect from a hospital room.

Harry sat in a low-slung armchair beneath the window, thumb moving rapidly across his phone.

'Hey,' I said. 'Any news?'

He glanced up, a quick flush filling his cheeks, and stood awkwardly, the sideways gait of one who has been sitting for too long. He waved at the empty expanse of floor. 'Nurse just left. The victim is on her way back from surgery now.'

I felt something in me brighten. 'She's ... so she's alive then, at the very least.'

He pulled a face. 'For now. Nurse said it was touch-and-go. That they nearly lost her a couple of times.' He reached his arms up above his head, a stretch that threatened to rip at the seams of his shirt, tugging at the fabric so that it was pulled taut across the muscles beneath.

I suppressed a sigh.

'Anything from your end?' he asked, lowering his arms, rolling his head in a circle. 'I saw the news. The family been in touch yet?'

'No.'

I leaned against the windowsill. 'The phones are going nuts. But no one knows her name. Just people who have seen her, out and about. We've got a couple of areas to look at, a bunch of calls have said she's a regular in Hampstead, a couple of other places.'

Harry rubbed at his neck and grunted. 'Thought it was always the husband in these kinds of things.'

I gave him a sharp look, but rather than seeing him, I was seeing her, walking quickly, with purpose, her gaze

46

ahead on wherever it was she had been heading. She had not looked back over her shoulder, had not seen him until it was too late. Impossible to tell then whether she knew him or not. He could have been an utter stranger, chancing on a likely target. Or he could have been the man who had promised to spend the entirety of his life loving her.

I thought of her gaze locked on mine. The word Wolf.

And, after all, Harry was right. You were far more likely to be harmed by someone you loved. But this way, in this place? When a husband killed a wife, he killed her in the bathroom or in the kitchen, in a place that he knew like he knew his own fingers, where his every move was a secret to be shared between him, her and the walls. Why in Brunswick Square Gardens, in a place of open ground, where anyone could happen by? It didn't make sense.

The high-pitched sound of gurney wheels pulled me back and I felt my heartbeat rise in time with it. A porter was angling the bed into the room, shooing us aside with a quick flick of his wrist. To say that she slept would be a lie, would make her near-death stasis seem almost gentle. Let's just say that her eyes were closed, that a tube had been inserted into the flesh of her neck, beneath the white packed wound on her throat, that her chest rose and fell with a mechanical forcedness, her fingers lying listless on the white sheets. There was still blood in her hair.

The porter slid the bed into position, a quick glance

at us, then, head down, dipped out again, his dancing steps interrupted with an ad hoc half turn as he met the nurse at the door.

'Harry? I've got the stuff you asked for.' She sounded thrilled with herself, younger than seemed feasible, with vivid blue eyes, large enough that it seemed there should be bluebirds following her wherever she walked.

I glanced at Harry, saw the flush begin to build from the base of his neck.

'This is my sergeant,' he said, voice unnaturally gruff. 'Alice.'

I gave him a flat look, sparing another for the narrow wedding band he wore, then turned towards the nurse. 'DS Alice Parr. How did she do?'

'She survived the surgery,' chirruped the nurse, 'so we're going to call that a win. She's sedated now ... it'll be a while before she comes out of it, if she does. I'm Gwen, by the way.'

I nodded. 'You said, if she does?'

Gwen sighed, expression heavy on the sympathetic. 'There was a lot of damage done, I'm afraid. The surgeons have done their best to put her back together, but in all honesty we just don't know how badly the oxygen flow to the brain was affected and what that's going to mean for her going forward.'

A worry I had not yet taken into consideration. 'You mean, brain damage?'

The nurse glanced up at me, bluebirds momentarily vanishing. She canted her head to one side. 'You really should speak to the doctor,' she said, softly. 'We just

48

don't know anything at this point.' She glanced at Harry, then back to me. 'Look, we'll know more when we try to take her off the sedation. If she comes round, then we'll be in a good position to judge how badly she's been affected.'

'And if she doesn't?' I asked, heavy with the feeling that I already knew the answer.

She sighed heavily. 'Then we'll know that too. If she slips into a coma ... Look, let's not go there right now. Let's just keep our fingers crossed we don't need to worry about that.' She smiled, but it seemed to require effort. 'I have her belongings here for you. They've all been bagged up.' She pulled the wheeled table away from the wall and set the see-through bags on top of it. 'Her clothing.' She pointed to the next bag. 'Contents of her pockets.'

A small set of keys shimmered beneath their casing. I picked them up, turning them over. House keys. But no markings, nothing to indicate where that house could be. And then, something else. My gaze caught on a bright fleck of colour through the sheet of plastic, and I picked up the bag, weighing it in my hands.

From beneath the plastic sheen, a small fabric doll gazed back at me balefully.

'Yeah, those were in her pocket,' offered Gwen.

The doll stretched the length of my hand, the roughened braid of her wool hair reaching just beyond my fingertips. She had cross-stitched eyes, a flowered pinafore, a wide stitched smile. I felt the body of her, squeezing the thinness of her between my fingers, and thought of Poppy and Charlie, with his damned zebra named Zee. I had bought it in the hospital gift shop, at a loss as to what one brought as a gift for a one-day-old. Zee had graced his crib, in a stony-eyed defiance of health visitor policy, his cot, his bed. Zee had travelled to Cyprus and Crete, had been left on the Northern line three times to my knowledge and had, over the years, developed an inextinguishable smell of vomit. Zee also felt thin, as if the very fatness had been loved out of him by the relentless adoration of a child.

'Someone loved this little lady,' I said, quietly.

The nurse glanced at Jane Doe, then leaned closer, lowering her voice. 'There's another one.' She pointed into the bag, beneath the first. A yellow stretch of fabric that ended in a rounded shape, a dog's head with a smiling mouth, a lolling tongue.

'She has children,' I said. I could sense Jane Doe, the she, on the periphery of my vision, could make out the inertness of her, and felt grubby for standing there the way I was, for clutching onto her child's toys, as if they were a mere trifle, not the beating heart and soul of the world for those who called her mummy. 'Shit.'

'Yes,' agreed Gwen. 'It is shit.'

I laid the bag back down carefully, studying the outline of it, pulling in a deep breath. 'No phone? Wallet? Anything with a name?'

'Nothing, sorry.' She moved the bags aside and picked up a small see-through plastic bag. 'There was this though.'

I squinted at it. 'What is that?'

She handed me the bag and I peered in, twisting the object so that the light fell as I needed it to.

'Is that a bandage?'

'Yes. A roll of bandage. It was inside her sleeve.'

I turned the bag over, studying the cream cloth, the edging of it dark with blood. 'Could it have fallen there? Been dropped when she was being treated?'

She shrugged. 'I don't know. I guess it would have had to. But look, there's something else ...' She leaned over me, adjusting the plastic in the light. And there, etched out in the dark blood on its clear plastic wrapper, was a shape. A fingerprint.

Chapter 4

I stood over my desk and let my gaze wander over Jane Doe walking down Hunter Street, Jane Doe lying in dew-soaked grass, her face caught in the moment of her almost-murder. Then on to the other photographs, of the crime scene soaked in blood, of the children's toys, dog-eared and adored, of the plastic-wrapped rolled-up bandage that no one could explain. Or maybe it didn't need explaining? Maybe it was a nothing, a red herring. And the soundtrack to it all, carving a groove in my mind, the word Wolf.

And yet a feeling had begun to settle over me, that perhaps I had been mistaken, perhaps in searching for a word, I had found one, my mind twisting empty air. The Outside Action Team had found nothing, had visited the list of names, the London Wolf Pack, with little to show for it bar short tempers and sore feet. I let my gaze flick up to my computer screen, to the blue edging of the Facebook screen, the steady stream of Wolfs beneath. So many faces looking back at me, yet with nothing to connect them to a bloodstained patch of grass in Holborn.

I sighed, took a large bite of Mars bar, the gripe in

my stomach reminding me that it was coming up to five-thirty in the afternoon, that I had eaten little more than a bag of crisps, an apple, all day. I turned away from the Wolf eyes, shifting my gaze up and out, from the horrors of the day to the nearby window and the patchwork sky beyond. I had the good desk. The one with the view, the one close enough to the radiator to keep it warm in the winter. The wind had settled now, leaving in its wake the remnants of a soft kind of spring day, of the sort that leaves people looking doubtfully skyward, clinging desperately to unused umbrellas, unable to believe their good fortune.

My stomach twisted as the sweet landed on the yawning emptiness of it, the density of the chocolate furring my tongue. I should eat properly. I should sleep properly. I should, I should.

'You should eat properly.'

It took me a moment to realise that the voice came from outside of me. I glanced up to see the DI watching me, his head tilted, all fatherly and concerned.

I grunted, mouth full of chocolate. 'My jeans agree.'

Noah moved closer, leaning in towards my computer screen with its stacked faces. 'Anything on Wolf?'

I shook my head. 'Maybe it's a nickname,' I offered, thinking that maybe in fact it was nothing at all.

Noah leaned across me, picked up the photograph of the soft toys. 'That's sad.'

I nodded, concentrating on my chocolate. It was a world removed from me. They say it changes you, the whole becoming-a-parent thing. That each case becomes more personal, that the involvement of children can twist the run-of-the-mill into the excruciating. But what makes a case personal, that is different for each of us. I studied the photograph of Jane Doe, the before one, where life was still as it should be. Because that was the part that did it for me, that unknowingness, that in a matter of seconds all would be tilted and that she would find herself in a fight for her life, and yet she stood, no idea she was standing on the edge of a precipice.

The door opened, flung as if by a hurricane wind, and Poppy came in the way Poppy always did, like she was leading an army. She blew out a heavy breath, sinking into the chair beside me. 'Okay, suffice it to say, if I never meet another Wolf again, I'll be a happy camper.' She shifted towards the DI, 'Oh, Guv? That last one, a Mr Reginald Wolf, aged 63, has advised me to inform you that he will be speaking to a solicitor with regards to police harassment. He also mentioned that it was the fault of immigrants.'

'What was?' asked Noah.

Poppy shrugged. 'Unclear, Guv. Everything, I think.'

I shook my head, my desk phone ringing from somewhere beneath the spread-out photographs. I followed the sound of it, sliding my hand beneath the slick sheets until I found it. 'DS Parr, Major Crime.'

'Hi, is that ... that's Alice, yeah?'

I hesitated. 'It is. Who's this?'

'Hi, yeah, it's Jake. From Green Java on Emerald Street?'

It took me a moment, brain slower than it should

have been. Emerald Street. I levered myself up in my chair, angling my head to look down to the street below, could just about make out the emerald flag of the Green Java coffee shop flapping in the wind.

'Oh, hi,' I offered, limply. 'What can I do for you?'

'Yeah, like, I saw the news. About that lady that got stabbed? Thing is, I'm sure I know her.'

My heartbeat had picked itself up, a trip-trap rhythm. 'Yeah? Where from?'

'Here. She came in ... I think Friday?'

I nodded slowly. 'Jake, I'm on my way down. Don't go anywhere.' I hung up, standing quickly and tugging my coat from the chair back. 'Pops, tip in from Green Java. Guy there thinks she's been in.'

The DI leaned, peering out of the window into Emerald Street below. 'Well ... that's ... handy?'

Poppy and I stood in the shadow of the nick, watching as the coffee shop door swung open and shut, open and shut, the smell of coffee and cinnamon rolling out towards us, and I felt my stomach growl despite the Mars bar.

Somehow, in my mind, I could not place her here, amongst the ordinariness of Emerald Street, in the Green Java – less a coffee shop, more an extension of Holborn station, albeit one that served legal stimulants and thickly topped cakes. I knew this shop. I knew the sound the bell made. I knew which floorboard creaked and which point at the counter the steam hit the loudest. I knew what time the good sandwiches went out and which server gave the most cream. To have her here, in my space … it would be like feeling a tap on your elbow and turning to find Jennifer Lawrence asking you to pass the sugar.

'You think this is a bullshit tip?'

I glanced at Poppy, the sudden disconcerting feeling of the world mirroring my thoughts back to me. 'Maybe. But it's a good excuse to grab a sandwich at least.'

I pulled in a breath, that smell of jasmine coming back to me again, and stepped into the stream of pedestrians, the thrum of people done for the day, hurrying towards the tube. I kept my eyes on the door, a salmon swimming downstream. A woman tutted, angling sharply around me, not breaking stride. I ducked in behind a parked-up Mercedes and contemplated flipping her off.

The bell tinkled. Come here often enough and that bell alone brings the taste of coffee to your mouth. Pavlov would have been so proud. It was quiet, a couple of people waiting in line, their gazes drifting over the brightly coloured sandwiches nestled beneath clear paper, as they tried not to look impatient, like all they wanted to do in the world was stand here, looking at those damn sandwiches. I slipped in behind them, my stomach clenching, a jarring reminder of the breakfast I had forgotten, my gaze running across the block-wood tables, two girls from the finance department, heads together, deep in conversation. A DC sat towards the back, top of his head visible above a magazine, *Triathlon Weekly*. A young mother, her eyes bloodshot and teary, her hair pulled up into a rough topknot. She was drinking coffee, sipping it through a thick mound of cream that hid her face almost from view. With her other arm she supported a baby – small enough to look brand new – to her breast, a tiny hand gripping the front of her shirt, as if to prevent her from running away. The woman looked up, must have sensed me watching her, and gave me a flat look, one that appeared right on the edge of tears. I felt myself colour, gave her a half-smile and then looked back at the sandwiches. Maybe the rest of the queue was on to something with this.

The barista was a reedy guy, one who couldn't possibly be as young as he looked, because he looked to be about twelve. He caught sight of me, his face flooding with relief. 'Hey, Alice. You want to talk down the end?' He had long since stopped noticing my scar, the novelty of it well past. In the months since the fire, that lack of interest alone had become enough to earn my eternal friendship.

'Hi Jake.' I knew his name from his name tag. He knew mine from my coffee cup. It was your quintessential first-world acquaintanceship. 'Please.'

I followed him down the counter to the end, the hiss of the coffee machine making my stomach tighten, and slid the still CCTV photograph of Jane Doe across the counter. 'So this is the woman you saw?'

He leaned closer to the photograph, studying it. 'That's her,' he said, triumphant. 'I knew it. Couldn't believe it! I mean, I saw it on the news right as I started my shift. I mean, you see these things happening, yeah? You never think it'll be someone you've met. Seems like stuff like that should only happen in films.' He shook his head. 'Yeah, so, I know her. Well, when I say know, I mean she came in here ... last week? Friday? Friday. I'm sure it was Friday. She was ...' he glanced up at me, a quick flush '... fit.' He looked away, cheeks slowly working their way to crimson. 'You know what I mean.'

I thought of her wide eyes, the cut of her cheekbones, her full lips. Fit. She was beautiful. But then someone sliced her throat open. The coffee machine began to shudder and burr and I glanced at it, wishing now I'd gotten him to make me a damn coffee first. 'Is she a regular?'

He shook his head. 'I'd never seen her before that day. Pretty sure I'd have remembered. I don't think she was English ...'

'What do you mean? Why?'

'She had an accent. I mean, she didn't say much, but I remember thinking that she must be, I don't know, Canadian, maybe? American? Maybe New Zealand?'

I swear to god I heard Poppy roll her eyes.

Okay, she had an accent. That was ... something.

'Did she give you a name?' I asked, gesturing to a toffee nut latte that had been slid onto the counter beside me, the name Jessica scrawled roughly across the side.

Jake grimaced. 'Well ... I mean, I'm sure she did, but, thing is, we serve a lot of people. Sorry.'

Poppy leaned in, interjected, 'You got CCTV?'

'Sorry,' he said again. 'We did have some outside, but some kids smashed them in a couple of weeks ago. My Guv is still waiting for you lot to catch them.'

I fought the urge to sigh.

'There was something though.' Jake looked back at the photograph. 'I remember her coming in.'

'What time was this?'

'I guess, I don't know, sometime around eight. In the morning, I mean. She ordered ... something ... not food, a drink. I remember passing the order over to Laura ...' He waved towards an imaginary Laura. 'I looked back at her, to take the money, you know, and she was just ... I mean, she looked like she'd seen a ghost.'

'What do you mean?' I asked, my heart beginning to beat faster.

'Well, she'd just kind of frozen. She wasn't looking at me, was looking out the window. I had to call her a couple of times to get her attention. And then she just, she said she'd changed her mind. She kind of backed away. To be honest, I thought she was going to cry.'

Poppy had leaned in, her jacket scraping against the film covering those damn sandwiches. 'What did she do then?' she asked.

Jake shrugged. 'I don't know. I mean, it was weird, but there were a bunch of people waiting. I didn't see where she went after that. I guess she left.'

'CCTV might help,' muttered Poppy.

I looked from Jake to the window and its endless stream of passers-by. Back again. 'You sure you have no idea what it was she saw?'

Jake shook his head. 'I've no idea. But whatever it was, it scared the shit out of her.'

Chapter 5

'Guys? Okay, it's late, so let's get this rolling.' The DI stood at the front of the briefing room. His hair stood on end, a coffee stain darkening the left sleeve of his once-white shirt. 'Okay? So, first thing to say – thank you for all your hard work today. Alice, you've been up to your neck in it – literally …' A brief, possibly sympathetic smattering of laughter. 'We're getting a lot of press interest on this one. There's a bunch of journalists still camped out outside the front door. If they catch you on your way out, just refer them back to the press officer. We need to carefully manage what information ends up in the public domain, so just a nice polite "no comment" and then move on. Got it?'

It was about ten, late enough that a heavy darkness had landed outside, and yet it felt to me like the middle of the day. I wasn't tired. I was … wired, I guess. I shifted in my seat, wanting to move, wanting to get back to work. Adrenaline is a wonderful thing.

'So, our victim. We still have no name on her, so currently to be referred to as Jane Doe. The hospital has reported her condition as remaining critical. They have not yet attempted to end her sedation, but I'm told that they will be doing that very soon ...' – he glanced at the clock – '... and they will let us know how they get on.'

He tapped a button on the mouse, the screen behind him flickered to life. 'Now, we don't know who she is, but thanks to our lovely friends at TFL,' a snort from somewhere in the room, 'we do know where she came from.'

Another touch, another image appearing, Jane Doe on an underground train. I shifted, leaning sideways to see past the heads that blocked mine. She had a seat beside the door, was wearing that same coat, the fur collar of it brushing her cheek.

'Is this today?' I asked.

Noah nodded. 'This footage was taken at 7.25 a.m., today. It shows our victim on a Northern line train heading into King's Cross.'

She looked lost in thought, her mouth pulled tight as if she had made a decision, was set upon a course of action. Blonde waves lay across her shoulders, her gaze trapped in middle distance. *Where are you going?* I wondered. *What are you thinking?* Then the bag. It sat upon her lap, looking just as it had looked the last time I had seen it. Only without the blood. Her arms were wrapped around it, a mother cradling an infant, pulling it to her, holding it safe. And there, clearly visible from the top of it, was a large shape, square and tan.

I stood up, movements unthinking, could feel heads turn to watch me. Moved up towards the screen, to where Jane Doe sat. 'Here,' I said, tracing the square with my fingers. 'Look, it's a folder. Or an envelope.

Something like that. She had it in the CCTV footage of the attack. But when we found the handbag, it was gone,' I said to the room at large.

The DI pursed his lips. 'Righto. We'll keep that in consideration.' He looked at me, pointedly, and I remembered myself suddenly, the weight of two dozen stares settling on me. I could feel myself flushing.

'Sorry. I ... I'll sit down.'

A brief laugh.

'What about the attacker?' called Poppy from her seat beside mine. 'Any sign of him?'

'No sign of him on the train. The guys finally picked him up coming out of the toilets at King's Cross. Hang on ...' He fumbled with the mouse, then the image changed, this time to the lobby of King's Cross Station. People flooded across the screen, moving this way and that. A group of teenagers hung by the turnstiles, poring over a map, forcing the crowd to bifurcate. I scanned the crowd, searching for a shape that looked familiar. Then finally it happened, a movement to the left of the screen, familiar in the heft of him. He slid out of the toilets, shoulders hunched, a large backpack on his back. He walked with a purpose as far as the doors, then, as if he had meant to all along, hooked a sharp turn, skimming the edge of the lobby, until he half vanished between a newsagent stand and a pillar.

'What's in the backpack?' I muttered to Poppy. She shook her head, not pulling her gaze from the screen.

We watched, the room silent. He was waiting, that much was clear. For her? Or for anyone? What were

62

the rules of this particular game of hide-and-seek? We watched him. Or, at the very least, we watched the pillar where we believed him to be, for long enough that people began to shift, the odd murmur springing up, the moan of a suppressed yawn.

A knot of anxiety had formed in my stomach. Had he slipped out? Had we missed him in the rush-hour fray?

Then Jane Doe coming through the turnstiles, her overstuffed bag tucked beneath her arm. She walked towards the exit, confident and clear, never a thought of where this might lead. And then it seemed that the pillar itself moved, a shape emerging from behind it, falling into step with his victim. Close enough that she could not slip away. Far enough back that he would not be noticed.

'He was waiting for her,' I said, softly.

'Certainly looks like it,' Poppy agreed, quietly.

I thought of the coffee shop on Emerald Street. Of the breeze that funnelled its way towards us, the groan of traffic.

'Maybe she was being followed,' I said to Poppy, as I stood before the window of Green Java, the chill snapping about my legs, the mercurial day changing yet again. She had seen something, from out of the window behind me. What was it? What had frightened her? 'Whatever she saw, it would have been here.' I glanced across the street. 'Here-ish.' The sodden sun glinted off the glass. The image of tables intersected with my own reflection, a Daliesque painting. Then I warped again and it was no longer my reflection but instead that of Jane Doe looking back at me.

What did you see? What were you afraid of?

The briefing room had begun to feel uncomfortably warm, too many bodies stuffed into too small a space. I shifted in my seat, watching as the DI bent forward, fiddling with the laptop on the podium before him, muttering under his breath. I leaned closer to Poppy, pointing to the image, frozen now on the stocky man, his long blond hair snaking from beneath the hat. 'You think it was him at the coffee shop? You think she saw him outside, that that's what freaked her out so much?'

Poppy glanced at me. 'Could be. But that means ...'

'That means that this didn't begin today,' I finished, quietly.

The coffee shop, that can't have been where he first saw her, where it all began, because then she would have had nothing to be afraid of. Fear is learned. A deer that's never seen a hunter has no reason to fear a gun. And yet our victim, she was frightened.

'Guv?' called Poppy. 'What's the point of origin for her journey?'

'It's Hampstead tube station,' supplied Matt, two rows forward.

I turned towards him. 'How did she pay for it?'

He snorted, twisting to face me. 'Typically, Ms Doe is the only person in London not travelling contactless. She bought a ticket. An actual ticket. From a ticket machine at the station.' He gave me a flat look. 'And she paid cash.'

64

Poppy groaned. 'I'm starting to think she's doing this on purpose.'

The DI glanced up from the laptop. 'The good news is that Hampstead being her starting point marries up well with all the reports we've had of sightings of her in that area. I'm betting she lives there.'

I thought of the coffee shop again, of the close-to-tears mother and the smell of cinnamon. 'Guv, our witness at the coffee shop, he said he remembered her as having an accent ...' I thought of the soft toys tucked inside her pocket. 'We've been wondering why her family haven't called in after seeing it on the news. What if they haven't seen it? What if they aren't here?'

'What do you ...'

'Well, maybe she doesn't actually live here. Maybe she's on holidays or just visiting. It would explain why everyone has seen her and yet no one seems to know her. It would explain why she's the only person in London using cash to ride the tube.'

The room fell silent, twenty heads chewing over what I had just said.

'I think we should check hotels,' I added. 'B&Bs, that kind of thing.'

Noah had folded his arms. He nodded slowly. 'Nice. I like it.' He thought for a moment. 'You know, whenever we go away, we Airbnb it ...'

'That's because you have forty kids, Guv,' put in Poppy.

'No,' he sighed, 'I don't. It just feels that way, is all. Al, you happy to take the lead on that?'

'As a clam, Guv.'

'Excellent. Guys ... whoever this is, he's dangerous. Our victim survived because of luck. He struck out of the blue, in broad daylight. We need to find this guy before he does anything else. Now, tomorrow ...'

'I'm telling you,' Poppy leaned in towards me, her voice low, 'it's the husband.'

I rolled my eyes. 'You're such a cynic.'

'Funny, that's exactly what the solicitor who handled my divorce said.'

I laughed, rolling it seamlessly into a cough, then waved my hand. 'Guv? Anything from that bandage I submitted?'

Noah frowned. 'Al, are you new? Whilst I appreciate your enthusiasm, I have been informed that the lab will attend to it with the utmost urgency, but only if I get you to stop harassing them.'

'What can I say? I'm keen.'

Noah sighed. 'Well, that's certainly one of the words we could use. Right, you lot. Go home. I'll see you bright-eyed and bushy-tailed in the morning. Eight a.m., please.'

A sigh swept across the room, one that sounded a lot like relief, then a flurry of chair legs scraping. I sat for a moment longer. The screen had returned now to the image of Jane Doe on the tube, that far-off gaze, that bag clutched to her knee. Where was she going? What was she carrying?

'Hey, you coming?' asked Poppy.

It took me a moment to pull away. 'No,' I said, 'not

quite yet. I'm going to top and tail a few things first.'

'Al ...'

'Pops.'

She rolled her eyes. 'Fine. Well, just don't work too late, okay?' She leaned over and kissed the top of my head.

I smiled. 'Yes, Mum. Give Charlie a kiss from me.'

I don't remember how long I worked, running down hotels, B&Bs, any places where a holidaymaker might stay. I sat hunched across my computer until my back began to seize up. It must have been midnight. There or thereabouts. I remember drinking Red Bull, my second can of the day, the sickly sweetness of it making my tongue thick. But I know that by the time I stood, my eyes had begun to weigh heavy, words on the screen dancing in front of me.

I walked towards the window, looking out across the London night, with its myriad lights, the eternal wakefulness of it all. I stood there for a moment, a thought sitting at the edge of my consciousness, just out of reach. What was that? I leaned my forehead against the glass, angling my gaze down into the valley of Emerald Street, quiet now, just puddled street lights breaking the darkness. Something had happened, out in that street. Something had caught Jane Doe's attention, had frightened her badly enough to make her run from the shop, to abandon her plans in favour of flight. Then another thought, hard on the heels of the first. That the coffee shop lay close to the police station. Not opposite exactly, but not far off. And that here, at Holborn nick, we prided ourselves on our CCTV.

I grabbed my notepad from my desk and ran up the stairs to the CCTV control room. It sat, small, empty and alone. It occurred to me briefly, worryingly, that I could just sleep in here. The plus side of that, no commute. I flipped through the cameras, pulling up the one covering Emerald Street.

'Okay,' I muttered, 'where are you?'

Friday, 8 a.m. People pour along the pavement in an inexorable tide. I leaned in, tired eyes straining to see more than ghosts. Where are you? Then a pedestrian hooked a sharp left and in the gap he left behind moved the narrow figure of Jane Doe.

My breath caught in my throat.

She walked just as she had walked today. With purpose, as if she knew exactly where she was going. And there, tucked beneath her arm, was that handbag with that large file sticking out of the top.

Was she working around here somewhere? Maybe some freelance thing, which would explain her lack of friends, colleagues, or at least friends or colleagues who cared enough to pick up the phone. Or … maybe she wasn't living in Hampstead. There were the international halls of residence. They were right there, right by Brunswick Square. But then, she looked old to be a student. Or was that impolitic to say? Think, I mean.

I watched her walk, already seeing her way ahead, waiting for her to join the line that had begun to stretch its way out through the open door of the coffee shop.

But, instead, she paused, looked left and right, then stepped out into the road.

'Where the hell are you going?'

She walked across the street, vanishing down Richbell Place. I sat for a moment, watching the flow of pedestrians left in her wake, something like a premonition stirring.

I changed feeds, pulling up the camera on the corner of Richbell Place and Lamb's. There she was, walking straight towards it. Only ... it was probably just my imagination, but it seemed to me that she was moving slower now, her head swinging from side to side, watching. Uncertainty where before there had been strength. Then she moved beyond the camera's reach.

I knew where she was going.

I changed cameras, this time pulling up the one that covered the front desk and the main door into the station. It had been busy at the front desk, unusually so for that time of day. A group of people stood at the counter, a family by the looks of things, a man at the front, his hands waving wildly as he spoke, a teenage girl at the rear, tucked into an older woman's arms. The girl was crying, her cheeks streaked with coal-black mascara. For a few moments, they caught my attention, the angst on their faces pulling me in, so it took longer than it should for me to realise what I was seeing.

For there, tucked up against the door, a powder blue handbag cradled across her body like a shield, stood Jane Doe.

I sat up sharp, vision clearing in a sudden spurt of adrenaline.

'Holy shit.'

She was here. Last Friday she had come here, into this police station.

I stared at the image, then, shaking myself, hit pause. The image shimmied and stopped, the face of Jane Doe frozen in a captured expression of fear. And then her hands. Half hidden behind the handbag was the dim outline of an envelope, A4-sized, its edges straining with whatever was held within.

I moved to grab my BlackBerry. There would be a report somewhere. Somewhere on the system would be the reason she had come. And with it would be her name.

But as my hand moved, a motion from the image stopped me. The man at the counter, his face contorted, apparently hearing something he didn't want to hear, slammed his hands down on the counter, the girl burying her face in her mother's coat. Trouble on its way.

And Jane Doe turned on her heels and fled back through the police station door.

Shit.

I reversed the image, watched it again. The impact, hand against desk. Then Jane Doe's flight. Not considered, far too fast for that, but rather an antelope sensing a lion. She vanished through the door, envelope still clutched tight to her.

I watched the lobby, full in spite of the loss of her, the man's arms waving widely about him, the older woman's narrow hand reaching towards him, useless. And beyond them, through the shimmering glass of the sprawling window, the distant outline of Jane Doe, head in her hands. Crying?

Why had she come here? The envelope. It had to be about whatever she carried within it. And yet the shape of her, all folded in on herself, the speed with which she had startled ... Her decision to come here could not have been an easy one for her.

I checked the time frame, a swift mental calculation. She had left the station, had gone straight to Green Java, already riddled with fear, her hackles risen. And there she had seen something else. Something that had made her bolt again.

And I thought back to this morning, to the CCTV footage of Jane Doe walking towards Brunswick Square and her inevitable destruction. The envelope standing proud from her bag. And in that moment I knew where she had been going this morning, where she was heading when she was almost murdered.

She was coming here.

Chapter 6

I slept little that night, just sporadic dips into and out of consciousness, each waking punctuated by the sense of wrongness and the awareness of a shape that loomed above me, a silhouette of a man, a knife in his hands. My dreams had a texture of franticness, of searching and searching and yet never really knowing just what I was searching for. I gave up, a little after five, pulled on some running clothes and set off along empty streets, down through Primrose Hill, a hard left by the entrance to London Zoo, its static lions and giraffes staring down at me, haunting in the early morning light. Pushing myself, harder, harder, so that my thighs burned, calves ached, the wide green of Regent's Park to my right, then a left turn, plunging into almost wakening streets. Running to something, even though it felt an awful lot more like running from something. Then the looming trees of Brunswick Square ahead, and suddenly I'm back there, holding her hands as she bleeds out, the smell of jasmine overwhelming, my footsteps matching the rhythm of my heartbeat.

I returned home feeling a little better.

I say home, use the word as some kind of linguistic

reflex, but in truth that place was not home to me. In a more generous frame of mind, I might have added a 'yet'. It wasn't home to me 'yet'. But deep down I think it would be reasonable to assume that the overfilled rental in Camden, with a penchant for chintz and the overwhelming smell of cat urine that worked its way up from the flat below, was unlikely to ever fill my heart with love. Harmless enough, but like the steady solid guy who comes along after the man who broke your heart, that flat would never really catch hold of me, entice me to go running back to it. Home. That would come later.

I showered. I applied my make-up carefully, easing the specialist concealer into the swirls of the scars, the sponge squeaking softly with the motion. I moved it around my eyes, pressing it hard into the blue-black bags beneath them, the sharp cheekbones that only served to exaggerate the dips underneath. I took a deep breath, thinking of the day to come and the crime to solve, and, in doing so, managed to forget about the face that stared back at me in the mirror.

I moved through the flat, checking rooms, switching off sockets, checking for an iron left standing, checking for candles left lit even though I had none.

And I stood there for a moment, in amongst that god-awful smell of cats, and felt it begin to roll over me, the smell of smoke, the weight, as if a mountain has worked its way on top of you.

My phone beeped, shaking me from my reverie, an incoming email, and I closed my eyes, offering up a brief prayer of thanks.

The gift of being Detective Sergeant Alice Parr. It allowed me to forget about having to be Alice.

I reached for my phone and scrolled through emails carrying adverts for holidays I would never take and clothes I would never buy. At the top of my inbox sat an email – Airbnb Hampstead. I frowned, pushing my thumb against it.

DS Parr,
In response to yesterday's email, I am writing to inform you that it is my belief that the woman whose picture you included is my current tenant.

I stared at the screen, my heart thundering, ran my gaze down to the phone number nestled beneath, the name A. Bean.

We had found her.

I punched the air, quickly dialling the DI. I think I have her. I'm going to Hampstead. There must have been more to it than that. There must have been niceties to offer, procedures to follow. But all that stood out to me was the fact that soon I would have a name for her. Soon I could find her family.

'Hey,' I said, 'have you heard from the hospital? Is she awake?'

'I haven't spoken to them yet. I've tried, but no one is picking up. I'll let you know.'

'If she is,' I said, 'if they've woken her ... do you mind if it's me? If I go interview her, I mean?'

The silence had stretched itself out so that I could read within it all that was unsaid.

Then, 'Of course, Al. I wouldn't dream of sending anyone else.'

I waited impatiently at the kerb, bouncing on the balls of my feet, watching as the traffic oozed by. Finally, after what seemed to be hours, Harry eased to a stop before me. I dragged open the door, clambering in.

'Sorry,' he muttered. 'Traffic's a bitch.'

A quick glance. His hair stood on end, by accident rather than by design, and his usually immaculate shirt looked wrinkled. 'You okay?'

'Yeah,' he answered shortly. 'Problems at home.'

I nodded, kept my mouth shut. The baby was three months old. The marriage six months older than that. And Harry had managed to retain his spotlight attentional capacity for any attractive female within a quarter-mile. As Poppy had said, I give it a year.

We worked our way through the early morning traffic, pulling into the narrow car park at a little after nine.

'Nice,' I offered. 'Bet these places cost a bit.'

Harry grunted in reply, taking a pull from his travel mug.

The car park was quiet. It was late enough that those residents who worked had already left. I leaned forward in the passenger seat, squinting up at the apartment complex with its loops of bay windows, Mary Poppins rooftops begging for a chimney-sweep chorus. Red-brick, faux Georgian, the doorways guarded by imposing

75

pillars, lined with flower beds that bubbled over with colour. I found myself straightening my blouse.

'What time did he say?' asked Harry.

'Nine.' I glanced at my watch. Nine-fifteen. 'He's late. But then,' I allowed, 'so were we.' I glanced up at the low-lying clouds. It had begun to rain, a false-start spring taking a sudden slide back into hard winter.

'He's late,' repeated Harry.

I glanced across at him. He had been in Major Crime for eight weeks. Had moved from puppy-excited to weary to oh-god-what-the-hell-have-I-done in two short months. I probably should have said something to inspire him, guided him like a supervisor should.

'Yup,' I concurred.

What can I say? I was distracted. It wasn't my finest teaching hour.

I shifted, tapping my fingers. Come on. A footpath worked its way between the trees, cutting across the low-trimmed grass. Did Jane Doe walk that path? It seemed now that I was seeing her face everywhere I looked. On crowded Holborn streets, on the Piccadilly line. In the newsagents on the corner of my road, her face looked up at me from tabloid rags – 'The Mystery Of The Fallen Angel'. I must have hesitated, had smelled jasmine weaving its way in between roughened newspaper, the low-level scent of chocolate. 'Terrible, innit?' The shop owner had shaken his head, dreadlocks clicking together until it sounded as if the store had been overrun by crickets. 'Thing is, when it's these drugged-up hoodlums as get stabbed, well, you think, it's nature, yeah? They put themselves out there. They know the dangers. But a beautiful girl like that. Awful. Just awful. Papers, they say she had money, yeah? You got to think, if someone like that, world at their feet, if they can't protect themselves, who the hell can, yeah?'

'You think this is him?' Harry pointed as a shimmering black Porsche whipped past us on East Heath Road, taking the corner hard, sweeping into the car park with a screech of tyres. He pulled into a bay close to us, halting the car with a groan of brakes.

I pulled at the door handle, sliding out into the grey of the day, flecks of rain puckering at my skin, the overture of a symphony to come. I arranged myself, closing the car door behind me, watching as the Porsche driver unfolded long legs from the sports car beside us. He was young and lean, wild blond hair with a kink to it. He slammed the door, like he wasn't driving a fifty-grand car.

'Police, yeah?' He snapped the words off, his gaze flicking quickly over Harry, coming to rest on me. Appraising. Then he took in my scar, raised an eyebrow.

I nodded slowly, studying the shape of him, the gait of him. Thinking now of the CCTV footage, of hunter and prey. Yet this man, he was leaner, his hair shorter than what we had seen. 'DS Parr,' I offered. 'This is DC Regan.'

He sniffed, shrugging the hood of his hoodie up over his head. 'Weather's shit.

'So, you are …'

He frowned at me, seemed confused by the question. 'Yeah, Anthony. Anthony Bean.' He delivered the words, triumphantly. Like they should have some value to me.

'Oh shit,' said Harry loudly, 'you used to play for Arsenal. Man, you were brilliant. I saw you play against Liverpool. That goal, mate, bloody hell.'

I stared from one to the other, studying the young man for any sign of familiarity, before giving it up as a lost cause. I had been raised on rugby, a proper sport, so my dad would say. 'Okay ...'

'So where you playing now, mate? Seriously, that goal though ...' Harry was bouncing on the balls of his feet, face lit up like a child at Christmas.

My eyes ached with the strain of not rolling them.

'All right,' I murmured, 'calm down.' I shifted my attention back to the man-child before me. 'Mr Bean, you said you thought you knew the stabbing victim?'

He shrugged, folded his arms across his chest and shivered pointedly. Another glance to the scar. 'Yeah, like I said, it's the woman who rents my place.'

'Okay ...'

'Thing is, like, I mean, I'm all for helping out the police and everything, but I got stuff to do.' His voice had an edge to it, his feet twisting away from me, like they were ready to run. 'I run my own business now,' he added, 'making protein drinks.' He looked up at the building clouds, the rain intensifying so that our words intermingled with the thumps on the pavement. 'Not being funny, but I'm getting soaked. We going up to the flat or not?'

I pulled the zip of my coat closed. 'Sure.' Slid into step

behind him. Watching his slouching walk, the swing of his arms, and trying to lay the shape of him alongside that of Jane Doe's attacker. Is it you? I checked my asp in my pocket, wrapping my fingers around it, just in case.

He slid a key into the front door, letting himself in and leaving us to follow. Harry was still fidgeting, looking from Anthony Bean to me, his eyebrows dancing up around his forehead. I gave him a flat look, easing my baton from my pocket, a flash of silver. I saw him clock it, his expression change in an instant. His shoulders squared with tension.

We wound round in a tight circle, one floor, two, Anthony Bean turning off the stairway onto the third-floor landing, not pausing to see if we followed. He shoved the hood down from his shoulders, sliding the key into the lock.

I caught Harry's eye, a quick nod. Be careful. Closed the front door tight behind me, the click of the lock catching, deafening.

A narrow hallway, glassed double doors flung open onto a bright living room, pulling in light even on this dullest of days. Anthony flung himself down onto the sofa, legs spread wide so that his boots rucked up the woven rug. I watched as Harry positioned himself in the armchair beside him.

'Nice flat, man,' he offered. 'Nice.'

Anthony shrugged. 'Whatever. Investment, innit? Don't live here. You, ah, you'd better sit down, yeah?'

I held back, watching as Harry stroked the leather armchair with the palms of his hands, still muttering 'nice'. I had a feeling he was going to need a bit of a lie-down after this. Or possibly a cold shower.

I wound past them to peer out the bay window onto the green of the heath. Had Jane Doe stood here, gazing out at the same views?

'So,' I said, 'I appreciate you calling us, Mr Bean.'

'Anthony.'

'Anthony. As you can imagine, it's very important to us to identify the victim in this case.'

'Yeah, well, hard to figure out who killed her if you don't know who she is, I'd say.'

I paused. 'Yes. Yes, it is …' An offbeat, his conclusion throwing me. 'I, ah, we need to make sure that the victim was in fact your tenant. Do you have anything we can check? Photographs, did you take any ID off her when she booked the accommodation?'

Anthony fixed me with a hard look. 'You're messing, yeah?'

'I …'

He let out a heavy sigh. 'Jesus wept.' He shifted, pulling an iPhone from his jeans pocket, and moved his fingers across the screen. 'Here.'

I took the phone from his hand, peering at an email. It took me a moment to focus, to understand what I was seeing. Embedded within the text was a passport photograph. A woman staring down the lens of the camera, her hair pulled up into a chignon, a swipe of dark red lipstick. She looked straight at me, the weight of her gaze feeling just like it had on the day I had held her hand as she lost her grip on life.

Jane Doe.

We had her. We'd found her.

I stared at the eyes that studied me, those full lips, the slight downturn of them, and I realised that my fingers had begun to shake.

I pushed the screen up.

Beneath the photograph, a passport number and, just beneath that, a name.

Holly Vale.

'Her name ...' I said, 'it's Holly.'

Harry had stood, was peering over my shoulder, all thoughts of his footballing hero forgotten now, back into the thrill of the chase. 'We got her,' he muttered.

I could not pull my gaze away. This was it, proof positive that the life of Jane Doe – Holly Vale – extended beyond an empty sleep in a lonely hospital room. That once she lived and she travelled and she did all of the things that the rest of the world did. I blew out a slow breath.

I fought to focus, pulled my gaze in on the words – country of origin. Three letters. USA.

Jake was right. Well, sort of right. She was American. That was why no one was looking for her. That was why there was no family knocking down our doors, no husband desperate to find her. She wasn't from here. She had been lost an awfully long way from home.

I bit my lip. We could do it now. Now that we had her, now that we knew who she was, we could find who tried to kill her.

The rain had begun to batter against the window,

bouncing hard off the glass. I turned towards the outside world and the shadowy wildness of the heath. A pigeon landed on the windowsill, looked at me, its head tipped to one side.

I could feel a knot in my shoulders begin to unravel itself.

'What can you tell me about her?' I asked, looking not at Anthony but hooked by the photograph gaze of Jane Doe. 'How long had she been here?'

'Three weeks. Had another three to go.'

'And did she happen to mention what she was doing here? A holiday? Work?'

He shook his head, another glance to his phone. 'Nah. Didn't mention it.'

'Do you know where in the United States she was from? Which state?'

He looked exasperated. 'Look, like I told the other guy, I only met her once – when she arrived. I do that with all of them, yeah, just like show them around, make sure they know how everything works. I stay away after that, 'cos you've got to, like, otherwise you get people saying on the reviews "oh, he was too pushy, always up in our business". I met her, thought she was fit, then I didn't see her again.'

Something felt wrong, a piece of the puzzle placed at the wrong angle, the air in the room stilling. 'The other guy?'

'Look,' Anthony leaned forward, his forearms resting on his knees, face hard. 'Like I said, I'm happy to help.

Community spirited me.' There was an edge to his voice. 'I give to three charities, like, serious money. But this is getting a bit much now. That other detective said you wouldn't need anything else from me.'

'This other detective,' I balanced my voice carefully, 'when did you see him?'

He stared at me. 'It was ... I don't know ... I woke up this morning to train, yeah, and I saw the email, the one from Airbnb asking if any of us had leased a place to this woman, yeah. So I reply, say yeah, that's me, and ... thing is, it was in my head then, y'know? So I figure I'll just come down here, early like, because, to be honest, I was thinking I must have made a mistake, y'know, just got carried away and all that. Only this detective, he's already here waiting when I get here, looked like he'd been trying the bells.'

'You let him in?'

'Sure.'

There are moments when time hardens around you, solidifies so that it feels that you will be stuck there forever.

I pulled my notebook from my pocket, aware of the slightest of shakes to my fingers.

'What time was this?'

'Maybe, ah, 6.30, 6.45.'

'He gave you a name?'

The footballer frowned. 'Detective Grey. What's this about?'

'Can you describe him for me?'

He stared at me. His skin was pocked, forehead marked

with old acne scars, eyes a glacial blue flecked with hazel-nut. 'Why?' It came out as a croak. 'Why are you asking me to describe one of your own guys?' He leaned closer, the smell of oak overlaying the merest suggestion of stale sweat. 'He wasn't one of your guys, was he?'

I studied him. 'No,' I said. 'No, he's not.'

He leaned back then, rangy hands scrubbing at his face, from superstar to little boy in one swift move. 'Fuck.'

I moved towards him, sinking onto the opposite end of the sofa, face a careful construct of calm. 'Anthony, it's extremely important that you describe for me the man you saw.'

'Ah, chunky, yeah. Belly on him. Blond. Glasses, I think?'

The man on CCTV. The hand that held the knife.

'He touch anything?'

It seemed to take a long time for my words to reach him. 'What? Yeah ... well, no. I mean, he put gloves on, like plastic gloves, yeah? To preserve the scene, he said.'

'He take anything with him?' My stomach twisted, a flare of pain.

Anthony nodded. 'Bunch of stuff. I didn't ask. I mean, police business, yeah? He was here a while, maybe thirty, forty minutes. Got what he wanted, said thanks very much, and off he went. I'd only just gotten home again when you called.'

'You see a car? Get a licence plate? Anything like that?'

The footballer shook his head. 'He walked round the corner. I don't know. I assume he had a car, but I didn't see it.'

'I'll call the office,' muttered Harry. 'Get them to check on ANPR.'

There was purpose here, a driving force beyond the mere exigencies of death. He had wanted something from her. I thought of the handbag, of the stark emptiness of it, of the missing folder. Had he gone after her, thinking she would be carrying something that he had wanted, only to be disappointed. Having to think on his feet, come up with a new plan. What was it he was looking for?

'Do you know ... did Holly have anything, any paperwork that she might have carried with her, documents with the address of this flat?'

'There's a business card. I got a stack of them out in the hallway. It's got the flat's address on it, postcode, phone number. The people who stay here, they can take it with them, that way if they need, like, an Uber or something, they got the right information.' He shrugged. 'I don't know if she took one, but ...'

But it could have been in her handbag if she did, could have led him straight here.

'You're thinking it's him? Who stabbed her?' He had folded in on himself, his knuckles white on the phone that remained tight in his grip.

It wasn't thought. It was cold, hard certainty.

I glanced at Harry, then back to Bean. 'It's too early to say, but it's always better to err on the side of caution.

We'll do a search, see if we can figure out what he took. Maybe it will help us get a better understanding of who he is and why Holly was attacked. I mean, the thing to bear in mind ...'

The sun had broken through the rainclouds, a brief interlude, spreading a glow across the dull room. Then, from the front door, a sound.

There are times when it seems that we have lived events through before, that we are caught up in some kind of feedback loop, so that our brains react before they should, kind of a déjà vu in reverse.

It was the metallic grating of the key in the lock.

'Who the hell is that?' asked Anthony.

I was running before he had finished the sentence, out of the living room, down the hardwood hallway, my low heels clacking against the floor. Grabbed for the door, fast but not fast enough, because now whoever had been there had fled, was thundering down the stairs.

'Stop! Police!'

I ran the way you do when you're a child, when running becomes a kind of frozen falling, feet always on the precipice of tumbling. I felt a gust of wind rising up the twisting staircase as the lobby door flew open, a thud as it hit the wall beyond. One floor to go. I ran faster, slipping on the third step from the bottom so that I slid down the last few, righting myself at the last moment.

The door hung wide open, the brief gap in the clouds past now so that rain that had built to driving was sweeping in through the door. I plunged out into it.

The rain swept across the car park. I spun, searching. For footsteps. For a figure. For anything.

I turned about on the pavement. Looking left to right. But whoever had been there was gone.

Chapter 7

We were an army seeking a ghost, a platoon in luminous yellow marching across the car park, fanning out into the surrounding buildings, onto the scrubby heath beyond, hunting for that one needle in this giant haystack.

He had escaped me.

A marked police car was angled across the car park entrance, its blue lights swirling in the tumbling-down rain. And, just beyond it, a clutch of figures, their umbrellas slanted into the wind that had begun to pick up, raincoats whipping out behind them like so many capes. When you call in the cavalry, you have to expect that the cavalry will draw an audience. The reporters had come from all over for this, flocking towards the death of the perfect victim, the everywoman. It is, one had said to me, an allegory for our time, how someone can seem to have it all and yet can be cut down one fine spring morning, leaving in our wake the sudden realisation that we never really existed at all.

'DS Parr, is this to do with the Brunswick Square Jane Doe case? Have you found something?' The woman's voice had been taken by the wind, twisted so that it came out thin and reedy. She was short – although perhaps petite would be the better word for it – a frame like a child's, dark blonde, her hair whipping in the wind so that it tugged across her face.

'We'll have a statement for you later,' I said to the reporter, infusing my words with confidence, little caring whether I was lying or not.

They did not matter. Crows around a carcass.

I had searched the length of the apartment grounds until my vision had blurred by the pouring-down rain. Had knelt down in puddles to peer beneath parked cars. I had walked until the rain had leached through my jacket – shower-resistant, my arse – until the fabric of my clothes was entirely sodden through. Had clambered over the wrought-iron gate into the perfectly manicured rear garden. Had felt my heart sink as I took in my surroundings. A neatly trimmed lawn, a bubbling riot of colour from carefully kept flower beds. And then, at the rear, a gate leading out onto the heath. Shit.

Then I had called for help.

'Nothing?' I asked.

'Nothing from house-to-house.' Poppy shook her head.

I let loose a low growl of frustration. 'Where the fuck can he have gone? I was seconds behind him. How the hell is it possible he simply vanished?'

Poppy squinted through the rain. 'Garden backs onto the heath …'

'But how the hell … I mean, I'm not that sodding slow.' I stepped out, my feet sinking into a puddle, and scanned the car park, blue lights reflecting off water. I moved away from the front door of the building, slow, sopping steps towards the few cars that remained.

'Your fella is a ghost,' said Poppy. 'That is,' she amended, 'if he is your fella. I mean, we don't know that the person who came to the door was the same one who stabbed her.'

'It was,' I said, quietly. 'I know it was.'

'Well, far be it from me to question that. Is someone doing the flat?'

'They've just gone up.' I tilted my head back, so that the rain worked its way in beneath my hood, trickling along my collarbone, and gazed up at the wall of bright-eyed apartment windows, vacant and unyielding. 'And we checked all the apartments?'

Poppy nodded. 'All the ones with people at home. Work day is in full swing. Lots of places empty. We've left contact details though.'

I watched the windows, wondered if behind them there was someone else watching me.

'Seriously, who the hell is this guy? I mean, look, the guy who stabs a woman, who slits her throat … I kind of get that guy. I mean, it's deeply unpleasant and seriously fucked up, but I know how to deal with that guy. But this guy … I mean, who does that, carries out an attack like that, then talks his way into that same woman's apartment and clears it of evidence. And then comes back for more. What the hell is that about?' I looked up, turning my face towards the rain.

'What more?' asked Poppy.

'Huh?'

'You said he came back for more. But he didn't get in, did he? So whatever he came back for, it's still in the apartment.'

I stared at her, my mind moving jigsaw pieces. 'You know what, you're right.'

'I often am,' said Poppy, sanguine.

'DS Parr!!' I looked back to the gathered crowd of reporters, all umbrellas and hooded faces, could see the small woman, waving wildly in my direction.

'Shit,' I muttered. 'I'm going to have to get past that crazy train.'

'Go,' said Poppy, grimly. 'I'll deal with that lot.'

'Pops ...'

'What? I'll be nice. I mean, I'll lie, obviously, but other than that I'll be delightful.'

I grinned. 'Good luck.'

'It's them who'll need the luck.'

'Who do you think I was talking about?' I patted her on the arm, spun on my heel, eyes front. I would walk past them, would not look sideways. After all, I had a job to do.

The rain had begun to beat down with a fury. It bounced up off the pavements, the upwards raindrops meeting the ones heading down on my shin, forcing my trousers to cling to my legs. Hard to walk with authority when your every footstep makes a rasping noise against the ground.

'Alice.'

Dammit. My traitor head spun of its own accord, my

body too well trained to the sound of its own name. Essentially, I'm a sheepdog.

The small blonde woman had separated herself from the crowd, was half buried beneath an oversized umbrella, but even so, her mascara had begun to run, leaving dark rims beneath her eyes.

'Alice, hi. I'm Naomi. Naomi Flood? I just wanted to introduce myself to you, and to say … Look, this is a bit weird, but I think you're a real inspiration.' She shuffled closer, the edge of her umbrella brushing against my scalp. 'I was there, that night. The fire at your house? I reported on it. Didn't think anyone would make it out alive from that thing. I just wanted to say, what you've been through … it would break most people. I think the fact that you kept going, that you picked up and just carried on, is incredible. You are a true hero.'

My mouth opened, and yet there were no words. I stared at her, her sympathetic brown eyes, and felt myself take a step back.

'So, this Jane Doe thing …' Her voice had shifted now, easing into a well-formed patter. 'Is this her?' She nodded up towards the apartment complex. 'I guess you have an identity on her now?'

I frowned. Tried to think of a quick response. But all that I could find was the rake of acrid smoke at the back of my throat, the distant crackle of flames. 'We … we'll be releasing a statement later.' I turned, walking with quick, slopping steps away from her. I walked slowly up the stairs, my footsteps echoing with the last time I had

92

trodden them, steps behind the vanishing man. I paused in the hallway and pulled on a forensic suit.

The apartment door stood wide open, the CSI beginning to set up to work on the handle. He stepped aside, grunting an acknowledgement to my thanks.

I slowed, concentrated on my breaths, on the in and the out. Told myself that Holly had stood here. That before she lay in an empty park in a pool of puddled blood, she had walked through this very hallway, had entered this kitchen.

I turned in a slow circle.

He'd come here for a reason. I ran my fingers across the walnut worktop. He had taken something from her, after slicing open her throat. Had stolen from her that envelope and all that it contained.

The tap dripped into the ceramic sink. She had something worth killing for. And yet somehow that hadn't been enough. I looked around me. What had he taken? And, more importantly, what had he missed?

I tugged open cupboards, running my gloved hands along the sides of them. But the kitchen yielded only itself. Plates and cups and bowls. Only the things that keep it running. No discarded scraps of paper with notes to remind you. No letters for the attention of.

But then, this was a fleeting home, wasn't it? A brief stop upon a journey.

I turned to face the kitchen table, the fruit bowl, apples beginning to brown and wither. Through the glass of the table, a flicker of red. I ducked down, pulling on a pair of gloves, and reached out to grasp it in my fingers,

93

a slip of card, *sorry we missed you*. I leaned back on my haunches, studying it. *Your letter required a signature*. It has been left with your neighbour at number 13.

My heart began to thump just that little faster.

'Harry?' I called.

The sound of footsteps, then Harry peered around the kitchen door. 'Yes, Sarge?'

I passed the slip to him. 'Can you check this out?'

He took it gingerly, scrutinising it. 'You think this is why he came back?'

I looked about myself. A scrap of paper, easy enough to drop as you gather together the final vestiges of a woman's life. And then, in the sudden realisation that you have seen something, but that something has not made it out with you, that you have left a trail ... yes, it would make sense to me that this could bring him back.

'Maybe,' I said. 'Go see if number thirteen can shed any light, yes?'

I watched his retreating back, mind instead on this so-called Detective Grey. What kind of confidence, what kind of arrogance, must this man possess? To return here. To chance his arm. Not once, but twice.

I moved through into the bedroom, the double bed neatly made, curtains pulled back. A small desk stood in the corner, a chair tucked up beneath it, its surface clear. A glass vase on the windowsill, a small bunch of daffodils that had twisted and browned, spilling a sodden sweetness into the room. I raised a hand towards their saccharine rottenness, and I thought of wolves, of the hunter and its prey.

I crouched down, my knees tugging with the movement, pulling out the drawers, disappointingly empty. There was a layer of dust beneath the desk, standing proud on the light carpet. And a flash of white. Gotcha. There, right at the back against the wall, doused in shadows, lay a coiled cord. I squeezed my way beneath the desk, re-emerged, a power cable clutched in my fingers. A MacBook by the look of it.

I pursed my lips, turned in a slow circle. Where was the computer?

I peered under the bed, pulling open the drawers of the bedside cabinet, behind the curtains, beneath the cushions on the chair. No sign of the MacBook.

The sound of plastic rustling footsteps and Harry reappeared. 'No answer at number thirteen, Sarge. I'll keep trying.'

I frowned. 'Yeah, let's keep on top of that one. Hey, Harry? You seen a computer about the place? I'm thinking a MacBook.'

'Nothing so far. You think he took it?'

I sighed. 'Looks like it.' I pushed myself up to standing. 'She should have a passport. If she's come in from the US ... Or flight information. Some kind of documents.'

Harry shook his head. 'There's a make-up bag in the bathroom, the usual toiletries and,' he flushed, 'you know, girly stuff. But nothing that could be used to identify her.' He fell into silence, then, 'You think ... you think he didn't want us to find out who she was?'

'Maybe.' But then, if Anthony Bean had told him he had her passport information, he would know that we would find out soon enough. What would be the point? What did she have on her that he needed to hide?

It was a jigsaw puzzle with pieces missing, a picture out of focus.

'Check the bed for me, yeah?' I said, moving back to the bedside cabinet, pulling out drawers, feeling around the edges of them for something, anything.

'Sarge?'

I paused, an uneasy feeling of premonition settling over me, glancing behind me. Harry had pushed the mattress up, placing his shoulder under it to expose the underside. And there beneath it, just below the level of the pillow, lay a kitchen knife, large and sturdy, all that a kitchen knife should be, apart from, y'know, being under a mattress.

Harry leaned in, peering more closely at it. 'Now, obviously I'm just a guy, but do all women sleep with carving knives within hand's reach?'

'No,' I said, quietly. 'No, we do not.' I slipped the knife into an evidence bag.

I thought of Holly, inert in her hospital bed. You were afraid, weren't you? My fingers felt sticky, the memory of her blood on them, the thought settling over me that in the deepest part of her she had a sense of what was to come. I raised the knife up to the light. Where there were doubts before, there were now none. This had been no random attack. He had come for her. And she had seen him coming.

I slipped one glove off, dialling quickly on my mobile. The DI answered on the second ring, voice harried.

'Guv,' I said, 'we need to have a guard placed on the hospital room.' In my mind, the echoes of retreating footsteps. 'I don't think he's done. She knew him. And he meant to kill her that day. I think he's going to try again.'

The DI didn't answer, for long enough that my stomach began to knot up on itself. Then, 'I'll get someone over there straight away.'

I hung up, the sense overwhelming that we were on the precipice, that a few more steps and all would become clear. I moved to the wardrobe, scanning the row of blouses, of trousers, all with discreet designer labels, all showing signs of wear. I slipped my gloved fingers into the pockets, feeling the fabric for any unexpected density. Then I froze.

'Harry,' I said, 'can I borrow your torch?'

I took the flashlight, crouching down low to peer between the forest of fabric.

'Sarge? What are you looking for?'

I didn't respond. Instead, I twisted my body, crawling half into the wardrobe to reach it. I tugged it forward, pulling a large cloth tote into the light of the room, could feel Harry looming over me, gaze hooked on it. I pulled open the bag.

Shit.

'What is that?'

I didn't reply, simply pulled out a dark swathe of hair. Followed by grey, short and to the point. Then an unremarkable brown. 'Wigs,' I said, shortly. Beneath that, a small box containing two pairs of glasses, one narrow and businesslike, the other overlarge and vaguely insectile. 'They're disguises,' I said, softly. 'She has disguises.'

Was it me, or had the temperature in the room dropped?

I glanced up at Harry, slack-jawed and nervous. 'Do me a favour?' I said. 'Give Poppy a shout.'

Harry gave me a sharp look, then slowly nodded, ducking out of the room.

I sat there, on the floor of her bedroom. Her. Jane Doe. Holly Vale. The victim. And I looked at the kitchen knife, large and looming. At the splayed-out wigs.

There could be reasonable explanations. There would be, somewhere just beyond where I could see. But, for now, I was swamped by a sense of foreboding, of having gotten hold of the wrong end of the stick.

I pushed myself up, moving closer to the window, the grey-green of the heath beyond it. The rain came horizontal now, the wind tugging a spatter of it against the glass. A row of books stood on the windowsill, all of them well read, their spines broken and broken again. The kind of thing that you find in a rental house, mementoes of the visitors that had gone before. I studied them, sensing something off. I ran my finger across their roughened edges. The last in the line was a copy of *Wild Swans*. There was something there, a wrongness with the shape of it. I touched the spine of it, creased only up to about the first quarter, the rest of it pristine. I pulled it out, letting the book fall open on my lap.

Time stopped.

There, in the centre of the book, where a thick wedge of pages should be, lay a sheaf of $100 bills.

I stared at them, letting one gloved hand run along the edge of the wad. There must be, what, a hundred? More. Ten thousand dollars at least.

'Harry said you wanted me. Shit.' Poppy stopped in the centre of the room, staring down at the book in my hand, at the brick of notes. She glanced up at me, back down again, then did a slow turn about the room, taking in the knife, the disguises. 'Oh, Al, this is not good.'

Do you know how much I hadn't wanted her to say that? How much I had wanted the woman who had lain bleeding in my arms to remain who she had been to me? An innocent. The fallen angel. Later, I would come to question why that was, why that seemed so important to me. But right then all I could think was that I had been wrong.

Poppy opened her mouth, closed it again, her gaze returning to the money in my hand. 'Al,' she said, softly, 'I don't think our Jane Doe is who we thought she was.'

Chapter 8

There are moments in each investigation, when the lens shifts, when all becomes clear. Even if the only clarity you find is the crystal-clear realisation that you are screwed, that you have wandered into a crime that is, for now, unsolvable. I stood beneath the trees, the rain thrumming above my head in an uneven chorus as it hit the leaves, the pavement, the bare skin on my cheeks, the weather bringing with it an early twilight, and scuffed my toe against a tuft of scrub, feeling the wind sweep up across the heath, tugging at me. The city had disappeared now, buried beneath low-lying cloud. It was only me on a wild moor.

I rubbed my face. I was getting delirious for want of coffee.

Jane Doe. Holly Vale. She was a ghost, a thread-thin figure that vanishes when you reach out to take hold of it. Only, she wasn't, was she? Because she had left behind her very real blood, that coated my clothing, worked its way into the creases of my fingers. And she was flesh and bone, lying in a hospital bed, hovering between life and death.

I told myself that we had a name. That she was Holly

Vale, and now we could begin to drill down, to really understand who she was, what she was doing here. Find out how a person lived and you will find out how they died. Or almost died.

Yellow jackets moved towards me, a swarm of them, on their way back from the heath. The search had been called off. Whoever had been there, he was gone now.

The press had begun to grow impatient. You could see it in the sway of their umbrellas, hear it in the jibber-jabber voices, questions flung out into the empty air, towards the forensic officer loading his car, the PCSO who stared past them, unmoving as a statue. They could sense that we had something, could smell the sea change. I ran my fingers through my hair and let out a sound that fell halfway between a laugh and a groan. They would be anticipating an outcome, would be justifying their damp trousers and ruined hair by telling themselves that they would have a story, that in minutes or hours they would at least know, what happened, who she was.

I turned back towards the car park, the wind from the heath gusting up behind me, pushing me onwards, my mind twisting, trying to find an angle in which the pieces added together so that it all made sense. That feeling of being stared at, of watchful eyes in the trees that surrounded me, wraithlike figures in the vanishing mist.

'Okay, Sarge?'

I started, my gaze sweeping across the sodden heath, finally picking out Harry. He had tucked himself be-neath an overhanging elm tree, his face hidden by the narrow tunnel of his hood, the glow of an optimistic cigarette breaking the shadow.

'Yeah. Fine.'

'Want one?' He held out the packet to me, Marlboro lights.

My body recoiled, snapping me backwards against my will. My scar ached.

'No, thank you.'

He nodded, sanguine. 'I got the details of number thirteen. Woman named Emilia Lucas. Tried reaching out to her on her mobile, but nothing yet. I've left a message.' He blew out a stream of smoke and gestured towards the apartment. 'What do you think? This Holly Vale into something she shouldn't be?'

No.

Yes.

'I don't know.' I watched him take a pull on the cigarette, the embers glowing brighter then fading. 'I'm going to head over to the hospital. See if there's any more news.'

'Sure. Want me to come with?'

No. 'You, ah, you stay and give Poppy a hand, yeah? She'll need extra bodies to finish up with the apartment.' I pulled my hood back up, too little, too late. 'I'll see you back at the office, yeah?'

I turned back towards the main road, my head aching, muscles twanging with the slingshots of adrenaline. Slipped along the narrow pathway that led back to the car park, keeping my head low, my face turned away from the waiting journalists. Across the expanse of tarmac, a small figure detached herself, her orange umbrella dancing merrily against the grey of the day, heading towards the first of the search team to make it back. Naomi Flood. That she would be frustrated gave me little solace.

Against the drumbeat of raindrops looped her earlier words. You are a true hero.

I thought of Jane Doe. Of myself. Neither of us are who we appear to be. And then, inevitably, I thought of that night – of the creeping wakefulness, being pulled from an unnatural sleep, of that sense of something being just that little bit off. Of the room, shimmering, the lines of it softer than it should have been, and thinking it was the wine, or the suddenness of waking. Of that slow, slow dawning awareness that no, whatever this is, it is not that. That something is wrong.

I snapped back to reality, pulling open the driver's door of the shitty little Ford Focus and climbed inside, vaguely aware of the orange umbrella turning, of the spotlight gaze of Naomi Flood finding me, the inevitability of what would come next. I jammed the key in the ignition and pulled out of the car park, fast enough that a passing motorist honked in righteous indignation. Well, there was one for Twitter. Police misuse of power.

I forced my foot up from the accelerator, the words of Naomi Flood twisting their way through my head.

Hero.

It was a Saturday when it all changed, or a Saturday night that had spilled over into Sunday morning. It was 3.05 a.m.

It is easy to forget, on the rare occasions when I tell myself this story, that there was a day that came before it, that life had a form, even then, without the fire and its scars to shape it. But these moments, the ones that take what we once were and flip it on its head, transforming us into someone new, they come from nowhere. They come from a perfect clear blue sky. From a calm ocean.

That day, it had been a good day. A date with a guy I met out running. Josh, I think? I don't remember much about him, not now, but I know that at the time it had seemed that there was ... something. That undefinable unknown that, when you are thirty and single and beginning to google things like sperm banks and escort services, you pray for. I was in a good mood that night. I had thought that it was the beginning. I had no idea.

What time did I get to bed? One, maybe? Or a little later?

I remember that I was still thrilling with too many cocktails, my skin prickling from the chill autumn air. That I struggled to fall asleep, my skittish mind pulling apart and reconstructing my day, my date, and, let's be honest about things, a future in which I was the wife of a barrister, had a litter of children with perfect dark curls.

Then a settling, a sinking, snaking tails of dreams ... then the waking and the sound and the murkiness of the room and that something that catches at the back of your throat, scouring at it. Your brain is addled, you don't understand. Or at least, *I* didn't. I didn't understand.

What came next? I think that I tried to sit up, but it

seemed that the room itself was pushing me, pressing me back into my mattress. Sleep then. I would close my eyes, for my body felt so heavy and my mind so reluctant. Sleep would help.

I shifted, turning to my side, and, for reasons that remain unclear to me, my eyes flickered back open, just for a moment.

That was when I saw it. The dark shape of the door, the thin orange line of light that surrounded it. My eyes closed, then opened again as my slow mind caught up.

My flat – my little one bedroom first-floor on a quiet street in Kentish Town, the first place I had ever bought, my home, my safety net – was on fire.

I remember a clawing pain, one that pressed from the top of my skull to the bottom of my jaw and then vanished just as quickly as it had come, leaving nothingness in its wake. I remember a sound that I took to be flames but later I realised was someone calling my name. I remember pressure, beneath me, around me. A dizzying sense of movement. Then a change in the air, as if it had suddenly been stripped bare, leaving it cold and clean.

Then nothing.

It had been a spark in the flat beneath mine, the home of Elsbeth Little, a missed connection from a cheap mobile phone charger that had frizzled with unconfined electricity, the grip of it catching at a throw. Then the spark had become a flame and it had spread and worked its way through her home, climbing up to mine. It was an accident. Nothing more. Could happen to anyone.

They had found the body of Elsbeth the following day. She had been killed by smoke inhalation in her bed, by all appearances had never even woken, her sleep merely shifting from deep to eternal.

By the time I reached St Mary's Hospital, the rain had slowed to a drizzle. I jammed the car into an unlikely space, turned off the engine and breathed deeply. Forcing myself to move then, opening the car door carefully, squeezing my way out into the rain.

I marched through the sliding glass doors like a conquering army.

The room was empty, but for her, Holly, lost in her cavernous sleep, the machines that kept her alive beeping and whirring. Her skin seemed smoothed out, the lines eased away by the power of her sleep, lips curled about the tube that gave her breath in a faux snarl. I moved closer, catching the shadow of a scent, jasmine in amongst the roar of plastic and ammonia.

Who are you?

'Oh, hello.'

I started, for a moment my uneven mind thinking that it was her.

'Sorry. Didn't see you come in. Alice, isn't it?' The nurse looked me over, taking in my dripping-wet clothes.

'Yes. Sorry. What's your ...'

'Gwen.' She waved towards the bed. 'I thought the sister had called you. As you can see, it hasn't gone terribly well.'

106

'It?'

'Ending the sedation. We had been hoping to bring her round, but unfortunately there's been nothing yet.'

I hesitated, my gaze falling on Jane Doe ... Holly. 'What does that mean?'

Gwen blew out a sigh. 'In itself? Not too much. She could just be taking her time. The concern, of course, is that her brain has been deprived of oxygen due to her injuries. The longer it takes her to regain consciousness, the more we have to consider whether some serious damage has been done.' She gave me a well-practised smile. 'Still, too early to think like that now. Was there something you needed?'

'I ...' What was I doing there? Why had I come? I played with the question, testing out the uncomfortable truth that I had come there to escape. 'I just wanted to let you know some good news. Well, maybe good is ... Well, news at any rate. We found her name. It's Holly. Holly Vale.'

'Oh, marvellous,' said Gwen, squeezing her hands tight together. 'I'll update her notes. Any luck with locating the family?'

'Not yet.'

'Well, that might be the thing that does it, you know, hearing her loved ones' voices. Anyway, now that you know who she is, I'm sure you'll be able to get hold of them soon. I bet they're sick with worry.'

I thought of the money hidden in a book, of the disguises and the knife.

'Yes. Yes, I'm sure they are.'

Chapter 9

The office was quiet now, the early morning flurry of outside activity well underway. I rubbed my hands across my face. I hadn't made it home last night, had reached the stage in proceedings at which the effort was greater than the reward, had slept for maybe thirty minutes, my head leaned back in the chair, and woken feeling worse than I had before. I had sank into my seat, pulled my knees up to my chest, had managed to find an old sweater stuffed in the back of my locker, an oversized thing, ragged at the cuffs and a pair of loose-fit jeans. Not much, but still preferable to my sopping-wet suit. I had stood in the locker room for longer than you would think feasible, had stared at myself in the mirror, my hair pulled up into a rough, rain-soaked topknot, my face slicked bare. The scar had looked angry, livid red swirling into bright white, like this day and this case had pushed it to its limits, like something was breaking free.

I held the paper coffee cup close – Green Java's finest latte, two shots of espresso, a hint of gingerbread – and wiggled the mouse, bringing the screen to life. The report on the Wi-Fi feed of Holly's Airbnb was lengthy and dry. I sighed, took a sip of coffee. According to the summary, she had spent a prodigious amount of time online, upwards of six hours a day. I scrolled through her inputs. Her time, it seemed, had not been spent like most of us do. Not dipping into and out of shopping sites, scrolling uselessly through Twitter, Facebook.

Instead she had focused on search engines.

I let my finger run down the screen, trying to make sense of the search before me.

Google.

Input – Ed Canning.

I searched the date field. It had begun upon the day of her arrival, the first search starting in the early hours of the morning. Jet lag, maybe?

Ed Canning London.

Then, after an hour or so, Ed Canning university. Then Ed Canning finance.

Who was he? And why was she searching so desperately for him? Night after night, her activity beginning at about 7 p.m., running through until 1 sometimes 2 a.m. But what was strange was that it seemed all she had was a name. Based on her searches, she knew little else about him. They ran the gamut, covering almost every industry you could conceive of. She had tried dating sites, Facebook, Twitter, all with the same end in mind. Finding him.

I flicked between screens, running a PNC check on the name Ed Canning in a brief moment of hope that ended abruptly. Whoever he is, according to us he doesn't have a criminal history. What the hell were you doing here, Holly?

'Hey.'

I started, the movement jostling my cup, sending a wave of coffee over my once-clean desk. 'Shit. Hey.' I glanced up at Poppy, grabbing a handful of tissues, began padding uselessly at the puddle. 'All wrapped up in Hampstead?'

'Yeah.' She sighed, holding out her arms in illustration. 'It remains a touch damp out there.' Her clothes hung from her, limp and sodden.

'Anything else?'

'Nothing. I've sent all the forensic stuff to the lab, so we'll see ...' She dropped into her chair with an uncomfortable squelching sound and glanced down at her phone, the screen lighting up with a photo of Charlie, smiling brightly.

'Where's young Charles today?'

'My mother had him overnight. She, and I quote, hopes that I won't make a habit of this working-all-hours nonsense, because "your son really should be your priority, you know".' She scrubbed at her face, smearing her mascara beneath her left eye. 'You'd swear I was ditching him to go sit on a street corner and smoke crack.'

I tilted my head, sympathetic. 'And are you?'

She shrugged. 'Well, you know, when the crack-train calls ... Whatcha doin'?'

'Wi-Fi. It looks like Holly was keeping herself busy here in London. She was looking for someone. An Ed Canning? That seems to be the focus of all her online activities.'

Poppy pursed her lips.

'What?'

'You know,' she said, thoughtful, 'that was one of the things I thought was weird on that search. There's no evidence anywhere in that apartment that she was a tourist. No brochures for attractions. No souvenir purchases. No receipts. Matt spent hours going through the admittedly shitty CCTV from the apartment complex, and each morning was the same. She gets up, leaves the complex at 8 a.m. Then, at about 6 p.m., she would return, not carrying any extra bags or showing any signs of a day spent on Oxford Street.'

'So …'

'So, I don't think she was here on holidays. I think she was here with a purpose.' She nodded towards my computer screen. 'Maybe this was the purpose.'

'Anyone get hold of the neighbour at number thirteen yet?'

Poppy shook her head. 'Still trying. We'll do another sweep tonight when more people are home from work.'

I nodded. 'Did Matt find any sign of our guy from the CCTV?'

'System only covers the car park. If you come out of the front door, take a hard right, you'll miss it. Looks like that's what he did.'

'And no footage from his meeting with Anthony Bean?'

Poppy shook her head. 'Bean said he saw him by the front door, yeah? Cameras didn't get it, didn't catch any sign of him arriving. It's almost like he'd planned it, like he'd thought through his entrances and exits, taking into account the camera's reach.'

I swivelled in my chair. 'Then ... he'd have to have been there before, checking out the lie of the land. Let's assume he did find the business card in Holly's bag, that that is how he knew where she was staying, that means he had twenty-four hours to scope the place out.' I gave her a pointed look.

She pulled her phone free, shaking her head. 'I'll call Matt,' she said. 'Tell him he needs to do the full twenty-four.'

I swivelled in my chair, turning to study the lines of text across my screen. Who the hell was this Canning guy and why was she looking for him?

'He's on it. He's delirious.' Poppy shuffled her chair closer, peering at my screen. She made a noise, a low, back-of-the-throat grunt.

'What?'

'I don't think you're going to like this.'

'What??'

'Something feels ... off about this, Al. The stuff we found in the flat, the visit to the station, the stalking of this guy. The disguises, the money. I think we have to consider the idea that there's more to Holly Vale than meets the eye.'

I turned to face her. 'You think she's into something criminal.'

A pause.

'It would explain an awful lot.' Poppy folded her arms. 'Think about it, Al. I mean really think. Like you just came on this case from the outside. What we've found. It doesn't make her look good.'

I glanced away, discomfited suddenly. Because when you pulled it all apart, Poppy was right. The evidence, the few pieces of the puzzle that we had stacked together, it was starting to suggest a theory. And yet my insides railed against that. Why?

The thing is, when you work a case like this, there are parts of yourself that you shut down, pieces you turn off. The victim – for right or wrong – becomes little more than an agglomeration of body parts, a puzzle that needs to be solved. It's easier that way, safer. It allows you to sleep at night.

But this case . . .

I never had that. Not with her. Whether because of my entry into her attack, because she held my hand as she fought for breaths, or because of what would come later. Whatever the reason, I never managed to do it with her, to maintain my distance.

'Okay . . .' I said, willing my voice to calm. 'What if . . .'

The ringing phone cut across me, a welcome reprieve, and I grabbed for it, overeager probably.

'DS Parr, Major Crime.'

'Ah, hello? Yes, hello. I hope you can help me.' The man spoke slowly, as if afraid of being misunderstood, his Scottish burr heavy and rolling. 'I am one of the managers here in Victim Support operating in the Greater London area, and I've been speaking with a lady involved in one of your cases, a Ms Edwina Clarke?'

'I …' I fought for a face, finally coming up with an oversized golden retriever, a small, rounded Jamaican woman with bright white hair. 'Ms Clarke. Of course.'

'Ah, yes, the thing is, Ms Clarke is particularly vulnerable, I'm not sure if she told you but she lost her husband some time ago and has recently been receiving treatment for a serious heart condition, so as I'm sure you can appreciate, she has a lot on her plate.'

'Oh, yes.' I glanced at Poppy, frowned. 'So …'

'No, well, the thing is, we've had a wee issue with Ms Clarke. She called us this morning, extremely agitated, said she'd been having nightmares and that she thought something was wrong, that she was having chest pains, but then the call dropped out. And I'll be honest with you, I'm worried about her, and I just can't find her address on our files here. So, look, if you can give me her address, then I can nip straight round there and make sure she's okay.'

I frowned, fingers moving to pull up Edwina Clarke's information. 'Okay, look, I'll get uniform round there as a matter of urgency, get them to do a welfare check. If you want to leave your contact details, I can give you a call back …'

'Well, you know, I think it would probably be easier if you just let me have her address myself? That way I can just nip straight round there. I mean, given what she's been through, I think it's important …'

'Well, I …' Something stopped me, something about the conversation ringing false. 'I'm sorry, I'm sure you said your name, but I missed it?'

'It's Kevin.'

I looked at Poppy, snapping my fingers to get her attention. 'Kevin what?'

'Kevin Walters.'

'And you're from what branch of Victim Support?'

There was a silence, the sound of wheels turning, then a click and dial tone.

'Shit.'

'Who was that?'

I looked at Poppy. 'I think that was him. I think that was the guy who tried to kill her.'

Chapter 10

I sat, holding the telephone receiver in my hand, suspended in disbelief. That someone would leap at a woman, stab her until she is just clinging to life, then vanish into thin air, only to reappear, a key in a lock in a place he should not be, then vanish again. Then this, a heavy Scottish accent, a probing voice in the guise of a caring professional.

Poppy had stood now, was hovering at the side of my desk, watching me, the phone, as if we were both in danger of exploding. 'You think it could be the press, chancing their arm.'

How to explain it? That stirring feeling in my gut. That sense of newness and familiarity all at once.

'It was him. I know it was him.'

As explanations went, it wasn't the most comprehensive. I placed the phone back in its cradle. 'I ... I know it sounds weird. But I'd lay money on it.'

'But then ...' Poppy stumbled, struggling for the words, 'how did he know the name of the witness? Yes, he'd seen her, but he wouldn't have known who she was. Unless ... they didn't print that in the papers, did they?'

I shook my head. 'I don't know.'

'The press was all over that place like cockroaches. And that Clarke woman, she was chatty. Would have been easy enough for a reporter to get her name out of her.' She lowered her voice, tone serious. 'That'll be it, Al. It'll be the media, trying a new tactic.' She said it like one would say 'step back from the edge', 'put down the gun', her gaze wary.

I didn't answer. 'We need to trace the call,' I said, quietly.

She nodded slowly. 'Okay. Sure. I'll get on it.'

I stared at the grey sky beyond the wide expanse of window. Thinking of the voice. It sounded fake. Or was that only in retrospect, an addition to prove my point? The clouds drifted, their shapes loosening, contrast lowering, rain to come, and a new thought moving in. That it was not impossible I was wrong. That the phone call had in fact been someone else, a cheeky journalist, but that the notion of him, with his ready knife, the ability to force your gaze to slide away, scared me. How many criminals had I dealt with? How many arrests had I made? And yet something in this had wormed its way beneath my skin, twisting shadows into figures in the dark. It was the intangibility of him, the there and then gone again, that to me made him seem to be everywhere.

I blew out a breath and picked up a pen, some paper. Drew a circle at the centre of the page, the words Jane Doe at the heart of it. No, not Jane Doe. Holly Vale. Cross it through. What do I know about you? American.

Married with children. I tapped the pen against my lip. $10,000 in cash. Knife. Disguises. Ed Canning. And the word wolf.

I studied that last word, pen hovering over it.

'Alice? Everything okay?'

I hadn't heard the DI slide into the room, and I struggled to focus on him, to look beyond my own thoughts.

'I ... yeah ...' I said, rallying. 'I'm fine.'

He perched on the desk beside mine. 'It's a nasty one this. Especially for you, being with her after it happened.'

I schooled my face, a careful construction of DS Alice Parr. 'I'm fine,' I said. 'Hey, Guv? Let me run something by you.' A diversionary tactic. I spread the papers out in front of him, the name Canning circled so many times that it seemed to sit in the heart of a tornado. 'She was searching for this guy, we have a whole host of computer searches on her computer, dating from the time she arrived and filling up most of her waking hours.' I pointed to the Wi-Fi report. 'Only that stopped, about ten days ago.' I turned to face him. 'So, I'm thinking ...'

'Maybe she found him.'

'Or,' I said, 'maybe he found her.'

'You think this is the guy? The same guy who attacked her?'

I looked back at my screen. 'I think we have to, at the very least, eliminate him as a suspect.'

Noah nodded. 'I agree.' He leaned closer, studying my notes, his gaze falling on the same word I was so focused on. Wolf. 'Did you ...'

'Nothing.' I sighed, heavily. 'To be honest, I'm

starting to wonder if I heard what I thought I heard. It was chaotic and she could barely breathe ...' I stared at the scrawl of paper, at the rough-hewn circles in red marker pen. 'Perhaps it means nothing at all.'

The DI's phone rang, his hand hurrying to it with an apologetic grimace. I turned my attention back to the screen, to Ed Canning and Edgar Canning and Edward Canning.

Say it was true. Say it was him. What did I know? Thickset, long blond hair. He knew who she was, was clearly waiting for her at King's Cross. So he was confident. No. Arrogant. Because if you're going to return to the flat of a woman you've tried to murder, if you're going to call the detective investigating her case and try and con information out of her, there must be a certain hubris, a certain belief in your own capacity for deception. He was calm. Had he panicked, someone would have seen him. There were certainly plenty of potential witnesses. But he didn't, he kept his cool and, despite severing a woman's throat, slipped away unnoticed.

Then a thought sliding in, cold and hard. He'd done this before.

A bang of the door and Poppy swept in. She'd changed into a pair of jeans, a loose-fitting T-shirt, had pulled her still damp hair back into a ponytail. 'Okay, so I chased up your Victim Support friend. You were right. No Kevin Walters on file. Call is tracing back to a throwaway phone. Harry's gone round to Mrs Clarke's to make sure she's safe, and I've told him to recommend to her that she goes to stay with a family member for a couple of days. Just to be safe.'

'Good,' I said. 'What about ...'

'Yes, I have also spoken to Matt. He says he has a migraine from all the shitty CCTV you have made him watch. He also said that he's picked up something in the early hours of the morning – around 3 a.m. He said you can see a figure approaching the apartment complex from East Heath Road. It's dark, figure is hooded ...'

'CCTV is shit, yeah, I get it.'

'Right, but he says whoever it is enters the apartment complex, walks round it. He said that he seems to check the periphery of the complex, pays particular attention to the location of the cameras, vanishes round the front to the front door – I'm guessing to see if he could gain entry without a key – then returns within a matter of minutes and is seen again heading back onto East Heath Road. I've got him checking out the surrounding areas, see if we can't find some better footage on him.'

I nodded, my mind bifurcating, on a dark figure on a Hampstead road and a man named Canning.

Edmund Canning. I typed quickly.

'Shit.'

'What?'

'I've got an address. Edmund Canning. I've got him registered in an apartment in Vauxhall.' I pushed myself up, grabbing hold of my coat. 'Come on. Let's do this.'

The rain had eased now, a torrent turning to a trickle, leaving behind a weighted day, a chill wind that whipped its way along the Thames. I pulled my stab-proof vest on over my sweatshirt and looked up at the straight spine of the apartment building, the glass of it reflecting the grey of the river. I paused for a moment, taking stock, and looked skyward, the fifty storeys of the Vauxhall Tower looming overhead, reaching up towards the massing clouds.

'Nice place,' I offered, checking the fit of the tabs, and slid my asp out, hefting it in my right hand, all the while trying not to think of the phrase 'bringing a stick to a gunfight'.

Poppy grunted from somewhere within her stab-proof. 'Rental agent says these flats go for a pretty penny.' Her head appeared out the top, and she grinned broadly. 'Pretty sure he'll be overwhelmed once he knows we wandered through there looking like this.'

I slammed the boot down, the gunshot ricochet of it making me jump. 'Yeah, well, he's extremely lucky it's us and not the tac unit.' I glanced up at the skyscraper. 'Maybe it should be the tac unit.'

Poppy racked her asp. 'Those boys with their guns? Like they have anything on you, me and a couple of metal toothpicks.'

'Great,' I muttered. 'I feel so much better now.'

I fell into step with her, walking into the lobby with a thousand-yard stare. Could feel the turn of heads following us as we passed, the open mouth of the receptionist, the dense sickly-sweet scent of the lilies that lolled over their cavernous crystal vase, my skin prickling with the sense of being stared at. Don't think, just do. And yet my mind bucked and shimmied. Was it him? Was Canning the man who had slit her throat, stabbing her again and again and again and leaving her to die in Brunswick Square Gardens? And if he was, what then? He would be expecting us to come for him. He would be armed.

I jammed my thumb against the lift button, the metal doors sliding open, myself looking back at me from the mirrored walls of the lift.

'Well,' I said, 'let's do this.'

I stepped in first, watched as Poppy pressed the button. Floor 32.

Poppy stood in front of me, her gaze on the floor counter, asp held tight in her hand.

30.

31.

32.

A quick glance back at me. Here we go.

The doors slid open to reveal a dimly lit hallway beyond. One door, two. Then apartment 324.

Poppy pulled up sharp beside it, a look at me, a quick nod. Then a sharp rap on the door. A pregnant silence. She rapped again, harder this time and for longer. I adjusted the grip on my asp, feeling my hands slick against the metal of it.

We waited, listening.

Then, 'I don't think he's in, Al.'

'Fuck's sake,' I muttered.

'I'll call the front desk,' said Poppy. 'See if they have a key.'

It took the building manager a full five minutes to reach

us, driven onwards by a heady steam of self-importance. He dressed like he was twenty, was probably fifty, and likely had more invested in his shoes than I had in my car. That was fine. They were ugly shoes anyway.

'I've tried contacting Mr Canning repeatedly since you called,' he said, sotto voce. 'But, unfortunately, I haven't been able to raise a response. Now, I mean, I have a key to the apartment, but obviously ...' He studied said key, very carefully not making eye contact 'I mean, we clearly have to be careful with our clients' privacy ...'

I smiled and tried to look like I meant it. 'I think, given that you haven't been able to reach Mr Canning ...'

'And we have reason to be concerned for his safety,' offered Poppy, flat-faced.

'Right. So, we're going to need to see inside the apartment. For Mr Canning's own protection.'

The man nodded mournfully, slid the key into the lock. 'I should say, I'm very uncomfortable with this.'

'Me too,' I said. 'Open it.'

A gusty sigh, and he twisted the key, swinging the door open. 'Mr Canning? Mr Canning? It's Piers Cole, building manager ... And the police.'

I moved past him, from the gloom of the hallway into a marbled lobby and then through into a spartanly furnished living room, one wall a window, a yawning expanse of glass that peered down onto the Thames, Pimlico and the rest of the sprawling city beyond.

'Mr Canning?' I tried, pushing my voice out, hearing it echo off the hard surfaces. 'You home?'

I glanced at Poppy, checked for my asp and moved into the apartment. There was little here to suggest habitation. A magazine on a coffee table. A chair left pushed back from the dining table. But as to anything else ... There was something, nibbling at the edge of my awareness, something that made my hackles rise. What was that? A sound? No. There was a smell, barely there at all. I raised an eyebrow at Poppy, nodding along the hallways. 'You smell that?'

She looked about her, eyes narrowed. 'I ... Is that smoke?'

I nodded. If anyone would know ...

'What's down there?' Poppy asked the building manager, quietly.

'Bedrooms. A bathroom.'

'Stay here,' I said. 'And don't touch anything.'

I moved past the length of window, sliding from grey daylight into the dimly lit hallway, aware suddenly that the smell was stronger there. Waited for Poppy to take up position alongside me, and then, with one hand on my asp, pushed open the bedroom door.

The room lay in darkness, the curtains stretched tight across. I ran my fingers along the wall, searching for a light switch, found it, then stood blinking as the room came into glorious technicolour.

Nothing.

I slipped inside, checking the en suite, and yet all there was as it should be.

I bobbed my head to Poppy, indicating further along the hall.

She opened the next door, careful. But the story remained the same. Twin beds this time, each neatly made.

And yet the smell had grown stronger.

'It's the last room,' I muttered.

We stacked up outside the door. I reached out a hand, laid a fingertip on the metal doorknob, waiting for heat, for a warning – do not enter.

I shook my head. 'It's cool. Ready?'

'Ready,' nodded Poppy, firmly.

I twisted the handle, shoving the door inwards, my body bracing itself, waiting for the ball of flame, for the clutch of smoke to wrap itself around me, finish what it had started. Instead, nothing. I frowned, stepped cautiously into the small room, this one set up as an office, a leather-backed chair, a desk and, on the top of it, a metallic container, the smell of smoke powerful now.

I inched closer. 'Well, I think I figured out the smell.' I peered into the container, insides blackened with a thick layer of ash, used my asp to sift through the debris. 'There's something in here,' I muttered.

I waited as Poppy pulled her torch free, shining the narrow beam of light into the darkness, watching as it bounced off twisted metal.

'Is that what I think it is?' asked Poppy.

I took the torch from her, lowering its heft down into the container, letting its beam illuminate the charred remnants of a computer, the skeletonised remains of an Apple logo.

'Yes,' I said shortly. 'It's Holly's MacBook. Or what's left of it.'

Poppy let out a low whistle, leaning closer. 'Who does that? I mean, seriously? Who starts a fire inside an apartment on the thirty-second floor?'

I pursed my lips. 'Someone with something to hide.'

Chapter 11

The building manager sat with his head in his hands. I dragged a chair out from beneath the desk of the recently appropriated ground-floor office, the legs of it scraping against hardwood floors that were probably worth more than my entire apartment. You could see the forensic unit van from here, parked up in an attempt to look innocuous, failing miserably, the pedestrians, slowing in their journeys as if pulled in by some gravitational field, their gazes hooked on the front lobby, the forensic team with their white suits heading in. A middle-aged man pushing a child on a scooter slowed to watch their progress, his face creasing up with tension. Then he hooked a hand around the child's arm, began to tow him away. I sighed. They would be thinking terrorism. They would be waiting for the other shoe to drop, for the next bomb or knife or car. I watched as they made their slow progress, the little boy crying now, trying to twist his arm free, and wanted to open the window, to call out, it's okay, it's fine. Just the home of a knife-toting madman. Nothing to see here.

I shifted my gaze back to the manager. 'I know this is tough ...' Did that sound sympathetic enough? Did

I sound like I cared? Because I'll be honest, my mind was well gone, was roaming through the apartment thirty-two storeys up, plunging back down and across the city to a flat in Hampstead, to Brunswick Square Gardens, was trying to tie these scenes together, create a picture that made some sense at least.

He looked up at me, the strain showing in the dark shadows under his eyes, the lines on his face that hadn't been there before. 'Seriously ... it really is. And the thing is, with the rental market the way it is right now, if Mr Canning has done a runner, we're going to need to rent that place asap ...' He shook his head. 'I don't believe this.'

I stared at him, attempting to shift his words into some sort of coherent order, before giving it up as a bad job. 'Yeah. The housing market. That's what I meant.'

'So, you think he tried to kill someone? Mr Canning?' he asked. 'I mean ... I heard some of the uniformed officers talking ...'

I hesitated, silently cursing the gobshites amongst our ranks.

'I don't know,' I said, honestly. 'But he is someone we need to speak to as a matter of some urgency.'

The manager was silent for a moment, then, in a burst, 'Who sets a fire in an apartment building? I mean, who does that? That's just ... it's irresponsible, is what it is. And I tell you one thing now, that man, he is not getting his deposit back.'

I stared at him. 'Uh-huh.' I leaned forward in my

chair. 'So, let's get this done, shall we? You knew the tenant? Mr Canning?'

'Huh? No. I mean, not personally. We have many people here, impossible to remember them all. You know how it is.'

Oh do fuck off.

'But you have met him?'

He frowned. 'See, now, I was thinking about this. I must have done. It's policy, you understand? To meet them when they first arrive, set them up and so forth. So I must have met him at some point, but … no … I don't really remember much. A bigger gentleman, I think.'

'Anything else? Height? Hair?'

He shook his head. 'Honestly don't remember. Nicely dressed, I think. Well spoken, well mannered. I think he might have been wearing glasses, but again I just couldn't say for sure. I could be thinking of some-one else.'

'How long has he lived here?'

'He rented the apartment in February last year, so a little over a year.'

'Alone?'

'To my knowledge, yes.'

I handed him the photograph of Holly Vale. 'You ever see this woman coming here?'

He studied it, shook his head. 'Sorry.'

'What about Mr Canning himself? I'm assuming you would have some sort of identification on file?'

'Well, now this is embarrassing … the thing is, it is

policy, but I checked this morning when you called and, now I don't know how this happened, but there's nothing in the file. I guess he was supposed to forward it to me and never did.'

Brilliant.

He glanced about the office, a quick look down at his watch. 'So, any idea how long this is going to take?'

'Oh, you can head off now. I have your details so I'll call you if there's anything further.'

'No, no, I meant the flat. How long do you think you will need to examine it? Obviously we're going to need to get a cleaning crew in there, get it back on the market ...'

I gave him a flat look. 'I'll make it my top priority.'

'Wonderful,' he said, cheerfully.

I ushered him out of the building, giving myself a mental high five for not booting him down the front steps, and then hurried back to the lift and to the thirty-second floor.

Poppy was loitering in the lobby, writing crabbily in her notepad. 'Hey. All done with Gordon Gecko?'

'Well, isn't he just a treasure? His concern was sincerely touching. How are the neighbours?'

'Out, mostly. However, number 326 says they rarely see Canning – she described a blond-haired man with glasses. Says he's very quiet and, on the rare occasion she has seen him, he doesn't speak to her. In short, the ideal neighbour. Number 322 on the other hand says that they've never met him but that they heard a loud noise coming from inside the apartment, yesterday lunchtime.

Said it sounded like a smoke alarm, but that it didn't last too long.'

I mentally shifted the pieces. Yesterday. He had gone to the Hampstead flat, had stripped it clean, or almost clean, and, after his abortive second attempt at entry, had come here, had immediately destroyed the computer he had stolen, along with whatever else had been in that container. The forensic team were sifting through it now, in an effort to identify anything else, their expressions universally doubtful.

'I'm assuming number 322 didn't call anyone? Go investigate to make sure everyone was okay.'

Poppy looked at me. 'Honey, it's London. And not just London. This is high-price tower living. *Of course* they didn't.'

I shook my head. 'You know, back home, if we forgot to put our bins out, the entire village would know about it by lunchtime.'

She snorted. 'Psh, you and your quaint Derbyshire country ways. This is the big city, missy.'

I grinned, tugged a forensic suit on. 'Shall we?'

Poppy sighed. 'My butt looks so big in polyethylene.'

The apartment looked much as we had left it. The only sign of habitation was the forensic case left sitting on the kitchen counter.

I stood in the doorway, surveyed the room before me. 'It's very ... neat.'

'I'd like to be neat,' offered Poppy. 'But the trouble is, I also like to be lazy. Oh, and I have a five-year-old. He does not like to be neat.'

I moved into the tucked-away kitchen with its high-gloss cabinets, granite worktops, and began to pull open cupboards, mostly empty. 'It's ... spartan. My mother would have a fit if my cupboards looked like this. What would happen if it snowed?'

'He'd starve. Although ...' Poppy stuck her head out from the freezer door, waving a bottle of vodka. 'There's vodka in here, so he'd at least be happy.'

'What about the fridge?'

'Um ... a pint of milk that ... yup, that's gone, Jesus.' She paused. 'And a bottle of Prosecco. So all the essentials.'

There was a coffee machine, tucked back against the wall, a grinder with beans in it, the residue of coffee grounds in its receptacle. A jar of brown sugar beside it. I frowned, the embryo of an idea beginning to form.

I moved across to the windows, the dizzying expanse of glass looking out over the grey London day. A speedboat shimmied its way along the Thames, the white-top waves kicking up behind it, passengers a collage of red waterproof ponchos. London on the water on a damp April day. What could be better?

'What's in there?' I asked, pointing to a door.

'Ah, toilet. There's an en suite off the main bedroom, a main bathroom down the hall.'

I stuck my head in. It was clean, although the faintest rim of turquoise soap had crept down the sides of the dispenser, leaving a circle on the white sink.

I closed the door behind me and stood for a moment, looking down at the grey of the river. Then I slipped down the hall, letting myself in through the open bedroom door, waving quickly to the forensic team. 'Sorry, guys, won't be a sec.'

The en-suite bathroom looked to be more of the same. Painfully white tiles, a rainfall shower. I scanned the room, gaze falling on the toilet-roll holder. The idea had gestated now, was taking on more solid form.

Interesting.

I squeezed my way out of the bathroom, waving to the CSIs, and took a right, down the wide-slung hallway towards the rear of the apartment. The main bathroom door stood wide open. A cavernous free-standing tub, a handbasin, a toilet. I stooped down, checking the toilet roll. The same.

'Poppy?'

'What?'

I hurried down the hallway, my forensic suit brushing against the walls. 'I have a question for you.'

She was kneeling in the living room, searching through a cabinet tucked up against the wall. 'What?'

'You ever fold your toilet roll over into points? You know, make like a triangle with the end of it?'

She looked at me. 'Alice. You have been to my house. You have been to my house many times. In all those times, has my house ever struck you as the type in which a person would fold the toilet roll ends into a triangle? I didn't have paint on my bathroom wall for six months.' She studied me, curious. 'Why do you ask?'

I thought for a moment, then, with quick strides, pulled open the toilet door. 'See this? This toilet roll

133

here? It's normal, yeah? Been left like … well, any sane person would leave a toilet roll.'

'Okay?'

'But the toilet rolls in both the en suite and the main bathroom, they have their ends folded over into triangles. Like you would find, say, if you were staying in a hotel. Or if you had only just moved in.'

She thought. 'But he hasn't just moved in. He's been here for …'

'A year. Precisely.' I nodded. 'But look at the cupboards. Empty. The only things in this place are tea, coffee …'

'And vodka,' said Poppy. 'Don't forget vodka.' She stood, a book clutched in her hand. 'So what are you saying?'

'I'm saying, what if this Canning guy, what if he isn't actually living here? The stuff that looks like it's actually being used … the toilet off the living room, the coffee machine … you would use that if you just came here occasionally. But the en suite – the toilet that you would definitely use if you slept here – it looks like new.'

'So, you think he's rented it for something else? Some other reason?'

I pulled a face. 'I don't know. But I'll tell you one thing I very much do want to know …' I checked off on my fingers. 'If he isn't living here, why pay the frankly huge levels of rent on this place? And, if he isn't living here, then where the hell *is* he living?'

Chapter 12

The sun had long set now, sending purple splays of light across the dark of the Thames. A heaviness had crept over me, lethargy of thought and action, neurons that once sparked now merely fitzing, brain clear in one thing, that I would have to sleep soon. I bit the nail on my index finger, feeling the edges of it ragged and torn against my tongue, looking out over the river.

'What are you thinking?' asked Poppy.

'I ... I don't know. I mean, she clearly knew him. Or ... she was looking for him at the very least.'

Poppy glanced down. 'You could almost say stalking?'

I pressed my lips tight together.

'Look,' said Poppy, 'based on what we got from her flat, something was going on with Holly Vale. I mean, who has disguises, $10,000 and sleeps with a knife under their bed?'

I shook my head, gaze still focused on the world beyond the window.

'Maybe she was into something,' said Poppy, 'with this Canning. Some kind of scam. Maybe he did a runner with the profit, and she came after him. Perhaps she tried to reach out to him, make him play fair, but when he refused, she decided to turn him in to us. Only he's not so keen on getting caught so he stabs her.'

I looked back at her, raised an eyebrow. 'You got that from three wigs and a carving knife?'

Poppy batted me away. 'I know, I know. But I'm just, you know, floating a theory.'

'Okay,' I said, slowly. 'Well, fine, but let's not get too caught up in that as a theory until we have some evidence to support it. We don't want to get tunnel-visioned on this thing. And this Canning, if he is the guy who stabbed her ...' I looked about, my arms extended. 'Look at this place. This is not cheap. And it's untouched. This isn't somewhere someone has been living for a year. This is a place that has been rented for a different purpose.' I glanced back at Poppy. 'Maybe this guy is using it as a safe house, a place to conduct business.'

Poppy pursed her lips.

'What?'

'No, nothing.'

'What? What are you thinking?'

'No, it's just ... now don't take this the wrong way ...'

'Oh god.'

'Only, it seems like ... now I'm not saying you're not brilliant at your job, because of course you are, but with this one, it kind of seems like you've ... personalised it a bit. Like you're personalising her – Holly. I mean, I get it, I really do. We spend so much of our time dealing with little shits trying to kill other little shits, it grinds you down, I get that. Sounds awful, but sometimes it's a relief to be dealing with a genuine victim. An innocent. It makes you feel like you're actually doing something worthwhile with your life. And I get that it's way worse for you. I mean, you were there right after it happened, you helped save her life. Of course you want her to be what you thought she was. But, Al ... look, I need to be honest with you here. I'm worried about you. Since ...' – she glanced up at my scar, a quick look away – '... since the fire, you're, well, you're more distant. And, of course, I get that. But ... I mean, in the months since the fire, you've been, well, awesome, like you always are. But this case, for some reason, it seems different, like it's getting to you more. I don't know, it's just, sometimes I wonder if maybe you're not doing as well as you pretend to be.'

I stared at her, my insides racing with competing emotions. Anger, that was foremost, a boiling-hot rage that it seemed to me now had been sitting inside the whole time, just waiting. Frustration, that she had not been there, had not watched the life seep out of this woman, that she couldn't possibly know. And, beyond it all, tucked away in a dark little corner, fear. That Poppy was right.

'I'm fine,' I said, stiff.

'Look, I'm just saying, it would be understandable if you were struggling to see things as clearly as you used to, if you were having a rough time. I mean, what you've been through ...'

'Poppy,' I said, my voice all hard edges and pointed

corners. 'There is nothing wrong with me. Jesus. If you're so determined to find drama, maybe look in your own house.'

Poppy railed back, as if I had slapped her. 'What the hell does that mean?'

'I mean you and Art, all those cosy chats and family gatherings. Poppy, he left you. All this hanging around on the off-chance that he'll change his mind, you think that's healthy? You think that's good for Charlie?'

Poppy's face had drawn pale, her mouth a round O, and I felt a rush of guilt follow right along through, pushing all else aside.

'I'm going to go search the rest of the apartment,' I muttered.

I stalked from the living room, back down the hall-way, driven by anger, guilt, all the usual bedfellows, the words circling around in my head. She was wrong, how dare she. She was right, what's wrong with me. I know what I'm doing. I'm falling apart. I let myself into the rear bedroom, pulling the door behind me harder than was strictly necessary, the bang as it hit the frame reverberating through me, sating the anger a little, but making the guilt worse. I pulled a chair out from beneath a desk and sank down in it, my head dropping into my hands.

I could feel tears burning at the back of my eyes.

Don't cry.

You are Detective Sergeant Alice Parr, and she does not cry.

I shoved the seat back from the desk and began to

pace, turning tight circles in that small little room. I was right and Poppy was wrong. Poppy was wrong and I was right. I paced until my toes touched the plate glass of the window, until it seemed that I had fallen through, into the amassing clouds, with their arching loops, their promise of rain to come. Clenched my fingers into fists, driving my fingernails into the palm of my hand. And I forced myself to breathe, forced my lungs to expand, to contract, told myself that this was merely a moment, like any other, that I would live through it, would begin again. Poppy's words, circling, circling. Only I couldn't look at them, couldn't let them in, because if I let them in, then all would fall.

I moved back to the chair. It was about Holly Vale and the man who had tried to murder her. I sat, working to steady my breathing, to slow my racing heartbeat. And then my gaze, seeking a distraction, landed on a cordless phone tucked into a receiver on the desk. A landline. How quaint. I picked up the phone, studied it for a second, then hit redial. A moment as the numbers dialled through, then a pause, then a ringtone I didn't recognise, something strained and tinny. Then came a click, which, for a moment, I took to be a disconnection, before a voice filled the line.

'You have reached the Owens Manhattan Medical Practice. We are sorry to say that after many years of serving our community, this clinic is now closed. We would like to wish all of our patients well in the future.'

New York.

I hung up, typing the clinic's name into the search

engine on my phone. A list of results popped up and I clicked on the first of them. The clinic's website. A photograph of a skyscraper, of a plush white office with skyline views, of smiling patients who, let's be honest, had to be high to be that cheerful about going to the doctors. I rolled down to the text beneath.

The Owens Manhattan Medical Practice was first established in *2010* by Dr Jacob Owens, with the aim of caring for the community. An award-winning health practice, this practice focuses first and foremost on the health and welfare of our patients.

I scribbled down the name on my notebook and rubbed my face. I was getting a headache again.

Why was he calling them, this Canning? Was this his doctor? Was he from New York too? Had Holly followed him all the way here?

My mobile rang in my hand, and I fumbled with it, almost dropping it. 'Hello?'

'Sarge? It's Harry. I'm down here in the basement going through CCTV. I've found something I think you should see.'

I pushed myself up. 'I'm on my way.'

There was no sign of Poppy as I walked through the living room, but, to be frank, that suited me just fine. I jammed my finger into the lift button, thinking that I would have to make peace, that it was just possible that my reaction had been far more about me than it had about her, that I would have to be a grown-up. But I was still angry and frightened and I wasn't ready to be a grown-up quite yet. I slipped into the lift, pressing the button for the basement.

It took me a few minutes to find Harry, lost in the warren of hallways. I finally unearthed him, drawn by the glow of blue light spilling out into the gloom. He sat beneath a bank of monitors, the image frozen on an area that looked to be the lobby on closer reflection. He was texting.

I cleared my throat.

'Oh, yeah, all right Sarge?'

'What have you got?'

He spun in his chair, waving at the monitors above his head. 'Watch this.'

The image jumped and now you could dimly see the shape of cars moving outside the lobby windows. I folded my arms, waiting. Then the door swung open. A man entered the lobby, his head down, a baseball cap pulled down low. But it was the glint of lightness that made my breath catch in my throat. That shimmer of light as he turned towards the lift. A blond ponytail that hung over his collar.

'It's him,' I breathed.

'Yup,' Harry said, smugly.

I stared at the figure, could feel my gaze wanting to slide away, and yet held it there, staring at the man-who-would-kill Holly Vale. Ed Canning.

'When is this?' I asked, my voice straining at the edges.

He turned to face me, grinning. 'Friday lunchtime. 12.58 p.m., precisely.'

I watched the man walk the way I had watched him so many times before, the sense of familiarity screaming at me. Only now it was different. Now he had a name.

'We need to put a call out, get everyone looking for an Edmund Canning in the attempted murder of Holly Vale.' I watched as he stepped into the lift, my mind far away. In a Hampstead flat. In a park in Holborn. So it took me a moment to notice the sound, to recognise it as my phone ringing. 'Yeah? Hello?'

'Alice? It's Noah.'

'Hey, I was just going to …' It worked its way through then, the sound of his voice, the edge to it. 'You okay, Guv?'

A quick laugh that he didn't mean. 'Um, yeah, things are … interesting. Look, I wouldn't ask if it wasn't important – I can send Poppy … but I need one of you to get to Hampstead.'

'Hampstead? Why?'

'Because the flat immediately adjacent to Holly Vale's has just been set on fire.'

Chapter 13

It was the sounds. The shouts of the firefighters, the muted roar of the water pump, the gush of water hitting flame, the murmur of the spectators, inevitably gathered to watch the show. It was the smells. Hard-edged smoke, the exhaust of the fire truck, rubber from the hoses, and something else, something tangy and ill-defined. It was the way the smoke crawled from the darkened window, the way it clambered up the red bricks, the way it broke free into the darkening sky, as if that had been its plan all along.

I stood, one hand on the driver's side door, like my commitment was in question, like I might still bolt. I'm not entirely sure that wasn't true. I tried to breathe, tried to slow down my thinking. My scar hurt, a low-down ache that seemed to come from deep inside me, and I could feel my limbs becoming heavy, unwilling.

'Alice? You okay?'

It took me too long to pull my eyes from the apartment, from the billowing black smoke, to arrange my features into a rough approximation of Alice, or what Alice used to be. The Alice before, with her smooth skin, her blissful ignorance of just how fast the world can change. And yet still I smiled. 'I'm fine, Guv.' No, I had said, still rolling in anger and stubbornness. I'm not sending Poppy. I'll do it myself. Because I'm fine. I'm Alice the hero. Remember? I turned towards the building, the licking black smoke. 'It's number thirteen,' I said, both a question and an answer.

The DI frowned at me. 'How did you know?'

'It was the parcel,' I said. 'The sorry-we-missed-you note. Something was delivered there for Holly. We haven't been able to get in touch with the neighbour.' I looked back to the building. I should have seen this coming, I should have understood. 'Is there a body?' It surprised me, the levelness to my voice. Because there was an inevitability to it. A knock on the door of number thirteen, a shoulder that barges its way in, the knife, the homeowner dead on the floor. And then fire. To cover. To cleanse.

The DI shook his head. 'I don't know. I'm waiting on the fire chief.' He opened his mouth, and I could see it coming, in the crease of his eyes, the furrow of his forehead, that I had been too slow, he had gotten a glimpse behind the curtain. Then, a reprieve. The high-pitched squeal of his phone, the sound weaving its way into the cacophony of water and flame. A rescue bell.

'I'll go find the fire chief,' I said, backing away as he patted through his pockets, distracted.

The smoke had begun to eke away, leaving behind the smell of it, that burn at the back of your throat. I moved past the fire trucks, an ambulance standing idle, the paramedic raising his hand in an acknowledging wave, bringing me back now to Brunswick Square Gardens.

Christian gave me a half-hearted grin, a here-we-go-again kind of look.

I moved past the ambulance towards the building, found the fire chief standing by the front doors, deep in conversation with a short, densely packed firefighter. The chief glanced up when he saw me coming, hand up in acknowledgement.

'Police, yeah?'

'DS Alice Parr.'

'Well,' he said, turning towards me, 'it's arson. Not a doubt. Strong smell of accelerant in the front hallway. Looks like a rag has been stuffed through the letter box and then set on fire. Neighbour spotted smoke, little after nine. Fire alarm was activated a minute later. Same neighbour reports seeing a figure run from the scene.'

'Description?'

'Big guy, baseball cap.'

That feeling again of an uneasy déjà vu.

'Was anyone in there?' It was a rhetorical question almost. Because hadn't I already seen it in my own mind's eye, the limp-limbed body of the resident of number thirteen, blackened and charred. And so it took me a moment to find the meaning in the shake of his head.

He sniffed. 'Place was empty. No sign of the owner.'

My stomach flipped, a new image taking the place of the one before, a knock, the door flying open, large hands wrapping themselves around narrow wrists.

I stepped back, hand moving to my airwave, thinking an attempted murder, an abduction hard on its heels. We'd need the CCTV. It was crap, but crap was better than nothing. My mind was galloping now, would need ANPR, because if number thirteen – Emilia Lucas – had been taken, then surely a vehicle would be involved, and speed would make the difference now, would determine life from death.

'Alice!'

I looked up to see the DI waving at me. 'I'm sorry, excuse me a sec.'

He stood beside a woman, one for whom the word willowy could have been invented. From a distance, I'd have guessed mid-thirties, but up close that shifted upwards, late fifties maybe.

'Alice, this is the lady who called the fire in,' said Noah. 'Mrs Lewis, I'm going to leave you in DS Parr's capable hands.' He gave me a quick grin, ducking away past a fire engine into the gathering night.

The woman, it seemed, had barely heard him, did not look at me, her gaze locked on what remained of the apartment. She gave a small sigh. 'This … it's just awful. I can't bear it. I mean, this is a safe place, or was at least. It's why I bought here. I'm on my own, see, and you know, when it's just you, you need somewhere that you're going to feel safe. Only now … And this so soon after what happened with that other girl … Has anyone told her?'

I frowned, thrown by the conversational flip. 'Unfortunately, Holly is still unconscious.'

'No, not ... Holly? Emilia.' She waved towards the blackened hole where a window once was.

'You know if she was home tonight?' I asked, my heart rate clambering a touch.

The woman gave a theatrical little gasp of the type that made me want to roll my eyes in the most powerful way. 'Oh gosh, oh no. Oh, you don't know, do you?'

'Know what?'

'Emilia's pregnant, due any day now. I saw her leaving, Friday I suppose it would be, with a suitcase, those, oh you know, those notes they carry. What do they call them? Maternity notes. I haven't seen her since. I'm assuming they took her into hospital. She's probably had the baby now, bless her.'

The adrenaline spiked, crashed. 'You know which hospital?' I asked.

She pulled a face. 'Can't say I do. I mean, I would assume the Royal Free, but ...'

I nodded, mind shifting to a different track now. 'No problem,' I said. 'We'll find her.'

The woman sighed again, shaking her head. 'I hope that's where she is, because that's where I told her ex.'

I stopped. 'What?'

'Oh well,' she leaned closer, face glowing. 'I was just popping out earlier, and there was this man at Emilia's door, so I said to him, well, there's no use waiting there, she's in the hospital.'

'He was waiting?'

She glanced at me, seemed surprised to see me there. 'Well, I assumed he'd been knocking, only he wouldn't have gotten an answer, would he? Poor love. And he was such a nice young man too.'

My brain had pivoted, turning to attention. 'So, you knew him? If he was Emilia's ex, I mean?'

'Oh well, no. I just … well, I assumed …'

A chill raced across my skin. 'Can you remember what he looked like?'

She frowned, turning to face me. 'Well, I … he was a large fellow, rather portly. He had a baseball cap on. He seemed awfully pleasant.'

I nodded, stilling my features. Because in my head I was seeing that awfully pleasant young man slitting open the throat of Holly Vale. I dug in my pocket for my phone, pulling up the CCTV still of Canning taken in Brunswick Square. 'Was it this guy?'

She squinted at it. 'Let me see … I … yes. Do you know, I think it was.'

Of course it was.

'And this was …'

'I suppose, oh, about six o'clock. I was just popping out for dinner with a friend and I was to be there for six-thirty, so, yes, six it would have been.'

I looked back at the building, at the smoke, diminished now, leaving behind charred blackness in its wake. Six o'clock. But the fire didn't begin until nine. 'Were there many people about at that time? You know, coming home from work?'

She rolled her eyes. 'It's always so noisy come about six, what with the doors banging, people talking in hallways …'

That was why. He had come, thinking to find Emilia returned from whatever job filled her day, thinking to get back the parcel, whatever it was that slip of paper had referenced. Would he have brought out Detective Grey again? Was that the plan? Only she wasn't there, and with the comings and the goings ... no, better to destroy it, to pour accelerant through the letter box, ensure that whatever had been taken into number thirteen would not be seen again.

'Thank you,' I said, tucking my notepad into a pocket. 'You've been most helpful.'

She looked at me then, for perhaps the first time, her gaze taking in my scar and hanging there. I forced a smile and turned from her, feeling the weight of her gaze upon my retreating back. But there was no time for that. It was irrelevant.

I'll go to the Royal Free, I told the DI. We need to know what was in that apartment, what he wanted destroyed. I'll go talk to the homeowner.

Another day. Another hospital. Although this time it was like gaining entry to a nuclear arsenal, with the buzzers and badge checks, the midwives' eyes following me, studying my shoulder bag as if they were assessing if it was large enough to hide a baby in. Which is probably exactly what they were wondering. The lights had been turned down now, curtains pulled tight around beds. From near the door came the sound of snoring, weighty and substantial, and then another sound, a smaller snore this time, that wove into it, creating an unlikely harmony.

Emilia, the midwife had said, was over by the window, the one with the light on. I hesitated outside the closed curtain, pondering the etiquette, raised my hand to knock on the flimsy fabric and then caught myself. I was more tired than I thought. I tweaked back a corner of the curtain.

'Hello?'

The woman lay back in the bed, propped by a heap of pillows, a mound of auburn curls spread out across them. A book was folded open on her upraised knees, the spine cracked dead in the centre, and above that a baby rested on her chest, its legs pulled up towards its stomach, chin tucked into the crook of her neck. She looked up, expression resigned, morphing to curious when she saw my suit.

'You're not a midwife,' she commented.

The baby shifted, giving a low snuffle, before falling back to sleep with a heavy sigh.

'No,' I agreed, 'my name is DS Alice Parr.'

Her expression shifted then, as I had known it would, dark eyes lighting up with alarm, and she adjusted one hand to the baby, clutching it tight enough that it gave a small mew of protest. 'What's wrong?'

'I'm afraid I have some bad news, Emilia,' I said, softly. 'I've just come from your apartment. There's been a fire. It's out now, but I'm afraid the damage is extensive.'

She stared at me, and it seemed like she was shifting through my words, testing them for an escape hatch. 'But ... but I'm going home tomorrow. We're going home. They said.'

'I'm sorry.'

She ducked her head, resting her lips against the soft down of her baby's dark hair, tears overspilling, splashing down her cheeks. 'What am I going to do? Tilly and me, where are we going to go? My mum ... she hasn't got room. Not since her girlfriend moved in with her kids. Oh god.' She shifted her gaze back to me 'What happened? How did it start?'

I braced. 'We have reason to believe it was arson.'

Emilia's colour leached into the mound of pillows. 'Someone ... someone did this on purpose?'

'We believe so.'

'But ... but why?'

'Emilia, is there anyone who might have wanted to do you harm? Anyone you have a problem with?' I said it like I meant it, like my mind hadn't already raced off in an entirely different direction. I had warned Poppy of tunnel vision, was not ignorant of the irony. I gestured to the baby. 'The baby's father perhaps?'

'No! No, god. I mean, we're not together, but he would never ... No. Absolutely not. There's ... I just don't understand this ...'

I gestured to the chair beside her. 'Do you mind?'

'No, please.'

'Emilia, I have to ask, are you familiar with your neighbour at all? In number fourteen?'

'That's ... it's a rental. Like an Airbnb thing? You see lots of different people coming and going there.'

'But,' I said, 'you took a delivery addressed to someone from there? The current resident?'

Emilia frowned at me. 'A delivery?'

A beat, two, then her face cleared. 'Oh, I forgot. There was a letter … It's just, see, it was the day I went into labour, and I took it, I don't know, first thing, and then, maybe an hour or so later, my waters broke, so I just, I clean forgot about it.'

I leaned forward. 'I don't suppose you remember what it was?'

She shook her head. 'No idea. It was … a letter, I think? But it had to be signed for, so I, well, I signed for it …' Her voice faded out. 'I'm sorry. I don't understand. This has what to do with my apartment?'

'I'm not sure yet,' I said. 'But, the letter. You never gave it to Holly, to number fourteen?'

'No.'

What was it? Did he know? Or did he suspect that somehow something in that letter could do him harm. I thought of the apartment, of the rolling flames, and felt a surge of frustration.

'And it was definitely left inside the apartment?'

'I put it in my bureau … Sorry, I don't understand. Why would someone burn down my apartment over a letter?'

'Emilia … a couple of days ago, the current resident of number fourteen was stabbed whilst walking in a park in Holborn. We have reason to believe that her attacker has been to her flat in the days since and, in the absence of any other logical reason, it seems likely that your flat fire is connected in some way to this attack.'

Emilia stared at me, not comprehending, then shifted,

retched. The baby let out a cry. 'Take her.' She pushed the baby into my arms, twisted in place and began to heave.

Shit.

I glanced about, seeking rescue, but it remained just me, her, the baby and the curtains. I hefted the alien weight of the child, grabbing for a bedpan and thrusting it into Emilia's hands. Another dry heave, then the loose-limbed sound of vomit hitting a metal pan.

The baby shifted in my arms, her eyes flickering open, forehead creased into a frown. She studied me, dark and intense, then let loose a heavy sigh, nuzzling closer to me and settling back to sleep. I lowered myself into the chair, shoulders straining with the weight.

'Is she going to die?' Emilia's voice came out slurred. She shifted to face me, a glance down at the vomit, her nose wrinkling in disgust. 'The woman?'

'I don't know,' I said, quietly. 'They've operated but … she hasn't regained consciousness yet, which is concerning them. I genuinely don't know what will happen.'

She was crying properly now, her breath coming in jagged little spurts. 'Do you think he was trying to kill me too? I mean, are we in danger? Tilly, me …'

Yes.

'I've already spoken to my DI. We have someone on their way here to keep an eye on you. Just in case.'

'So, we are? In danger, I mean.'

I measured my words. 'We are acting from an abundance of caution, Emilia. Better to be safe.' I glanced down at the baby, at the soft curve of her cheeks, gentle flutter of lashes. 'I'm sorry,' I said. 'I know this is an awful time for you ...'

She shook her head, her fingernails digging into the starched sheet that lay across her legs. She blew out a slow, long breath. 'No. Please. I want to help. I mean, someone who can do this, they have to be stopped, right?'

'Right.' I handed her my phone, the CCTV footage of the attacker, of Canning, on the screen. 'You seen this guy before?'

She pulled it into her, studying it closely. 'No, I'm sorry.'

'Look,' I said, accepting my phone back from her. 'I'm sorry, but I have to ask this. Is there any chance at all that your ex-boyfriend was at your front door earlier on today?'

Emilia shifted, reaching her arms out towards me. I lowered Tilly back into them, the baby moulding herself towards her mother like they were two parts of a greater whole. 'My ex is in the Marines. He's out in Afghanistan. Bagram.' Emilia studied the sleeping Tilly, then glanced up, frowning. 'You know, that's so weird. The midwife ... she told me that someone called, a couple of hours ago, that he said he was the baby's father, wanted to check on us. She said that she'd bring the phone into us, so I could talk to him, and then, she said he said no, then the line went dead. Only, the thing is, Neil, he's been calling me on my mobile. So I don't understand why he'd do that. Unless ...'

'What time was this? What time did that call come in?'

'I don't know, maybe, I guess a little before nine.'

Nine. Minutes before the start of the fire. I watched the mother and child, the thought settling over me that he had been checking, had been making sure that it was true, that they were in hospital, were away from the flat. That he had confirmed it, had heard what he needed to hear. Then he had set it alight.

Chapter 14

I stepped into the ruined remnants of Emilia's apartment. It was today. It was eight months ago. The smell clawed at my throat, making my heart race, my abdomen contract. Now I was on fire, was lying in a bed, in a burning apartment. Now I was stepping, each footstep a gamble, on blackened floors, ducking to avoid collapsing joists. I flicked my torch, concentrating on the destruction beneath my feet, carefully placing my heavy boots, pouring everything I was into just that moment so that I would be forced to stay there, in the ruined remains of Emilia's apartment, refusing to be tugged back in time to where I didn't want to be.

DS Alice Parr. I'm DS Alice Parr.

You imagine how it would go, when the world crashes down around you, when all rests on your capacity to think, to survive. You. I. I had imagined how I would be, in that moment of true crisis. In a plane crash or a terrorist attack. I had reasoned with myself that I had seen the worst of humanity, that there was little left now that could shock me, and so, when tested, I would of course rise. Saving myself and others along the way. In short, I had lulled myself into thinking that, were I ever to be tested, I would be a hero, just as Naomi Flood said.

I was wrong.

When the fire came, I did not leap from my bed, did not fashion a rope ladder from bed sheets, nor combat-crawl into the flames to reach the door. Did not abseil into my downstairs neighbour's – Elsbeth Little, eighty-two years old – flat, pulling her willing body to safety.

I thought that I would be the hero. Instead, I lay back down on my bed and I closed my eyes.

You see, this is the thing, we think that we know people, we think that we understand who they are because of how they look, the way they behave and what they say. But it turns out that none of that means much, not really. Not when it comes to truly under-standing what a person is, deep down in the heart of them. Because, until we are tested, until we are put to the flame, we do not even know ourselves.

I have asked myself what I was thinking on that night, why I did what I did, what could have led me to do, in fact, nothing at all. I have comforted myself with platitudes, that I was confused, that the smoke had affected my reasoning, that I just didn't know what I was doing. The truth is, none of that is true. I knew.

I made a choice. Not to fight for survival. But to give in, to yield. To accept my time as over.

I lay down. I made a choice to allow myself to die.

The firefighter hovered before me, bringing me back to Emilia's apartment, back to the present, had flicked

157

his torch back round to pick me out in the gloom. 'You doing okay back there?'

I didn't look up, pulled in a smoke-stained breath, just concentrated on moving my feet, steps like I was walking on a rolling sea. 'I'm fine.'

You could smell it, the raking scent of gasoline. It filled you up, battling against the smoke itself to overwhelm you.

'He's done a thorough job,' I said, simply to have something to say.

The firefighter grunted. 'He has that. Prick. Lucky it didn't spread to the other apartments. Extremely lucky no one was in here.'

Lucky. Only it wasn't luck, was it? He rang the hospital to check. It was something else, a plan I did not understand.

I couldn't breathe. The inside of me had filled up now, stifling me with the smell of it, with the breathless hopelessness of it all, and so I walked straight into the back of him, torch hitting him in the ribs.

'Oof.'

'Sorry.'

He held up a hand, smiled widely. 'I'm a big boy. I can take it.'

I returned the smile, water-thin and distracted, and swept my torch across the living room, or what little remained of it. 'Holy hell.'

'Yeah.' He sighed.

The ceiling had collapsed down into the room itself, so that the entire flat seemed to be the remnants of some forgotten war. The walls were puckered up, a deep carcinogen black, that clawed its way downwards towards the assaulted floor. A cold wind swept in through the window, the dangling shards of glass swinging with it, catching the light from our torches.

'It's destroyed.'

'It is,' he agreed. 'Homeowner won't be coming back here any time soon.' He swept his torch across the destruction. 'Arsehole, eh?'

'Yes,' I said, quietly. 'Arsehole.'

Anger rolled in my insides. Ed Canning. The man in the CCTV, following so close behind Holly as she made her way around Brunswick Square. The thick Scottish burr of a victim support manager who did not exist. The baseball cap pulled low, striding into the lobby of the Vauxhall Tower. The fictional father pining over his partner and newborn child.

Who the fuck are you?

He was everywhere and he was nowhere. It was as if a tap had been turned on that morning in Brunswick Square and that my entire life now was made up of him and the reflection of him, there but not there.

He was a ghost.

And now an uncomfortable question clawed its way to the surface. If these were the times at which I had figured him out – the father ploy, the victim support ploy – what if there were more? What if there were times that I had missed?

There were no records of a Canning, nothing to draw us closer. I breathed in the ruined air and tried to orient myself, to keep myself here, in this hellhole, to avoid being pulled back into that other place, my greater hell.

He had wanted something here. He had burned this place because he couldn't get it. That meant it was really important to him that nobody saw it. Maybe it led back to him.

I turned in place, scouring the alien landscape around me, looking for anything that resembled a bureau. Or anything that resembled anything at all.

The ringing of my phone broke through the quiet, and I pulled it free, answering it quickly.

'Is that Alice? Alice, it's Gwen, the nurse from the hospital? I'm taking care of Holly?'

I stood for a moment, reorienting, struggling to equate the clean lines of intensive care with the carnage around me. 'Hi Gwen. What can I do for you?'

'I'm sorry to call you so late. I didn't wake you, did I?'

I laughed. An actual laugh. I felt the firefighter turn to watch me, the beginnings of a smile teasing at the corner of his mouth. 'No, Gwen. I'm not sleeping. Is Holly okay?'

She sighed, and my heart sank. 'That's why I'm calling. Look, I'm really sorry to have to say this to you, but I'm afraid Holly is in a coma. Her score is lower than they would like, which is giving them some cause for concern about her long-term prospects. But we aren't going there yet. She may still surprise us. But I wanted to let you know.'

I nodded slowly, then realised she couldn't see me. 'I

see. Okay. Thank you, Gwen. I appreciate you taking the time to let me know.'

I hung up the phone, closed my eyes briefly and inhaled. The hung-over fumes of smoke and gasoline raced into my nostrils, making me gag. I flicked my eyes open to see the firefighter watching me.

'You okay?'

I sighed heavily. 'Sometimes I hate this job.'

He looked around himself grimly. 'Right there with you.' A pause, then, 'You, ah, you look like you have some experience with this kind of thing.' He gestured towards my scar.

I turned away, feeling the flush building across the smooth of my cheeks to the ruching of my scar.

People say scars represent battles fought and won. Not this scar. This scar represented only what had been lost, the innocence, the optimism, the arrogance, all the ways in which I had turned out to be less than I had hoped I was, a bitter reminder that the me who had come before, she was dead, if, in fact, she ever existed at all. And this one who was left, a sham of an Alice.

'Yes,' I replied, briefly, 'I do.'

He was watching me, or perhaps not me, perhaps just my scar. 'Seriously, though,' he offered. 'To be back, doing what you're doing after something like that. That's some serious cajones right there.' His gaze flicked away. 'You ... you're pretty impressive.'

I turned, running my torch across the window, following the shape of the room. It was in a corner. She said the bureau was in a corner. 'I'm not impressive,' I muttered. 'I'm surviving, that's all.'

'Sometimes that's the most impressive thing of all,' he said, quietly.

No one ever asked me what happened. My parents, my brothers, Poppy. They seem to think that I was unconscious, unaware. I haven't told them the truth. That my body, the body that I trusted, that I cared for and worked on, that I believed could handle itself, simply gave up. That something in me had determined that the hour of my death was then. There. I haven't told them the truth because I do not understand it. That something in me was prepared to die. And not for a worthy cause, not as a hero, in the saving of another, but simply because I could not muster myself to get out of my damn bed. I have allowed them, these people that I care for above all others, to operate under an illusion, that I remain the person I have always pretended to be. Capable and resilient and, above all else, a survivor. They do not know that Alice died that night, and that I, the one who remains, am a mere doppelgänger, a mimicry of what Alice used to be.

I shook my head, like I was trying to dislodge a gnat from my ear. The ceiling had come down just across from the window, sheets of plasterboard twisted with the heat. I ran my light across them, could dimly make out a shape beneath.

'Hey, I think I have something.'

It was buried, beneath a pyramid of destruction, the wood of it blackened and warped.

'Shit,' I muttered. 'The bureau has collapsed.'

I stood back as the firefighter tugged at it, shifting its position so I could see inside.

'Dammit!'

'You looking for a letter?'

'Yeah.'

He snorted. 'Good luck.'

At the bottom of the bureau's carcass lay a mass of pulp. Where the wood of the bureau was charred, the paper that had been held within had mostly survived burning, the fire eking out before reaching it. But what fire had spared, water had reached, and that which had not been burned had been thoroughly soaked, turning it into so much papier-mâché. I ran my gloved hands through the stodgy pile, allowing my light to shine on it. Flecks of what could generously be called paper remained, although little of any use.

Shit. Shit. Shit. He had done it. He had gotten what he wanted. Shit.

Then, in amongst the pulpy mess, my torchlight flicked on a patch of colour. I leaned in closer. 'Hey, can you give me some more light here?'

The firefighter crouched down beside me, angling his torch so that our beams overlapped.

'You see that?'

I ran my finger across a shape, broken down but just about visible.

'I see it. What is it?'

I pursed my lips. 'This ... it may not mean anything.

It may not be what we were looking for. But … that's a double helix.'

'Okay?'

I looked up at him, grim. 'The kind that DNA companies use as their logo?'

Chapter 15

I sat at my desk, the photograph of the twisted helix staring back at me. I had gotten to bed a little after two, and, in spite of all the odds, had fallen into a ravenous sleep, the kind that stretches out for unmoving hours but that, when you awaken, seems to have taken only a moment. I didn't remember dreaming, but then that was probably a good thing.

A breeze twisted in through the open window, break-ing free from an effortlessly blue sky, and I opened my mouth to speak, attention shifting to the rod of Poppy's back at the desk in front. But it was in the tightness of her shoulders, the hard clack against the keys. I was not forgiven.

She had smiled at me when I came in, a compulsory social smile, had quickly looked away, her lips pursed, suddenly busy with who knew what. I should apologise. That was what a grown-up would do, what a profes-sional would do. But what would that look like? I'm sorry I lost my shit with you. It was mostly because I figured you were probably right, seeing as my life has become little but a game of dress-up, splitting seamlessly into two halves, before the fire, after the fire, nothing seeming real to me, including myself. That I can't let go of the fact that I wasn't who I thought I was, and now I'm trying so so hard to force it, to make myself who I wish I was, that I'm becoming a bitch, even to my best friend. Sorry about that.

Instead, I sighed and pulled the desk phone close to me, dialling the mobile number Emilia had given me last night. The young mother answered quickly, her voice sounding thick, with sleep or with tears.

'Emilia, it's Alice. Alice Parr?'

'Hi.'

'Are … are you okay?' And there was my dumb-arse question quota met for the day.

Emilia let loose a short bark of a laugh. 'I guess. I have my health, right? Although the doctors have said my blood pressure has gone back up, so I have to stay in. Honest to god, when they said that I just laughed in their faces. Blood pressure. I'm surprised I haven't had a bloody stroke.'

'I'm sorry,' I said, thinking of Tilly, the warm weight of her.

'Whatever. I mean, it's not like I have anywhere to go … Sorry, you didn't ring for this. Is there anything I can help with?'

I picked up the photograph of the helix. 'I just need to check something with you. I went to your flat last night …'

'How bad is it?'

'It's …' a bombsite '… not great. I think it's going to take an awful lot of work to get it put back together

166

again.' I hesitated, my request suddenly callous-seeming. But then there was Canning, and if there was something he didn't want me to see, then I was damn well seeing it. 'I found a piece of paperwork. Well, you can hardly call it that any more. It's pretty badly damaged. But I was able to make out what I think is a company logo. Now, obviously, I don't know if this was the letter Holly signed for, but I figured if it wasn't yours ...'

'Of course. What's the logo?'

'It's a double helix. Like a strand of DNA? Now, I don't want to jump to conclusions, obviously. And with you just having had Tilly, I was thinking you could have ...'

You know when you say something and as you're saying it you can feel your shoe entering your oesophagus, and so you try to stop saying it, but your mouth just keeps on trucking?

There was a silence on the line that lasted far longer than it should. 'No, I haven't had my baby's DNA tested, if that's what you're asking me,' Emilia said, voice cold. 'I am fully aware of who her father is, thank you very much.'

'No, I ...'

'Was there anything else?'

'Well, no, but ... so, you think this could have been Holly's letter?'

'As I have already said to you, I don't make a habit of snooping in other people's mail. However, I can tell you now that I have no communications whatsoever with any DNA companies, so if that's what it is, then it didn't come from me.'

'Okay,' I said weakly, 'thank you.'

She hung up the phone with a click.

Bugger.

'Well, that didn't go well,' I said, to the room in general, or to Poppy's back in specific. She ignored me.

The door opened, Harry slinking in. He looked tired, heavy with the lack of sleep affecting us all, his face slack with sulk, his shirt unironed, face unshaved.

Don't ask. Don't ask. 'You okay?' Dammit.

'Tired,' he answered, briefly.

My gaze landed on a spot on Harry's jacket shoulder, a small circular stain of yellow. He followed the direction of it, glancing down.

'Shit. Mila was sick earlier. I thought I got it all.' He scrubbed at it with a tissue, expression close to tears.

I watched him, no longer seeing, mind instead on that phone call to the maternity ward. I had held Holly's hand, had watched the blood spill from the puncture wounds that littered her chest, the gaudy bloodline that traced her neck. Canning was willing to kill. So, the thought that he might have been checking no one was home before he set fire to the place, that made no sense. Right?

I sighed heavily, turning back towards the computer and jiggled the mouse to bring the screen to life. A helix. It wasn't much to go on. After all, how many DNA companies were there in the world? And given what I had learned about Holly Vale so far, I wouldn't like to narrow it down to a country. I typed DNA-testing companies into Google and began to trawl through the seemingly endless list of sites.

It took the better part of two hours, sparing a moment every now and again to glance up at Poppy. She did not move, did not spare any of her glances for me. My hands had begun to cramp, a tight line of pain tracing across my shoulder blades, and I had just begun to think that I would have to move soon, that my body and brain had reached their tipping point, when there it was, a DNA-testing company based in Haringey, North London. DNA4U. The company name made me feel slightly nauseous. I pulled up their postcode, grabbed the car keys.

'Hey, Poppy?'

She didn't answer, just looked up at me, her expression hard.

'I'm going to go visit this DNA service. It's out in Haringey.'

'Okay?'

'You want to come?'

For a moment I thought she was going to break. Then she shook her head. 'Sorry. Got too much to do with the ANPR data from down by Vauxhall Tower. I'm sure you'll be fine though. Like you said, it's not your first day.'

I opened my mouth, the 'oh do fuck off' right there on the tip of my tongue, and then closed it again. After all, I had probably asked for that.

The drive out to Haringey hurried by in a thousand

repetitions of our cross words, a thousand different routes we could take next. Unfortunately, none of them seemed particularly palatable at the moment. By the time I reached the lobby of the frankly horribly named DNA service, my mood was decidedly bleak.

'DS Parr. I need to see a manager.' I thought for a moment. 'Please.'

The young girl behind the desk looked at me through heavy framed glasses, seemed startled and slightly fearful, which, given my mood, was hardly surprising. 'Yes, just a sec. Please, have a seat.'

I slumped in an oversized leather chair in the modest, whitewashed lobby. I would have to apologise. Poppy ... she could be your fiercest ally or your greatest foe, little in between for her. I could just say I was having a bad day. She would take that, would think little of it. But the thought had jagged edges to it, because it wasn't true. I wasn't having a bad day. I was having a bad life, one that began on the same night it almost ended. And the thing is, I'm not sure Poppy would want to hear that. I had seen it in the hospital, from my parents, from my brothers, from Poppy herself, that watchfulness, that fearfulness, as if they are studying you, waiting for you to break. So you don't break. Instead you pretend. You tell them that you are fine, that yes, you are scarred but scars are a part of life and you're moving on. And then their faces ripple with relief, and their bodies unknot from it, and you know that you have done something good, that in lying to them, you have protected them from a truth they don't want to hear. And you shrug it off, because

170

they love you and they want you to be happy, and that's a good thing, right? And it's only later, after months of scattergun sleep, after feeling yourself living day after day teetering on the edge – you don't know the edge of what, but you know it's nothing good. It's only at the end of that, when you have been stretched out just as far as a person can be stretched, and when the inside of you is bursting with the need to just say it – I can't cope with this – that you realise, there's no one who wants to hear. They all love you too much to want the damning truth.

'DS ... Parr?'

I started, looked up into a woman's lined face, heavy with make-up, a blouse that tugged across her wide bosom, the cerise of a bra peeking out between tautly strained buttons. She examined me, her voice doubtful, reached out a heavily ringed hand. 'Heather Beresford. Would you like to come this way?'

I stood, sparing a smile for the receptionist, and followed the woman, the quick clack of her stilettos on the tiled floors excruciating and fascinating both. How the hell did she walk so fast on those things? I struggled to keep up in barely heeled pumps. I slunk through the office door behind her and into the seat she waved me towards.

'Please ... would you like a tea? Coffee?'

'Nothing, thank you. I appreciate you seeing me at such short notice.'

She sank into a seat behind a wide slate desk. 'What-ever we can do to help. I'm not sure what this is in relation to ...'

'I have reason to believe that a victim in an extremely serious attack has been in communication with your company,' I said. 'As I'm sure you understand, in order to build a full picture of what happened, we need to gather as much information as we can about our victim and those involved, which brings me to you.'

She nodded, swivelling her chair so that it faced towards a computer. 'Name?'

'Holly Vale.'

She typed slowly, long fingernails clicking on the keys. 'Ah ... okay, here it is. Yes, we have been running some tests for a Ms Vale.'

'What kind of tests?'

'She came in ... let me see ... about ten days ago, and asked us to run a DNA comparison against an item.'

'Item?'

'Hang on ... She submitted the hair of a subject and requested that we run a comparison test between that sample and ... ah, a plastic spoon.'

'And the results?'

'They were a match.'

'So ...'

'That is to say, the sample of hair was confirmed as belonging to the same person who had provided the spoon.'

I floundered. 'So, do you know whose DNA it was?'

She shook her head. 'Sorry. That's all the information I have.'

I stared at her, my mind racing. What was she doing? Whose DNA was that and why the hell did Holly need to have it tested? Was this related to Canning?

My phone rang in my pocket, startling me out of my confusion.

'Sorry,' I said. 'Hello?'

'Alice? It's Poppy.'

'Oh, Pops, I ...'

'I have some information for you,' she said, her voice clipped. 'I've found CCTV footage of Canning leaving through the front lobby of Vauxhall Tower at 3.20 p.m. on Tuesday. I've located a car leaving the car park at 3.25 p.m., a black Audi A4, and running the plates, it leads back to Everdrive car rental. They've confirmed that the car was rented by Canning.'

'Okay, great ...'

'I've alerted the control room to put the car on everyone's radar. I just thought I'd better keep you informed.' And she hung up.

I stared at the phone and briefly contemplated throwing it at a wall.

'Everything okay?' the woman asked, leaning closer in anticipation.

I looked up at her. 'I have no idea,' I said.

Chapter 16

The journey back to the nick looked much like the journey from it, with me driving far too fast in traffic unwilling to accommodate my mood, mentally rehearsing all of the home truths I would share with Poppy on my arrival. And if that failed I had a cup of coffee in the console that had long gone cold that could be put to far better use than drinking.

By the time I returned, however, the office was all but empty, everyone else off with better things to do than mutely receive my anger.

I threw myself into my chair and glared across at Poppy's desk, as if that would do anything.

God.

I shook myself, scrubbing my hands across my face. It didn't matter. None of it. All background noise to an almost murder, and ... whatever the hell else this was. I leaned back in my chair, thought about the apartment in Vauxhall Tower. I tapped my pen against my lip. Then leaned forward, googling the Owens Manhattan Medical Practice, this time taking my time over its photographs of cheerful medical staff, apparently deliriously happy patients. Moved the mouse to the latest news tab and clicked on it. The top post, the most recent, read, We are sorry to inform you that OMMC has been forced to close its doors. We have loved serving this community and we wish you all the very best for the future.

That post had been added last May, a little less than a year ago. Why had Canning called them?

I clicked on the next tab – About us. The page listed a contact name – Chloe Hodge, Office Manager.

I shimmied the mouse, pulling up a new search screen, and opened the Whitepages, typing in Chloe Hodge. Five listings, one in Georgia, one in Wisconsin, two in California and, thank god, one in New York. I closed my eyes, offered up a brief prayer and hit the information tag, which revealed a phone number and address in Brooklyn.

I punched the number into the landline. Distant, shimmering beeps, then a click and a robotic-sounding voice. 'There is no one available to take your call. Please leave a message after the tone.'

I sighed, waited for the protracted beep. 'Ms Hodge, this is Detective Sergeant Alice Parr from the Met police in London. England,' I added redundantly. 'I'm working on a case that I think you might be able to help me with, and I'd like to speak with you in relation to your work at the Owens Manhattan Medical Practice. I'd appreciate it if you could call me back at your earliest convenience.' I reeled off the phone number and then hung up with a bang. This day simply would not sort its shit out.

'Alice?' Harry stuck his head around the office door.

By the looks of it, he had failed in his quest to remove the stain. 'Sorry, just wanted to let you know, the phone records are in from Holly Vale's Airbnb. I'd go through them myself, only ...'

I waved him away. 'It's fine. No one wants to talk to me anyway.'

'What?'

'Nothing. Go, it's fine. I've got it.'

My desk phone rang and I grabbed for it, a silent prayer that at the other end I would find an American accent. 'DS Parr?'

'Yes?'

'Heya, I've got the results back on that bandage you submitted?'

I felt my skin freeze over. The bandage that had been tucked within Holly's sleeve, the fingerprint marked out in blood. 'You've identified the print?'

'Yeah, that's a match to the victim in the case, uh, a Miss Vale?'

Yup. That was the way my day was going.

I thanked the distant voice, doing my best not to batter the phone against my desk, and turned my attention back to my computer. I pulled up the document, staring at the swirl of numbers, beginning with the day Holly had arrived in the Airbnb. She had, it appeared, begun to busy herself on the phone almost straight away. I frowned. Seriously, the woman had been living on the phone for the first few days. I selected the first number. St Thomas' Hospital. The next, University College London Hospital. Then London Bridge Hospital.

What the hell was she looking for? I thought about the Wi-Fi report, about her relentless search for Canning. Had she reason to think he'd been hospitalised?

I bit my pen, the plastic jabbing into my gum. Was this something to do with the DNA? Was she trying to confirm his identity somehow?

I sighed, checked the next number, expecting the same result. This time, though, it was different. The number tracked back to EuroDespatch, the luggage management service out of St Pancras. The home of the Eurostar.

'Holly, you little sod,' I muttered.

I pulled the phone closer, dialling the number for Eurostar, rattling off the spiel at top speed. Did you have a Holly Vale travelling? Why, yes, we did. Fantastic. What did she want with EuroDespatch? Well, you'd really better try them.

'Oh,' I said, 'one more thing before you go. Could you check another name for me?'

A sigh. 'Go on.'

'Edmund Canning.'

'Ah ... yes. We have an Ed Canning ... he travelled with us, but it was some time ago.'

'How long?'

'Last year? February.'

I stared out of the window into the blue of the sky. It was there, the answer sitting just out of reach. What was I missing?

I picked up the phone again, dialling EuroDespatch. 'Hi. My name is Detective Sergeant Alice Parr. I'm conducting an investigation and it has come to my attention that the victim in our case called this number on twenty-third April. I was wondering if you could give me any information about that call?'

'Okay, sure ... do you have a customer number?'

'No. Sorry.'

'Okay, what about a name?'

'Holly Vale?'

A long silence, then, 'Yes, according to our records, that customer lost a bag onboard the train and contacted us to try and locate it.'

I held my breath. 'And have you?'

Another pause. 'Oh yes, it's still here waiting to be collected. Will you be picking it up, DS Parr?'

I punched the air.

St Pancras thronged with people, towing suitcases behind them, their gazes fixed up high on information boards. I moved carefully round a toddler, a little girl with a pink party dress and bunches, lying prone on the floor, her father standing beside her with folded arms, a long-suffering expression on his face, and ducked down a branch off the main causeway towards the EuroDespatch counter. A queue had formed at the desk and I slid in behind it, waiting with what we'll call patience.

The woman before me, a slight ephemeral whiff of a thing with long grey hair piled up high on her head, and a faint, but unavoidable smell of pot, sighed heavily. 'Oh dear,' she murmured, glancing about her. Her gaze fell on me, mouth opening like she had found someone who would give a shit, then it did what they all do, took in my scar. I stared at her, folded my arms and seriously contemplated the logistics of picking her up for use of illicit substances. Apparently my poker face needs some work. She baulked, looking quickly away.

I waited whilst she drifted through her life crisis with the admirably patient guy at the desk, thumbing through my phone. In truth, I was looking to see if Poppy had been in touch. Or at this stage in the game, anyone would do. I'd even have been briefly excited by a text from Harry. Yet, in keeping with the spirit of my day, my phone remained resolutely contact-free.

The woodland sprite of a woman concluded her business, clutching onto a sheaf of paperwork with a stellar show of tears, before drifting away with another glance back at me and my scar.

I allowed myself a moment to scowl at her, before marching to the counter. 'DS Parr,' I said, waving my ID at him, voice clipped. 'We spoke on the phone?'

The clerk nodded, 'I have it here. I just need you to sign ...' He twisted a clipboard towards me and vanished towards the rear of the booth, re-emerging with a black backpack.

He hoisted it up onto the counter, making a show of studying my signature, checking one more time the ID on the bag.

'So, um ... this thing you're investigating, is this, like ... is this, like, terrorism or something?'

I smiled brightly, my tone set for reassuring. 'Oh no, nothing like that.'

His face fell.

'It's attempted murder,' I offered.

His mouth formed itself into a perfect O, eyes widening. 'Great,' he said. He stopped for a moment, colour beginning to flood to his cheeks. 'I mean ...'

I waved him away. 'Yeah, I know. Thanks for this. You have been a tremendous help in this case.'

His face shifted, smile widening. 'Oh. Great!'

I hefted the backpack, lifting it down from the counter, and winked at him, manoeuvring my way through the queue, feeling the touch of its straps, rough on my fingers. My fingers. Holly's fingers with their perfectly manicured nails. I moved towards a row of metal chairs. When she held this last, she would have no idea of just what was to come, of how far she was about to fall. I placed the bag down, pulling a pair of forensic gloves from my pocket, and sliding them on I tugged the zip open.

I'm not sure what I was expecting.

I think that I had fooled myself briefly that this would be the key, this would bring forth the moment of revelation. I peered into the shadowy interior of the bag.

There were clothes in there, some toiletries. A pair of striped deck shoes, their toes scuffed, the fabric at the edge of them beginning to fray.

Something. Something to tie the threads together.

I lifted the bag up, allowing the light into its dark insides. There was a zipped portion at the back of it, tucked away almost out of sight. I reached in carefully, opening the zip, and pulled out a small white card, the name Detective Gabriel Otero printed on it, a number beneath that. Then, at the bottom, NYPD.

I studied the card. 'Well, Detective Otero. Now just who in the hell are you?'

I tucked the card back inside. There was something else, tucked away inside the zipped pocket, something small and bookish.

A passport.

I pulled it out, and my thoughts then were along the lines of how worried she must have been that she had lost her passport, how at the time that must have seemed like the worst thing she could have to contend with. I was thinking this, was thinking of Holly, as I flipped through the passport's pages, coming at last to the identification page, to the picture of her, her hair shorter, carefully styled.

It took me a few seconds to look at it. I mean, really look.

Because it was clearly her. That photograph, it was clearly Holly.

Only it wasn't.

There, beside the photograph, read the name Erin Owens.

Chapter 17

No one spoke. Noah and Matt and Harry and Poppy, with her lips still pursed, cheekbones still tight with anger, they all just stood round the plastic-spread table and stared at the contents of the bag laid out before them.

'Well, shit,' muttered Matt.

'Yeah,' agreed Noah. 'Shit.'

He looked back up at me, looking lost suddenly. 'So who is she? Holly Vale or Erin Owens?'

I shook my head. 'I don't know. Eurostar had her registered as Holly Vale. So did the Airbnb. So, she has a passport registered to each name.' I looked at Poppy, resolutely not looking at me, and for a moment wanted to smack her. 'Poppy? What do you make of this?'

She started, seemingly surprised at being addressed. 'I think what I've been thinking.' She glanced at Noah. 'Guv, no one has two identities if they're not into some seriously dodgy shit. The stuff we found in her apartment – the knife, the money, the disguises. Now this. She's into something. And she's into something bad.'

She looked at me as she said it, as if expecting me to react, to jump to the victim's defence. But I was all out of jumps. I was tired, and had suffered a catastrophic loss of the righteous indignation that had powered me through. And, after all, what was there to say? Poppy was right. Holly, Erin, whatever the hell her name was, she was into something she shouldn't have been into.

'Guv, the Canning apartment ... the last number that was called from there was to a medical centre in Manhattan. The Owens Manhattan Medical Practice.' I studied Noah. 'I have trouble believing that two instances of the name Owens in the same case is a co-incidence.'

'You think she's related to that place somehow?'

I nodded. 'I'd lay money on it. I've got a call in with the clinic manager, but I'm going to chase, see if she can shed any light on this.'

I moved round the table, my gaze hooked on the items spread out before us. There were toiletries, a small purse of make-up, a change of clothes – different than her usual, in that they were basic, none of the high-brand names I had come to associate with her. These were simply functional.

Laid out next to the clothes was a receipt. I picked it up with gloved hands. 'This is ... Anyone looked at this properly? This isn't in English. It's ... Spanish?'

The DI leaned over my shoulder. '*Grazie per aver soggiornato con noi*. That's thank you for having stayed with us. It's Italian.'

I stared at him.

'What?'

'You speak Italian?'

He shrugged. 'I'm a complex man.'

I looked at him for another couple of moments, frowning, then shook my head, shifting my attention back to the receipt. 'Villa Tramonto.'

'Sunset villa,' Noah supplied.

'That's quite impressive, Guv.'

He shrugged.

Harry waved his phone. 'I've googled it. It's in Rome.'

'Dated three days before she arrived in London,' I said, studying the receipt. 'She has had herself quite the grand tour, hasn't she?'

'What's that?' asked Harry, pointing at the business card.

'It's a detective in the NYPD.'

I'd tried calling him from the car. That damn twisted dial tone again, followed by a snap straight to answerphone, a soft voice that sounded like anything other than a New York detective – This is Gabriel Otero. Leave me a number. I'll call back.

Because apparently no one in New York answered their phones.

'A detective?' asked Noah.

I fixed him with a flat look. 'Homicide,' I said, quietly.

He stared for a moment, then turned to Poppy. 'Looks like you were right, Poppy. This is not looking good. Not at all.' He shook his head. 'I spoke to the hospital again, but no change. Of course, the way things are shaping up, Ms Vale ... or Ms Owens ... or whatever

184

the hell her name is, might be quite lucky if she stays unconscious. We have everyone keeping eyes out for the car Canning rented, and we've got an alert out at all ports and airports.' He shook his head. 'Let's get back to it then.'

I stood for a couple of seconds, staring down at the passport, at the face staring back at me, that name seeming to loom larger than it should. Then shook myself, strode round the table, grabbing hold of Poppy's arm as she turned to go. 'Can we have a quick word?'

I didn't wait for confirmation, just walked out of the office to the corridor beyond and waited. It took Poppy long enough that I thought she wasn't coming, but come she did, her face still set, teenage mutinous. I could still smack her.

'Poppy, I'm sorry I snapped. It was inappropriate and unfair.'

She reacted, looking up at me, doubtful.

'I have no excuse for my behaviour, except that I ...'

What? That it's becoming painfully obvious that my entire existence is predicated on a bullshit assumption – that I know what I'm doing, that I'm capable, cool under pressure, that I can read people. Except the truth of it is that I'm falling apart.

'I was having a bad day.'

She scrutinised me, in the manner of one watching the earth rip apart, wondering if that fracture will continue to tear, creating a Grand Canyon in its wake. But I had been practising my poker face as well as my contrition, and so finally she smiled.

'Whatever. You can buy me a beer next time we're out.' She waved back towards the office. 'So what do you think?'

What did I think? I thought that, in spite of all I had said, I had fallen into an investigational tunnel, that I had been lulled into safety by a beautiful face, my need to prove myself painting everything a different colour.

'I think you're right,' I said, firmly. 'She's into something. This Canning thing. I think ... I think she hunted him, she followed him, across an ocean, across Europe, and then ...'

He killed her for it.

'She's still got the guard on her?' asked Poppy.

'Yes.' Only whether now it was to protect her or prevent her flight was unclear.

Poppy clapped me on the shoulder. 'Come on then, you pain in the arse,' she said, brightly, 'let's get on with it.'

I followed her into the office, could feel my mind screaming as it pulled itself in a thousand different directions at once.

My desk phone rang, the sound jarring me to attention, and I grabbed for it. 'DS Parr.'

'Oh, hi Alice, it's Naomi here. Naomi Flood, with *The Times*? I know you must be very busy, but I was just wondering if you had any comment on the fire last night out at Hampstead? It's my understanding that the property owner is in hospital having had a baby, and I was thinking ...'

'Naomi,' I interrupted, 'I'm sorry, but I can't give

you anything. You're going to need to ring the press office.' And then I hung up. Because it had been that kind of day.

Poppy frowned at me, curious.

'That reporter from *The Times*,' I said, gesturing at the phone. 'By the way, how the hell did she know that Emilia is in hospital? Seriously, the woman has ears like a damn bat.'

Poppy shrugged. 'Snooping is literally what she does for a living.'

I shook my head, almost instantly forgetting about the questing voice of Naomi Flood. 'The thing is,' I said, thinking, 'okay, so we know who she is now. We know who attacked her. At some point, Canning is going to show up on someone's radar, whether he tries to leave the country or gets picked up for something else, but sooner or later, we're going to get hold of him. But that still leaves this enormous question out there.'

'Why?' supplied Poppy. 'Why was she following him halfway around the world? What did she know that he tried to murder her for?'

I nodded, considering. 'And the envelope. What was in that? What was she planning on bringing to us? I'd lay money on the fact that he went after her to stop her handing that in. But what in the hell was it?'

Poppy shook her head. 'You think it could be about the money? I mean, that place Canning was living. That's a pricey place. With the disguises, the false identity – maybe she was blackmailing him? It would explain the ten thousand dollars we found.'

'Maybe,' I said, quietly. I thought of the flat, of the money tucked inside the book. 'He, Canning I mean, he can't have found the money. I mean, it's ten K. If he had, surely he'd have taken it.'

'In fairness to her, it was a pretty good hiding place. And he would have had the footballing legend waiting for him to finish up, would have been under time pressure. I guess he missed it.'

The photographs remained spread across my desk, of Holly – Erin – of the toys in her pocket. I pulled them together, placing them into a folder. They represented a different investigation, one viewed through a different lens. Instead, I spread out other photos – the knife from beneath her pillow, the disguises, the money, the false identity.

Each set of photographs represented two victims, but the same woman.

I pulled out my chair, sank into it, closing my eyes for a brief moment. I was tired now, all energy drained from me, and, for the first time in months, I longed for my bed, with a bone-aching homesickness.

I opened my eyes, took a long pull of water from the bottle that stood on my desk and ran a White Pages search for Holly Vale in the area of New York. One woman, listed in her 60s, the spelling different ... not our victim then. I considered, then ran my gaze across the rest of the screen – birth and death records for Holly Vale. V-a-l-e.

I clicked on the birth records. A Holly Vale, born in New Jersey, 1986.

Interesting.

'Anything?' asked Poppy.

'Maybe.' I studied the page. 'Okay, I've found a Holly Vale. Right age. Right area. Well, next state over, so right area-ish.'

'But?'

'But,' I said reading the report, 'she's dead.'

'Ah. Probably not her then.'

I studied the numbers. This Holly Vale, she would have been the same age as our victim, had she lived. But she hadn't, had died aged two of causes unspecified.

I bit the end of my pen, considered. If I needed to be someone else, I might find that useful – a dead child in the same age range as me. I might apply for a birth certificate for the sadly deceased Holly Vale – it would be easy enough to knock up an ID that could pass muster when attached to an email. Once I had that birth certificate, then the whole world would open up to me. A driver's licence with my own photograph on it, social security number. A passport.

I leaned back in my chair, the certainty settling over me. 'Holly Vale is a false identity.' I said it softly enough that I wasn't sure if I had said it for anyone else, or merely for myself, if I was testing the words to see if they would bear up under the weight of scrutiny.

'What?'

'It's ...' I twisted the computer monitor towards Poppy. 'There's a Holly Vale who died at the age of two. She used her information. She stole her identity.' And now another thought. I typed quickly, waiting for long moments as the screen flickered before me. I blew out a breath, reading quickly. Then, god help me, I began to laugh.

'What?' Poppy pulled her chair closer to mine. 'Are you having some kind of stroke?'

'Okay,' I said, 'so I'm thinking, right, if Holly, Erin, whatever the hell her name is, if she's from the US and has been following Canning, that maybe he is too, yeah? So ...' I turned the screen to face her. 'Meet Ed Canning.'

Poppy leaned closer, studying the screen. A birth record from Madison, Wisconsin.

'Okay, so ...'

'Wait,' I said. 'There's more.' I clicked to a second window. The death record of Edmund Canning. 'They've both done the same thing. They've used other people's identities. Our guy, whoever he is, he is not Ed Canning.'

Poppy leaned back, let loose a hard bark of a laugh. 'You have got to be fucking kidding me.'

I rubbed my hands across my face. 'Okay, so ... so, we have CCTV footage of the attacker, but no real name on him. It's not beyond the realm of possibility that he will use the Canning identity again, but he's going to know we're after him.'

'Which is why he cleared out from the Vauxhall flat.'

I thought of the burned contents of the container. 'He set fire to anything incriminating.' I shook my head. 'And then we have our victim. She's been using an identity we now know to be false.' I collapsed the window down, pulling up the Owens Manhattan Medical Practice website. Erin Owens. 'The founder of the clinic is one Dr Jacob Owens,' I read. 'Pops, see if you can get an address on him.'

'Hang on.' She scooted over to her desk, typing hurriedly. 'Nothing in Manhattan ... okay, here we go, I have a Dr Jacob Owens listed in Setauket, Long Island. Other residents ...' She pumped her fist. 'Other resident is Erin Owens,' she said, triumphantly. 'Husband and wife. They've got to be.'

We studied one another for a moment, then Poppy shook her head. 'I don't get this. I don't get this at all. If she really is Erin Owens, wife of a successful medical practitioner in Manhattan, what the hell is she doing in London, chasing after some dodgy guy who has a thing about fire starting and slitting women's throats.'

'Well, let's ask her husband, shall we?' I thought of the soft toys, of the children waiting. Whatever their mother was, whoever she would turn out to be, they deserved to know what had become of her. 'You got a number there?'

Poppy pursed her lips. 'Not listed. I'll try the clinic website.' She frowned, scrutinising the screen. 'Oh my god. Look at this.'

I leaned closer to her, using the arm of her chair to pull myself in, taking a minute for my eyes to adjust, to read what had been buried within the heart of the website.

We are heartbroken to have to inform our patients of the tragic death of Dr Jacob Owens. Dr Owens and his two children were killed in a car accident over the weekend. A memorial service will be held in the Presbyterian Church of Setauket, Long Island on Wednesday 1 February, 2017.

I held on to the edge of the desk. The soft toys that she carried in her pockets. She carried them there because the children who should have carried them were dead.

Chapter 18

The car jutted awkwardly from the frozen river, its tail lights just visible above the solid sheen of grey ice. The photographer, whoever the photographer had been, had captured a moment, the bank built up high with snow. A couple of police officers stood looking down, one with his hands on his hips, his gaze hooked on the frozen bay. The other his head bowed, in prayer or contemplation.

I clicked the screen, enlarging the photo. Beyond the car, if you could pull your gaze away, off in the distance, there was a line of definition, a distant shore across the iced-over water.

What must it have been like? That moment when their day had gone from ordinary to over? When the thoughtless road had suddenly become their greatest nemesis, the car's wheels loose suddenly on the piled-up ice. I thought of this man, the husband of a woman who now lay dying, the sudden realisation that everything was going awfully, catastrophically wrong, twisting the wheel, pumping the accelerator, trying with everything in him to save them, to keep them away from the large looming bay. Knowing that the water was coming and that it was cold, and that going in there would mean not coming out, and feeling the presence of his children, right there behind him, knowing that their lives depended on these next seconds, on what he did to save them.

According to the news reports, the Long Island winter of 2015 had been a long, bitingly cold one. A wave of low pressure had swept its way down from the north, bringing with it frigid Arctic temperatures, roaring blizzards and bitter, bitter cold. And, on the way to a birthday party with his two small children, a boy of six months and a girl of two years old, the car of Dr Jacob Owens, noted physician and highly respected member of the Long Island community, had gone off the road, plunging into the murky waters of the frozen Great South Bay.

'My god,' said Poppy, quietly. Her face had changed, softening into the other her, the one that she became when Charlie was near. She glanced up at me. 'That poor woman.'

I caught a hint of jasmine in the air.

'We wanted to know where her family was, why they weren't looking for her. This is why. They're dead.'

I nodded and allowed myself a moment to close my eyes. What happened, when you entered a coma? What did you become? Was it a state of emptiness, one that you just couldn't pull yourself out of? Or was it more like sleep, where your dreams roll over you, again and again and again. My insides clenched with the thought of that, of what that would be like, to have my dreams ever-present, with the heat and the overwhelming sound of encroaching flame, of not being able to pull myself free from that. And I opened my eyes, looked back at the photograph before me.

What about her, Holly, Erin, whatever we were calling her now? The fire, that was my darkest hour. This, this moment when her entire family plunged into the frozen ocean, this would be hers. Was that where she was now, locked in an inert world, living over and over again the worst day of her life. Was she trapped there, forever encased in that feeling of wrongness, the recollection of that knock on the door, the phone ringing in the dead of night, the eternal image of a car encased in relentless ice?

Death would have been a mercy for her.

I stood up, my movements sudden enough that Poppy started, and walked to my desk, grabbing the phone, punching in numbers with a heavy hand. The international dial tone again, that rang and rang.

Then, 'This is Gabriel Otero. Leave me a number. I'll call back.'

Shit.

I dumped the phone back into its cradle, feeling like my skin was crawling off me, that I had to move, had to flee.

'Want a coffee?' I asked Poppy, my tone suspiciously light.

She looked at me, sharp.

'I'm knackered,' I offered, with a shrug. 'Need a pick-me-up. And the Guv frowns on coke use in the office.'

She gave me a quick smile. 'Yeah, please. Grab me a chicken salad sandwich too?'

I barely heard her, was gone before she had finished, out of that office with its pressing-down spectre of grief, down the empty staircase, the sound of my heels reverberating across the whitewashed walls. I was running. I can admit that now. And yet somehow I had reached the point at which running away seemed like progress. I wasn't standing and fighting, yet neither was I laying in a smoke-ridden bedroom, waiting for death. I had progressed from freeze to flight. Hurrah.

I hit the ground floor at speed, shoving the door so that it flew open, hitting the wall behind it with a satisfying thud, and pulled in a breath dense with car exhaust and diesel. I kicked the door closed behind me, allowed myself to lean back against the bricks.

I had been right. She was a decent woman, a grieving mother, a widow.

I had been wrong. She was a criminal, juggling multiple identities.

She was Jane Doe and Holly Vale and Erin Owens.

I wanted to keep running. I wanted to run and run and run, until I had left London behind me, until all that was before me was wide-open spaces. I wanted to run all the way home to the clambering hills and the empty skies of the Peak District, to return myself to my childhood bed, to weep until I was spent. I'm done. I can't be who they need me to be. I never could. I wanted to lay my head down in my mother's lap, to have her stroke her palm against my cheek, to tell me that it was okay, that I didn't have to try any more, that I could give in, retreat, give up.

I leaned over, feeling a heat rising through me, my vision swirl.

Had it begun there, on that cold February day in the Long Island Sound? Was that where Erin Owens had lost herself, the person that she thought she was stripped away, grief tipping her from the life she had had before into this other life entirely. And, somehow, in the midst of that had emerged the shape of Canning, or whoever else he might prove to be, and something about him had pulled her along in his wake, had led her to abandon what life she had left, to chase him from continent to continent, so he could murder her in a London park.

A pressure began to build in my chest, the burgeoning weight of panic.

I watched the traffic ooze its way past me and felt something cold steal over me. He would not stop. Whoever she was, none of it mattered when thrown into this sharp relief. What mattered was this man, the casualness with which he dealt out death, the quiet confidence that spoke of someone who had done this before. I watched as a Passat pulled up sharp, missing the Volvo in front of it by inches, an ear-shattering parp of the horn, its echoes bouncing from the surrounding buildings, that told the world that the Volvo driver was not happy. And the realisation crept over me that I had made a mistake. I had been looking at her. Trying to understand her. Because for some reason it had mattered to me what kind of a victim she was. When the truth of it was it should have made no difference at all. She was a victim, and there's an end. But I had spent all my energies, all my focus, chasing the truth of her, whilst ignoring the inescapable conclusion that had been sitting right there before me throughout. That this man was a would-be murderer. That she lived because of Edwina Clarke's timely arrival, not because of any soul-stirring sense of mercy. That if I did not find him, stop him, he was going to kill again.

I stood up, the movement causing my head to swim, told myself to breathe. We knew what he looked like. We knew what car he was driving.

We would find him.

I watched the coffee shop across the street, the door of it swinging open and shut, bringing with it the heady scent of coffee, and pinched the bridge of my nose. I could say I wasn't feeling well. I could return home, crawl under my duvet. Not home, but Camden home. Or ... I could ... I could actually go home. I could be at Euston in an hour, be on the Manchester Piccadilly train, change to the northern line to Sheffield, get my dad to pick me up from Hope. I could do it. I could retreat into myself, or whatever was left of myself, admit that I was falling apart.

I blew out a long breath.

Coffee. I had promised Poppy coffee. And a chicken salad sandwich.

I couldn't do much, but perhaps I could do that.

I shoved myself away from the wall, walking slowly to the pavement's edge, one foot on the kerb, when something caught my attention, a black Mercedes, E-class, its driver hunkered down low, frowning down at something. I thought back to yesterday, to the day before, a memory I hadn't known I had, of the same Mercedes, parked in the same place.

I stepped out into the road, scaring the shit out of an elderly woman driving a red Toyota Yaris. What do you know? Guess there was a devil-may-care part of me left in there somewhere.

I weaved my way towards the opposite pavement and hurried towards the car, my hand questing in my back pocket for my warrant card.

'Hey.' I rapped on the window, the sound making him strike a black mark across the page, gestured for him to roll it down, waving my warrant card at him.

He obliged, wide-eyed with alarm.

'You're fine,' I said. 'I just need to ask you something. You're here a lot, right? I've seen you about before.'

'Yeah, I mean, I have a client, I drive him, I'm a driver, yeah? And I do a regular pick-up from that office there.' He pointed a little further down the street. 'I got a boss and everything. You can check. I'm not a terrorist or anything like that.'

I frowned. 'Okay, good news. Pop your door open for me, yeah?'

He hesitated, then flipped the passenger-side door open. I slid my way inside.

'So, you're here every day?'

'No, well, yeah. On weekdays, like. No weekends. I'm a singer on weekends.'

'Right.' I pointed to a small black box at the top of his screen. 'This is a dashcam?'

'Yeah ...'

'You here last Friday?'

'Yeah.'

I looked at him. 'You see where I'm going with this?'

He stared at me for a moment, then started, fumbling his mobile phone from a holder on the dashboard. 'You want my footage from Friday? Yeah. Yeah, I can do that. I mean, anything to help, know what I mean? You know, I know you're just doing your job and I ...'

'Yeah, singer. Got it.' I took the phone off him.

'The camera will stream footage to the phone. Just press play there. Should be about right.'

He had been parked in the same spot, there or thereabouts. Could just about make out the doorway of the coffee shop. But the camera held an unobstructed view of the opposite side of the street. If Canning had stood there, then we could get a clear shot of his face, could plaster it all over the media. Tough to hide when you're everyone's favourite poster boy.

I watched the crowd funnel past the car, picking up a familiar figure, the fur of her coat brushing her cheek. Watched her move across the flow of people, vanishing into the coffee shop.

The other side of the street remained steadfastly empty.

'Come on, you bastard,' I muttered.

Then, as if summoned, a figure appeared on the corner of Richbell Place, his back to us. He hovered there, seemed that his gaze was fixed on the coffee shop, a baseball cap pulled down low. He stood, watching for a minute, two, then he looked, left, right, a glance back at the police station behind him, then turned, walking down towards Theobalds Road.

'Is there any way to zoom in on this?' I asked.

'Sorry. It is what it is.'

I pursed my lips. We were too far away, just the murkiest of outlines. I rolled the footage back, watching it unfold again. Only this time, I stared at the spot I knew he would appear, did not let myself be distracted by the figure of Erin or Holly or whoever the hell she was. I watched him as he rounded the corner, as he took position across from the coffee shop and as the slightest of movements of his coat revealed a flash of light. I replayed it again. A knife.

He had stood across from the coffee shop, had waited until she had seen him. And he had shown her how he meant to kill her.

'You fucker.'

'Sorry?'

'Not you.'

I thought of Emilia, of the call to the hospital. Was this a threat? Or was it something different? A warning. Back off. I don't want to have to use this.

My phone rang, startling me and startling the singer next to me, who dropped his crossword puzzle.

'Yeah?'

'Al?' said Poppy. 'Get your arse back here. We found Canning's car.'

Chapter 19

The black Audi A4 sat desolate, a lone ray of sophistication in a Hounslow industrial estate. It had been parked up near a warehouse, so that if you were not paying attention, just driving past, say, you might not have noticed it. Fortunately, our uniformed officer was paying attention.

I slammed the car door, tucked my coat around myself as a cold wind spiralled from nowhere.

'How did he find it?'

'Said he's been here a couple of times before, calls to stolen cars. Struck him as a handy place to dump a vehicle, so when the alert went up, he came for a look. Paid off, evidently.'

'Remind me to buy him a beer,' I said. 'Or a car.'

A low rumble like a tank crossing a bridge and I looked up at the belly of an A380 as it lined itself up with a Heathrow runway just a couple of miles away.

'See now, the stupid part of me was about to ask why you would come all the way out to Hounslow to abandon a rental car?'

Poppy stopped, looked up at the plane. 'And the smart part of you?'

I sighed heavily. 'He's doing a runner, isn't he? We need to contact Heathrow, tell them that we think he's on his way through there.'

'I'll get his description out to them, see if the AFOs can look out for him on their patrols, try to pick him up. Of course,' she muttered, 'would be a damn sight easier if we knew where he was heading.'

'Yeah, well, this job would be a damn sight easier if people would stop committing crimes.'

'That would be nice, wouldn't it?'

My phone began to ring, and I answered, turning my back on the wind. 'Alice Parr.'

'Hey Sarge. It's Harry. Sorry, just thought I should let you know, we've managed to find a mobile phone linked to Erin Owens.'

I hesitated. 'You're kidding. Is it ...'

'It's running off a US network. I've managed to speak to them and they say the phone is currently turned off.'

'Have they ...'

'They're working on getting the phone records to us.'

'Oh.' I looked back towards Poppy. 'Okay, let me know when they come in.' I hung up, moving back towards Poppy. 'Harry's tracked down her mobile. We're waiting on a call log.' I looked back at the car. 'You ready?' I asked.

'Born ready.'

I pulled my gloves on and shone my torch through the driver's side window of the Audi, revealing little but what you would expect. 'Looks clean enough,' I muttered, trying the handle, with little hope of success. It gave in my hands with a loud click.

I glanced up at Poppy and pulled the door open wide.

'It's been emptied out.' I peered into the door pockets, running my gloved hand beneath the seat. 'Shit. We need a CSI to process this, see if maybe we can get some hair, prints, something that he's missed. Dammit.'

I checked the back seat, the glovebox, all faultlessly clean, then stood to face Poppy.

'Boot?'

'Boot.'

I confess that my expectations were low. Which just goes to show that policing is the enemy of expectation.

I popped open the boot and stood there, flicking the torch around the dark interior. It was empty, for the most part, just a disappointingly vast expanse of beige carpet. I ducked down, shining the torchlight into the farthest reaches of the boot.

Then the light caught on something, a mounded shape half hidden towards the rear of the space.

I shifted my torch from hand to hand and pulled it forward, a black bag bunched up tight, opened it carefully.

'You've got to be kidding me.'

Poppy leaned closer. 'Is that ... Oh god.'

I opened the bag wider, revealing a long blonde wig and something dense and soft.

'Is that a cushion?'

'No,' I said, words tasting like ash in my mouth, 'it's padding.' I looked up at her. 'He was wearing a disguise. Every image we have of him ... it was all a disguise. We have no idea what he looks like.' I dropped the bag back into the boot, tugging my gloves off hard enough that they tore. 'Holy shit. We have nothing.' I turned away from the car, facing into the tugging wind, anger balling my hands up into fists. 'He's done this on purpose. This,' I waved back at the black bag, 'this is a message to us, a great big fuck you.' I rubbed my hands over my face, torn between laughter and tears. 'Jesus Christ, Poppy. Who the hell is this guy?'

'Al ...'

'Fuck.'

My phone rang and I tugged it from my pocket, inches from throwing it at the wall, just because I could.

'What?'

A silence on the other end, then a small voice, 'Sorry ... I ... DS Parr? It's Gwen. The nurse from the hospital?'

I blew out a slow breath. 'Sorry. Yes, hi Gwen.'

'I'm really sorry to disturb you, but ... Look, this is probably nothing and I shouldn't even be calling you, but you know when something just strikes you as odd?'

'Sure?'

'Well, see, I just took a call from one of your detectives. Or ... he said he was one of your detectives and he wanted to know how Ms Vale was and what the doctors were saying about her chances. And, I mean, I told him that I'd need the password before I could give out any information and he, well, it sounded like he kind of panicked, and then he hung up. As you can imagine, that made me nervous, so I thought best give you a call.'

I stopped. 'Did he give you his name?'

'Detective Grey.'

Son of a bitch.

'You didn't give him any information?'

'Nothing. She's still got the uniformed officer in with her so she's fine. I just thought it was best that I let you know. And also, I've just spoken to the doctors,' she said, 'and the latest assessment shows that her condition has improved a little. It's far too early to tell anything at this stage, but the doctor said he's encouraged by today's test.'

I breathed out slowly. 'Is he there? The doctor?'

'Um ... yeah, well, he's here somewhere. He's doing his rounds so he'll be about for the next hour or so.'

'Okay, I'm going to come in and see him. I'll be there as soon as I can.'

I pocketed my phone, took off towards my car.

'I'm going to St Thomas',' I yelled back at Poppy. 'They said she's improved slightly. I'm going to try and get more information out of the doctor.'

She made to follow me. 'I'll come.'

'No. You go to Heathrow.' I yanked open the car door. 'Focus on the American flights. But, remember, he likes playing dress-up.'

I pulled out of the car park, faster than one could feasibly expect to drive in London traffic. Had made it as far as the defunct Battersea Power Station when my phone rang again.

'Hello?'

A pause, then, 'Is that Detective Parr?'

I hesitated, easing my foot off the pedal as the traffic slowed in front of me, and picked the rolling American accent from the quiet voice. 'It is.'

'This is Gabriel Otero. You left a message asking me to call you.'

'I ... yes, hi.' The traffic began to move off again, easing slowly forward, buildings giving way to a snapshot of sunlight glinting along the Thames. 'Thanks for calling back. It's ... I'm investigating an incident here in London, and we found your business card ... I was wondering if you would be able to fill in some blanks for me.'

'If I can,' said the distant voice. 'Who had my card?'

'We think her name is Erin Owens. But she also goes under the identity of Holly Vale.'

A hefty silence this time.

'I don't know a Holly Vale, but, yes, I do know an Erin Owens.'

'Okay ...' I said, steering round a Boris bike, its middle-aged rider swaying precariously into the road. 'You know her how?'

'I knew her husband. Well, knew might be a bit of a stretch. He was an acquaintance. I kind of remember giving him my card, but I mean, wow, this would be a couple of years ago now. It's funny you're asking this ... the number you called me on, it's my old precinct. I haven't worked there in, I guess, eighteen months? When they called me to tell me you'd left a message, they said there's another message on the system too. That Erin Owens had called, on, I don't know, Friday? I've been off a couple of days, so they were only just able to get hold of me today.'

I slowed, struggling to concentrate on the traffic coming across Vauxhall Bridge, the cyclist nudging his way forward in blatant disregard for life and limb. 'Okay,' I said, going for calm and almost achieving it. 'What did Erin say?'

'Ah …' the distant sound of typing, 'not much. Just that she needed me to call her back as soon as I could. She left a cell number.' He paused, then said, 'Did you … did you say she was going under a different identity?'

I squeezed past the bike, watching in my rear-view mirror as the rider took a hard right, causing the BMW behind me to slam on his brakes, releasing a stream of invective through the window.

'Yes. It's … it's complicated. So, do you by any chance know an Edmund Canning? We have reason to believe it may be an alias.'

Another silence, the sound of typing. 'I'm not seeing anything on the system. So, what's going on with Erin Owens?'

I tugged the car into the car park of St Thomas', faster than I should, the tyres squealing against the tarmac. 'She was stabbed, walking in Central London. She's alive, but only just. Look, I'm just heading into the hospital now. But we have reason to believe that her attacker may be trying to leave the country, either under the name of Canning or some other alias. Can

I get you to keep a lookout your end? I have no idea where he's headed, but we believe he has connections with New York, so …'

'I'll pass it on to Customs and Border Protection. You got anything else on him?'

'I'll forward over the files.' I slowed, waiting for an elderly woman to manoeuvre a tiny car into an enormous space. 'But Captain Otero? I need to reiterate – whilst this man hasn't yet killed anyone, that is not through the lack of trying. Based on his actions here in London, we believe him to be a highly dangerous individual.'

A silence, then he said, 'Do something for me? Send me everything you've got on Canning. I'll do some digging my end.'

I pulled into a space, leaving mere inches between me and the car next door. 'Yes. Thank you. I'll get that over to you as soon as I get back to the office.'

And then I promised to call him when I had more, let myself out of the car and walked slowly into the hospital.

We had nothing, no idea where to begin. Our images were so much dress-up. And so, if he was rabbiting, where the hell was he rabbiting to? To New York? To Paris? We know he had been there at least once because he came across on the Eurostar. And from there, where?

I could feel my legs, heavy, as if they had made the decision for me, that it was over, time to give up.

Detective Grey. Detective Grey, you cheeky son of a bitch. Who did that? What kind of criminal had those balls, that confidence in their own invulnerability?

I pushed the door open slowly, walking as if in a dream. So it took me a moment to piece together the alarms that were sounding, the running of feet, the white coats flying out behind the rapidly retreating backs.

But when I did finally get there, when I pieced it together, it was almost as if I'd been expecting it, that I had known all along how this would end.

I rounded the corner into her room. Jane Doe. Holly Vale. Erin Owens.

They surrounded her, engulfing her in a wall of white. The alarm shrieking, movements quick and urgent. One, two, three, four. One, two, three, four. A young PC stood, back pressed up against the wall, shooting for equanimity, achieving instead a look of abject terror.

I stood there and I watched as what little life that remained inside of Erin ebbed away.

I stood there, time warping and contracting and expanding until I had no idea who I was, how long it had been, the moments only measured by the fingernails that dug into the palm of my hand, the sharp shards of pain all that connected me to this moment, to this twisted reality.

I stood there and I watched as, finally, the white-coated backs stepped backwards, as their shoulders sank. Someone turned off the alarm.

Then a voice, from somewhere within it all, 'Time of death, 3.46 p.m.'

Part Two

Chapter 1

My eyes swam, exhaustion making the lobby of the NYPD First Precinct buck and shimmy. I pushed myself up in the chair, feigning an alertness that had left me somewhere in the middle of the Atlantic, and took a long pull of coffee, stronger than I was used to. But then, that was no bad thing in the grip of wicked jet lag, riding on the back of three hours' sleep.

I glanced across at Harry, bright-eyed and preternaturally enthusiastic, leaning forward in the hard-backed chair, a runner just desperate for the starter's gun.

'How the hell are you so awake?'

He grinned. 'I love New York. Don't you just love New York? So much energy here, so much life.'

I grunted, buried my face in my coffee again, my guts twisting around on themselves. Because, the thing is, I had made the decision. On the day that followed the finale of the long drawn-out death of Erin Owens, after a night of endless wakefulness that nonetheless somehow brought with it dreams, of smoke and flame. I couldn't cope with bed, not on that night, and so I had lain on the sofa, as if that way I could cheat my nightmares, like they couldn't find me there. It hadn't worked. Then, at

4 a.m., I had run the shower, turning the dial up so that the heat of the water fell like arrows against my skin, and had cried, in a way I'm not sure I had cried since I was a little girl and the end of the world could be brought about by a skinned knee, or silence from a friend. At 7 a.m. I called my mother. I've made a mistake. I shouldn't have come back to work. I'm not ready. A long drawn-out silence on the other end of the line, and I imagined her, standing with bare feet on that always cold kitchen floor, choosing her words with care. What can I do to help, Alice? What do you need? And then crying again, I need to come home, Mum. I need to stop.

What did I feel then, as those words spilled out into my empty Camden apartment? Was it relief, the exquisite forgiveness of finally letting go, admitting to yourself and to the world that you are irretrievably damaged? Looking back now, it's hard to tell. All that remains to me is the emptiness left behind on the disconnected call, the hollowness. It was set, done. I would go home. Run? No. Not that. A tactical retreat.

I remember the reverberation of my footsteps, echoing in the breeze-blocked hallways of Holborn Police Station. The feel of the cold metal door handle beneath my fingers.

It was an ending, a cessation of all pretence. Detective Sergeant Alice Parr was dead. And I didn't know who this was that had been left behind. All I knew was that, whoever she was, she couldn't do this job. All her instincts, everything she had thought she knew, all wrong. Wrong, wrong, wrong.

And yet …

The next morning I had opened the door on an office fizzing with energy. I could feel it in the air, that something had changed.

'What's going on?'

Poppy had looked up from her computer, shook her head quickly. 'Erin Owens' phone. It's been switched back on within the last hour.'

I stood stock-still. 'They got a location?'

'Yes,' said Poppy, expression grim. 'New York.'

It had taken an impressively short space of time for a decision to be made. Someone needs to go to New York. Harry's hand had shot up, like we were in comp and someone had started handing out Jägerbombs. Because, of course, it's New York, and who doesn't want to go to New York? Me. I didn't want to go to New York. But for the rest of the world, it is a dream opportunity. Only there are partners to consider, and children and workloads. Unless, of course, you are Harry and such considerations are beyond your current levels of maturity. Or me, with no one to consider but herself.

I watched Poppy, her head down, her thumb repeatedly pressing her phone, the screen lighting up again and again with Charlie's face.

'I'll go, Guv,' I heard myself say, the words settling on me with an inevitability. Because it had to be me, didn't it?

And so, there I was, on an uncomfortable seat in a chilly NYPD precinct house.

Harry shifted in his chair, watching the NYPD uniforms as they walked towards the back of the lobby. 'You know,' he offered, 'I came here on a stag do a couple of years ago. Epic, man. Epic.'

I turned a bleary gaze towards him.

'You been here before?' he asked.

I looked down, taking a sip of my coffee, watching as they punched in a code, disappearing through a door, one saying something to the other, a loud burst of laughter. 'I've been as far as Lanzarote if that helps?'

The door hung open, fingers appearing round the edge of it, a figure emerging into the lobby. I watched him scan the lobby, took in the height of him – 6'3, I would later learn – but his shoulders rounded so that he appeared smaller, that black hair, the caramel skin. Nose like a beak. The thing is, much of recollection becomes rough-edged over time. Uncertain. But what remains clear to me is that I thought he was attractive. I know this because it made me spill my coffee in my lap.

'Oh, dammit!' I jumped up from the chair, watching as the pool of coffee in my lap widened and stretched, running down towards my thighs.

'Detective Parr?' The voice was soft, low enough that I only caught the tail of the words. 'I'm sorry. Did I startle you? Kitty? You got a cloth?' He grabbed a wad of tissues from the middle-aged woman behind the counter and handed them to me.

I dabbed at the rapidly widening coffee stain, attempting to feign serenity. 'Oh, it's fine. Don't worry. I'm just jet-lagged that's all. A barbarian horde could have crept up on me.' I stuck out my hand, trying to ignore the damp patch that pressed itself against my leg. 'Alice, please. This is Harry.'

The man smiled widely. 'Gabriel Otero.'

I nodded. It's possible I blushed.

Possible.

Inevitable.

'Come on through. Thanks, Kit.' He turned, leading us past the main reception desk, into a warren of corridors. 'So, you been here before?'

'I have,' offered Harry. 'Great city. Great. Just so … alive, you know?'

I didn't roll my eyes.

Gabriel nodded, thoughtful. 'Alive. Sure.' He caught my eye, the briefest flash of a grin and I felt myself colour again. Dammit.

He opened an office door and guided us inside. 'Have a seat, please. You guys get coffee?' He glanced down at my trousers. 'I mean … you want a coffee to drink instead of to wear?'

I smiled. 'Yes, please. Coffee to drink would be great.'

'Let me just grab those.'

I turned to study his desk, empty for the most part, just a computer, a desk phone and a neat stack of papers. A framed photograph sat on a shelf to the right-hand side, a small boy with wide dark eyes, a mop of black hair. I wondered if he was married. I mentally slapped myself.

'You know,' said Harry, quietly, 'I'm going to see if I can have a go at a gun range while I'm here. I've never been shooting before.'

I nodded, the wet patch on my trousers sticking to my thigh, and wished like hell I'd come alone. Then quickly chastised myself for being so impatient. The boy was keen, I'll give him that.

The door swung open and Gabriel set three cups of coffee down on the desk, sinking into the chair. 'I didn't know what you'd like, so I guessed cream.' He dropped some sugar packets on the desk in front of me. 'And you might need this. This stuff doubles as tar for the highways crew.' He shook his head. 'I was sorry to hear about Mrs Owens. No one deserves to die like that.'

'So, you knew her?' I emptied a sugar packet into my cup, hesitated, then added a second.

He took a sip of coffee and grimaced. From the memory or the coffee was unclear. 'I knew her a little. From before. She used to live out in Setauket with her husband. Long Island. I lived a couple of blocks away.'

I nodded, took a sip of the dark coffee and suppressed a shudder. God.

'Her husband and I ... we used to walk our dogs in the same park. Nice guy. Of course, that was before ...' He glanced down, voice trailing off. 'I heard about the accident. It was a couple of months after I left Long Island, moved down here to First Precinct.' He shook his head. 'That lady, she had a hell of a lot of tragedy to live through in one lifetime.'

I nodded, the smell of jasmine vying against the bitterness of the coffee.

'So,' said Otero, 'I've done some digging. Erin has been living in an apartment in Brooklyn, has been working out of the Morgan Stanley Children's Hospital, paediatric nurse. She qualified eight years ago but gave up work after she had her first child. Apparently, she had kept her certification, so after the accident she returned to work. Now ...' – he checked hand-scrawled notes on the desk before him – 'it seems that she left the country on March first, so just over a month ago. She flew from JFK to Fiumicino in Rome on a Delta flight. After that, nothing. As to Mr Canning, I can't find any record of him. No sign of him leaving the country, no sign of him coming back in.' He shifted through the papers, pulling one from the pile and sliding it across the desk towards me. 'That is a record of all the Ed Cannings in the state of New York. We've already looked into them and they're solid. They all have alibis covering the time period we're looking at.'

I nodded, feeling a twist in my gut. 'If we are right in thinking that Canning, or whoever he is, originated here, then it could suggest he only began using the identity once he reached Europe.' Which means we had no idea who he was before, who he was now.

A bubbling ring broke through the momentary silence that followed and I sat there, disoriented.

'Alice ...' prompted Harry.

'Oh shit.' I flushed, glanced up. 'Sorry. Can you excuse me?' I grabbed the phone, ducking out onto the empty corridor. 'Hello?'

'Al, it's me.' Poppy's voice gave me a jolt, and suddenly it hit me again, the need to hide, to run home, to stop pretending I was something I wasn't. For the briefest and most foolish of moments, I wanted to cry.

'Hey, Pops,' was all I said.

'How's the Big Apple?'

'Appley. Hey, how about I put little Harry on a flight home and you come out and take his place?'

'Getting on your nerves?'

'We've been here thirteen hours. I'm not placing any bets on him reaching fourteen.'

Poppy laughed. 'Al, he's new and excited. You know, like a puppy.'

'Yeah, well, if he pisses on the carpet, I'm rubbing his nose in it. So ... what's up?'

'Well, I have some news. We just got the post-mortem results back on Erin Owens. According to the coroner, her death was unrelated to her injuries.'

'Meaning what?'

She sighed heavily. 'Meaning, he thinks she died from an overdose of morphine.'

Time stopped then, the flow of it pulling itself up to a hard halt, me trapped in it, the seconds swirling around my legs.

'How?' I breathed. 'No ... the uniformed ... she was there, the PC was there, in the room. I saw her, when they were trying to revive Erin.'

'I just got done speaking to the PC,' Poppy said, grim. 'She swears she never left the room, that a doctor came in while she was there, that he was very pleasant, made some small talk, administered an injection into Erin Owens' IV line, then left. About three minutes later, all hell broke loose.'

'Oh my god.'

He had killed her. After all that, the effort and the chasing and this man who appears and disappears, he killed her right there in front of us. And I was looking the wrong way, was chasing a blond-haired fat man across London.

I had been right. When I had told myself that I had lost it. I had been fucking right.

'I'm on my way to go through the CCTV, see if I can catch a glimpse of him. The PC gave a description, dark hair, glasses, medium build. We've got her working up a composite sketch as we speak.'

'Okay.'

The line hung empty and for a moment I thought that she had gone. Then, 'Just ... keep the faith, sister.' A click, then true silence.

I stood there in the hallway, allowing my thoughts to buffet me. I could just leave. Could go, get on a plane. Tell the Met to do one. What could they do? Arrest me?

I closed my eyes briefly, pulled in a breath and pushed open the door, Harry's voice billowing out at me, all high-pitched and keen. It trailed off when he saw me.

'Everything okay?'

I walked slowly, conscious steps like a drunk woman feigning sobriety, lowered myself into the chair, waiting until I was sure I could speak.

'That was London,' I said, addressing Gabriel. 'The post-mortem on Erin Owens has revealed that she was killed with an overdose of morphine in her hospital bed. I think our conclusion has to be that it was him.'

Harry let loose a low whistle.

I watched Gabriel as he leaned forward, his forearms resting on the desktop, forcing the checks on his shirt to buckle and warp. 'And now,' he said, 'he's somewhere in New York.'

I nodded, not trusting myself to speak.

Gabriel considered for a moment, then shifted in his seat, gesturing up at a map tacked high on a wall – New York and its surrounding environs. 'This here,' he said, indicating the jagged-edged peninsula jutting out into the Atlantic, 'this is Setauket, out on Long Island. Erin Owens' phone pinged off a tower right about here.'

I twisted, studying the map, thinking of the White Pages, of the first unveiling of Erin Owens. 'That's where Erin was living, right?'

He sank back into his seat, expression grim. 'It is. We've been trying to get a further read on the phone's location, but it's been switched back off again. But,' he said, 'the phone company has managed to get the records associated with that phone over to me.' He slid a piece of paper across the desk towards me. 'Erin didn't use it much after she left the US. At least not until about two weeks before she was attacked. Then she called her old next-door neighbour from out in Setauket, a Kate Weland. According to the records, they spoke extensively over the course of the following weeks, the final call going from Erin to Kate on the night before she was stabbed.'

'He has Erin's phone,' I said, quietly. 'He's going to know who she talked to.' A roar of fear worked its way

222

up my sternum. 'He just walked into a hospital, killed Erin in front of a police officer. We have to assume that he represents a substantial threat to anyone she's been in contact with. Kate Weland isn't safe.'

Gabriel's lips flattened and he pulled his mobile phone towards him, standing with a rush of movement. 'We need to go.' He punched a number into his keypad, one eye on the phone records before him, the dial tone loud in the small room, his face becoming grimmer by the second. I followed him from the room, step quick, my heart thudding, could hear Harry's trotting steps behind me.

'Shit. No answer.' Gabriel shoved open a door leading to a staircase, voice echoing about us. 'I'll get someone local straight over there.'

My phone began to ring again and I answered it quickly.

'Al? It's Noah.'

'Hey, Guv.' I hung back, let Harry go ahead, slipping through the door after him into the underground car park.

'Um, Al ... look, something's happened. Well, I mean, I can't be sure, but ...'

'What's going on, Guv?'

He sighed windily across the ocean. 'Al, there was a call, this morning, from the hospital. Guy says he was one of the doctors treating Erin Owens. Admin picked it up, and they just ...' He sighed again. 'Al, they told him that you weren't here. That you'd gone to New York.'

I let the door swing closed behind me, the clang of it loud in the quiet car park, a chill creeping across me. A premonition of things to come. 'It was him, wasn't it?'

Noah's voice was taut with strain. 'I only just heard about it. I called the hospital. Alice, I'm so sorry, but no one there had rung.' He paused, a tremor in his breath. 'Al, before he hung up, he told her to tell you that he'll be seeing you really soon.'

My footsteps slowed, stopped, a knot forming heavy in my stomach. Then, the sound of Gabriel's voice breaking in. 'You've got to be kidding me.'

I shifted the phone to the crook of my neck. 'What?'

He shook his head. 'We have to get to Setauket. Now.'

Chapter 2

She lay prone on the kitchen floor, bare legs stretched out, long and tanned, from a thigh-length dressing gown. Her feet had begun to turn blue. She had done her make-up, perfectly pink lips gently parted in what should have been a sigh, her lashes long and dark. There was a single bullet hole in her forehead.

'Alice, Harry,' said Gabriel, softly, 'meet Kate Weland, Erin's friend and neighbour.'

I crouched down low, tilting my head to see the ruination that lay beneath her. The back of her head had been destroyed, auburn hair turned black with blood. A mug lay shattered beside her, dark coffee spilling out, staining the cashmere of her robe. Brain matter splattered across the cabinets.

'Shit,' I muttered.

Her eyes were open, frozen in an expression of stunned disbelief. Had she seen it? Her understanding quick enough that she knew what was to come, and yet too slow to do anything about it? I twisted, looking up, in my mind, raising her from the dead, placing her back where she would once have stood. She had been drinking coffee. She had been standing here, at her kitchen window, looking out over a finely kept garden, a pool of azure blue, all curves and rock formations, looking ill-equipped for actual swimming. I studied the window, the spiderweb bullet hole, the narrow slivers of glass that lined the kitchen sink.

'It was him,' I said, softly.

I looked at the dead woman, at the parting of her lips, like there was something she simply had to say. Erin had been right. He was a wolf. And they were the prey.

What did you know?

'Who's this now?' A detective, all long and lean, gleaming mahogany skin, her hair shorn short to her scalp. She frowned at me, taking my measure.

'I've got a guy wanted on a murder in London.' I pushed myself up to standing, handing her my phone, the CCTV footage of Canning, all dressed up in fat sheep's clothing. 'The victim was this lady's friend and former neighbour.'

The woman squinted at the image. 'You put out a BOLO on this guy?' she asked, addressing Gabriel.

He nodded. 'Already done. He's been operating under the name of Canning. No sign of him entering the country, so odds are he's under a different name. And they've found evidence that he's in disguise in that picture.' He looked about the kitchen, the dead woman on the floor. 'Who found her?'

The detective sniffed. 'The daughter. She's off at Penn State but was home for the weekend. Said she was out for a run this morning, came back and found her mother like this. She's pretty cut up. Obviously.' She consulted her notes. 'Time is estimated to be around 9.15 a.m. First responders found footprints in the flower bed outside that window.' She pointed at the kitchen window. 'We got a shell casing, found outside, 9mm. And a bullet hole in that wall there, suggests she was standing right at the window when the shot was fired.'

'Neighbours see anything?' asked Gabriel.

She pursed her lips. 'Couple of people said they heard the shot, but no one saw anything suspicious. The houses, they're set pretty far back off the street here, so wouldn't be hard to move about unnoticed. One house, down there on the corner, the resident said she noticed a jogger go by, around about the time of the shooting. She didn't think much of it at the time.'

Gabriel looked to me.

'It would fit with his MO,' I offered.

'Is there anyone else?' asked Harry. 'What's going on with the husband?'

'We've picked him up, patrol are bringing him in to the station. He's a lawyer in the city. He was in a meeting with fifteen other people at the time, so his alibi is solid, but still . . .'

'The daughter?' asked Gabriel, quietly.

'We've swabbed for gunshot residue. She's clean. Couple of neighbours saw her running when she said she was, so alibi checks out. She may be involved, but I'll be honest and say I don't think so. She's pretty cut up. We've got her down at the station right now.'

'We need to speak to her,' said Gabriel. He nodded to the detective, a glance to me. 'Shall we?'

I looked one final time at what remained of Kate Weland, a feeling massing in the pit of my stomach. Was this what an antelope felt in the presence of a lion? I looked through the shattered remains of the kitchen window, seeing a shape beyond that was not there. Him.

Dammit.

Through the once glorious house, through the press of people, of police, forensic teams, all with their best business faces on, and with each step thinking, it could be you. It could be you. Training my gaze on each of them, so that they were forced to look at me, so that I could see, what? What would be there, differentiating this wolf from the sheep he hid amongst? Telling myself that I would know if I saw it, but deep down knowing that I was lying.

We stepped out into lurid sunshine. A news crew had arrived, had set up shop across the street from the house, a camera already out and rolling and trained on us. I looked down the lens, already seeing myself on the evening news. He'll see you really soon. I looked beyond the camera, to the man behind it, his face hidden, hair a mass of curls, and suddenly I was walking. Not walking, striding. Towards the looming black lens, the part-hidden frame of a man. Could feel Harry, footsteps close behind me, not asking, just letting me lead. Pulled out my warrant card, like that meant a damn thing here.

'Police, can you stop filming for me, please?'

The man trained the lens on me, his head poking out from behind the mass of it. 'I'm pretty sure you're asking me to suspend my first amendment rights there, Ma'am.'

Gabriel sighed heavily behind me. 'Don, don't be a dick. Just put the camera down, hey?'

Don rolled his eyes, ostentatiously switching the camera off and lowering it to his waist. He eyed me, his gaze skirting across my scar, lingering on my breasts. 'You're not from around here.'

I looked back at Gabriel. 'You know this guy?'

Gabriel folded his arms, nodded. 'I have had the pleasure. Don here is from Channel 92.'

I nodded, took a step back, tried to breathe. Because that was the thing, he was everywhere, was everyone. He was a victim support worker, a doctor, a jogger. Is it you? Or you? Or you?

'You know, if you're new to the area ...'

'Take a breath, Don,' said Gabriel. 'Alice, you ready?'

I nodded, bile rising up in my throat, and fell into step with him, feeling Don's eyes burning into the back of me and trying not to see the uniformed officers that stood beside cars, the gardener two doors down, the entire world of wolves. Beyond that, the houses, the two tragic homes, of Kate Weland and, once, of Erin Owens. Separated by sweeping lawns, high hedges. Kate's had a steepled roof, a columned front, yawningly wide bay windows, Erin's a flat frontage, a wood slat façade, a row of front-facing windows. An entire world and a whole socioeconomic group removed from my sad little Camden flat.

I turned back towards the car, pulling the door closed hard, tried to catch my breath, felt Gabriel slide in beside me. Harry pulling the rear door closed, the impact of it leading to reverberations. One beat, two.

'You okay?' asked Gabriel.

I thought I was going to be sick. 'I'm fine.'

We pulled from the kerb, taking it carefully on the residential streets. I could feel the questions just oozing from Gabriel's pores, could feel Harry's judgement rippling forward from the back seat. Did he know it too? That I wasn't up to this. That whatever shit I had, it was long gone.

I leaned forward, for a moment forgetting that I was not alone, pulled the passenger-side visor down and studied my face in the mirror, my fingers teasing at my scar. This man, he was a symptom, an indication of something that had fractured within me. I told myself that if it were not him then it would be someone else. That he was nothing special.

I studied the circular patterns, the red-raw skin where the make-up had rubbed away.

Thought of the irony, the vicious symmetry of it, of Canning, dipping into and out of this investigation, each time his identity shifting, until it seemed that everywhere I turned there he was. He played with it, this notion of identity. Whereas I – I ran my finger across the raised ridge where my hairline should be – I grieved for mine, for what had been taken from me by the fire and my own inadequacies.

The thing is, I had thought that it was about Erin, that this case had gripped hold of me because of who she was. That she was the victim I had needed, one who could allow me to justify my being. But maybe I was wrong. Maybe instead it was always about him, who throws away what I would kill for with a sense of wild abandon.

I sighed, allowed my fingers to drop to my lap and looked at the shape of myself in the narrow mirror, at the whole of it, the damaged, the smooth, suddenly aware again, of the movement of the car, of the heady silence from the two men beside me, the click of the road beneath us, a squall of a seagull overhead.

I'm going to find you.

Chapter 3

The small station thrummed with activity. I fell into step behind Gabriel, Harry's heavy tread right at my heels as we moved through the corridors. I watched Gabriel, a quick smile here, a nod there. The women, their heads pivoting to watch him pass, backs straighter, smiles brighter. And then taking in me, with my hangdog jet-lagged looks, my scar. I smiled brightly at them, tried to pretend I wasn't dreaming of my hotel room, of a thousand years of sleep, of escape from the spotlight stares.

Gabriel slowed as a detective met us coming the other way, a dark-skinned man, a shock of white hair, about as wide as he was tall.

'Well, well, well, Rudy. How you been?'

They reached out to one another, did that complicated man hug, handshake thing that men will insist on doing, while I stepped back, mentally calculating how long I had left until sleep beckoned.

'I'm good. I'm good. You? Hey, how's Isaiah? He still doin' that karate?'

Gabriel nodded, a wide smile. 'Yeah, purple belt now. You know he's down in Boston, right? Nancy got tenure at BU.'

Rudy hesitated, a clammy silence descending. 'No. I'm sorry, man.'

Gabriel shrugged, a glance back at me. 'It's ... you know. Whatever. He's doing great though, so that's all that matters, really. Hey, Rudy, I'd like you to meet Detective Sergeant Alice Parr and Detective Constable Harry Regan. These guys are over with us from London.'

Rudy grinned broadly, encasing my hand in his bear-like paws. 'Well, it's a true honour. You keeping this guy in check?'

I nodded. 'I come from the land of Mary Poppins. I'm well trained in handling unruly kids.'

Rudy gave a loud guffaw of laughter, clapping me on the shoulder with a heavy hand. I glanced at Gabriel, his grin wide, eyes dancing, and shrugged.

'She's good,' rumbled Rudy. 'I like her. So, I'm hearing you guys are invested in this here murder?'

I nodded. 'We have reason to believe the shooter might be our suspect from a London murder.' My gaze fell on the clipboard he was holding, a plastic evidence bag stretched taut over an iPhone. 'Is that by any chance Kate Weland's mobile?'

He glanced down. 'Huh? Oh, her cell? Sure. I was just gonna take a look. Come on.' He led us into an empty conference room, setting the phone down on the table and pulling on a pair of gloves. 'So, London, huh? This guy's got some ambition then. Most of the assholes we deal with don't get more than three blocks from their mom's front porch.' He punched a lock code number in. 'The daughter gave us this. That girl,

233

she's crushed. Even if it turns out not to be your guy, it wasn't the kid. I'd lay money on that. We've got the father in interview right now, but so far it looks like his alibi stacks up. Okay now, let's see here.'

'Is there any communication from an Erin?' I asked, sinking into the seat beside him. Harry sat down beside me, back poker straight, fingers bouncing off the table in an irritating beat.

'Ah ... okay ... yeah ... perhaps best you take a look yourself.' Rudy swivelled the phone towards me, passing me a pair of gloves.

I began with the conversation at the top of it, the initial text dated two days after Erin's attack.

Erin, what the hell is going on? Seriously, I'm freaking out. Text me back. I've been calling and calling you. I know we said about waiting, but if I don't hear something by tomorrow, I'm going to call that Otero guy. I'm seriously worried about you. CALL ME!

The reply came quickly, perhaps twenty minutes later.

I'm fine. Sorry. Phone's all messed up. Have some amazing news. Will call as soon as I can. Don't go to police. It's all been dealt with.

'I'm guessing that wasn't written by Erin?' murmured Gabriel.

'Erin was in a coma by then,' I said. 'We never found her phone. It has to be him.'

Another text from Kate followed, a day later.

234

> Can you call me yet? Dying to know what's going on.

The reply:

> Patience! I have a surprise for you. Give me a couple
> of days.

It felt like being back watching the CCTV of Erin
walking, utterly oblivious to the danger that stalked her,
mere feet away. I thought of Kate Weland, of what these
texts would have meant for her. Was she reassured by
them? Excited? She would have had no idea that each
one of them was a step closer to her inevitable demise.

And then, yesterday, a text coming from Erin's phone
to Kate's:

> I'm in New York. Will you be at the house tomorrow?
> I want to come and see you. I have something to show
> you.

> Squeal!!!! Yes!!! You're here? What's going on? What's
> the surprise? Is it what I think it is? I'm here. I'll be
> here. I'm so excited!!!!!

> Ha! Wait and see! I'll see you tomorrow.

'He lined her up,' I said. 'He manoeuvred her to be
where he needed her to be so that he could kill her.' I
looked up at Rudy. 'Can I talk to the daughter?'

He nodded, face an Easter Island mask. 'Sure. But
she's skittish. Had a rough day. Best just you and Gabe.'
He glanced at Harry. 'No offence, kid. Come on, I'll
get you a coffee.'

Gabriel looked to me, inclining his head towards the interview room. 'You ready?'

'Let's do it.'

The interview room was empty, but for the girl. Quinn Weland sat, her knees drawn up close to her, an oversized hoodie pulled low over skintight leggings, looking far younger than her eighteen years. Long dark hair hung, curtains around her face, her eyes shot through with red, face padded by so many hours of crying. She looked up at us as we entered, and it occurred to me that in another setting, she would be beautiful, with her mother's narrow figure, thick dark hair and chocolate-brown eyes. But grief takes so many things, beauty being one of the first. The girl tugged her sleeve across her fist, dragging it beneath her nose. I offered her a smile, in lieu of anything useful, knowing all the while that she wasn't really seeing me at all, that I was little but a screen onto which her mind was projecting the image of her dead mother lying sprawled across their kitchen floor.

'Quinn? Hey. I'm Gabriel. This is Alice.' Gabriel pulled a chair out, gesturing for me to do the same, his gaze hooked on the young woman that sat across from us. 'I'm so sorry for your loss.'

If she heard him, she gave no indication. Tears built up around those chocolate-brown eyes, spilling down onto the hoodie.

'You think you can answer just a couple more questions?' asked Gabriel.

She turned then, movements underwater-slow,

bringing him into focus. 'You're going to find whoever did this?'

'Yes,' said Gabriel, firmly.

She wiped her nose again, shifting her chair closer to the table, the tears on her cheeks catching the light. 'I'll answer anything you want to ask me. Just catch this guy, okay?'

Gabriel nodded, carefully turned the cover of the file he had carried in with him, scanned the page in front of him. 'Detective Schumer said you didn't see anyone?'

Quinn shook her head, her mouth held taut, gaze off in the middle distance. 'I was running,' she said, quietly.

Gabriel nodded. 'Okay, now, look I don't want to go over old ground for you. I know you talked to my colleagues, and they said you did a great job. I need to ask you some other things ... Quinn, have you ever heard of someone named Ed Canning?'

A beat, two, as the words worked their way through to her, then she shifted, attention pulled back to Gabriel now. 'No ... I don't think so.'

I thought of Erin, of her rasping breath. 'What about Wolf? That mean anything to you?'

'You mean, like a name? No. I'm sorry.'

I handed her my phone, the CCTV still of him. 'You recognise this guy? Look closely, he likes to change his appearance.'

She leaned in, then shook her head, wiping her sleeve against her nose.

'Okay,' said Gabriel, nodding slowly. 'Your mom got any phone calls recently she wasn't expecting? Anyone come to the house? Anything that felt just a little bit off to her?'

Quinn dipped her head, tears welling again. 'She said to me that she thought someone was following her. She saw this car ... I don't know, like two days ago, said it seemed to be everywhere she went.'

'You know what car it was?' I asked.

'A blue Chevrolet,' she said quietly. 'Thing is, I blew her off. I even ... I laughed. I said she wished someone was stalking her ...' The tears bubbled up again, spilling down her cheeks with a new vigour.

I nodded slowly. Why were you following her? A different man this from the one who had chased down Erin, slashing her throat without mercy in a Holborn park. This watching, waiting – was he planning? Designing his attack? Or was it something else? I thought of Emilia, of the calls to the hospital, almost like he was making sure that she wouldn't be there, clearing the decks before he struck. Was he stealing himself to kill?

My stomach knotted up, the sense descending on me that in spite of all I knew, sometimes it seemed I knew nothing at all about the man I was chasing.

'Quinn,' I leaned in towards her, my voice soft, 'you couldn't have known.'

She looked up at me, like I was a life raft and she was on board a sinking ship.

'Life,' I said, quietly, 'sometimes it twists into something we could never have imagined, right in front of us. And we beat ourselves up for not having seen it coming, but really, how could we possibly? We do the

238

best we can,' I said. 'That's all we can do.' And then I felt Gabriel watching me, felt myself colour. 'The car,' I said. 'Did your mother see who was driving it?'

'She said it was some guy. She couldn't get a good look at him, though. It spooked her, you know?'

Gabriel jotted a note on a pad in front of him. 'Quinn, I'd like to talk to you about your mom's relationship with Erin Owens.'

Quinn shifted her gaze towards him, struggling to follow the conversational shift. 'I ... Erin? Why?'

'We think ...' Gabriel hesitated, 'it's possible it may be related to your mom's murder.'

'My mom loved Erin,' Quinn said distantly, worrying at the cuff of her hoodie with her lips. 'We all did. Erin was good to me.'

'And after the accident,' said Gabriel, 'did her and your mom stay close?'

Quinn thought. 'I think ... it was hard.' She sighed. 'Erin, she kind of fell apart. I mean, to have something like that happen ... to Jacob and the kids. Mackenzie, she was this little ball of energy, just the cutest kid. And Levi, he was just so small.'

'What was Jacob like?' I asked, curious.

She shrugged. 'He was just a really great guy, you know? Just really cared. I mean, he had this thing, I don't know how he did it, but it was like he always knew if you had a problem, he could just tell, and he would just ... he'd need to help. It was like he couldn't live with himself if he didn't.'

I studied her, felt a flash of premonition. What was

239

your problem? What did you need Jacob for? She glanced up at me, seemed she could hear my thoughts, coloured.

'I ... fine, look, I used to cut.' She pulled up the sleeve of her hoodie, exposing a narrow arm traced with a pattern of thin scars. 'I mean, not for years now, but ... it was Jacob who figured it out. He found a psychiatrist for me, got me help.' She pulled her sleeve back down. 'This is ... this is all confidential, right? I mean, you wouldn't ...'

'There would be no purpose in us sharing this with anyone, Quinn. It's okay,' said Gabriel softly.

New tears bubbled up, spilling over. 'It's just ... it was so sad, I mean, they had everything, you know? Like, the clinic, was just, like, totally huge. I guess he was making a lot of money from it, they always had new cars, amazing holidays, but the thing is, no one resented him for it, because he was just such an awesome doctor. His patients ... You know, there are some people around here who would travel all the way into Manhattan, just so they could see him. I mean, the old people, like my grandma's age. They totally thought he was just awesome ... it was like hero worship with him. They were talking of expanding, they were so popular.' She scrubbed at her face, her gaze dropping to the sodden hemline of her cuff. 'My mom, when it happened, she was worried Erin might try to kill herself. She kept saying she had nothing to live for.' Her voice fell away. 'Mom tried,' she said. 'She really did, but Erin, it was like she couldn't handle being around people any more.'

'Did Erin have any family?' asked Gabriel. 'Anyone else supporting her?'

Quinn frowned, considering. 'I ... I know her dad died, back before Mackenzie was born. She wasn't from around here. Grew up out in California. Near San Francisco, I think, so she never really had family about. I don't think she was close to her mom, I kind of remember hearing that they fell out, around the time Erin and Jacob got married. So it was pretty much just her and Jacob and the kids. Then it was just her.'

'You said Erin couldn't handle being around people any more,' I said. 'What do you mean?'

The girl's gaze moved towards me. 'She just big time withdrew, you know? Got so she wouldn't answer the door, even though you knew she was there. Mom kept trying. Said that whenever Erin was ready to accept her love, she'd be there with it. It was bad, though. I went over there one day to drop off some mail that had been sent to ours by mistake, and I kind of wasn't expecting her to answer, you know, because of how she'd been, but she did and she was ... well ... she had turned the entire house upside down. I mean, I could see it from the front step. Papers were spread all across the floor, she'd pulled drawers out. You've never seen anything like it in your life.'

'Did you ask her why?'

She shook her head. 'She just stared at me. She'd been crying, I could see that. I offered to help her clean, put things back together again, but she just pushed me out, slammed the door in my face. She left the following day, moved out.' Quinn looked down. 'She didn't even say goodbye, just stuck a note in our postbox, said she was moving to Brooklyn.' She shook her head, a brief flicker of the girl beneath the grief. 'Brooklyn!'

'When was this?'

'Um ... I guess, May? Last year. The house sold pretty quick, I guess. Some family looking for a second home. They're never there. Mom hated that. She said it was a family home, that it deserved to have a family in it, replace some of the joy that was lost after ... you know.'

'Did your mom hear from Erin after she moved away?' asked Gabriel.

'No ... not for a long time. To be honest, it made me mad. That devastated my mom. She didn't have a ton of friends, you know, it was just her and Erin. So when she left ...' Quinn shook her head slowly. 'It's weird. We haven't heard from her, for maybe like a year. You know, she just kind of vanished. Then, maybe two weeks ago, I was at college, was trying to call Mom, like calling and calling for hours, and I couldn't get through. Turned out she'd had a call from Erin, that they'd been on the phone that whole time.'

'You have any idea what they were talking about?' asked Gabriel.

'No. But when I spoke to my mom, it sounded like she'd been crying. She did say that she had to go into the city the next day, that she'd promised Erin she'd get something for her.'

I sat up straighter. 'You know where she went? What she had to get?'

'No. I asked, but Mom wouldn't tell me. Said that it was something private that Erin needed help with. I was … to be honest, I was kind of pissed. I mean, Erin had, like, dropped her, then she comes back around and my mom is running here, there and everywhere for her.' Quinn's voice tailed away. 'I told her …' Her voice cracked, 'I said she was being an idiot.' She gave a little sob. 'And my mom, she said that if being an idiot meant that she was the kind of person who stood by her friends when they needed her, then she was okay with being an idiot.'

Quinn dropped her head into her hands and sobbed, tears twisting their way through her long fingers and splashing to the table before her. Gabriel and I shared a look, the question unspoken. Had we pushed her too far, gone further than she was able to go on this, the worst of all possible days?

But then I thought of Erin Owens, her endless struggle for this life that seemed so determined to cast her off, and the needle that finally struck the decisive blow. And I thought of Kate Weland, a woman who loved her enough to forgive the silence, who, even after a year, would drop all she had to help a friend, a single bullet hole through her skull.

'Quinn …' I said, carefully. 'Honey, you're doing really well. Okay? Just a couple more questions and then we're done. I promise. Quinn, what happened after that? Did your mum hear from Erin again?'

She pushed herself back in her chair, her breath coming in short, sharp bursts. 'I … yeah … I think they talked, like, every day after that. My mom wouldn't tell us what they talked about, but she was pretty, I guess, preoccupied? Then the whole thing about her being followed started.' She looked down, a flush of guilt across her features. 'Thing is, I said to my mom, I said maybe she needed to stay away from Erin. I mean, yeah, I loved her. But we hadn't seen her in a long time, and you know, with the rumours and stuff ... thing is, people change, don't they? I told my mom she needed to be more careful. That she didn't really know her any more.'

The temperature in the room changed, everything slowing down, as it seemed that time itself snagged upon the hook of her words.

I leaned forward. 'What rumours, Quinn?'

The girl shook her head, sighed heavily. 'Okay, look, I don't know if there's anything in this ... only my mom, she bumped into Erin's housekeeper, the one they had before the accident. And, I mean, so she knows the family pretty well, yeah, she's, like, there every day ... Thing is, she told my mom that, before Jacob died, that Erin was cheating on him.'

Chapter 4

We stood at the window of the police station, watching as Teddy Weland led his daughter towards the unmarked police car, a detective waiting for them, holding open the rear door. The older man seemed to be struggling, was walking as if the earth was bucking and rolling beneath him. But then, I suppose it was.

'Where will they go?' I asked.

'Teddy's mom has a place out in the Hamptons. They're going to stay with her until we can release the house.'

I watched as the father guided the girl into the car, his arms about her shoulders like she were a child. Theodore Weland hadn't provided us with much, his voice made distant with shock. I work a lot. I'm often not there. Yes, she mentioned speaking to Erin. No, she didn't tell me what was said. No, there is no one who would want to hurt her. No, I haven't seen anyone hanging around. All delivered in slow motion, his mind stilled with the suddenness of his changing world.

'What do you think?' I asked.

Gabriel shook his head. 'He can't have pulled the trigger. Still doesn't necessarily mean he wasn't involved.

We'll chase it down.' He shrugged. 'I guess it is still possible that all this stuff with Erin is a coincidence.'

I didn't answer. Because in my mind it had already settled that it was him, his gun and his bullet, an assassin of shifting identities.

Teddy Weland closed the car door on his daughter, carefully, as though any sudden movement might shatter her. He leaned forward then, resting his hands on the roof of the car, his head down. Even from this distance, you could see it, the will it took to keep himself together, to not collapse beneath the weight of his grief.

'That son of a bitch is removing people,' I muttered, 'getting rid of them because they inconvenience him.' I watched as the widower took one final breath, pushed himself up to standing, fighting forward, carrying on because he had little choice. 'He has to have done this before,' I said and, in that moment, knew it to be true. 'He's too calm. Too organised.'

Gabriel shifted his gaze back to me. 'Okay, let's say that's true. The crimes that we know about, they're all over the map right now. Figuratively and literally. London, Long Island. A knife, a needle, a gun.'

'It's functional.' I looked at Gabriel. 'And yet, he made sure that Erin's neighbour Emilia was out of her apartment before he set fire to it. For some reason, he didn't need her dead,' I said. 'He kills because it serves his greater purpose.

'Which is?'

I shook my head, watching as the car made its steady way from the car park. 'I have no idea. But the only

246

other person I have ever met who knew anything about this man was Erin. We need to know what she knew.'

'Alice?'

I hadn't heard Harry enter, took a moment to pull myself back. 'Hey, sorry.' I forced a smile. 'Everything okay with you?'

'Yeah,' said Harry with an enthusiasm that felt a million miles removed from me. 'Look, I was just talking to Rudy. You think it would be okay if I helped out with him on this Kate Weland thing? I mean, if we're assuming there's a connection, might make sense to split up, cover both angles.'

I worked hard not to look too relieved at the opportunity of a free babysitter. 'Sure. Good idea.' And, in spite of myself, I looked beyond him to Rudy. 'You sure that's okay?'

'Oh for sure.' The older man's face split into a dizzying smile. 'Anything to help our friends across the pond.' He nodded towards Gabriel and patted me on the arm. 'Now as long as you can make sure that one doesn't get in any trouble, you hear?'

I gave a small salute. 'I shall do my best.'

Another burst of laughter. 'She's got you, man.'

Gabriel nodded, grabbing his coat from the chair back. 'All right then. Alice, you ever been to Brooklyn?'

It took a solid hour, our pace slowing dramatically as we neared the city. We crept slowly across the Kosciuszko Bridge, and I let my head drop back against the headrest,

247

watching the city glide past, with its never-ending peaks and spires.

Where the hell are you?

I shifted my gaze across to the red station wagon that kept pace with us, to the driver, his dark glasses flecked with orange as he drove into the lowering sun; studied his chaos of curls, the shape of him. Is it you? I stared, waiting for him to sense me, to turn to me, for his lip to curl and then, then I would know. Right? Because this man, he is evil, and when one stands before evil, you can feel it. How could you not?

Right?

The driver glanced up, his gaze drawn by the pressure of mine, frowned slightly, speeding up, leaving us behind. As the car surged forward, I caught a glimpse of a toddler in the back seat, of a toy waving wildly in the air.

I shook myself, was letting him get inside my head, seeing nightmares in shadows.

'You think what Quinn says is right?' asked Gabriel. 'About Erin having an affair?'

'Whatever she did,' I said, 'she didn't deserve what happened.'

'No,' he said, quietly, 'of course.'

We rode in a pregnant silence for long moments, then Gabriel said, 'So do you think that explains it? Who he is? Why he's so hidden? Could he have been the boyfriend?'

I glanced at him, thinking of Erin, of that moment of seeing him, of the knife plunging in, the realisation of just how big a mistake she had made. 'I guess there's a fine line between love and hate.'

Gabriel steered up before a red-brick row house, set back a little off the street, pulled the car tight into a kerb. 'There it is. That's Erin's apartment,' he said, gesturing towards a white metal staircase, leading from the pavement up to a second-storey porch. 'The landlady,' he said, retrieving a key from the glovebox, 'has said that she would trust me with this, but only because I have an honest face.'

I smiled, pushed open the car door and stepped out onto the Brooklyn street, a stiff breeze channelling its way between the buildings, tugging at my coat. 'You think we're the only ones to have been here?'

'You mean him?'

'I mean him.'

Gabriel walked slowly up the metal staircase, one hand on his sidearm, his gaze swivelling, left to right. He hunkered down before the front door, studying it. 'No sign of forced entry here,' he offered. He slid the key into the door. 'I'll check the windows from inside.'

He pushed the door, holding it open for me.

The setting sun spilled across the living room, casting shadows across the corners of it. Gabriel moved towards the light switch, flipping the light on. I turned in place. It was small, faux-wood floors, a living room that spilled into a narrow kitchen. Paint had begun to chip from the skirting boards, the floor scuffed and scarred.

'Well, this isn't Setauket,' I muttered.

'You aren't kidding.'

A small stack of books balanced on the arm of the sofa, a jacket slung across the back of a dining chair. It looked like she had just walked out the door, as if it was waiting for her, that any minute she would walk back in, reclaim the life she'd left behind.

Gabriel checked the window locks, moving through the small place with a steady tread. He stopped, his attention caught on a tall bookcase tucked into an alcove.

There were no books, just row after row of photographs of a little girl and a baby of indeterminate gender, at the beach, before a Christmas tree, cradled in their laughing mother's arms. Mackenzie and Levi, frozen in time. I felt an ache, that these children would never age.

'It's a shrine,' I said, quietly.

Gabriel didn't answer, just allowed his finger to stroke the tilted edge of an image, the little girl holding her baby brother on her lap, face split into a wide smile.

It seemed to me that the grief oozed from the walls of the place, that there was only so much sadness any one place could take before it became a permanent feature, a scar left behind.

I shook my head. 'You notice there are none of the husband?'

Gabriel stepped back, studying the shelves. 'That's interesting.' He looked over to me. 'You think that lends credence to Quinn's rumour?'

'Maybe.'

Or maybe something else. Maybe in death Jacob Owens had ceased being her partner, had instead become the vehicle for her world's destruction.

'What did you think? How was their relationship? Before he died?'

He shook his head. 'I knew them to say hi to but not much more than that. I know some of the guys who worked the accident. They said she had to be sedated when the word came down that they were gone ... It's a hell of a thing.'

I turned away from the wide-open faces of the children and moved back through the apartment. The bedroom was tucked away at the rear, small enough that the bed felt cramped in it, that you had to squeeze to one side to pull open the wardrobe door. I ran my gloved hands across the rack, women's clothes, all carefully hung.

'Look at this.' A large box had been shoved towards the rear of the wardrobe and I crouched down, pulling it towards me. A flash of red, glint of gold.

'What?'

'Christmas presents,' I said, shaking my head. 'She still buys the kids Christmas presents.'

I crouched down lower, ducking into the rear of the wardrobe. Plastic tub boxes, all stacked up. I pried the lid open on one.

'It's stuff from her old life. Before the accident. Kids, clothes, toys.'

Gabriel shook his head. 'Damn.'

He moved away from me and the box of unopened packages, towards the empty desk, pulled open a drawer and drew a sheaf of paper from within.

'Well now.' He held up a letter, the letterhead indicating it was from the DMV. 'It's addressed to Holly Vale.'

I moved towards him, taking the letter from his out-stretched hand. 'This was part of the process for her. The setting up of a new identity.' I looked up at him. 'Seriously, who does that?' I let the letter drop to my side. 'Why did she ask Kate to come here? What did she want her to collect?'

'She'd have needed to gain access,' said Gabriel. 'Presumably through the landlady. I'll go have a chat with her, see what she knows.'

I watched the door swing closed behind him, then moved through into the living room, carefully removing the sofa cushions, one by one. I had reached the final one, when a scrap of something caught my eye, a curl of paper that had wound itself up into a ball, tucked down the rear of the sofa and forgotten. I held it up to the light. It had been shredded, edges of it clean-cut, symmetrical. I ran my gaze across the printed letters, and there, towards the bottom, was the word wolf.

I stared at the strip of paper, back now in Brunswick Square Gardens, my fingers slick with the blood of Erin Owens. And suddenly I knew, that I hadn't imagined it, that I hadn't been wrong. She had said wolf.

I turned the paper over, over again. But what did that mean? I stared at the letters until they dissolved, now just etched shapes on a background of white, as if it was some kind of optical illusion and that if I could only look at it long enough, then I would understand.

When my phone began to ring, my brain barely registered it. My hands moved without thought, pulling it free from my pocket, hitting connect and lifting it to my ear.

And suddenly there it was.

'Hi Alice,' said the voice on the line. 'I think you're looking for me.'

Chapter 5

It was fingers of ice down my spine. I gripped the phone, suddenly aware, in the most painful of ways, of my position. In a lighted house on a darkened street, the window unfettered before me. I thought of Kate Weland, of the phone in her hand, the single gunshot through the kitchen window. A perfectly lined-up target. I moved quickly, snapping off the light, slid to the side of the window to where the curtains hung limp and peered beyond their folds into the twilight street.

'Mr Canning.' I forced every ounce of calm that remained within me into my voice. This is a surprise. Who are you? What the hell do you want? 'What can I do for you?'

'I understand you've been looking for me?' His voice was steady, even. The American accent rolled and I struggled to place it, diving in amongst the knowledge I had gained from watching television, trying to find an in. 'It was dedicated of you to come all the way to the States for me.' It was like the embryonic American accent, a sampler, no specificity that I could find. But then, perhaps I just hadn't watched enough Netflix.

'It's no problem.' A man walked beneath a street

light, a phone held in one hand, his thumb rapidly moving across the screen. So not him. I leaned further towards the glass, trying to see into parked cars, through the plunging shadows. 'Murder is an important thing.'

He was silent for a moment, and I glanced about the shadowy living room, a sudden thought that I had been had, that this was all a distraction, something to allow him time to corner me. Could he have a key?

'Murder ...' said the voice on the phone. 'Yes, I suppose it was.'

The room behind me remained resolutely empty.

'You suppose?' I asked, genuinely curious.

'She just wouldn't let things be,' he said.

'You mean Erin?' I hazarded.

He sighed. 'Yes.'

'And Kate? Was her death necessary too?'

'Yes.'

'Why?'

I thought he wasn't going to answer, but then, 'Because Erin talked too much.'

A car drove slowly down the street, its headlights casting me into an unwelcome spotlight, and I ducked back behind the folds of fabric.

'Look, Mr Canning, we both know how this is going to end. Co-operation would go a long way for you at this point, so why don't you come on in and we can get this whole thing straightened up?'

A laugh. 'Straightened up? Is that cockney rhyming slang for something other than a long-term prison sentence? I'm sorry, no. I'm not coming in.'

'So why call me then? What do you want?'

He seemed to choose his words carefully. 'I'll be honest with you, I don't want to have to kill anyone else. I don't like it. It's ... messy. I just want to be left alone to live my life. That doesn't seem so much to ask, does it?'

'I'm sorry, you know I can't do that.'

'You know, I've been reading up about you. You're quite the celebrity, the detective who survived, scars and all, back in work three months after the fire, cracking cases. Your colleagues, they say you're a shoo-in for inspector if you wanted it.'

I felt that cold tingle again. 'You spoke to my colleagues?'

He gave a studied laugh. 'This is what you need to understand about me, Alice. I have been doing this for a very long time. I can go anywhere I want to, be anyone I want to be.'

A thought landed on me, hitting me hard, and I bit my lip.

'The thing is,' he said, 'it's true. You really are a true hero, Alice. And like I said, I don't want to kill anyone else. It really isn't my thing. But I will do what I need to do.'

I started as the door opened, Gabriel looking up, his mouth open, probably to ask what the hell I was doing hiding in the dark. I gestured to the phone, mouthed the word Canning.

'That sounds a lot like a threat.'

Gabriel moved quickly, soft steps, and positioned himself beside me, his ear resting against mine.

'I know.'

I took a deep breath. 'We know about the others, you know.'

A long pause, then, 'The others?'

'Yes,' I said, quietly, praying that the ice on which I stood wasn't busy fracturing beneath my feet. 'The ones from before.'

He didn't answer, the silence taking on a meaty quality, and I pulled a face. Dammit. I had gone too far.

'Leave me alone, Alice,' he said, softly. 'Don't make me kill you too.'

There was a click and the phone went dead.

Chapter 6

I stood, the phone held uselessly to my ear, could feel pins and needles rush through me. 'Well,' I said. 'That was ... unexpected.'

The words of Canning were ringing in my ears.

'What?' asked Gabriel.

'Nothing.' I studied the shape of the shadows, a car passing, throwing light across them, its departure leaving them darker than they had been before. 'He got my phone number,' I said, redundantly. 'He's gotten in among my friends, the people I work with.' And there it was, that flash of fear. 'He's been moving about them, hiding in plain sight.' I thought of Poppy and her son, Charlie. I thought of Noah, the wife and gaggle of children that followed along. Even Harry. Although frankly I was less worried about him.

'How do you find someone who could be anyone at all?' I said. To this man, identity was not who you were, it was what you could be. 'We were right.' I looked back at Gabriel, watching me in the gloom. 'About him having done this before. When I said that, he didn't like it, it freaked him out. Whoever he is, this is not his first time. He has a history.' I stood up and felt my way over to the bookshelf, the row upon row of photographs of Mackenzie and Levi, and picked one up, carrying it over to the window, to the orange glow of the street light. 'Erin was coming to us. On the day she was attacked. She was bringing us information.' I thought of the envelope clutched tight to her chest. 'I don't know how he connects to her, how she found him, or even why she did, but she did. She tracked that bastard down. We just have to follow her lead.'

'So ...'

'So,' I said, 'I want to know everything there is to know about Erin's life before, and anyone she might have had contact with. If she was in fact having an affair, we need to know with who. We don't know of any family, or anyone else she was particularly close to, so I want to start with the people she worked with, work our way out from there. Erin, she's going to lead us to him.'

Gabriel nodded slowly. 'Then that's what we'll do.' He moved closer, stood next to me, looking out into the darkened street. 'The landlady, she said she had a call from Erin a week or so ago, said to let Kate Weland in, that she was collecting something to send to her.'

'What?'

'She doesn't know. But she did say that whatever it was, it was small enough to fit inside Kate's purse.'

'What about him? Could he have been here?'

Gabriel grimaced. 'Turns out the phones cut out, day before yesterday. A repairman shows up, says they're working in the area, only he needs access to the apartments to fix the problem.'

I turned to face him, letting the curtain drop. 'It was him.'

Gabriel nodded.

I held out the evidence bag, the scrap of paper, the word wolf, visible through the plastic of it. 'But he missed something,' I said.

Chapter 7

I watched the road rush by, the interstate cutting through a channel of trees. White tuft clouds scudded across a pale blue sky, and a seagull swooped low, keeping pace with us for a few brief moments before pulling upwards and away.

A knot had formed, heavy in my stomach.

It occurred to me then that I had forgotten it, that urge to retreat. That I had tumbled last night into a turned-down bed, without bothering to take off my clothes, and had plunged into a drowning kind of sleep, heavy with dreams of towering glass and car horns. That I had woken to the alarm, had showered and dressed and eaten, and that not once during that time had I felt that fear grip my insides. Not once had I felt my body tense itself up, ready to run away. Perhaps it was something to do with a multiple murderer threatening to kill me if I stayed.

My mother always said I was contrary.

I shifted my gaze, focusing on the passenger-side mirror, on the road behind us as it flashed away, could just make out a white sedan, the headlights of it glinting in the sun. It kept pace with us, leaving a car length or two between. Is that you?

'It's a woman.'

I started. 'Huh?'

Gabriel glanced across at me, his voice soft. 'The car behind. It's a woman.' He shifted, peering into the rear-view mirror. 'I'd say early fifties.' He gave me a wry smile. 'I'm guessing that's not your guy?'

I snorted. 'Mr Chameleon? At this point, nothing would surprise me.'

I turned back to the mirror, watching the sedan's indicator flick on, the car moving across onto a slip road on the right, and my shoulders slumped. Proof positive at last.

'So,' Gabriel grinned, 'how'd you sleep?'

'Like the dead.' I glanced at my reflection in the visor mirror. 'As you can see.'

I pulled at the dark circles beneath my eyes, at the corner lines that seemed deeper today, and sighed, sliding the mirror shut. Some things were best left unseen.

Gabriel flipped the indicator on, a look over his shoulder and a quick left turn, and I caught a wave of cologne again. 'And your partner? How is his jet lag?'

I snorted into my coffee. 'He knocked on my door at midnight. Midnight. I was already asleep. Asked if I wanted to go dancing with him at Cielo.' I pulled a face.

'So, I'm guessing you went and drank tequila till dawn?'

'In fact, I'm still drunk.'

Gabriel laughed.

Poppy had called first thing, had interrupted the ringing of my phone's alarm clock. I checked the CCTV at the hospital. I've found our doctor friend, the one who decided to finish off Erin Owens. We've got him entering her room, exiting.

Let me guess, I had said. He's wearing a disguise.

Surgical scrubs, said Poppy, hair hidden underneath a paper cap, pair of thick glasses. And for the kicker, he walks all the way along the corridors deeply absorbed in the paperwork he is carrying.

He never looked up, I said.

He never looked up, agreed Poppy. A long pause, then, Are you doing okay? Poppy's concern giving her voice a stiltedness I was unused to.

I had lain in my bed, had thought of the dark-timbred tones of Canning on the other end of the line, and I had lied. Of course, I had said. I'm absolutely fine.

I looked back down at the sheaf of papers on my lap. All of the Wolfs within the New York area. Needle, meet haystack. I shook my head. 'Anything on the Weland investigation?'

Gabriel eased us to a stop as the light turned to red. 'Couple of people saw the jogger, but no one saw where he went after he left the immediate vicinity. My guess is he had a car stashed somewhere, but tough to say at this point. We're working on tracing the call to Kate Weland's phone, see if that will give us anything, but frankly, odds are he'll have used a burner.'

'That's what I'd have done if I were him,' I muttered.

'Right. We're running down leads on the blue Chevrolet Kate saw.' He gave me a sideways glance. 'You got any idea how many blue Chevys there are in this state?'

'No,' I said, with interest. 'How many?'

He floundered. 'A lot.' Gabriel slowed as the Buick in front braked hard. 'So … any issues?'

'You mean did our man attempt to murder me last night?'

'Yes.'

'No,' I said, flatly.

'Excellent.' Gabriel flipped his indicator to the right and guided the car onto the slip road, the sun ahead of us now, making my eyes tear. I leaned back in my seat, watched the globular trees as they sailed by us, the radio humming, just on the edge of my awareness.

Don't make me kill you too.

I looked down at the papers, the word wolf, again and again. There was a possibility that this was little more than an errant trail, but my gut forced a focus on the word. I heard once that our brains are tuned to detect that which would threaten us, that when we see something that represents a danger, our attention will hone in on it, will narrow down, keeping it in centre focus, lest it kill us. I rolled the word around in my head. That was where I was now, unsure that I was right and yet afraid to look away.

Wolf. It meant something.

I leaned my head back against the rest, thought of him, of what I knew. I knew that he was someone who liked to be in control, who was used to having the gaze of those around him slip right off him, that he could move through a crowd, as invisible as if he truly were a ghost. I knew that he was fierce in the protection of that which he deemed a secret, that he would kill for it.

I felt the car begin to slow, the click, click, click of the indicator again, as Gabriel steered us off the road, edging the car into a narrow patch of scrub that lay alongside it.

He released his seat belt and gave me a steady look. 'I'm waiting for Erin's manager to start her shift at the hospital, but, while we're waiting, I thought you should see where the accident happened.' He pushed open the door, vanishing into the blue day, and I sat for a moment, spun suddenly from my world of thought. It took me a moment to centre. I took a deep breath, released my belt.

We had come to a stop mere feet from the water, a stretch of greying blue that reached out into the distance, to the left of us and to the right. The road that we had been on, if we had stuck with it, that bisected the water, climbing in a soft curving arc of man dominating nature. Salt came to rest on my lips, an easy breeze sweeping across the water, tugging at my hair.

I walked closer to the water, coming to a stop beside Gabriel.

'Where are we?' I asked.

Gabriel gestured at me to follow, working his way through low-lying scrub until it finally gave way to a hillock of stone that petered out in the water below.

'This is Great South Bay,' he said, the rhythmic roar of car engines vying with his soft voice.

I stepped closer so I could hear, caught a hint of the cologne that he wore, weaving its way into car fumes and the sea.

'If you follow the causeway all the way along,' he pointed out across the water, 'you'll reach the Atlantic.' His finger traced the arc of the road we had just left, his movement following the curve of it as it seamlessly slid from road to bridge. He turned, his back to the water, looking back towards the car we had left behind. 'This is where Erin's husband, her kids ... this is where they died.'

I looked at him, sharp, suddenly seeing a newspaper report, a car being pulled from the water, and turned about, thinking. That was where the police officer was standing. The photographer, the photographer must have been back there, closer to the road. But it was all just procrastination really. Eventually I let my gaze fall on the water that lapped against the stones. And that. That was where they died.

'That winter,' said Gabriel, 'there was construction going on, repairs. You see that guard rail?' He pointed to a low metal barrier that edged the road. 'It had been taken out, an eighteen-wheeler, its driver texting at the wheel. He'd drifted, taken out a whole bunch of those barriers, just a couple of weeks before.' Gabriel shrugged. 'But you know how things are ... the repairs went onto a list, and then they got delayed ... What it all added up to was that, on that day, there was only some plastic cones up there to protect them from the water.'

He walked towards the water's edge. 'It was January twenty-first, last year. It was a bad winter. Had about ten inches of snow, total white-outs in some areas.' He waved out across the water. 'The bay itself had frozen over. The entire place, it looked like it had just been whitewashed.' He wasn't looking at me, but down into the waters of the bay. 'Erin, she said that the kids had been invited to a birthday party out in Babylon, just a couple of miles from here. Well, Mackenzie – she'd been invited. Levi, he was just a baby. They were all supposed to go, the whole family. But the previous evening, Erin had begun to feel unwell, sleepy, said she figured she had the flu coming on. She'd gone to bed and had pretty much slept the clock around and then some. Said she woke, about 11 a.m., house is empty, Jacob and the kids have gone.' He shrugged. 'She told me later that she hadn't been worried, not then. He'd left her a note, saying he'd take the kids to the party, that she should rest. Jacob placed two calls, the first at about 10 a.m., to a fellow parent, a dad that he knew from his softball days, checking that he was going to be there. According to this other dad, he'd made it as far as Nesconset. But he said that the roads were a mess, that the weather was making driving tough. We also know that he called the hostess, a little after ten twenty, to confirm her address, and that he said the same thing to her, that he was concerned about driving in the weather.'

'Why didn't he just turn back?'

Gabriel shrugged. 'The hostess told him to. Said that they had received a bunch of cancellations, that the roads were pretty well iced up down in Babylon too. When they didn't show, the hostess assumed he'd turned around.'

'And Erin?'

'It took her a while, to get concerned. She said that she was still feeling unwell, so she had fallen asleep on the sofa again, and that it was only when she awoke again that she realised how late it was, that she hadn't heard from Jacob. She began calling him, I guess around 5 p.m. I mean, it was dark by then and the weather had closed in. It was snowing pretty hard. She spent maybe an hour trying to get hold of him, then she finally called the hostess, thinking that perhaps the party had run long, that he was holed up there because of the weather. That was when she found out they never made it.

'When the call came in, a father and his two kids missing … thing is, they all assumed they'd find them, that they'd hit ice, gone into a snowbank. They rallied quick, because in those temperatures, you don't want babies sitting out in that just waiting to freeze to death. So, within an hour of the call going up, there were maybe thirty volunteers, all driving the snowed-up roads, all looking for Jacob and his kids.' He shrugged. 'He was a popular guy. Lot of people wanted to help.'

I nodded, could not seem to pull my gaze from the lapping waters of the Great South Bay.

'It was only when one of the search teams went off the road, hit a tree up on the 25 that they called it a night.' Gabriel stared down into the water, his voice flat. 'They found the car, late the following day.'

I looked down towards the water below.

'He fought. Jacob, I mean. He fought to save those kiddies. When they got the car back, the driver's side window was all smashed in. They found a car hammer – you know, one of those things you keep in your vehicle to break a window in an emergency? That was in the footwell.' His voice dipped, almost vanishing in amongst the cawing of seagulls. 'The baby's hat was under the pedals, both kids' car seats were unbuckled.' He looked back at me. 'Looks like he did it, that he got them from their seats into the front and somehow managed to get through the window, pulling his kids through after.'

'They were swept away?'

He nodded. 'The current. It's wicked strong right around here. And Jacob, apparently he wasn't a good swimmer, had always been deathly afraid of the water. And with the cold ...' He shook his head. 'Poor guy did his best. It just wasn't enough.'

'Jesus,' I muttered.

I looked back at the road, seeing a car driving towards me, seeing driving snow, ice beneath it, and then, what? Maybe something darted out in front of him, an animal, his wheels losing traction on the ice, and then the car is sliding, hitting the cones that mark the edge of the road, and he's trying desperately to do something, anything. To brake, to steer, to keep his family away from the icy plunge. And yet nothing is enough and then it's over and he's in there, and the kids are screaming, and his head is racing as fear takes hold, only he can't be afraid, can he, because he has to save his children. So his desperate fingers grab hold of the car hammer, the one that he bought from an abundance of caution because, really, things like that don't happen to people like him, and maybe his wife laughed at him, and maybe he felt slightly silly, and yet resolute nonetheless. A loud crack as the car hits dense ice, and then bitter cold water pours in, and he smashes the window because time is short and he has to at least try. And he twists his frame round in the driver's seat, cursing the steering wheel and the seat belt and his own body and all the gods who allowed this to happen, and he reaches back, awkward, clumsy, unbuckles the little girl, dragging her into the front with him and she's screaming and screaming, and then he reaches for the baby, only he needs two hands for this one and the car is sinking and uneven and the water is climbing higher and higher. Yet somehow he does it, squeezing his unyielding body through the gap in the seats and tugging his infant son free from that which was supposed to save him but is now dooming him, and then …

What? He squeezes himself through the broken window, into the shockingly cold waters of the Great South Bay. Is he telling himself he's almost there, that they're almost safe, just a little way more to go. When does safety take a sharp left turn, escape becoming more deadly than entombment?

I looked out across the water and wondered if he had seen it coming. Had there been a moment for Jacob Owens when he knew that it was over, that he had played and lost?

I hoped not.

I do not know how long we stood there, our toes hovering above the rippling waves that lapped against the rocks. I know that it was long enough that the breeze across the bay had begun to chill me and that I could taste salt with each breath in. And I found myself wondering if Erin had come here, if she had stood where we stood, the yawning expanse of the Great South Bay taking the place of a headstone. I looked down into the bubbling water and wondered if she had ever cast flowers into it, if she had sunk down onto the scrub beneath her feet to weep for the family who had left her behind.

Then came the ringing of Gabriel's phone, the real world crashing back in on us with ungainly speed. He shook his head, gave me a wry smile. 'Otero.'

I walked away, tracing the rocks at the water's edge, the dark greying blue of the water beyond. The sun danced across the top of it, throwing shards of light in every direction. And I thought of the bodies. Were they still down there, trapped beneath the waters, unrecognisable now from what they used to be? Or had they been yanked away, dragged in an unrelenting current out into the endless Atlantic Ocean?

'Okay, yeah, that's great. No, I appreciate it. We'll come right away.'

Gabriel's voice pulled me back, and I turned to look at him.

He hung up, looked at me. 'Erin's manager has just agreed to meet with us. Let's go.'

Chapter 8

We spoke little on the drive there, each of us weighted down by the dark waters of the bay, the memory of a family lost beneath the ice. I strained to look up at the Morgan Stanley Children's Hospital as Gabriel pulled the car into the car park. The hospital's entrance overlooked a bank of trees that, if you weren't paying attention, could convince you you were somewhere other than in the heart of the city.

We climbed from the car, riding the lift up to the lobby, dazzling in its rainbow colours. I found myself caught up in it, this splash of joy in so unlikely a place. But then, if you were a child doused in the terror of a hospital, a parent bound up in the suffering of your little one, even the smallest amount of joy would likely be a valuable thing. Gabriel made our introductions, while I glanced about the lobby. At a man, my age perhaps, sitting on a bright arching chair, his head in his hands, shoulders shuddering in a wave-like rhythm. Crying? Or perhaps simply breathing, trying to find the strength for what would come next. I looked away quickly.

'Up the stairs, on the right. Her line manager will meet you there.'

I followed mutely in Gabriel's wake, my gaze pulling itself back again and again to the man with his head in his hands.

We jogged up the stairs, luxuriating in the fact that we could, that we weren't bound here but merely passing through. Passed a woman, her hand wrapped tight around a small girl, a shock of white-blonde hair, her arm held out in front of her, sparklingly white in plaster cast. I smiled at the little girl, and she grinned back, holding her arm out further to ensure it would be noticed.

On to the next floor, this one just as vivid as the one before. Somewhere, I could hear the sound of children laughing.

Gabriel glanced back at me. 'I hate places like this.'

I nodded mutely.

A woman stood beside the desk, ostentatiously waiting. Taller than Gabriel, her skin the colour of oak, limbs painfully thin. 'You're Captain Otero?'

He nodded, reaching out to take her slender hand. 'I am. This is Detective Sergeant Alice Parr from the Met.'

She studied me. 'Something's happened, hasn't it?' Her voice was sing-song, a Nigerian uptick to her words. 'To Erin?'

'Perhaps,' said Gabriel gently, 'we should speak in private.'

She stared at him for a long moment, then ducked her head. 'Of course. Please.' She led us away from the desk, the scent of vanilla wafting over me as she moved past, leading us to a door beneath a blazing orange sunrise, punched in a code to the keypad. The room beyond had been set up to be comfortable, large overstuffed cushions, effortlully harmless art. A desk had been pushed against the rear wall, a computer waiting in idle. She waved us towards the sofa, sliding into an armchair.

'I'm Leila. Her supervisor. What is it? What has happened?'

'I'm sorry, Leila,' I said, quietly, 'but Erin has passed away. She was attacked walking in a park in London, and later succumbed to her injuries.'

The woman dipped her head. Her shoulders heaved, a low muttering that I later realised was a prayer. When she looked up, tears stood proud on her cheeks. 'She was a good person. An even better nurse.'

'In what way?' I asked. 'Who was Erin?'

'Erin ... she was kind. She worried about people, not just her patients. She wanted everyone to be happy.' She wiped a tear away with her fingers, then looked down at her hand, scrutinising it as if surprised by its presence. 'I do not understand though, you said that she was killed in London, yes? Why then are you asking questions here?'

I selected my words with care. 'We have reason to believe that her attacker may have been known to her, that she may have had some contact with him before she left the States.' I handed her my phone, the captured image of him on the screen. 'Do you recognise this man? Though I should add that we believe he was wearing a disguise in this photograph.'

She studied me, a heavy frown, as if trying to read beyond the police speak, get to the truth underneath. Then she looked at the picture, taking long moments to scrutinise it. 'No,' she said. 'I am sorry, but I do not believe I have seen that man before.'

I nodded. 'Okay, no problem. I need to run some names by you. Do you know an Ed Canning?'

She stood suddenly, walking towards the computer, tapping the keys with long, quick fingers. 'Personally, no. But ... no, we have no one by that name on our staff. None of our patients have the surname Canning either.'

'What about wolf?' I said, my heart rate climbing.

'You mean like the animal?' She typed quickly. 'No. I am sorry, but there is nothing.'

She stood, a delicate movement more like a dance from her, and returned to the armchair.

'How long has she worked for you?' asked Gabriel.

'She came to us about nine months ago. In July of last year. My understanding is that she had done little nursing since her children were born, just enough to maintain her registration. But, after they died ... it gave her purpose, I believe.'

'And, in that time, she didn't mention a man?' I asked. 'Someone she was concerned about? Or any mention that she was trying to locate someone?'

Leila shook her head. 'She and I, we were ... I think friends would be the wrong word. Erin, I think she was too much lost in her grief for true friendships. But we were as close as she could come to friends at that time. I heard no mention of a man.'

'Why here?' I asked, thinking of the juxtaposition, of the modest Brooklyn apartment laid out alongside the sprawling Setauket home. 'I mean, she was living in Setauket. Why not look for something closer to home, something that would have allowed her to keep the house?'

The woman hesitated, a guarded look as she picked her way ahead. 'I ... I must be honest and say that I have never asked. Money. It is not my business. But I ... well, I got the sense that Erin, you see, she worked a lot of overtime, whenever she could. She brought her meals from home. I never saw her spend so much as a penny on herself.' She glanced down at her lap. 'In truth, I got the sense that money, it was not an easy thing for her.'

I raised an eyebrow at Gabriel, thinking of the $10,000 in Hampstead, the value that must have lain within that Setauket home.

'Okay,' I said, 'her trip to Europe. How did that come about?'

She shook her head. 'I knew nothing about it until she came to me. If I am being honest, I would not have believed that she would have the means to fund such a trip. And,' she said, 'I had thought that she was happy here. Or, as happy as she could be, after what happened. And yet, one day, she simply walked into my office and handed in her notice.'

I sat up straighter. 'She quit?'

'A day or two before Christmas.'

She wasn't planning on coming back. Or, at the very

least, she could not have predicted how long she would be gone.

'And there's nothing you can think of that could have precipitated that?' asked Gabriel.

She sat, lost in thought for long moments, then, 'The only thing I can think of, it was a short time before she left us, December of last year. I was coming in through the lobby and I saw her and this woman – a big woman, older – and she was shouting at her. Saying that she should have done something about it. That she needed to take responsibility. And everyone, you know how people are, they are just watching like it is some kind of television show or something, so I go to her, to try to help. And the woman gets right up close to Erin, and says, "You should be ashamed of what you have done."'

'Did Erin tell you who she was?'

Leila shook her head, long hands folded neatly into her lap. 'She did not. And I did not ask. We see it here, sometimes. People ... they want you to work miracles. And sometimes, when you cannot, it makes them angry. But not everyone can be saved.' She shook her head again. 'I would have not thought of it, only ... she asked that day if she could leave early. Erin never left early. But that day ... she came to me, said she had a headache and could she leave a little early ... Of course, I said yes.'

'And then?'

Leila shook her head, sadly. 'Then nothing. She called in sick for the next three days, and the next time I saw her was when she came in to hand her notice in.

I tried to get her to stay, to talk to me about it, but she said she didn't have a choice.' She ducked her head. 'I'm afraid ... I said to her that she was giving up. Please understand, I was worried about her. I begged her to go see our psychologist. To talk to me. But she only shook her head. Then ...' She sighed. 'Then I said that to give up, it wasn't right. That her children would want her to live her life for them. And she looked at me then, said, "I'm doing this for my children."' A tear slid down her cheek. 'I never saw her again.'

Chapter 9

I watched as Washington Heights slid past, the tight togetherness of downtown Manhattan yielding, the exhalation after the deep breath, the apartment buildings lower here, more room for the sky. Gabriel eased off the accelerator, an array of red lights ahead glowing a warning. I glanced up, traffic lights flicking to red, then shifted my gaze back down to the folder of notes on my knee.

'Okay,' I said, 'so, according to Erin's boss, she was broke. According to Quinn, she was minted. So the question is ...'

'What the hell does minted mean?' finished Gabriel.

I grinned. 'You're clearly not up with the urban youth. Loaded, um ... has a surplus of wealth.'

The traffic lights changed, a quick dip back to green, and we began to drift forward, our progress stunted by the mass of cars ahead.

'Right,' said Gabriel, 'so either Quinn was wrong about the money ...'

'Or the money went away.' I tugged the financial report from the folder. 'Shit. Well, we know how Erin paid for her trip to Europe.' I waved a sheet of paper at Gabriel. 'Looks like everything went onto a credit card.' I studied the printout. 'She was up to $12,000 and climbing, making only minimum payments.'

I stared at the figures, long enough that my vision began to blur. How did a woman this reliant on credit cards accrue ten thousand dollars in cash? And what was she keeping it for?

The car filled with the sound of Gabriel's phone ringing.

'Otero.'

'Hey Cap.' Rudy's rumbling bass drowned out the roll of the engine. 'How you doin'?'

'Ah, you know, can't complain.'

A throaty laugh. 'Sure you can. You're just not trying hard enough. So, I got something on the Weland case, just wanted to let y'all know.'

Gabriel glanced across at me. 'What you got?'

'Resident a couple of blocks away from the Weland house, says she saw a jogger getting into a car. Guy fits the description of the jogger seen leaving the scene. White and under fifty. Not going to do much to narrow it down for us. But she did remember the car. A new model Chevy, metallic blue. We're on our way now to see if we can dig up some CCTV on it.'

Gabriel pursed his lips, guiding the car smoothly up the slip road onto the 195. 'Let us know.'

'See ya, Cap.'

I shook my head. How many people had seen this man and still not seen him? 'The Setauket house, that had to be worth a fortune. Where did that money go?

Also … wouldn't you think a guy like Dr Owens would have life insurance?' I riffled through the pages. 'Wait, here it is. They were insured with Liberty Mutual.' I punched the number into my phone, putting it to speaker.

'Good morning, Liberty Mutual.'

'Oh hey, wonder if you could help me …'

I flipped through the pages, only half listening as Gabriel explained the situation, confirmed that he had a warrant, that it should be recorded on the system. Erin had spent the entirety of her time in London hunting this guy down. That hunt, it had begun somewhere, and that somewhere had to be amongst these shards of her former life.

A sound pulled me from my reverie, Gabriel clicking his fingers at me. 'Just a second, Ma'am. I'm going to get you to repeat that for my partner.'

A rolling southern accent filled the car. 'So now, I can confirm that Mrs Owens placed a call to us on March second at 2.48 p.m. According to our files, she was enquiring as to the payment of due benefits on her husband's life insurance policy.'

'And what did you tell her?' asked Gabriel.

'Ah … unfortunately, it looks like my colleague here had to inform her that particular policy had been allowed to lapse.'

Gabriel and I shared a look.

'It had been allowed to lapse?' he repeated.

'Yes, sir. The premiums on that particular policy had not been paid in … let me see … a little over five months. The system shows that we had written to Mr and Mrs Owens on multiple occasions to remind them of the need to keep up their payments if they wished the policy to remain valid, but according to what I see here we never got a response.'

'So,' I said, 'the policy wasn't actually terminated?'

'No, Ma'am. They just stopped paying their premiums.'

'What was Mrs Owens' response when you told her there was no insurance?'

'According to what I see here, Mrs Owens became quite upset. My colleague was ultimately forced to terminate that call. We have a strict policy that our staff will not tolerate harassment of any kind.'

'Of course,' murmured Gabriel. He hesitated. 'Ma'am, I want to thank you for your help on this.'

'Oh, not a problem. Y'all have a good day now.'

A click and a heady silence in its wake.

I pursed my lips, gazed out the window, the city giving way now to Long Island openness. An idea beginning to form. 'Quinn, she said the house sold quickly, yes? She said she found Erin, upset, house turned upside down, then a couple of days later, she was gone.'

'Okay?'

'Like things changed quickly for her?'

'I'm not following?'

'Give me a minute.' I flipped through the financial files, pulling free the details of the Owens' bank. Dialled the number, bouncing through endless levels of automation and button pushes to find a human. Then, a harried-sounding man, who listened to my request, sighed heavily, put me on an abrupt hold. The sound of Rachmaninov.

Then, 'Ma'am? Yes, based on the warrant submitted by NYPD, I've had confirmation from my supervisor that I can answer your question. You were interested in the mortgage of the property in Setauket?'

'Please.'

'Yes, Ma'am. That property was defaulted on.'

The air in the car stilled, Gabriel and I drawing in simultaneous breaths.

'It went into foreclosure?' said Gabriel.

'Yes, sir. According to our records, payment had not been made on this property since August 2016. Multiple attempts were made to contact the family in an effort to reach a resolution, but all were unsuccessful. A final notice was delivered to the house on May nineteen, last year.'

The May day that Quinn had mentioned, Erin in tears, papers strewn about the house.

I nodded, mute, forgetting that the quick-voiced man on the phone could not see me. That was what had happened to her, that was what had changed. The world that has already shattered, shattering yet again.

Chapter 10

It was a single-storey, wood-slat shoebox of a house, the narrow window of it half buried behind a swathe of hydrangeas. Gabriel flipped through the folder. 'Okay, Carol McGilly, aged fifty-eight. Mother of three, grandmother of two. Worked for Erin and Jacob Owens for three years before being let go.'

I glanced across at the paperwork. 'You think maybe that was part of the whole financial collapse?'

He shook his head. 'Maybe.'

I climbed out of the car, looking about the quiet street. The clouds had drifted away now, leaving the day to begin in earnest. There was little traffic here, little sign that one of the most populous cities in the world was but half an hour away. I closed the car door gently. How does a family go from mansion-rich to repossession-poor so quickly? And what did this have to do with him?

I stood, scanning the street, empty but for us.

'We weren't followed,' said Gabriel, low. 'I was keeping a watch.'

'No,' I said, oddly uncomforted. 'But he knows where we're going before we do.'

Gabriel glanced up at the house. 'Kinda hoping that's not true.'

A woman with a bowling ball of a pregnant belly jogged towards us, a spaniel running alongside her, its gaze not on the ground before it but up at its owner. Definitely not him. I fell into step with Gabriel, up the short flight of stairs to the front door, a good solid police officer's knock and then we listened as what sounded like twenty dogs barked on the other side of the door. I looked at Gabriel and grimaced. Footsteps drew closer and the front door was tugged open, revealing a woman who looked closer to forty than sixty, shoulder-length blonde hair, a knee-length skirt that gave way onto black knee-high boots.

'Mrs McGilly?' asked Gabriel. 'I'm Captain Otero, this is Detective Sergeant Parr. We spoke earlier?'

She nodded, her features carefully aligned into a beatific smile. 'Of course. Please.'

She pushed open the door, leading us along a narrow hallway towards a living room bright with early morning sunshine. The twenty dogs turned out to be two bichons, who sniffed and yapped about our feet, all white fluff and attitude.

'Don't mind them,' she said. 'They're not keen on strangers.'

Them and me both.

'Please, sit.' Carol McGilly eased herself into a wing-back armchair, the slightest of winces crossing her features and giving away the truth about her age. The two dogs arranged themselves around her, their gazes darting between us two interlopers.

I perched on the edge of the sofa beside Gabriel and tried a smile. The larger of the two dogs stared at me, one corner of its mouth rising in the beginnings of a snarl.

I always did prefer cats.

'You said you needed some help on a case?' murmured Carol, one hand scratching at the ear of the smaller dog, as the other one looked on mournfully. 'I'm not sure what help I can be.'

'Well,' said Gabriel, with a reassuring smile, 'we'd actually like to talk to you about your work for the Owens family.'

She frowned, forgetting about the dog now, much to its disgust. 'The ... Why? Has something happened?' Her hand hung in mid-air, the dog looking up at it hopefully.

'I'm afraid we have some bad news, Mrs McGilly,' I said, choosing my words carefully. 'Erin Owens was murdered in London last week.'

The woman stared at me, her mouth moving wordlessly. She shook her head. 'She ...' She looked from Gabriel to me. 'How? I mean ... who would have done something like that?'

'That's what we're trying to find out,' I offered.

I had expected tears. Some show of sorrow, at the very least. Instead, the housekeeper stood, walked to the window. 'I'm sorry. That's ... terrible. Of course, I need to be honest with you. Truth is, I never really liked her.'

Oh. No tears then.

'She was never one for people. Wouldn't talk to me. Not really. She'd go out of her way to avoid me. I guess maybe she was just quiet, but I always got this feeling, like she thought she was better than me. Not like Jacob. I liked him, a good man, kind to a fault. He always made time, you know, to stop and pass the time of day with me. Truth was, he relied on me. Used to say, "I don't know what I'd do without you, Carol."'

'So,' I said, carefully, 'you weren't a fan then? Of Erin, I mean.'

She pulled a face. 'Is that bad? My son, he always says I need to stop and think, not just say the first thing that pops into my head. But I say honesty is best. Don't you think?' She looked from Gabriel to me, the question clearly not rhetorical.

'Sure,' I said, thinking that so often honesty and bitchy can end up looking oh-so alike.

'You didn't like Erin,' said Gabriel. 'Did other people feel the same?'

She picked an invisible fleck from her cardigan. 'Hard to say. Didn't exactly move in the same circles. She was very … insular. I know she was close to …' she waved her hand, 'that neighbour. Kate? But, other than that, I never heard of any other friends.'

I handed her my phone, that same CCTV footage, the man hiding in plain sight.

'You recognise this guy? He may look different from how he looks here – hair, build, that kind of thing.'

She took the phone, frowned up at me. 'How am I

supposed to recognise him then?' She peered at it. 'No, I ... No, I don't think so.'

A sudden shot of adrenaline. 'You're not sure?'

She held the phone further away, squinting. 'No. No. I don't know him.'

'Does the name Ed Canning mean anything to you?'

She peered up at me. 'Should it?'

'What about wolf? Does the word wolf ring any bells with you?'

She shook her head, sniffed. 'No. But then, like I said, that woman, she kept herself to herself. Not for me to know who her friends are. Were,' she added as an afterthought.

'So you don't know of anyone who might want to hurt her?' asked Gabriel

She sniffed, the dog taking the opportunity to lick her cheek. 'Like I said, we were hardly close.'

'Okay. And, forgive me, this is awkward,' said Gabriel, apologetically, '... I understand that you were let go from your position with the Owens.'

Carol McGilly sat back down in the chair, beatific smile now just a distant memory, face hard now, back ramrod straight. 'I was.'

'When was this?' I asked.

'January tenth. Last year.'

Just a couple of days before the crash.

'And why was that?'

'*She* said she didn't want me there any more.'

'She being Erin?'

'That's right.' The larger dog stretched its front paws

out, attempting to clamber up onto her lap, and she shooed it away.

'Why would she say that?' I asked.

She pursed her lips, the upper one curling so that she reminded me powerfully of her dog. 'Jacob, he was devastated. Hated having to break that news to me. Like I said, he relied on me. But he said she was insisting, that he'd tried to talk her out of it, only she wouldn't listen.' She sniffed. 'I think she knew I could see through her little princess act. You know she was cheating on him, don't you?'

'We have spoken to Kate Weland's daughter. She said that you told Kate that Erin was having an affair.'

'Yes, well, didn't like it that I knew, did she? And Jacob, well, god love the boy, but he couldn't see what was right underneath his nose. The times he said to me that she hadn't come home, that they were getting hang-up calls. She would disappear for hours at a time, he said, would leave him with the babies and just vanish, and Jacob, he said he thought maybe she was depressed, that motherhood was getting on top of her. But I knew. The things he said, they were just ... classic.' She looked down to her empty ring finger. 'My ex-husband ... let's just say I learned to recognise the signs the hard way.' She sat up straighter. 'I said it to him, too. Jacob, I mean,' she said, proudly.

'You did?'

'I did. I told him he needed to watch his back, that she wasn't to be trusted.'

'And what did Jacob say?'

Carol McGilly shook her head. 'He just laughed at me, said that was ridiculous.'

'Was that when they fired you?' I asked.

She glared at me. 'They *let me go* months after that. It was ... It came from nowhere. I don't know what happened, or why she got her panties in a bunch, but just, one day, Jacob came to me and said that he was so sorry, but Erin wasn't happy with my work, that they were going to let me go.' She leaned forward, her voice lowered confidentially. 'Mind, I often wondered if it wasn't more about the money. She was awful for it, would spend like it was going out of fashion. You know about her debts, right? She had been racking up huge credit card debt and hadn't told him. He was so upset about that. He said it was always money with her, that she just couldn't see the value in it.' She shook her head. 'And him working so hard to provide for them too.' She glanced down at the dogs, face coy. 'I mean, look, I shouldn't be talking about this, and I wouldn't, if you weren't the police and all. But you know she kept an apartment, right? In the city?'

I sat up straighter. 'What do you mean?'

She sniffed. 'For my money, it was a little love nest for her and her boyfriend. Right under Jacob's nose too.'

'Okay,' I said, 'so if that's true, if she did actually have a secret apartment, how would you know that? You said you weren't exactly the best of friends.'

She flushed. 'I found a letter. Addressed to Mrs Owens, but the address wasn't the Setauket one. That poor man, poor, poor man. To go through all that and then, the accident, and those poor babies ...' She gave me a hard look. 'I see you judging me, for not being all broken over that woman's death. But let me tell you, what she did to her husband, the way she betrayed him and lied to him ... I'm sorry, but she doesn't deserve my sadness.' She glared at me, fierce.

'So, you're saying that Jacob had found out about the apartment?' interrupted Gabriel.

'Well, I would assume so. I found the letter in his study. It had slipped down the back of the desk.' Her voice had grown higher, strained at the edges.

I watched her, the way her gaze had dipped now, dancing around the level of my knees, the way her fingers danced across the arm of her chair. 'What are you not telling us, Mrs McGilly?'

She flushed. 'Look, I don't ... that is to say, my honesty has never been called into question ... only, I must have had the letter in my hand and then I got distracted and somehow it ...'

'You kept the letter,' I said, my heart leaping.

She nodded. 'I did.'

Chapter 11

A truck roared by us, a tide of sound funnelled between skyscrapers, and I felt the scrape of its fumes scratching at the back of my throat. I ducked round a scaffolding pole, following Gabriel down a shadowed tunnel, boardings blocking the view of the workers from the street, but you could hear the sounds of the drill, a radio burbling. I looked up, could make out the tip of the Chrysler Building peeking between its neighbours. But in my head, the vision of it was overlain with bold-faced print, Carol McGilly's narrow fingers clutching it tight enough that the blood leached from the tips of them. Mrs Erin Owens. It had been a foreclosure notice, the words marked out in a stark, scary print. And on the envelope, an address – Mrs Erin Owens, East 44th Street.

Gabriel shivered, nodding his head towards a high-rise slightly higher than those surrounding it. 'It's right up this way.'

It had taken mere moments, a quick investigation into the address, to reveal that it identified not an apartment building, but rather an office block.

We joined a flock waiting on a walk light. I felt a movement at my side, Gabriel bouncing on the balls of his feet. I glanced up at him and he sank back down, sheepish. I grinned. The walk light came on, the crowd surging forward into the street, onto the opposite pavement. Past a Le Pain Quotidien that made me feel like I was on the South Bank rather than buried amongst towering buildings on the island of Manhattan. Coming to a stop at a sandstone office block.

The revolving door spilled us out into a dimly lit lobby, long and rectangular, a high-shine floor, dark tiled walls. A reception desk sat at the rear, opposite a bank of lifts. A middle-aged man in a security guard uniform, with close-cropped grey hair, a pronounced roll of a belly, sat, watching us approach.

'Hey, there. Captain Otero, NYPD,' offered Gabriel, smiling brightly. 'This is my colleague, Detective Sergeant Alice Parr from the Metropolitan Police in London.'

The man straightened, attempting to suck in the gut that lolled forward onto the desk before him. 'Captain. Detective … Sergeant?' He looked at me questioningly. 'Ernie. I was NYPD. Finished up about ten years ago. Worked out of Hoboken.' Shook his head. 'Great job, man. Great job.'

Gabriel leaned forward, resting his forearms on the desk, voice taking on a conspiratorial tone. 'We're investigating a double murder that took place in London, hence my colleague's interest in this … One of your offices has come up in our enquiries. I've spoken to the company that owns the building and they've given their permission. Said they'd email you about access …'

The guard nodded, face pulled into a look of heady concentration. 'Just a second there ... Okay, yeah, there it is. Sure. It's suite number 229. You guys want that I should show you?'

Gabriel smiled. 'No, no. I don't want to put you out. If you could just give us the key ...'

The guard sighed, disappointed, and handed over a single key on a fob.

'While we're here,' I said, 'you remember anyone coming or going from that office?'

He thought for a minute, then shook his head. 'We get a lot of traffic through here. A bunch of business start-ups that don't make it out the gate. You know how it is. Economy, am I right?'

I smiled. 'So, you don't remember a woman ever coming here?' I pulled a photograph of Erin Owens from my pocket and placed it before him. 'You recognise her?'

He hesitated, pulling the picture closer. 'Yeah ... yeah, I do. I mean, come on. That's not the sort of face you forget.'

I laughed obligingly. 'When did you last see her?'

'Oh ... I don't know. Maybe a month. Maybe more.'

'You don't get people to sign in?'

He shook his head. 'We got CCTV. But, to be honest with you, system's crappy, rewrites every twenty-four hours, and I know it was longer ago than that.'

'She didn't say anything to you? Nothing about her struck you as odd?'

He thought. 'She ... I remember she looked a bit

lost. I thought she must have been in the wrong place. But then I thought, well, maybe she's on a modelling assignment. I mean, we get that sometimes. We had one guy rent a space, set himself up as a photographer, turns out he was getting underage girls in here, getting them to put on this frilly stuff, lingerie and things, just to get his rocks off. Asshole. Yeah, so, I mean, I paid attention because you can't be too careful … But she had a key, so I figured … if she wants help she'll ask for it.'

'Nothing else?'

He shook his head. 'I remember she was here for a long time. Like late. I know the first time I saw her, she came in, what, maybe about 2 p.m. I finished my shift at 8, and I hadn't seen her leave. I figured she'd taken over the lease on the place.' He looked thoughtful. 'She did come to see me, maybe a day or so later, to say that she'd had the locks changed. All our tenants have to leave us a copy of their keys in case of emergencies. I remember her being concerned about that. She said to make sure we didn't let anyone else in.' He looked us up and down. 'I'm going to assume she wasn't talking about you.'

Gabriel nodded. 'And has anyone else tried to gain access? Other than this lady?'

Ernie frowned. 'Let me …' He reached beneath the desk, pulled out a large-format leather-bound book. He ran his finger down the handwritten pages, stopping at a midpoint. 'Here it is. Yeah, you know, we did have an issue. It was about two nights ago. I wasn't working, but a colleague of mine, he was doing his rounds, late, maybe 2 a.m. He gets to the twentieth floor, and there's this guy there, trying to jimmy the lock of suite 229. When he sees the security guard, he takes off. He made it out of the building, just vanished off into the night.'

I felt a breath on the back of my neck, my shoulders tensing. 'Your guy get a good look at him?'

He shrugged. 'Nah, he was a white guy, average build, baseball cap. Not too much to go on. Thing is,' he said, confidentially, 'some of the guys who work here, they're out of shape, not as fast as they should be.'

'Uh-huh.' I nodded, my gaze irresistibly drawn to the belly that tugged at the buttons of his shirt. 'We, uh, we need to get that door checked for prints.'

The security guard looked at me, sympathetic. 'My guy said he wore gloves.'

'Of course he did.' I sighed, sparing a look for Gabriel. 'We need to check surrounding buildings. See if their CCTV is any better. He hasn't been back since?' This last to Ernie.

Ernie shook his head. 'We're all keeping a sharp eye out. Probably afraid to come near here now.'

I sincerely doubted it.

'You know anyone by the name Canning?' asked Gabriel.

'Ah, let me see here . . .' He entered the name into the computer, one dense finger laboriously pressing against the keys. 'No Canning.'

'What about wolf?' I asked.

He nodded, tongue snaking out between narrow lips, carefully entering the letters. A delay and then, 'Sorry.'

296

I handed him my phone, the CCTV footage, one more act of hopeless optimism. 'This look like the guy that paid you a visit?'

He glanced at it. 'I didn't see him. You'd have to ask Billy.'

I nodded, made a mental note to track down Billy. 'Last question, was Mrs Owens up to date on her rent?'

The guard snorted. 'If she hadn't been, building owners would've had her out on the street. No sympathy with financial issues.'

'So,' said Gabriel, 'the rent is still being paid?'

'Let me look now ...' He twisted back towards the computer, typing with painful slowness. 'According to this, rent was paid a year in advance. Last payment, ah, last November.' He shifted back, looked down at the photograph of Erin. 'What's she done, anyway?'

Gabriel smiled. 'It's just part of an investigation. Okay if we go on up?'

The guard waved us towards the bank of lifts, his gaze staying with us as we walked. Gabriel jammed his finger on the call button, and we waited, the sense of being stared at omnipresent. A ping, and the lift door opened, we ducked inside.

'What do you think?' I asked.

'This guy ... he's everywhere,' muttered Gabriel. He looked up as the numbers clicked by.

'Erin must have seen this coming. She knew he would try to get in there.' I rubbed my face, tired suddenly. 'The trouble is, we've already seen what he does when a property contains information he doesn't want anyone to see.' I gave Gabriel a meaningful look. 'There's a mother and newborn baby in London with nowhere to live, thanks to Mr Fire Starter.'

'I'll mention to our friend downstairs to keep a look-out.' He looked up to the counter again. 'Pretty sure he was dying for us to ask him to come and play cops.' The counter slowed, stopped on the twentieth floor. 'Here we go.'

We stepped out onto the twentieth floor, a wide corridor, a symphony in beige, giving way to door after door. Suite 229 was positioned about two thirds of the way along it. Gabriel inserted the key, letting the door swing open, one hand resting easily on the weapon that sat in his holster.

He grinned at me. 'Just in case.'

I baulked. 'Oh, please ... after you.'

He reached inside, feeling for a light switch with his left hand. Pop. A blinding burst of light spilled out into the hallway. Gabriel moved in through the door, both hands on his handgun.

'Oh.'

'What?'

I followed him in through the door.

'Holy shit.'

We stood in the doorway, staring about us. Where there should have been a floor, there instead lay a snow-drift of white, slender shards of paper so that it seemed a tornado had landed, had taken every sheet of paper in the building and torn them into minuscule pieces, before depositing them here for us to find. I stepped forward cautiously.

'Okay ...'

There was a desk there, somewhere beneath the flurries, a chair. Three filing cabinets all standing in a row. I inched my way closer, the floor crinkling beneath my feet. The skeletal remains of a browned ficus stood on the windowsill, its tendrils twisted and snarled. A coffee pot on a shelf. Across the room, there was a window, giving out onto the street beyond, the view yet another building, the same office windows reflected back.

Beneath the window, a shredder.

I looked back at Gabriel. 'Wow,' I said, quietly. 'Someone really didn't want us to read whatever was in here.'

He crouched down, lifting up the shards of paper and allowing them to trickle from his fingers. 'You're not kidding.'

I studied the floor, a rock climber gauging the crevasse before him, and took a wide step, towards the desk and the window beyond. Then stopped.

'Gabriel ...'

The flurry of paper. It ended once you reached the desk. The desk chair had been pushed back beneath the window and a little nest of empty floor had been created. I felt an uneasy trickle race its way up my spine. There, beneath the overhang of the desk, lay sheets of paper – not shards this time, but sheets – dense with Sellotape. I pulled a pair of gloves from my pocket, bent and lifted the top sheet, the plastic of my gloves sticking to the tape edges.

'Someone has been here before us.' I held up the sheet of paper. 'Look at this. Someone has been trying to piece this back together.'

He studied the scene, quiet. 'Shit,' he said, softly. He retraced his steps to the office door and slid it open, checking the edges of it, running his fingers across the lock. 'I can't see any evidence he actually managed to force this lock. That means, if he did get in here, then, somehow, he got a key.'

I was back in the apartment in Hampstead, the heath spread wild outside, hearing footsteps on the stairs, a key in the lock, a sense that everywhere you went, there he had already been. My skin sparked. I watched Gabriel, leaning his tall frame out into the corridor, one hand on the gun at his hip, and could see it in him too, in the tension in his shoulders, the muscles that stood proud at his neck. He eased the door closed again, flipping the lock to closed, and offered me a small smile, 'Just in case of unwelcome visitors.'

I nodded. It was the shift I had been waiting for, a feeling washing over me, a strange, unruly heat. I turned to embrace it, a long-lost friend. Hi, fear. Where've you been? Electric shocks raced across my skin. Why now? Were you always there, just waiting in the wings? My gaze moved towards Gabriel, the Glock at his hip.

I wanted a gun. I was a little girl from Derbyshire and, for the first time in my life, I wanted a bloody gun.

Okay, calm now. Try to think.

I blew out a slow breath, and I forced myself to turn away, to turn my back on Gabriel, shifting my gaze to the pieced-together paper shards, raised it to the light, paper crunching beneath my feet. Erin had rented this place for a purpose. She had been renting it for at least eighteen months and was so confident of her ongoing need for it that she'd paid the rent in advance, even in the midst of total financial collapse.

Why? What was it for?

I studied the patchwork quilt of paper, tried to focus, pick out the printed words in between the shimmering lines of tape. What secrets were you hiding here, Erin?

'What is that?' Gabriel had moved closer.

'It's ...' I read slowly, 'a receipt for a hotel. In Boston, Massachusetts. Dated two years ago.'

'Any name on it?'

I shook my head. 'Why would anyone shred this?' I looked up at him. 'I mean, it's a receipt. Let alone spending hours piecing it back together.'

Gabriel stepped gingerly into the sea of paper. 'I guess, if you're looking for something in this mess, you won't know it until you find it. The only way would be to put everything back together.' He turned in a slow circle. 'Holy hell, that's a job.'

He was here. He had gotten here before us, another round of chasing your tail for Alice. He knew enough about what was buried in amongst this haystack to go digging around for a needle.

'I'll get a forensic team in here.' Gabriel blew out a breath. 'Could take a while though. They're flat out and

301

the priority is going to be up at the Weland residence.'

I nodded, my gaze still hooked on the small pile of papers on the floor, each a mosaic of tape. 'You're right.' I sighed, shrugged off my coat.

'What are you doing?' Gabriel asked.

'If he has gotten in here, if he did this ... he thinks there's something in here worth knowing. If he thinks it's worth knowing, I want to know it.' I waved at the mounds of paper. 'He's only just begun. My guess is, he's coming back.'

'We'll tape off the room ...'

I gave him a wry smile. 'You think that's going to stop him.' I looked about me, was going to sit where he had sat, do what he had done. Because that was the thing, wasn't it? That so far he had felt elusive, beyond understanding. I sank onto the carpeted floor, pulling my legs up underneath me, the sense of sitting where he had sat sending ripples across my skin. 'I'm going to start piecing it together,' I said. 'If you want to shoot off, I won't take it personally, I swear. I'll check in with you later.'

Gabriel stood, studying me for long moments, then gave a weighty sigh. 'Yeah.' He pulled his jacket off. 'Did I ever mention I used to be my school's jigsaw champion?' He sank to the floor beside me, pulled a handful of paper shards towards him.

I grinned. 'I bet you got all the girls with a line like that.'

He winked. 'You know the ladies love a man with skills.'

The sun lowered in the sky as we sat, our laps filled with paper, splaying an orange light across the room. It felt gargantuan. An impossible task. But then, my mother always told me that impossible is simply a state of mind, and after an hour, perhaps two, a collection had begun to form, of letters that spilled one from another, that looked at in a certain light created words. When the sun had set, leaving the room doused in twilight proper, Gabriel stood, back creaking, wincing, and switched on the light, returning with a roll of tape. So our own collage began, letters turning into words again, words into sentences, and slowly, what had been hidden began to be revealed.

I laid the last piece of tape down across my artwork. 'Bank,' I said, quietly. 'The mortgage notices that the family ignored. They're all here.' I passed the sheet to Gabriel.

'She was hiding them,' said Gabriel. He studied the letter. 'Why?'

I shook my head, leaned back against the wall. 'I'm starting to think that everyone does everything just to piss me off.'

Gabriel called the bank, a tortuously winding call through an automated system, culminating in a disappointed-sounding woman, who confirmed that, yes, the Owens family had all their mail redirected to the office address, that this had happened late in 2016, a couple of months before the accident. That there was a note on the system, that this information was to be kept confidential and was not to be released to any third party. 'I'm gonna go ahead and assume that your warrant overrides that request,' she said, drily.

I watched as Gabriel hung up the phone. 'Why?' I asked. 'What was the point of this? And to emphasise their need for confidentiality – who did she think was going to come looking?'

Gabriel shook his head, gestured to the reconstituted sheets on the floor. 'Someone did. Suggests to me she knew that was a risk.'

My stomach growled.

'Yeah,' said Gabriel, 'I'm hungry too.' He set the sheaf of papers he was working through down on the floor and stretched his arms high above his head. 'There's a noodle place around the corner. You want me to go get some takeout?'

I sighed. 'Yeah. Noodles would be good.'

He pushed himself up, dragging his coat on, and I looked from him to the door, and felt it again, that creeping prickle of fear. It would be easy now to play it up, to say that I needed a breath of air, that maybe I'd go with Gabriel, just for the exercise. But then I thought of him, of the identities that he wore by choice. Today, I shall be this person. My hand drifted to my scar. I could not return to who I had once been, but maybe instead I could choose to be someone else.

And this woman, she was afraid, but would keep going anyway.

Fuck you.

'I'll stay here,' I said.

He studied me for a moment, then nodded. 'Lock the door, yes?'

I grinned. 'Yes, Dad.'

I watched him leave and I considered. But this woman, this version of me, whoever she was, she would not be cowed, yet neither was she a moron. I clambered to my feet, deadened legs making my movements awkward, stepped carefully over the undulating paper mountain that remained and flipped the deadbolt.

I turned, looking about the room, at the impossible pile of paper.

'Impossible is a state of mind,' I muttered.

I rolled my eyes, returned to my spot of clear floor, turning my attention back towards the slivers of paper before me. This one ... it looked like a newspaper clipping, the colours, the font of it. I ran my fingers through the pile, looking for anything that looked a good fit, lining them up, one beside the other. Yes. A cutting from a newspaper, a picture, its edges neatly trimmed. I leaned further forward, willing the image to take shape. A photograph. Maybe it was me, maybe my past had primed me to see what sprung out at me, but I swear the fire leapt out at me before it should have, when it was only a few paltry strips of meaningless red. I felt goosebumps stand proud along my arms, forced myself to focus, to find the red in the sea of white, to lay the strips, one beside the other. Until the truth was irrefutable. It was a fire, what looked like it had once been a barn in the centre of a wide field of land, caught up in an inferno of ravenous flames.

I shook my head. It was merely my imagination or my trauma or whatever the hell we were calling it these days. I tried to ignore the slight shake in my fingers as I laid the tape down in vertical lines.

What was that? Where was that? And why the hell would anyone shred it?

I studied it, the shape of the once-was building, the form of the flames. And, strangely enough, rather than thinking of my darkened flat, that line of red that traced the door, I thought of something else. Of a car park in Hampstead, a ruined window from which flames clambered. And then of a Vauxhall apartment, of a metal container incongruous on a desktop. And I knew. That wherever this was, whatever it once had been, that the flames had come from Canning's hands.

Because Gabriel was right. The murders, they had no connection, no ties to bind them together. A knife. A gun. A pillow.

He had said to me that he didn't want to kill. But he wanted to hide – although hide what, I had no idea. And when he needed to hide something, he used flames.

I leaned back, studying the image. That would be where we would find him, in this trail of paper destruction Erin had left behind.

I laid the re-formed image alongside me, could still feel the heat glowing from it, and delved back into the shards, pulling free a strip with narrow printed letters. I shifted through the piles, looking for anything that matched. Found another strip, then another, the shape of a word working its way out. Ed Canning. My fingers awkward suddenly, unwieldy. I studied the collage. A hotel booking. A logo, at the top of the puzzle, of a sinking sun, yellow splaying into red. Villa Tramonto. It was the hotel in Rome. The one that Erin had stayed in. I studied it. Breathe. The proof that she had followed him, from here, to Rome, then on to London.

I was getting closer. I could feel it.

I taped the pieces together, setting them to one side.

Next, a white strip, a block of black ink at the top. I studied it for a moment, then laid it down, delving back into the pile, searching for anything that might match it. Another, then another.

Then a sound from the corridor outside, footsteps, and my heart began to race. Then, a sharp knock and Gabriel's voice. 'Alice? It's me.'

I blew out a breath, stood awkwardly and tugged open the door. 'About time,' I said with mock fierceness.

Gabriel studied me. 'You freaked out a little, didn't you?'

I pursed my lips, taking the brown paper bag from him. 'Absolutely not. You see, in the UK, we don't need guns. We police with words.' I considered. 'And a metal stick.'

It sounded thin even to me.

We ate seated at the desk, cardboard cups of noodles in a spicy broth. I slid the fire photograph across to Gabriel, carefully spooning noodles into my mouth. 'Any ideas?' I asked.

Gabriel wiped his mouth with a napkin, pulled the

image closer. 'Looks like a barn … You don't know where this came from?'

I shook my head. 'For whatever reason, someone shredded it. Which is enough to make me curious.' I reached down, pulling the pieces I had been working on up to the tabletop, lining them up again.

'That's the DMV logo,' said Gabriel, suddenly. 'Department of Motor Vehicles.'

I slid some more pieces into place, reaching for the tape, but as my hand moved across it, a word caught my eye.

Wolf.

My breath caught in my throat. I studied the reconstituted page.

Dear Mr Jackson Wolf,
Please find enclosed your replacement driver's license.

'Gabriel?' I breathed. 'I found him. I found Wolf.'

Chapter 12

'Wolf. It's him. Canning, Wolf ... they're all the same person.' My breath felt short now, stopped up in my chest. The scent of jasmine overwhelming. 'She tried to tell me, that day in the park. She was solving her own murder. Only ... Only he hasn't used that identity within the UK.' I studied the paperwork, willing my heartbeat to slow. 'Look, this is from fifteen years ago. That's why we haven't been able to turn up anything on him as Wolf. He hasn't been Wolf for a long time.'

Gabriel was already dialling. 'Check the state on that.' Then into the phone, 'Yeah, hey, it's me. I need someone to run down a suspect. Jackson Wolf. Yeah, like the animal. I got a record of him coming out of ...'

'Massachusetts,' I supplied, looking at the DMV letter, the state seal.

'Massachusetts. Yeah, soon as you can.' He bit his lip, waited.

I moved through the pile of papers, the ones already pieced together, looking for something I'd already seen. There.

'Gabriel ...' I held up the hotel receipt. Boston, Massachusetts. 'Boston. Two years ago.'

He reached across, plucking the paper from my fingers. I turned, studying the flecks of paper with a new eye now, a sudden sense of urgency. That I was within a finger's reach of him. I crouched down, sifting through the strands of paper with my fingers, looking for that one word.

Wolf.

Then, as my hand dove deep into the paper mountain, coming back with a fistful of shards, I saw it. The w. The o. I studied the print, bold and rolling, the colour of the paper, yellowed with age, the lines of the font, wide-spread and spacious. A twisting, clawing sensation in my gut. I leaned in closer, looking for more of the same. There. And there. And there.

My hands stilled, looking at the sketched-out pattern before me.

It was a birth certificate. Jackson Henry Wolf. Born 28 March, 1978. Bloomington, Indiana.

I had him.

I sat back on my heels, only half listening as Gabriel relayed the updated information, my phone in my hand. That feeling of knowing something before you know it, of knowledge that is so insidious, so creeping, that it feels almost like instinct instead. Because I knew what was coming next.

I waited as my phone loaded the screen, typed with clumsy figures, correcting, typing again. And when it came, when I saw it, it felt like I was asleep, dreaming of what had come before.

'Gabriel,' I said again, handing him my phone. I said

nothing else, mostly because words had by then escaped me. A bubble of something in my chest that looked like fear but, when you looked closer, would seem instead to be laughter, absurd and unwieldy. That son of a bitch.

'You're kidding me?' Gabriel looked from me to the phone, back again. 'You are fucking kidding me.'

I shook my head, taking the phone back off him. Looking at the screen again, just to be sure, even though it seemed that I had known all along. And, sure enough, there it was, the death certificate of Jackson Henry Wolf. Aged eighteen months.

It was a dance. I step forward, you step back. I run, you run faster.

I sat, my phone cradled in my lap, and that wild laughter broke free as a hiccough of sound. I shook my head, rubbing my hand across my eyes. He was all of them. He was Canning, he was Wolf. He was a detective, he was a worried father, he was a victim support worker and a telephone engineer. And he was none of them at all.

'Uh-huh. Yeah, I'm still here.' Gabriel clicked his fingers at me, gesturing me towards the notepad and pen that sat on the floor beside me.

I passed them upwards, my fingers still wrapped tight about my phone and the tragic death of Jackson Wolf. Another thought flitting by, that there were families out there who still mourned children, little knowing that they, or those that would claim to be them, moved with wild abandon throughout the world. I watched as Gabriel scrawled loose-limbed words across the blank page.

'Okay, yeah. No, I appreciate it.' He lowered the phone, looked at me. 'Okay, so we have information on the Jackson Wolf identity. We have him registered as living in an apartment in the South End area of Boston, back in 2003. But what's really interesting is that, around that time, a warrant was issued for his arrest.'

I stared at him. 'For what?'

Gabriel grinned. 'Would you like to guess?'

I looked across at the patched-together papers, my gaze flicking its way to the flecks of red and orange. 'Arson.'

'Correct,' Gabriel agreed. 'Warrant eventually timed out under the statute of limitations. Apparently, our friend, Mr Jackson Wolf, he rents this apartment, same place for going on three years, is a model tenant. Then one day the fire department gets a call, place has gone up in flames, no sign of Mr Wolf. Evidence of an accelerant and Wolf is seen leaving the premises moments before the fire is spotted.'

'Let me guess,' I said. 'No one ever saw him again.'

'No they did not.'

'He became someone else,' I said, softly.

Strands of paper littered my lap, my knees beginning to cramp. I moved my fingers, a swift flick to push them away, stayed by a single strand of baby blue, the letters on it penned with swirling cursive text. I picked up the piece, holding it up to the light.

'What?'

'I don't know.' I leaned forward, sifting through the spools of paper, picking free blue from in amongst white, handing them back to Gabriel, who laid them out on the desk, one strip at a time. We worked steadily, piece by piece. And when we were finished, we had found where Erin had begun.

Chapter 13

... thing of all is that we trusted you. That we believed what you told us when you said you cared. We understand now that our trust in you was misplaced. Perhaps you think we're stupid? Believe me when I say this is not the case. The loss we have suffered is the responsibility of you and of the Owens Manhattan Medical Practice. You should be ashamed of what you have done.

A Lee

Chapter 14

The Owens Manhattan Medical Practice had once lived in a suite of offices, a floor of windows housed in a tower of glass on the Avenue of the Americas. Gabriel strode up the short flight of steps leading to the main door, his long legs making it look effortless. I hurried to keep up, briefly wishing my already pretty long legs were just that little bit longer. The world had begun to swim now, tiredness nibbling at the edges of it. It had been a little past two when I had fallen into bed, a little past six when I had crawled out of it. I had begun to feel drunk from the lack of sleep. Gabriel held the door open, allowing me to step into a marbled lobby, banks of black leather sofas arranged in groups in the cavernous space.

'The office suites have been relet,' said Gabriel, voice low. 'Landlord says the Owens left pretty much everything behind, all the furniture, files. Said he didn't know what to do with it all, so he boxed it up and stashed it in the basement.'

I nodded, the click of my heels reverberating through my skull. 'What time is the clinic manager meeting us?'

Gabriel glanced down at his watch. 'Fifteen minutes.'

I gestured towards a small shape, tucked up in the corner of the ceiling. 'CCTV.'

He stopped, looked up. 'Well, let's see if the damn thing works ... Hello, hey.' This to the narrow post-teen, wearing a suit and yet still somehow looking homeless, behind the front desk. 'You got CCTV?'

The kid rolled his eyes. 'You got a warrant?'

Gabriel gave him a flat look, reached into his pocket and slid his badge onto the desk in front of him. 'I have a badge if that helps?'

The kid's colour drained, an already lily-white boy turning the colour of snow. 'Shit. Sorry, man. I didn't know ... yeah ... yeah, we got video.' He tugged his jacket further up on his neckline, attempting to cover a dark sweat stain that ran along the collar of his shirt. 'You need footage? When?'

Gabriel looked at me, the slightest of eyebrow raises. 'When?'

I frowned, briefly flummoxed. Then my gaze fell upon a large leather-bound book in the centre of the desk. 'Hey, do you do sign-in sheets?'

'Oh, yes, Ma'am.' The teen bobbed his head, the smell of stale smoke billowing towards me, his earlier snark in full reverse. 'Everyone who comes into the building has to sign in. Strict policy.'

'Can I see?' I asked, hands outstretched.

'Sure. Sure.' He thrust the book into my hands re-treating back to a respectful distance.

I flipped through the pages. There. 23 December. I thought of what her manager had said, of the confrontation with the woman at the hospital, of her leaving work early. I thought of A. Lee and the single solitary page of a hand-scrawled letter. My gut had been right. A. Lee was that woman. And whatever she had said to Erin had sent her straight here, to the Owens Manhattan Medical Practice. I pointed at Erin's signature. 'Twenty-third December. 4.11 p.m.' I looked up at the receptionist. 'You know where she went?'

He swivelled the book to face him, studying Erin's name, the scrawled note beside it. 'That's my writing.' He squinted at it. 'Basement. Aw, yeah. I remember. Like, we don't normally let people down there, yeah? But the owner, she'd been in touch with him, and he's like, yeah, let her go down there, she can get rid of all that stuff they left hanging around.'

'And did she?' I asked. 'Take the stuff?'

The young man snorted. 'Nah, my manager was pissed. It's all still there.' He thought for a moment, giving all the appearance of strain, then, 'You mentioning that, the files and all, some guy called me, I guess maybe a couple of weeks ago. Says he's from some medical council, yeah? That he's found out we've got these patient files, they're confidential, yada, yada, and that he needs us to destroy them.'

The call from the flat in Vauxhall. The last phone call of Edmund Canning.

'What did you say to him?' I asked, breath tight.

'I said I wasn't destroying nothing. That he'd have to talk to the landlord.' He shrugged. 'Stuff's still there, so I guess he didn't.'

317

My insides unfurled, just a little. I handed him my phone, the photograph again, little hope now of any response. A quick glance. No, I've never seen him. Canning? Nope. Wolf? Nope.

'So you want to see the cameras?' he asked. 'System is in the back office. I'll let you in, but you know, I got to stay here. Like I said, strict policy.'

Gabriel grinned, patted him on the shoulder. 'At ease, soldier.'

We let ourselves into the back office, little more than a closet, one wall covered with a bank of screens, and Gabriel pulled the chair up closer, typing the date and time into the system. I stood behind him, watching the lobby collapse, reform, the revolving door standing static. Then movement and a familiar figure came into view, sunlight glinting on her blonde hair.

'There she is,' I said, pointing to the figure.

Erin walked towards the front desk, steps cautious, tentative seemingly. Paused long enough to sign her name, an exchange of words with our friends there at reception, then she turned, heading towards the lifts.

'What about in the lifts?' I asked, bouncing on the balls of my feet. 'Are there any cameras in there?'

'Ah ...' Gabriel studied the system before him, 'here you go.'

I watched as the screen changed, a mirrored lift came into focus, Erin standing beneath the camera's lens, her back pressed against the wall of the lift, head tilted back, face creased in concern.

The lift slid downwards and it seemed that Erin shook

her head, her face smoothing itself out. She pulled her coat around her, expression sliding into neutral in time for the opening of the doors.

'I can't see any cameras within the basement itself,' said Gabriel, drumming his fingers on the desk.

'What about when she leaves?' I asked. 'Can we see that?'

Gabriel selected the lobby camera again, hit forward, and we watched as the lift doors opened and closed, open and closed. Time raced by, but no Erin.

'What the hell is she doing down there?' I murmured.

Then, finally, five hours after she arrived, the lift doors slid open and she stepped out again, not stopping to sign out, but walking with long strides towards the doors, as if she could not bear to be stopped, as if there was nothing she needed more than air, freedom.

And then she was gone.

'What about the lift camera?' I asked.

Gabriel switched images, setting the time parameters for the lift camera, bringing into view a mirrored wall, cerise carpeted floor. Then the doors slid open and in she came, with her shoulders back, head high. She turned, looked towards the doors as they slid shut and then, like a marionette with its strings cut, slumped backwards against the mirror. Her head sank into her hands, her shoulders heaving.

'She's crying,' said Gabriel.

It felt cold in the centre of me, watching this woman so privately fall apart. She had no idea that, a matter of weeks later, someone would be watching her in her private misery to try and solve her murder.

The counter ticked up – B, 1.

As the lift reached the lobby, she moved, lowering her hand, slender fingers twisting to slide something into her handbag. A fleck of gold. Then she raised her head, wiping at the hollows beneath her eyes with her fingertips, and strode out into the world.

'Wait,' I said, 'go back. Bit more. There. Look. What's that she's got in her hand?'

I leaned in closer, studying the way that her fist had balled itself up, the flash of gold briefly visible between her fingers. 'Is that a key?'

Chapter 15

Back in the cavernous lobby, a woman stood, looming in staggeringly high heels. She was younger than one would expect a clinic manager to be, mid-twenties at the outside, with the kind of good looks that looked like they required an inordinate amount of upkeep. She glanced at me as I entered, her gaze heading straight to my scar and staying there.

'Chloe?' said Gabriel, extending a hand towards her. 'Hey. I'm Gabriel Otero. We spoke on the phone.'

She reached a limp hand towards him, gaze locking on his.

'This is Detective Sergeant Alice Parr from the Met Police in London.'

I nodded, but she wasn't looking at me, the entirety of her attention caught up on Gabriel, her gaze soft.

'Thank you for meeting us here, Chloe.' I glanced back at the receptionist, who snapped to immediate attention, his gaze searching for somewhere to land that was ostentatiously not on us. 'Hey,' I said, 'you got an office we can use?'

'Uh, sure, sure. You wanna ...' He gestured for us to follow, back past the reception desk, into an office, the desk spread wild with paperwork, a couple of hard-backed chairs pushed up against the walls. 'I mean, you can use this, it's my manager's place, but I guess ... it should be fine.'

I smiled. 'Perfect. Thank you.'

'Ian.'

He hovered in the doorway, gaze flicking between us.

'Thank you, Ian,' I said, firmly, ushering him out, closing the door tight behind him. 'Shall we sit?' I suggested.

Chloe sat, her gaze still hooked on Gabriel as he folded himself into the chair furthest away from her.

'So, Chloe,' I said, my voice cooler than I intended. 'How long did you work for Dr Jacobs?'

She shrugged, long blue fingernails threading their way through her cinnamon-coloured hair. 'A year,' she offered, 'give or take.' She folded long legs, one over another, and I felt my gaze dawdle over her. The thought surfacing that she was someone you could not help watching. And I thought of him. Of the Wolf, as I had begun to think of him. With his seeming omniscience, a shadow that leads rather than follows. Was he watching her too?

Gabriel cleared his throat.

Was I staring?

I coughed, thrown suddenly. 'How did you find working here?'

She blew out a sigh. 'Look, it was hardly *Vogue*. I mean, no little girl grows up saying, I want to work in a doctor's office. But it was fine. I mean, it was a job.'

'And Dr Jacobs? How did you get on with him?' asked Gabriel.

She turned back to him, face blossoming into a smile. 'He was really nice. I mean, a really nice guy. All his patients, they just loved him. And, like, a lot of guys, they kind of try it on, you know ... but he wasn't like that. Not at all. He was kind of like my dad.'

I did a swift mental calculation and worked hard to stop my eyes from rolling. Sure he was.

'Like, the thing is, before ... a lot of people, they look at me, and they figure I've got to be dumb, right, because, you know, I'm attractive and all ...'

I did not snort. I remain extremely proud of that.

'Jacob, he said he could see it in me, that I was smart, that I was more than just a hot body.'

Okay, maybe just a teeny, tiny snort.

'He gave me a chance, pushed me to go back to school. Said he figured I could do anything I set my mind to.' She flicked her hair back. 'I appreciate that, yeah? It's more than my actual parents ever said to me.'

I nodded, working hard on my poker face. 'Were you aware of any problems within the clinic? We have information that some former patients might not have been particularly happy with their treatment.'

Chloe shrugged. 'You're never going to please everyone though, are you? I mean, sure. We had complaints. Every doctor has them. People think you can work miracles and they get really upset when they figure out you can't.'

'What happened to complaints that came in?' asked Gabriel. 'Would you have kept records of them?'

She flicked her gaze back to him, a winning smile. 'Sure. I guess. They'd be with the rest of the stuff.'

'You remember any that stood out to you?' I asked, thinking of large looped writing on fine blue paper. You should be ashamed.

Chloe shrugged. 'People complain. It's what they do.'

'You remember any complaints from anyone by the name of Lee?'

She frowned. 'I'm not sure. I think that one ... Look, you'd have to check the files, but I vaguely remember something. Some woman complaining about her father's treatment. Thought he should have had some tests done ... because she's a doctor, obviously. I don't know. You'd need to check.'

'The name Jackson Wolf mean anything to you?' asked Gabriel. 'Or Ed Canning?'

'Sorry. We have a lot of patients.' She shook her head. 'I just ... I can't believe she's dead, you know? When you said on the phone ... I mean, you just don't expect it.'

'You were close?' I asked.

'No.' There was an edge to that, a decisiveness that made me wonder. 'She'd come in from time to time, but I think Dr Owens liked to keep his family and work separate. I mean, I know she'd trained as a nurse and all, but they decided that it wouldn't be good for the family to have them both work here. Besides, I guess she wanted to stay at home with her kids.' It was dismissive that last, a judgement call on the decision of another woman. 'She had plenty to keep her busy, what with shopping for those designer clothes, all those handbags of hers,' she said, her lip curling ever so slightly.

I glanced at Gabriel. Another to add to the not-an-Erin-fan list. I thought of the letter, of the woman shouting at Erin. 'So, Erin wasn't involved in the clinic?'

'No. Not really.'

And yet, we know that Erin came here. That from the outside it would appear that this was the beginning for her, or rather perhaps the end. That she came here and that, after that, everything changed.

I was getting a headache.

'What about the clinic itself? How were things going here?' I asked. 'Was there anything here that would have given you cause for concern?'

She shook her head. 'We were doing well. Booming, in fact. Dr Owens, he was looking to expand the place, bring in a new doctor. He'd found someone, he said, someone who he thought would be perfect for us. He went out to meet with him, a bunch of times, said he was going to get the ball rolling on adding him to the staff.'

'You got a name?'

'Sorry. Dr Owens, he said he wanted to make sure he was the right fit before he introduced him to us. He was planning on bringing him in, the week he died.' She shook her head. 'It was so ... because I mean, obviously, we needed someone then, like seriously, so I tried to find this guy's information, see if he'd be interested in coming in as a locum. You know, like Dr Owens wanted …' She sighed, a swipe of her hand across her cheek, and I wondered, tears at last? 'Anyway, it didn't work. I could never track him down.'

Gabriel and I exchanged a glance, the hairs on my arms standing on end. A man, there and then gone again. Now, who did that sound like?

I watched as Chloe picked at an invisible fleck of thread from her sweater. 'Chloe, I need to ask you, have you had any problems lately? Strange calls? Anyone contacting you unexpectedly? Anything that worried you?'

She sat up straighter at that, her attention finally fully on me. 'No. Why? I mean, am I in danger?'

Gabriel held up a hand, his voice soothing. 'We're just advising all those involved to be vigilant until we are able to catch the man who killed Erin. So just be a little extra careful, yes? Let us know if anything seems off to you.'

Her overlarge brown eyes grew larger still and she nodded, mute.

'What happened to the clinic?' I asked. 'After Dr Owens died? I'm guessing it's hard to run a doctor's office without the doctor.'

She sniffed. 'We closed our doors on 23 May. We had a locum in, for a little while, just while we figured out what came next. Then one day we come in and the locks have been changed, the building owner is saying the Owens have stopped paying the rent. I reached out to her then, Mrs Owens I mean, but she … I don't know, she sounded like she'd been crying, and she just says, there's no money left, I'm sorry, and then she hangs up on me.'

May twenty-third. Four days after she'd received notice of the foreclosure on the house.

Chloe sighed heavily, a pointed look at her watch. 'I really have to get back to work. I'm at *The New York Times* now, you know.'

I nodded, impressed despite myself. 'You're a journalist?'

Chloe had the decency to flush slightly. 'Receptionist.'

I watched as she pushed herself up to standing, swaying on her too-high heels like a baby giraffe learning to walk. 'Chloe, just one more thing. We've seen the CCTV of Erin leaving the building one night, just before Christmas. Apparently she went down to where the files were being stored. She was down there for quite some time and, when she was leaving, it appears that she was carrying a key? Small. Gold. Any ideas?'

She looked at me blank for a moment, then a change, some recollection settling over her.

'What?'

She flushed, pulled her bag up on her shoulder. 'Well, no, it's just weird, is all. You mentioning a key. Only, the thing is, back before the clinic closed down, I was sorting out some paperwork, and I'd put the files up on top of the cabinet, you know the way you do? Only I must have jostled them when I was reaching for them, and one slipped down the back of it.'

'Okay?'

She drew her words out, every appearance now of one who is enjoying their own show. 'Well, I just mention it because, when I pulled the filing cabinet out to get the file back, I found a gold key that had fallen down the back of it.'

Chapter 16

A dim orange light swathed the basement room, stacked boxes, sentinel filing cabinets, casting deep valley shadows. It spread the length of the room, the remnants of a once-was medical practice, all accolades vanished now.

'You think he's gotten down here?' Gabriel stepped softly, tread squeaking against the wide-checked linoleum.

I stepped further into the twilight gloom, allowing my eyes to settle, adjust. 'I don't know.'

'You think it was him? The locum?'

'Yes,' I said. 'I do.'

I followed the length of the filing cabinet wall, fingers brushing light on cold metal to the end of it, the cessation of metal creating an artificial corner, the light from the insubstantial bulb puddling there, a little corner of brightness in the dark.

And there it was, a secret den built of low-set cardboard folder towers, stacked one beside the other.

'Here,' I said.

This was where she had come. When Erin had straightened her shoulders and marched forward towards whatever would greet her. I could see her, long legs folded beneath her, delicate fingers working their way through unruly sheets.

'What was she looking at?' asked Gabriel.

I crouched before the paper towers. 'Patient files.' I looked to the second. 'Billing information.' And, beside the stacks, a thick leather-bound book. 'And the clinic's sign-in book.'

Gabriel ducked down beside me, gaze moving across the folders. 'What the hell do you think she was looking for?'

'I don't know,' I said, pulling the patient sign-in book towards me. 'But that woman, that Mrs Lee, something she said sent Erin here.' I opened up the cover, a waft of dust billowing outwards. 'And whatever Erin found here, it changed everything for her and it sent her on a collision course with Jackson Wolf.' I blew at the dust, sank to the ground, crossing my legs before me. 'She found something here that led her straight to him. Let's see if we can do the same.'

Gabriel grunted, selecting a file from the pile. 'You owe me a drink after this.'

'Deal,' I said.

It was a mountain of paper, another one in a seemingly never-ending range. In the hours that passed, I thought often of Erin, of her sitting here, in this spot, looking at this same turret of paper. But her alone. What had she been looking for? What had she found that had spun her life so out of control?

I began at the beginning. With the name of Lee. Yet no matter how hard I searched, I could find no files relating to it, no mention that such a person had ever existed, until, there, one small scribble in the patient sign-in book. Frederick Lee.

I held the book out to Gabriel. 'There's a Lee here, but no files associated with it.'

'What are you thinking?'

I was thinking of Erin, standing in the lobby of Holborn Police Station, a large envelope clutched to her chest. 'I'm thinking Erin took it.'

'Why though?'

I shook my head. 'Don't know. Not yet.'

It was approaching evening when I finally saw it, when a growing suspicion floating up from endless words and numbers finally coalesced, creating a picture where before there had been none.

'Oh my god,' I muttered.

Gabriel looked up from the file before him. 'What?'

I leaned across the sea of papers that lay between us and passed him a file. 'Meet Mr Leo Zimmerman. Eighty-two years old. Had a heart attack two years ago, followed by the insertion of a stent.'

'Okay?'

'Now, looking at Mr Zimmerman's file, he's been through a number of procedures in recent years, including an endoscopy and a subsequent biopsy to examine a nasty-looking polyp.'

'Poor Mr Z.'

'Right? So, if you look at the billing, sure enough, you find that the insurance company covering Mr Z's health insurance has been charged for those procedures.

Adds up to about nine thousand dollars. However …'
I pulled the patient sign-in book across the table, spinning it to face Gabriel. 'This is the date on which these procedures are listed as having taken place, in this clinic. You see Mr Z on there anywhere?'

Gabriel leaned forward, studied the list of names, then turned to stare at me. 'You're kidding?'

I shook my head. 'I thought I'd missed something. Or that maybe Mr Z forgot to sign in.' I flipped open the top cover of file after file. 'But I've managed to locate everyone else who was on that sign-in log for that day and confirm they were in the office. So how come he managed to dodge signing in. Now …' I pointed to the open folders. 'Meet Mrs Selby, Mr Harris, Mrs Wu … the list goes on. And the same thing is true of all of these people. Each one of them is listed as having undergone a medical procedure on a day on which they were not actually in the clinic.' I looked at Gabriel. 'It's insurance fraud. The clinic has been charging the insurance company for procedures it hasn't been performing. You know how everyone has been saying how well the clinic was doing, how much money it was pulling in? This was why.' I stabbed the files in front of me. 'They were cheating the system.'

Gabriel was silent for a moment, staring at the papers in front of him. Then, 'Who was it?' he asked quietly. 'Who signed off on these?'

I shuffled through the papers, pulling a billing form free and slid it in front of him. 'Dr Jacob Owens.'

Chapter 17

'Well ... shit!' Harry looked older than he had when we arrived, the cumulative effect of a solid effort to drink away jet lag and a steadfast refusal to grow up gracefully. He had somewhere along the way acquired a beard, a scraggly, wishful-looking affair that swathed his features, making him look like a Dickensian fisherman. He pawed through the pages on Gabriel's desk, shaking his head, and I caught a whiff of stale alcohol, B.O. coming hard behind it. We would need a little chat, Harry and I, about the way one presents oneself in other jurisdictions.

Rudy peered over Harry's shoulder at the papers before him, the heft of him nudging my arm as he leaned in. 'And you're sure?'

'We're sure.' Gabriel had leaned far enough back in his chair that it threatened to tip, his feet stretched on the desk in front of him. He looked older too, the late nights, early mornings telling in the creases in his face. In his defence, he didn't smell. 'We were there till gone midnight. Jacob Owens was the only one who had access to all the available systems. No way could a scam of this magnitude have been pulled off without his say-so.'

Harry sank into the chair behind me, groaning softly. 'Is there any logic by which this has made things simpler?'

I snorted, burying my face in my mug. I'd actually started to like the precinct's coffee, shit though it admittedly was. 'Nice one,' I muttered.

I should have been tired. I had tumbled into bed a little after one, had been up by six, had spent the intervening hours with my head racing, moving pieces and players. One thought rising its way up through the morass. That I had been both right and wrong. That one twist of the kaleidoscope and all the pieces shift into a new picture. I had lain there, with my curtains open, the textured lights of Manhattan spilling in on me, had thought of the Erin we had begun with. Jane Doe. Our good victim. A turn of the lens and she's gone, leaving something darker, more sinister, in her wake. And now here, one more turn, and there she is again. Just as she had begun.

'So, the wife – Erin – had no knowledge of this?' Rudy looked from Gabriel to me, back again.

I shrugged, feeling my back twinge from a night of restless half-sleep. 'While we can't say for certain, it's beginning to seem unlikely.' I leaned forward, set my coffee cup on the desk and began ticking off on my fingers. 'According to the mortgage company, she had no idea that the house wasn't being paid off. She also didn't know that the life insurance had been allowed to lapse.' My voice cracked, an appalling step from professionalism. But the thing was, I was there, in that house, on that day, watching Erin, who had lost her husband, had lost her babies, who had been living the life of her dreams, only to wake one morning and find that it had vanished, that she remained behind like some kind of ghost, haunting the world she used to know. And then that fateful day, the crashing realisation that not only has your husband died, but that he had never been who you thought he was. Another death then. Of your beliefs, of what your past had been.

'So,' I said, clearing my throat in a manner that was unlikely to fool anyone, 'she realises he's lied to her, that for whatever reason all of their money is gone. And, in fairness to her, she rallies. Realises she needs to go back to work, to find somewhere she can pay for on her own.' She needs to become necessary again, to someone, even if only to strangers and their suffering children. And maybe ... maybe she needs to build a new identity for herself, to replace the one that was destroyed by this discovery. No longer the widow of a good man, now the foil of a liar. This was her fire. These were her scars. 'So, she moves to Brooklyn, begins work at the hospital, and for a while life is bearable. Only, then, she meets someone, a patient from the clinic.'

Gabriel spun himself round in his chair, pulled a fawn-coloured folder from the windowsill. 'Complaint letters. It took some serious digging to find these. Most of them, the usual grumblings.' He lifted the top sheet, a handwritten letter, and handed it to Rudy. 'This one, this came in after Jacob's death. So the clinic manager, either she thought it didn't matter because he was dead already, or she just couldn't be bothered ...'

335

'My vote is for the latter,' I muttered.

'Right. So, she just shoved it in the file, forgot about it.'

I watched Rudy as he read it, brow heavy in concentration. I didn't need to read it again, seemed to me that I had memorised it, the sad, sad story of Frederick Lee, who had reported to his doctor with stomach ache that just wouldn't go away. And his doctor, Dr Jacob Owens, told him it was anxiety, prescribed him Ativan. Only that wasn't what he told the insurance company. He told the insurance company that he had run an extensive series of tests, including endoscopies, biopsies, blood tests, and that he was seeing Mr Lee on a weekly basis. Shortly before the accident that killed Dr Owens, Mr Lee collapsed while doing his weekly shop, was rushed to the hospital, the doctors there revealing a tumour the size of a grapefruit in his stomach. He died a week later.

Harry looked up at me. 'So, the woman who had a go at Erin ...'

'This guy's daughter, Adrienne. We called her last night and she confirmed it,' I said. She had wept on the phone to me, the kind of tears that come from the very core of you, had asked me, again and again, why? Why would someone do this. I hadn't answered. Money didn't seem like the kind of answer that would ease her pain much. 'We dug through the clinic's financials,' I said. 'A year ago, that place was worth about three million. But, over the period of the next three months, almost ninety per cent of the clinic's money was filtered away, via deposits into various different accounts. We're still trying to figure out exactly where. By the time Jacob died, there was almost nothing left.'

'Okay,' said Rudy, the bass of his voice rumbling across the room, 'so the doc here, he's defrauding the insurance company for millions. Only his wife died broke and homeless. So the obvious question is ...'

'What happened to the money?' supplied Harry.

'It's him,' I said, softly. 'It has to be.'

Rudy turned to face me. 'Okay, Al, what's your theory?'

'I think he introduced himself to Jacob as a fellow doctor, that he worked him, and that somewhere along the way he figured out that Dr Jacob Owens was himself no saint. Now he's got something huge to hold over him. I think that he blackmailed him, that he took that family for everything they had. Until ...'

'Until there was nothing left,' finished Gabriel. He passed a folder to Rudy. 'I did some more digging into Jackson Wolf. Turns out that fifteen years ago, he not only lived in Boston but was registered as a student at the Boston University School of Medicine.'

Harry stared at him. 'So he is actually a doctor?'

'Well now,' I said, 'that's where it gets interesting. He registered. He did not graduate. According to the university's records, Wolf was there for three years – doing pretty well for himself actually – and then he just vanished.'

It had come to me at about 3 a.m. as I had lain in bed, staring at the office building across from the hotel, a lone office lit in the darkness, a man in his early middle age, perhaps, sitting at a computer, never looking up. I had watched him but had been thinking of Erin Owens and Wolf. What did we know of him? Hadn't he told me himself? He didn't like people who knew of his past. And he was willing to kill to keep hidden that which he deemed deserving. He had done it twice that we knew of.

'I don't think it was an accident,' I said, quietly. 'Jacob's car going into the bay.'

'You thinking suicide?' Rudy folded thick arms over the mound of his chest, eyes narrow. 'With them kiddies in the car?'

'It happens.' Gabriel wasn't looking at him, his gaze down towards the floor, expression loaded. 'This guy, he'd lost everything. If we're right, if Wolf took it all from him, if he had complete financial ruin, a prison sentence hanging over his head ... maybe he did do it, drive that car into the water himself. Maybe it seemed like the only way out.'

'Or ...'

They turned to me then, the three men, their gazes dragging, minds heavy with the image before them, two children, death by parent.

'Or what?' Harry looked to be on the verge of tears.

'Or Wolf killed them.' I let the words hang there for a moment, the weight of them settle over us. 'We've said before, he has no one method of killing. That he will do what is expedient. What if Jacob, what if somewhere along the way he learned something about

338

Wolf, something that Wolf didn't want anyone to know. We know that is enough to make him kill. And,' I said, once more seeing Erin standing in the lobby of the police station, holding her life in an envelope in her hands, 'if Erin found out about this, if she made the same connections we are making right now, then it would explain why she would be willing to give up everything to go after him.'

The silence rested, long and pregnant, then Gabriel sat up straighter. 'Goddammit. The key. We got it backwards. The office that was rented in her name, the one on 44th, Erin had no idea it existed. She must have found the key at the clinic ...' He paused. 'Give me a sec.'

He pulled his phone out, a quick conversation, a long pause, then his fist pumping in the air. He hung up, looked about triumphantly. 'Bank confirms it. They had a call off Erin Owens on 24 December, looking to confirm they had the right postal address for her.'

'They gave her the office address?' I asked, sitting up straighter.

'They did. There was a note on the system about the need for privacy, but she's on the mortgage, address is in her name, guess they figured that any secrets weren't secrets from her.' He looked at me. 'We've had it all backwards, right from the start. Whoever shredded all that information, it wasn't Erin. She was the one who found it, who was piecing it all back together. And the stuff she found in there, even assuming that she took a lot of it with her, that she was planning on using it as evidence of ... I don't know fraud or ...'

'Or murder,' I offered.

'Or murder,' Gabriel said, quietly. 'Whatever she found, the information must have told her the same as it told us. That her husband was into some seriously dodgy shit. And that, somehow, this mystery man – Canning, Wolf – that he was involved.'

I thought of Wolf's voice, of the dark throatiness of it across the phone line, so close it seemed that he was there, pressed up against me. I don't like to kill. I turned the words, twisting them to allow the light to fall on them. Because the thing was, I had believed him. In spite of what I knew, that he lied like I breathe, I had found some truth in those words. His murders, they were not gleeful, there was no sense within them that he killed for the sheer joy of it, it was necessity, pure and simple. And whichever way you twisted it, there was no room within that logic for the death of two children.

'He didn't know they were in the car,' I said, the truth of the words making them sound like inescapable knowledge rather than the guess that they were. 'He meant to kill Jacob. Not the children.' I looked up at Gabriel. 'You tell me,' I said. 'Is there any way in which this could be true? I mean, the investigation, was it conclusive in the crash being an accident?'

Gabriel tapped the file on the desk in front of him. 'I spoke to the investigating officer. From what I can tell, they treated it as an accident, pretty much from the start. There was nothing to suggest otherwise. No one had any motive to kill him. There were no witnesses, no evidence of tampering with the car. But,' he said, 'it would be the easiest thing, on a day like that, when the road is slick and it's snowing, to just follow, come up alongside, a little swerve in just the right place and they're in the water.' He shook his head, staring into space. 'Shit,' he muttered.

I concurred.

'Rudy,' I said, 'you said you had something for us? Please?'

Rudy stood up straight, tugging at the waistband of his trousers. 'Well, we found the blue Chevy, picked it up on CCTV leaving Setauket. Got a pretty good shot of the plate, and tracked it back to a rental agency in lower Manhattan.' He gave me a grin. 'Your hunch was right, Detective Sergeant Parr. Car was rented in the name of one Jackson Wolf.'

'He's returning to the Wolf ID,' I said, slowly. 'He has to know we have the Canning one. But he can't have figured out that Erin had made the connection, that she had managed to trace him back to Jackson Wolf.'

'There's been nothing on Wolf in fifteen years and that warrant for his arrest has well and truly run its course. Probably figures he's safe.'

'Does he still have the car?'

'Nuh huh. Returned it a couple of hours after the shooting. Car-rental place commented that it was "impressively clean".'

'He had it detailed,' said Gabriel.

'Looks like. We're on our way out. Figure he's got to be staying somewhere, so we're checking hotels in the

341

area of the car-rental place, see if we can turn him up. Good old shoe leather, hey kid?' He cuffed Harry across the shoulder, let loose a bellow of a laugh.

'He likes to play dress-up,' I offered. 'Don't forget, you're not looking at the external features, the hair, even the weight, he can change all that. Focus on the things he can't change, his height, face shape.'

Harry pushed himself up to standing. 'Got it, Sarge. We'll let you know.'

Rudy gave me a pat on the shoulder. Like being patted by a gorilla. 'Hang in there, kid.'

I watched as the door swung shut behind them, seeing not the shape of it thudding into its frame, but rather an ice-covered bay.

'She found him,' I said, softly. 'Erin ... she found Wolf. She trailed him across an ocean, across a continent. She tracked him down, because he was the man who had destroyed her life.' I looked up at Gabriel. 'We're going to do the same.'

Chapter 18

The rest of the day slid into the black-hole life of Dr Jacob Owens, favourite doctor, family man, all-round good egg, each moment punctuated with the inescapable feeling that there had to be something there, buried within the story of him, that could explain this sharp turn to the left. How did a good man end up doing something so terribly bad? And then, the unavoidable next step – how did his wife manage to miss it, how did she not see this change? Because it's what we do, isn't it? We blame the victim. Because if we can find some way in which she was wrong, some fundamental error of judgement, some oversight that the wiser amongst us would never have made, then we are magically protected, the same cannot happen to us. And yet the truth of it ever was that this magical thinking was akin to the counting of magpies or the refusal to step on cracks in a pavement.

The feeling began to settle over me as the day passed into afternoon, nudged towards evening, that whatever had happened here, Erin had little blame for it. She had been the victim of circumstance, of a lying husband who had flipped from good to bad, spun by the process of greed. Of a manipulative conman who placed a higher value on the money in his pocket than the lives of the innocents, who had stripped her of all she had, just because it was expedient for him. And following on from that came an overwhelming sadness, for what this woman had gone through and how much she had lost and just how hard she had fought for justice in its wake.

We finished early, the sun barely grazing the top of the surrounding buildings, because Gabriel had a meeting with a prosecutor, one that could not be rearranged, and I found myself wandering alone through the Manhattan streets, stopping in Sbarro for a slice of pepperoni pizza that dripped cheese onto my lap and stained my hands orange. Watching the ebb and the flow of it all and thinking that I felt alive, properly alive, for the first time in a long time. And more than that, that I was an I again. That somehow it no longer mattered that the I from now looked different from the I before, that all that mattered was that I was here and I was breathing.

I walked slowly back towards the hotel, pausing outside a bodega, considering picking up a bottle of wine, thinking of the dark red richness on the back of my tongue, and the softness it would add to my thoughts, turning to go inside, and then a flock of starling teenagers pirouetting past me, filling the narrow space with their flighty figures, high-pitched calls. And so instead I turned back towards the hotel, telling myself that I could do without wine, that I wasn't that bad, after all.

And then the lobby of the hotel, so full that the sounds seemed to rebound from each wall, hurtling back towards me at thunderous speed, and just wanting to be alone and quiet, and most of all to sleep. The lift – the elevator rather – those same mirrored walls, and thinking unavoidably of Erin and her quiet, private collapse. Then the shush of the doors, and my quiet corridor, and the empty sanctuary of my room.

I don't remember if I locked the door.

The sun had begun to splay shards of purple across the sky, nuggets of colour peeking out at me between pillar-box buildings. And there, standing proud on the table set before the window, a narrow-necked bottle of Vino Nobile de Montepulciano, 2011, a slender-stemmed wine glass standing sentinel beside it. A card had been set before it – From Gabriel – and a flush of heat rose up through me.

I opened the wine.

And then … what then?

Playing with my phone, checking Twitter, Facebook, the news, the weather. The thought that I had not heard from Wolf since, that it seemed remiss of him, lax to not have made full use of my number to create in me that sense of prey. The sky turning ochre beyond my window and wondering if I was too late, if he was fled already, was now someone new.

Because that was the thing with him, wasn't it? By the time you understood who you were chasing, he was someone else entirely.

Pouring a second glass.

From there, there are only fragments. Of heaviness and a weighty inexorable need for sleep. Of my face, pressing into the pillow, the angle of my neck odd, uncomfortable, and yet not having the will to move. Of dipping into blackness and then a sense, as of one struggling against a rip tide, only it is too powerful and there is no way back to shore, and then the blackness again.

Somewhere, deep inside me, the understanding of having made a dreadful mistake.

It was a dream, or rather the memory of a dream. That flash of light, that crackling sound that, if you listen hard enough, could almost be words. It was that smell, that grating of smoke that scratches at the back of your throat.

It was clambering from the blackness long enough to remind myself that I had been in this dream before, again and again, that if I concentrated hard enough, I would wake and find that all was as it should be.

It was a silent roar, deep from the centre of myself, powered by an impotent rage, one that drove up through the blackness that had once again closed over my head, that forced my eyes to open, my mind to come back to life.

Only this time, it wasn't a dream.

I was in it. It was in me. Those sounds and smells and sights that had become so common as to be a part of my DNA. The heat from fire, the scouring of smoke. And something else. I struggled to focus, to get my eyes and my brain to co-operate and pierce the darkness of the room.

And then the glint of light, a flash of metal, the shape

of a knife. The figure standing at the end of my bed, the shape of him carved from the darkness by the light of the fire. Watching me. Watching the flames that crept across the duvet, the heat of them reaching out towards me. Hello old friend. We missed you.

I tried to lift my hand, my arm, only they were simply too heavy, weighted down by the blackness that still swirled about my feet, pulling me, begging. Just close your eyes. You know you want to. Just close your eyes and everything will be okay. And my eyes closing, obedient to the last. And being distantly aware of a sound, was it screaming? High-pitched and relentless. Then another sound, buried within that, a click. And not knowing what any of it meant, only that I was so so tired.

Then a voice. It would perhaps be tempting to attribute the voice to some kind of deity, or at least it would if I were a different type of person. But I am not and so I will say I heard my own voice, stirring from somewhere deep inside me, telling me to get up, to get out, that I was going to die, and listening to it because, frankly, it seemed like the kind of voice that needed to be obeyed. And somehow, from somewhere, finding the strength to lift my leaden limbs, to raise them from the bed, to force my limpid body into a roll that spun it away from the crackle and the marching flames and plunged me onto the floor.

The shock of the fall, the voice itself, both of them combined to snap me back into the present, and I staggered up to standing, my brain and eyes working hard to understand the scene before them, the bed well alight now, the flames eating ever closer to me, the smoke thick enough to turn everything opaque. That screaming – the smoke alarm – and then, buried somewhere within that, the fitzing of a sprinkler, its head caved in, sending useless drops of water into the inferno below.

The door. I had to get to the door.

Only between me and the door there was fire, a path of it that led down from the bed, trailing to the opposite wall, a curtain of heat. And then the fear raged up in me, that I had to get through those flames, that if I didn't get through them then I was going to die, and the realisation hard on the heels of it, that for the first time in a very long time I very much did not want to die.

I spun in place. The window. But it did not open, and besides, if it did, we were thirty storeys up. Then I saw it, the door connecting mine to the one beyond. Had barely noticed it before, and yet now it seemed to scream to me.

I pulled my sleeves down over my hands and tried the handle. It was stuck fast.

Felt a sob well up in me.

'No.'

I stepped back from the door, turned my shoulder and ran at it, driving my shoulder hard into the catch of it. A shooting pain raced across my shoulder, down my back, and yet the door remained in place.

I felt another sob. The smoke was denser now. I could no longer see the window, the world beyond.

'Fuck you!' I screamed, running at the door again, throwing myself at it, because honestly, what the hell did I have to lose? A sharp shock of pain, and then I was falling.

'Oh my god! Are you all right?' I felt a hand grab hold of me, pulling me up to standing, had a vague sense of a dense southern drawl, a man with a lion's mane of white hair.

I leaned on him, feeling the pain arching across my shoulder. Then pushed past him, yanking open his bedroom door – he'd remembered to deadbolt it. Smart. And out into the corridor, smoke-filled now, doors open all along it, heads leaning out in various states of confusion.

'Hey ... what ...'

I shoved my way past them to the fire extinguisher that hung midway down the hall, ripped it from its holder and ran, hefting the weight of it on my hip. Back past the bewildered man with his wild white hair, into my room, rolling smoke, a rippling glow of orange. Pulled the nozzle free, aiming foam into the inferno. A sound behind me, a fitz, fitz, then the sprinklers from the adjoining room burst to life, the water soaking the back of me. I pushed on, foam drenching flame. Then a figure beside me, another fire extinguisher, the white-haired man aiming wildly into the smoke.

And finally, orange gave way to grey, the fire ebbing and ebbing until it finally went out.

I lowered the extinguisher to the floor, arms shaking,

glanced up at the man beside me. He stared at the remains of the room, shook his head. 'Fuck.'

I laughed. Because sometimes you either laugh or you cry.

Chapter 19

The pain pulsed from my shoulder, the heat of it radiating out from my back, arcing its way down my spine, threatening pinpricks of tears at the back of my eyes. I wouldn't cry though. I breathed out slowly, a long, concentrated breath, blowing out through my mouth, that landed on the nurse's face as she levered my arm into the sling. She glanced up, startled, then smiled.

'You can cry if you like,' she whispered. 'A dislocated shoulder hurts like hell.'

The pinpricks threatened to become a torrent, a rainstorm brought about by permission and sympathy, but instead I shook my head.

'I'm fine,' I lied. 'As you can see, I've survived worse.'

The nurse nodded, looping the brace around my neck. 'Yes. But it's not a competition. You're allowed to be in pain.'

I did it then, let a single tear escape, for a moment considering giving up, just letting the whole cascade fall. I wiped it away with my good arm. Because the thing was, she was right, I was allowed to feel pain. But I was also allowed to feel the rest of my emotions. The major one being that I was really, really fucking angry.

'I'm not going to cry,' I said, confidentially, 'because I need to go out and get the son of a bitch that just tried to kill me.'

The nurse grinned. 'Good idea.'

Footsteps, and the curtain jostled aside, Harry, unshaven and with bedtime hair, dressed to the nines in jogging bottoms and a loose-fitting T-shirt. He looked like he needed to cry even more than I did.

'You okay?' I asked, fully embracing the irony.

'Yeah,' he said slowly, entirely missing it. 'Yeah, I'm okay.'

The nurse gave a low snort, gathered up her things. 'I'll just go get your discharge stuff.' She glanced at Harry, back to me, 'You've both had a tough night.' She winked, ducked beyond the olive curtain.

'I spoke to the DI,' Harry said, sinking into the chair that had been tucked into the corner beside the gurney. 'He wants you back home. Says it's getting too dangerous. I told him I'll get us on a flight out tonight.'

The pain burrowed into my socket, arching up my neck. 'Yeah. No,' I said, adjusting my sling. 'I'm staying.'

'Alice, the DI … he said …'

'Don't worry about Noah. I can handle Noah. This bastard thought that he could scare me off and when that didn't work, he thought he could kill me. I am telling you now that I am not done until the day I cuff him.'

A roar of sound rippled from beyond the curtained wall, a scream of rage, of pain, it was impossible to tell. Another voice, school-teacher firm. 'Now, that's enough. Sit down and stop shouting.' I heard the squeal of metal chair legs on linoleum, the heavy sound of someone throwing themselves into it.

I looked at Harry, attempted a wry smile. 'Besides,' I said, 'who'd want to miss this?'

More hurried footsteps from the other side, and the curtain shimmied. Gabriel's face was pale, his eyes heavy with concern.

'Alice, are you okay?' His gaze took in my sling-supported arm, my wild soot-soaked hair. 'What the fuck happened?'

I looked at him, steady. 'Wolf happened.'

He had moved closer to me, was studying me as if through gaze alone he could spot injury. I'm not sure he'd even noticed Harry.

'I'm fine,' I said, as convincingly as I could manage. 'Besides,' I said, really going to town on this forced jolliness thing, 'Harry here is the real victim.' I lowered my voice. 'He had to leave his hotel room without his hair gel on.'

No one smiled.

I hurried on. 'We're getting close,' I said. 'He's panicking. He's said it himself, he kills because it's become necessary. He must feel that we've gotten close enough to him that it's necessary now.'

Gabriel pulled a face, apparently little comforted.

'We need to see if that wine bottle survived intact,' I said.

'Wine bottle?'

'When I got back to my room last night, there was a bottle of wine there waiting for me.' I flushed, thinking of the label, of what I had thought. 'I ... It said it was ... well, the label, it said you'd sent it up to my room.'

Gabriel started, forehead creasing into a heavy frown. I heard Harry shift in his chair, and once again briefly considered bursting into tears, more as a distraction than anything else.

'He drugged it,' I said, soldiering on. 'I don't know what it was, but it was enough to knock me out, for a little while at least.'

'You know what I don't get?' offered Harry. 'Why didn't he just kill you?' He waved a hand. 'I mean, no offence, but he's got access to a firearm, we know that from the Kate Weland murder. Why not shoot you? Or stab you, like he did to Erin Owens?'

I thought of light glinting from metal. 'He had a knife,' I muttered. 'He had a knife with him.'

Loath though I was to give too much credit to Harry Golightly, he was right. Wolf had stood there, at the end of my bed, for long enough to light a fire, to ensure it caught. He must have watched me sleep, must have been there whilst I was at my most vulnerable. Why not simply plunge that knife into me? There were so many ways in which he could have dealt out death for me, and yet he chose fire. And, of course, there was the issue of its unreliability. I mean, twice now I had survived a death that fire should have dealt out for me.

My thoughts snagged there.

'That was why,' I said, quietly. 'He chose fire because

he understood what that would mean for me. He knew about what had happened to me before. It's personal. It's a message. That he is smarter than me, that he understands my greatest fears, that he can make them come true.'

'Wait,' said Harry, frowning, 'but, I mean, if you're dead ...'

'I don't know if killing me was the most important thing to him. Like you said, if he just needed me eliminated, there are so many more efficient ways he could have done that. Fire, it sends a message. I think that the thing that mattered most to him was that he scared me, badly enough that I would walk away.'

Could Wolf have understood that, how close I had come to throwing in the towel, to running back to the comforting embrace of my mother, of the farm? I had told no one, other than my own mother. Impossible then that he could have had that knowledge. Or did he simply see more than I had credited him with. Could he tell somehow from the front I had adopted that it was all a façade, that one gust of wind would be enough to blow my house of cards down? I sat up straighter. Because the thing was, Wolf wasn't the only one whose identity could shift, who could choose to become someone new.

I had almost died by fire. Again. And it had firmed things up for me, made clear that which was once opaque.

That whoever I was becoming now, she had no intention of dying.

Gabriel shook his head. 'Whatever he was thinking, this guy is done.' He turned to Harry. 'Can you get her discharge stuff sorted out, get her back to the hotel and make sure she has a new room? I'm heading back there now to interview the staff. I want to know how the hell he knew which room you were in and how he got in.'

I manoeuvred my feet closer to the floor, the metal ridge of the gurney digging into me. 'I'll come with you.'

Gabriel stared at me. 'Alice, you need to rest.'

I shifted my sling. 'I'm coming with you.'

We stared at each other for long moments, two alley cats waiting to see who would win, then finally Gabriel sighed. 'Fine. You're impossible, you know that?'

'So I've been told,' I agreed.

The fire truck was still in position at the front kerb of the hotel. A small crowd of onlookers, a complicated mixture of young drinkers and elderly homeless, had gathered to watch, although there remained little to see. The crazy-haired guy and I had been mostly successful in soaking the fire out. Gabriel led our little trio into the lobby, the ballroom space of it thronging with people in nightclothes, the high-pitched chatter reverberating from the vaulted ceiling. We worked our way through the crowd towards the front desk, a man in a sharply pressed suit darting back and forth, moving quickly, achieving little.

'Hey,' called Gabriel. He flashed his badge. 'Need to speak to a manager.'

The man stopped dead, looking fearful. 'I'm the manager.' His gaze tracked across us, landing on me, his eyes as big as saucers. 'It was you? In the room? Wow. I mean, are you okay?'

I waved my sling at him. 'Just peachy.'

He nodded, his gaze moving to my scar, and I sighed heavily.

'Believe it or not, this is not my first time,' I said. 'So, couple of questions ... how did our friendly neighbourhood arsonist gain entry to my room?'

He paled, his gaze now hooked by something around the region of my knees. 'I asked the staff, and, look, you have to know this is a very unusual set of circumstances, we run a very tight ship here, very tight, and we are, by no means ...'

'Spill it,' said Gabriel.

The manager looked up, baulking. 'Okay, well, like I said, I asked the staff ... a guy came in yesterday, he was dressed in a nice suit, introduces himself to the duty manager, tells her he's from corporate, that he's doing a spot check of all our systems. He gave her ID,' he said, defensively. 'It was all legitimate, as far as my staff were aware. He was allowed unfettered access to our system. I'm assuming that at some point during that period he made himself a key card for your room.'

I sighed heavily. 'Wonderful.'

'I just spoke to corporate,' the manager said, quietly. 'They didn't send anyone, didn't know anything about it.'

Gabriel turned to look at me, shook his head. 'This son of a bitch. Okay,' this to the manager, 'you got CCTV?'

'Yes,' he said, relieved to finally be able to say something positive. 'Only ...' his face fell, 'I've checked the footage, you know, because I knew you'd need it, and he keeps his back to the camera the entire time. I'll get it for you, but ...'

'What about when he went up to my room? You know, to set fire to it ...'

The man flushed. 'Yes, we do have him on there. But his head is down, and he's wearing a baseball cap.'

'Aren't you supposed to say spoiler alert before you tell us stuff like that?' I muttered.

'We'll take a look anyway,' said Gabriel.

The manager led us into his office, gestured towards a screen. 'It's already set up for you.' He toggled the mouse. 'If you look here, this is when he came in, pretending to be from corporate.'

The cameras had captured a medium-build figure in a well-fitting suit with dark hair, neatly trimmed. But he had not gone in blind.

'He knows exactly where the cameras are,' I said.

He kept his back to them, carefully and concertedly, never giving us more than a view of shoulders, a dark head of hair.

'What about this evening?' I asked.

The manager selected a new recording. 'Okay, so we can't find any evidence of him coming into the hotel. If he copied your room key, he might also have gotten hold of the access key to the rear door. We don't have any cameras out there, nor in the staff stairwell.' He looked from me to Gabriel to Harry. 'And I assure you

358

that I will be raising this matter with corporate first thing in the morning and making clear to them that we need better security.'

I nodded. 'Well done. So, what about the corridor outside my room?'

He pulled the screen up, the image showing an empty corridor, and then a man approaching from the furthest end of it, baseball cap pulled down low. I watched, could feel my stomach writhe. I was behind that door, drugged, no idea what was coming.

Then I sat up straight.

'Wait ... did you see that?'

The man had stopped, slipping his key card into the lock, quietly easing his way inside.

'What?' asked Harry.

'That wasn't my room,' I said, my heart thundering in my chest. 'Look, I'm the next one down. Oh my god.' I leaned over, head in my hands. 'Oh my god. It was him.'

'Who?'

'The guy in the next room, the one with the crazy white hair. The one who helped me put the fire out. It was Wolf.'

Chapter 20

Dense steam filled the bathroom, stoppering up my lungs. And yet still I could smell it, the smoke that had burrowed its way into my nostrils, my throat. I buried my face in the towel, wet hair dripping down my bare back, and breathed out, a long breath, right on the cusp of becoming a cry. But it didn't, it just stayed there, hovering.

Twice now. I wiped off the mirror with the towel, then tossed it over my hair, studying my reflection, my face pale, scar vivid. Twice now fire had brought me to the brink of extinction. Twice it had failed. I pulled another towel around my torso, winding it tight like a swaddling blanket. It was starting to develop a feel of the absurd about it. I stared at myself staring back, and, instead of seeing my scar, I saw my features, the large eyes, the high-cut cheekbones. The me that dwelled beyond the scar.

I heard a door open, close, felt my heart rate spike. Then Gabriel's voice, 'It's just me. I got the breakfast.'

'Okay. I'll be right out.'

The hotel had given me a new room, a suite this time, by way of a sorry-we-allowed-someone-to-try-and-kill-you, up on the 58th floor with sprawling views of the Hudson, the Statue of Liberty standing to attention off in the distance. Harry had lost interest, somewhere around 3 a.m., had retired to bed, still muttering that we should go home, that it was all just getting too dangerous.

I pulled on a pair of jogging bottoms sourced from a sympathetic receptionist, a loose-fit T-shirt, and wondered where clothes shopping would fit into my busy schedule of not being killed.

'Hey.' Gabriel waved me towards the dining table. 'I got you bacon, eggs and French toast. And the biggest coffee they did.' He examined me, silhouetted against the early morning light. 'You okay?'

I nodded, damp hair sending water droplets soaking into my T-shirt. 'I'm fine. I'm hungry.' I sat across from him, took a large gulp of coffee. 'So, what do you think?'

'I think the guy's nuts,' muttered Gabriel through a mouthful of eggs.

'Well, yeah, but apart from that.' I bit into my French toast, hot syrup and cinnamon oozing out. 'I have a theory.'

'Go on then.' Gabriel leaned back in his chair.

'I think that the fire was a message for me. It was his way of telling me that he knew exactly who I was. That he understood my deepest fears, and that at any time he could use them to get to me. I think Wolf was trying to tell me, I can make your greatest nightmare come true.' I took another bite of toast. 'And another thing, he wanted to prove to me that he could be standing right in front of me, that he could literally take hold of my hand, and I would have no idea it was him. I would accept his help and be grateful for him saving my life.'

I felt my stomach knot as I spoke, the food burning in my gullet. Because that was the thing wasn't it, I had said I was chasing a ghost, and it seemed that I was, that he could be anywhere, do anything, even right before me, and I would never know. I pulled my legs up underneath me, suppressed a shiver. Was this how Erin felt? Had it been the same for her?

'He must have done it when he went into the computer system as a member of corporate – found out what room I was in, made the key. Then booked himself into the room next door.'

It had been booked in the name of Eduardo Alvarez. No credit card information. No passport. Shadows and games.

'I think …' I said, 'It's almost like this Wolf isn't a person, doesn't have one fixed identity. He is whoever he needs to be for any given period of time. Then, when that identity is no longer of use to him, he sheds it, like a snake sheds his skin.' I took another sip of my coffee. 'It's like, you and I, we think of ourselves as a single identity. I am Alice. When the fire happened, when … when I found out I wasn't who I thought I was … when the way I looked changed, it shook me, fractured my sense of who Alice was.' I set the coffee cup down, the truth of my words suddenly settling. 'See, the thing is, I was thinking of identity as like this permanent thing, that you are who you are, and if something comes along and changes that, then it's ... shattering. But for him, for Wolf, identity isn't like that at all. It is a coat you wear until you don't need it any more. He was Wolf for a while. Then, when that no longer suited him, he became someone else.'

I sighed, took another bite of bacon. It snapped into shards in my mouth, trickling pungently sweet syrup along my tongue. 'You know what I don't get though? He should have left by now. He has had time to build a new identity, or at least begin the process. By hanging around here, by doing things like he did last night, all he's doing is increasing his odds of getting caught. But then,' I allowed, 'maybe he is arrogant enough to think he can't get caught.'

Gabriel studied me. 'I think maybe that's a part of it. But I think the real reason he's sticking around is you.'

'What do you mean?'

'I mean, there are other people involved in this case, your friend Poppy, me, Harry. Why hasn't he been in touch with any of us? Why is it only you who has gotten texts or calls ...'

'Or drug-filled bottles of wine ...'

'Precisely. It's like he's fascinated by you.'

I felt my stomach drop, forced a smile. 'Well, I am pretty interesting.'

Gabriel grinned. 'Yes, yes you are. And, for some reason, Wolf knows this. I think he has begun to enjoy this game the two of you are playing, you seek, he hides. And he can't resist but make it just that little bit more exciting for himself by hiding right in front of you.'

I thought of Wolf's voice across the phone, of standing in the darkness of Erin's Brooklyn apartment, and a sudden shiver ran across me.

'He called me a true hero.'

'Well ...'

'Back in London, when I was dealing with the Hampstead fire, Naomi Flood used those precise words – true hero. She's a journalist – and it was ... a weird term to use. It's not something anyone has said to me before. I mean, let's be frank. I did nothing heroic in that fire. I just didn't die.'

'Yes, but ...'

I waved him away.

'My point is, he said that, he used the same words ... what if he was there?'

Gabriel baulked. 'Could he have been?'

'There were a lot of people there that night. Journalists, emergency services, residents. It was raining, so umbrellas, hoods ...' I stood up, pacing backwards and forwards. 'I've spoken to him, Gabe. I don't know when or how, but I just know I've spoken to him. That son of a bitch!' The movement made my head spin, and I slumped back down into my seat, took a long pull of coffee.

'You okay?'

'Yeah, I just ... whatever he gave me, I feel like I could sleep for a week.' My own words circled around me, reverberating through my skull. 'Did ... Wait ... on the day of the accident, when Jacob and the kids died ... you said to me that Erin Owens was meant to be going to that party with her kids, but that she hadn't felt well, that she'd gotten really tired the night before and slept all day?'

'Yes …' Gabriel looked up at me, eyes wide with alarm. 'Wait, what are you saying?'

'What if he drugged her too? We know that there's a certain MO he uses, of fire, the whole switching identities thing. He drugged me. What if that's why Erin was so unusually tired that day?'

'But … why? To keep her out of the car?'

'We've said he only kills when it's necessary. Maybe he figured that if Erin appeared sick, the kids would stay home too, that the only one in the car would be Jacob?'

Gabriel pulled a face.

'Or maybe the only one he was concerned with keeping alive was Erin … I don't know. I'm getting a headache.'

'Or maybe she was just sick?' suggested Gabriel.

'Maybe.' I turned my eggs over, over again. 'See, this is what he wanted, wasn't it? To get our heads spinning with it all.'

A hard buzzing cut the air, and Gabriel reached for his phone, an apologetic smile. 'Captain Otero. Yes. Oh, hey. How are you? Okay … okay … hey, Quinn, do me a favour, I'm just going to put you on speakerphone so Alice can hear this as well, okay? Hold on.' He raised an eyebrow at me, set the phone between us on the table and hit speakerphone. 'Quinn, we're here. Would you mind just repeating that last bit?'

'Hey, yeah …' Quinn Weland sounded older now

than she had a mere matter of days ago, her mother's death ageing her. 'I was going through my mom's stuff, and I found something, and, I mean, I don't know if it means anything, but I just thought …'

'Quinn,' said Gabriel, 'anything you can give us would be great. I really appreciate you calling.'

'Okay, so, my mom, she keeps … kept … a bunch of papers in her desk, like all our official stuff, documents, you know, the important stuff. So Dad, he was going through it last night, and he found … I don't know, it doesn't mean much to me, only I know you mentioned his name …'

'What did you find, Quinn?'

'Well, you said about Jackson Wolf, yeah? You asked me if I knew him?'

'Right.'

'Well, I don't. Only, when I was going through Mom's stuff, I found some paperwork. It was, like, a receipt from Americar rentals, you know that car-hire place out in Brentwood? And, it took me a minute, you know, to realise what I was seeing, but it had that guy's name on it. That Jackson Wolf.'

'Okay … so, he hired a car from Brentwood, and your mom got a copy of the receipt?'

'Yeah, I guess she must have gone there a couple of days before she died. She said, I don't know, maybe like two days before, that she'd been to Brentwood to get something for Erin.'

'So, your mom must have known that Jackson Wolf was back on Long Island?'

'No, see, that's what I thought, but the receipt is dated from ages ago, and I didn't figure it out until I woke up this morning. The receipt is dated from the day before Jacob and the kids had that accident.'

I stared at Gabriel, mouth open. He was there. This was it. Conclusive proof that Wolf was in the vicinity around the time of the accident.

'Quinn, this is so helpful. Now, if I ...'

'Wait, there's more. Okay, now, I don't get this, and I don't know why my mom has it, but there's a photograph in here as well, looks like it's a shot from their security cameras over at the car-rental place. It's time-stamped the same time as the receipt. Only ... well, I don't get it. Look, I'm in my dad's study. Can I ... I'll scan it and send it to you, yeah? See what you think?'

'Okay.' Gabriel reeled off his email address, and we sat in silence, listening to the distant whirr of the scanner, of the clack of keys.

'Okay, it's sent. I mean, like I said, I don't get it, but I mean, I'm not a detective.'

A ping from Gabriel's phone, a message coming through.

'Hang on, there it is. Just a second, Quinn.' He shifted screens, pulling up his inbox, sliding open the attachment.

A blurry picture filled his phone's screen, of a long counter, of a waiting area, a couple of customers milling about, and a man standing at the counter. I pushed my chair back, hurrying round the table, anxious to get my first real look at the man once known as Jackson Wolf.

Then I stopped. Because the man in the picture, a large man with jet-black hair, jowls, that man was Dr Jacob Owens.

'Holy shit,' I said. 'They're the same person.'

Chapter 21

The Long Island Expressway flashed by us, Gabriel weaving around the cars ahead, no more than brief flashes of colour and then gone. It felt like a dream, like being underwater. Ed Canning, Jackson Wolf, Jacob Owens. One man, so many different identities. Who the hell was he?

It was the knowing and yet still the not knowing. Because you could have him, could hold his identification in your hand, and yet have it mean nothing. Because there was no who. He was a mirage, an optical illusion in real time.

I had reared back from the screen, from the image of Jacob Owens and Jackson Wolf, had felt the floor buck beneath me, an arcing pain lancing along my shoulder a reminder that I was awake and this was real. A dim recollection of Gabriel thanking Quinn, of the call disconnecting, yet thinking only of them, of Mackenzie and Levi, Erin's long-lost babies. Because if Jacob Owens was Ed Canning and Jackson Wolf, and if he wasn't dead, then it would follow that neither were they.

'What the fuck ... why didn't they look for the

bodies, Gabe? What the hell were they doing out there? How could they miss this?'

'They did. They spent days out there on the water, but the current ...'

I felt ice-cold, I felt searingly hot. The children, babies. They were dead in a frozen tomb. They were alive ...

I had raked my one good hand through my still wet hair. The DNA. That was what she had tested. She must have had Kate collect something from her apartment, something belonging to one of the children. She found them, Gabe. They're somewhere in London.

I studied the blinding blue of the sky as it hurried past, rocking with the motion of the car, seeing not the scudding embers of clouds, but rather Erin, waking from an unnatural slumber. That sudden sense of wrongness. That inevitable spiral into panic, of suspended disbelief. That it couldn't be true, that her husband, her children, that in moments, minutes, they would return through the door. That surely all would be well. Then that moment, hearing the news, the car has gone into the frozen bay, then the pain, like having all of your organs torn out at once, reality suspended, your future vanishing in an instant. Of the weeks and months of ... what? The word grief hardly seems sufficient. But then, what word would be when you are left alone in a world that your children have already left? Did she think about dying? Did she think about ending it all, maybe filling her pockets with rocks, walking out into the Great South Bay, simply giving up? Or was there something deeper, something that I couldn't possibly understand? Some whisper that said, no, hang on. Did a mother know? I thought of Poppy and Charlie, of the knowledge that seemed to work beyond the senses. Was that true for Erin, that even in amongst the torture of her grief she lived, knowing without knowing that her job wasn't done yet?

'When do you think she figured it out?' I asked, watching as we sailed past an eighteen-wheeler.

Gabriel's jaw was tight, his expression stone. 'Maybe she started to suspect something once she realised how much her husband had lied to her, how much of what he had said was a fabrication. The foreclosure on the house, the lapsing of the insurance policies. I guess she realised then that the man she had married wasn't who she thought he was. But even then … I mean, who could imagine that someone you loved could do this, fake the deaths of your children?'

I watched as trees flashed by, but to me they hung heavy with snow. Jacob or Ed or Jackson – or the Wolf as he had come to be inside my head – driving along an ice-encrusted highway, his children buckled into the back. And then? 'You know,' I said, 'the stuff we found in her flat, back in London. Disguises. The money. That was why. She would have wanted to find him, find her children. But she had to have understood that she was in danger. And so perhaps she disguised herself.'

'Well,' said Gabriel, 'she did learn from the best. And the money?'

I shook my head, a seagull diving low overhead. 'Maybe she was going to try and bribe him? She must

371

have known how important money was to him, what he was willing to do for it. Maybe it was all she could think of, offering to pay him for her children.'

I thought then of the rental car. Had he parked it ready, had it waiting on a nearby street? Had he transferred his children, one car to another, leaving them alone in the arctic cold, the tumbling-down snow, because he had a stage to set. A car window to smash, a baby's hat to drop into the footwell. And then the slow roll of the empty car down into the blue-black waters of the bay.

'You know,' I said, 'he played everyone. It wasn't only his identity he changed but Erin's as well. He made people believe she was a cheat, that she had led them into financial ruin. And all along he was building a smokescreen to cover his tracks. Make him appear to be the perfect victim.'

'So that when he vanished no one would ever suspect it was anything other than an accident.'

I nodded. 'Because he was a "good" guy. And if Erin said anything, if she got suspicious, he'd already planted the seeds of doubt in anyone who might listen to her. I mean, how? How can anyone be that convincing a liar?'

Gabriel shook his head. 'Think about it. The people he convinced, Chloe, Mrs McGilly, even Quinn, they all had their own reasons not to like Erin in the first place. Chloe, well, I guess jealousy is the only word for it. Mrs McGilly didn't like the fact that Erin wouldn't let her in like Jacob did, kept her at a distance. And Quinn, she said herself that she was pissed, that she felt

Erin had pretty much abandoned her mother. He took those minor resentments and added fuel to the fire.'

'He even had the office rented in her name so that any subterfuge would be connected to her, not him.' I offered, 'That's why she didn't go to you straight away, why she followed him, gathered the evidence, so that it would be clear, so that we would have to believe her.' I looked across at him. 'You think that Adrienne Lee was the tipping point, the thing that made him decide to run? If he realised that she was onto him, that if she pushed hard enough then she would bring the whole fraud tumbling down ...'

Gabriel's face was grim. 'That son of a bitch,' he muttered.

Erin. What a price you paid for one simple mistake, placing your trust in the wrong man. How much you have suffered for that. And yet still, you brought us here. You did all this before us.

'You know what I don't get?' said Gabriel. 'The office. Why shred it? Why not burn it?'

I allowed my head to lean back against the headrest, thinking. 'The flat in Vauxhall,' I said. 'It didn't look like he was living there, more like it was a safe house, maybe. What if that's his MO? That in order to spin this elaborate web of identities, he needs this one place where he can funnel everything, somewhere that he is sure no one else will discover.'

'You're saying he was planning on returning to it. That he shredded the documentation, just to be on the safe side, but ...'

'But he was confident enough to believe that no one would ever find it. He can't have known that he had dropped the key. That the bank would give out the address to Erin. I mean, once you set fire to a place, you're done. He was leaving the country. Maybe he wanted somewhere he knew he could return to. Only he gets there and …'

'She's had the locks changed.' I shook my head. 'Well, that must have pissed him off.'

Gabriel steered us fast off the exit ramp, down into the outskirts of Brentwood, green fields giving way to solitary houses, a set-aside wood-slat church, proclaiming Jesus as king. We took a left, grass turning to the concrete of car parks and strip malls.

American rental agency sat on its own, surrounded by a sea of cars and concrete, an orange flag waving boisterously in the breeze, and as we drove in I was both myself and someone else. It would have been snowing on the night that Jacob Owens came here. I wondered what he was feeling, where his thoughts would have been. Was he sad, leaving behind a life that he had built? Or did it simply not work that way with him? Was the normalcy of human emotions somewhere beyond his capability? We slid into a space close to the entrance, and I wondered if this was where he had parked that night. Or had he walked here in the driving snow, the bitter cold? How had it all worked for him?

I pulled open the door, an uncomfortable feeling settling over me. Because in all that we had seen of him, all that we knew, it seemed inevitable that the choices he had made here had not come from the clear blue sky, that his entire life had dissolved into a series of plans, identities creating stepping stones in a fast-moving stream. That he had known that he would end up here, the night before his 'death', that in the roots of his relationship with Erin was the knowledge that it would end in the betrayal of her.

The manager waited for us, a middle-aged woman, her fingers resting on the taut lump of her pregnant belly. 'I pulled the files as soon as you called.' She led us to a table set to the side of the showroom, papers already spread across it. She sank into one of the chairs, waving us towards the others. 'I checked with the staff who were on that day. I'll be honest, I wasn't optimistic anyway. I mean, it was a long time ago and we see a lot of people.'

'No one remembered him?' I asked.

She shook her head, long auburn hair billowing about her face. 'No. They remembered the day though. It was a bad night, they were planning on closing up early. The two staff members who were working said they remembered having to stay open because a customer came in, but they couldn't tell me anything about that customer.'

I thought of Holborn, of the witnesses, everyone seeing Erin, no one seeing the man who walked a matter of feet behind her. 'No,' I said. 'He's not the kind of person you pay attention to.'

She shuffled through papers, sliding a receipt towards us. 'According to our records, Mr Wolf rented a five-door sedan. He also rented two baby seats.'

'When did Mr Wolf return the car?' Gabriel asked, his voice far away now.

She shook her head. 'According to my records, he didn't return it here. It went back to another one of our branches the following day.'

'Where?'

'Logan Airport. Boston.'

Chapter 22

Gabriel tucked the phone under his chin, watched me as I paced a groove across his office floor. 'Immigration have no records of him travelling from Logan under either the Wolf, the Owens, the Alvarez or the Canning identity. Yeah,' he said, this last directed into the phone, 'look, I'm going to send you over everything I have on this guy. Do me a favour and see if you can dig anything up on him.'

I stopped, turned towards him. 'Get them to check flights into Rome. Erin had come from there before she got to London.'

Gabriel nodded. 'Flights from Boston to Rome on that date. He would have been travelling with two children, a boy and a girl, but young enough that he could have passed them off as a different gender.'

I started as my phone rang, Harry's name flashing up on screen.

'Sarge.' His voice hurried, the low roar of traffic in the background. 'We're on our way to the Hilton in Tribeca. We think we've traced the rental car used in the Weland murder there.'

I grabbed Gabriel by the arm. 'We've got to go. They

have the car. Harry,' I said, this last back into the phone, 'we're on our way. Do not let him get away from you.'

We ran from Gabriel's office, slip-sliding past people in the hallway.

'That cheeky asshole,' he muttered. 'He was staying right around the corner the whole damn time.' We ducked out of the door, running up Beach Street.

And as I ran, that thought, that he had done it again, had positioned himself right beside me, without me ever having a clue. He had been watching me. I knew it like I knew my own name. Had placed himself a block from the station in one direction, a block from my hotel in the other. I ducked round an elderly man walking a pug. It should have frightened me, the thought of his proximity should have sent chills arcing through me. But instead it was something else, a thrill almost. That this was a game and I was inside it, and true, though it had begun as his game, perhaps with a couple of little tweaks it could become mine.

Then a smell, one so familiar that at first I thought I had imagined it, of drifting smoke, and then a sound that followed, the hard parp of a fire truck, the roar as it overtook us, hanging a hard left turn on the corner of the Avenue of the Americas.

'You've got to be fucking kidding me,' I muttered.

We rounded the corner in time to see the fire truck slow at the low-slung form of the Hilton, squeezing its way into the alleyway just beyond it. Followed it down the side street, a nothing lane of garages and emergency exits, a cloud of smoke billowing from just beyond.

378

Then a figure that I recognised, Harry running his fingers through his hair.

'What the hell is going on?' I bellowed.

'There's a fire in one of the garages.' He looked at me, face pale. 'Someone set a bunch of stuff alight in a metal bin. Just like in Vauxhall.'

I watched as the firefighter unspooled the hosepipe, then looked back at Harry. 'You get his room key?'

Rudy rounded the corner, holding up a key card. 'Got it.'

'Let's go,' said Gabriel.

We took the rear stairs two at a time, silent but for the ringing sound of our running feet. Each of us thinking the same thing, that we have seen this before, that time and again it has shaken itself out this way, of fire, this man slipping through our fingers. Gabriel tugged open the door onto the fourth-floor corridor, gun in hand.

'You two stay back,' he muttered to Harry and me, waving Rudy forward.

We moved carefully, past one door, two, pulling up to a halt outside room 432. I watched as Rudy slid the key card into the slot, the light changing from red to green, then pushed down on the handle, swinging the door inwards, Gabriel ducking inside, gun pointing into the dimly lit room. He moved from side to side, checking the bathroom, the wardrobe, the bed. Only I already know what he's going to find.

We were too late.

The smell of bleach scraped at the back of my throat.

The bed lay, not just empty but stripped, the linens on it pulled away.

'Has the cleaner been through here?' I asked Harry.

He shook his head. 'Wolf hasn't checked out.' He looked about him. 'He must have done this.' He let his gaze fall back on me. 'I think we missed him, Sarge.'

I let my hands fall to my scalp, felt a scream build up inside me. I could feel Gabriel, close to me.

'We're going to get him, Alice. No matter where he goes, or who he becomes next. We're going to find him.'

Was he gone? Was it over? Would he vanish now into the great wide world, someone else entirely?

'We need forensics in here.' My voice seemed to come from far away. 'I'm going to go talk to the fire crew.'

I had the sense of eyes on me as I left the room.

The smell of smoke hung heavy in the air, winding its way through the scent of exhausts. I worked my way by the fire truck, introducing myself to a firefighter. He shrugged at my question, his gaze lingering on my scar, before abruptly tugging away. 'Looked to be a bunch of papers used as a fire starter. There was some fabric, looked like bedding at the bottom.'

Fire, to wipe all things clean.

I nodded, turning away from the ashen smell, the sense of falling, your fingers grasping out for that last handhold, questing, failing.

Are you already someone else?

I walked back, towards the roar of traffic, cold certainty

closing over me. That we were midway through an illusion – the great vanishing. That Erin had done what I had not, had found Mackenzie and Levi. Were I to fail again, here, now, they would disappear again.

I rounded the corner, a bored-looking doorman studying the parked-up police cars with disdain. I waved my badge at him, hoping he would not recognise the futility of this.

'We're looking for a guy.'

'Uh-huh. So I see.'

'He would have come from the back of the building.'

'Where the fire is?'

'Where the fire is,' I confirmed.

'What's he look like?' the doorman asked.

I laughed. It had been a long week. 'No idea.'

The man frowned at me, a quick glance, up and down, subtle step back, just in case the crazy lady completely lost it.

I shook my head, rubbing my fingers across my forehead. 'Late thirties. Likely about six foot.'

The doorman's gaze tripped past me, out onto the swirl of traffic. 'Guy got into a cab. Maybe a half-hour ago. Suitcase. Baseball cap. He your guy?'

I felt my hackles rise. 'Which way?'

The doorman shrugged. 'Didn't see. It was Frank's cab though. Guy does regular pick-ups all up and down here.'

'You know how I can get hold of this Frank?'

'Concierge will have his number.' He waved me towards the slender desk tucked inside the door.

I ducked back inside, a thrill of something, hope perhaps? I explained myself to the concierge, a narrow, pale-looking woman, waiting as she typed, nails drumming on the desk, my head turning, left, right, studying everyone in my path. He had taught me well, hadn't he? That he could be anyone, be anywhere.

The concierge picked up the desk phone, dialled a number, and I turned, half facing her, half facing the lobby with its myriad strangers. Perhaps you haven't left at all? Are you here?

'Hey Frank, its Ellie at the Hilton. Hi. Yes, I have the police here. They're looking for information on that passenger you just picked up from here.' She listened intently. 'Okay, hold on, Frank.' She leaned across the desk to me. 'He said he dropped him off at Newark. At the airport.'

I remember the movement of her lips, the cerise of the lipstick she wore, and the shape of them as they formed the words. Frank says he's on his way back. He's about ten minutes out. Then the lift doors opening, and Gabriel walking towards me with long strides, and a sense of the floor swaying beneath me.

'You got something?' he muttered quietly.

'He's at Newark,' I said, voice low. 'He's rabbiting.'

And Gabriel's face grim then, voice hard on the phone, every inch the police captain now. 'He may be travelling under any of the following aliases – Ed Canning, Jackson Wolf, Jacob Owens. Or possibly Eduardo Alvarez. I'm sending you a picture of him, but please be advised he's likely to be travelling in disguise.'

A pause, for what I imagine was disbelieving laughter. 'Yes. Yes, I know.' A look to me, pleading almost. 'Where's he going, Alice?'

I thought of all that I knew about Wolf, of all that I had heard and come to understand of him. And I thought of what he had said to me, that he was willing to kill to defend what mattered most to him. He could have left his children, that morning when he ventured out into a snowy escape. How much easier would life have been for him then, if he had simply vanished, leaving them behind in their mother's care? Would she even have looked for him then, if he hadn't taken it just that one step too far? 'He's going back to London,' I said, settled in my own certainty. 'He's going to go get his kids. Look for flights into England. London, Birmingham, Manchester. He could even fly into Paris and go across on the Eurostar. He's done it before.'

I watched as Gabriel relayed the information, the sounds strangely distant.

'Excuse me? Detective Parr? Frank is back.' The young woman pointed to the front doors. 'He's just pulled in.'

I touched Gabriel's hand, gesturing to the yellow cab, and then darted across the lobby, that sense following me, that it could be that man or that man or that, that fire had failed, that when fire failed, Wolf killed. I moved in a wide arc through the milling people, waiting for a sharp pain to my ribs, for the hollow snap of a gunshot.

And yet where there should have been death there

was nothing, only people watching me, wondering at my wild-eyed looks.

I ducked out into the air again, a breeze whipping up the avenue, sweeping by me. The cab idled, its engine rumbling in a low-throated purr, and I leaned in to the open passenger window. 'You're Frank?'

The man studied me, then gave a quick nod. 'Yeah, I'm Frank. You the cops?'

I nodded. 'Where did you drop him?'

'Terminal B,' he said. 'International terminal,' he added, helpfully.

I stood up, looked back in through the door to where Gabe watched me, phone still pressed to his ear. 'Gabe,' I shouted, 'he's at terminal B.'

Gabriel didn't react for a moment, was piecing together the movement of my lips with the sound pulled from the traffic, the whipping wind. Then he nodded, waved, turning his attention back to the phone.

I leaned back down to the cab. 'Do me a favour, can you describe him for me?'

The man pulled a face. 'I can do better than that.' He leaned over, popping open the passenger-side door, and gestured for me to climb inside.

I hesitated, thinking of the white-haired man who had pulled me to my feet in the hotel, who had stood beside me as I extinguished the fire, that sense again that Wolf could be anyone, anywhere. And yet Frank was pushing seventy, his features laden heavy with the years, and even though Wolf was good, I doubted he was that good.

384

I climbed into the passenger seat of the cab.

Frank gestured up at the dashcam tucked at the top of the windscreen. 'This is New York,' he growled. 'You just can't be too careful.'

That was when I realised, that there were two, not one. One camera facing out, the other facing in, capturing the expanse of the back seat. I felt my heartbeat begin to rise, as Frank pushed at the screen with awkward fingers.

'Ah ... stupid thing ... you know, I hate technology. Damn stuff. Going to ruin the world one of these days. There it is.' He angled the screen towards me.

It showed a man, his arm stretched across the centre rest, his face in profile as he watched the city scud by. He was slender, his dark hair cut short.

He was Jacob Owens, only stripped away, the weight gone, jowls pulled back into the hard line of a chin, the mass of the hair shorn back.

And he was the man who had raised me from the floor, with his wild white hair and his fearful face.

And he was the man on a Holborn street, sprinting towards his target, his coat pulled taut with padding, a blond wig billowing out behind him.

And he was someone else.

Because, as I stared at the image, I realised that I knew this wolf.

My breath caught in my throat, as I felt damp grass beneath my knees, the iron-rich smell of blood in the air. Erin Owens scrabbling at her slashed-open throat, almost like she's trying to push away the helping hands of the paramedic. I thought of his words: 'hold her hands for me', of the bandage that she had somehow slipped up her sleeve, as if she had believed that somehow I would figure it out, that I would understand.

And I looked at the image of that same paramedic as he sat calmly in the back of a New York taxicab.

'Christian. You son of a bitch.'

Part Three

Chapter 1

Looking back now, it seems that life split apart there, right at that moment, the following hours and days speeding up, slowing down, time slipping into an uneven shimmy, so that by the end of it I had lost the form of what had passed. All that remained to me were peaks, moments that had risen above the melee, embedding themselves on my memory. A rough flight, rolling turbulence hitting somewhere in the middle of the Atlantic that made the plane buck and shimmy, the elderly woman in the seat across the aisle crossing herself, a low droning hum of the Lord's Prayer. Harry's face, green with the motion, his fingernails gripping on to his armrests like that way they would steady the plane's relentless bucking. The smell of Gabriel's cologne, his face poker straight, like he hasn't even noticed the vibrations.

London, spread out below us like some great grey blanket of civilisation, and wanting to leap from the plane, plummet to the land below, and, in amongst that eight million people, my fury and my horror drawing Wolf, Christian, Jacob forth. That feeling in the pit of my stomach that I was woefully late.

Poppy waiting for us at arrivals, her face grim. We've been to Christian's house. They've gone.

It had been thirty-six hours. There was a sense then, in that Major Crime office in Holborn, of suspended disbelief. That this should come to pass, that it would shake out like this. It seemed that Noah had shrunk in the intervening days, the bags beneath his eyes pronounced now, his movements languid and weary. I watched Gabriel, watching us, my gaze drawing his, a quick grin, there and gone again.

'What do we know?'

'We know,' said Poppy, her face grim, 'that he's married. And that you know his wife.'

Time standing still again, that sense that one has just before a fall. 'Who?'

'That reporter from *The Times*. Naomi Flood.'

There should have been surprise. But instead all I felt was a kind of world-worn weariness.

'I talked to her colleagues at the paper,' said Poppy. 'Carefully, obviously, but I did some subtle asking about. They married in September last year. It was a whirlwind romance, apparently. They met five months before that, at a fire, which I thought was deeply romantic. He brought two small children into the marriage. He told Naomi that their mother died giving birth to the youngest.'

I thought of Mackenzie and of Levi, of the shrine their mother had made to them, and felt an unfurling in my chest, that they, in spite of all odds, had survived, that their father, whatever darkness he had buried at the heart of him, loved them enough to protect them, to keep them with him.

But Naomi ... He had already killed two women that we knew of. Was she about to be the third?

'He knows we're right behind him,' I said, quietly. 'He's got to figure there's a very real risk we know what identity he's currently using. And Naomi, she's going to be a gold mine of information, especially if she's figured out that all is not well here.'

Poppy blew out a breath. 'If you don't want your spouse digging where they shouldn't, maybe don't marry a reporter?'

'Alternatively,' I offered, 'if you're looking for someone who can feed you information about people, say detectives, it's a pretty solid shout.'

Gabriel was looking down at the floor, had steepled his fingers in front of him, thumbs pressed together tight, bled white from the pressure. 'If he thinks she knows anything that could hurt him, he's going to kill her.'

The DI paced, backwards and forwards, shoes squeaking on linoleum floor. 'They're not at their London home. The car is there, so we can't use ANPR. The kids haven't been in crèche, neither Naomi or Christian ... Wolf ... whatever his name is ... have been in work.' He looked at me, dull-eyed. 'I hate to say this, but we could already be too late.'

I stared up at a London map tacked to the wall, locations of interest to the case of Erin Owens marked out in red. Brunswick Square Gardens. That was where it had begun. I thought of him, of Christian, of Wolf, of his frantic movements, hands working their way across her body to save her life. It is amazing the effect a uniform will have on your perceptions. Because twist the lens, just a little, and you see something different, his hands moving to restrain her, to check her, is there something she's hiding, something he'd missed?

It was midway across the Atlantic, just as the ping sounded, the seat-belt sign finally flicking to off, that the pieces slid into place. That in all of the CCTV footage I had viewed, I had never seen Christian arrive at the scene. That he had told me he had been right round the corner, that if that were true, he would have been visible running to the scene just as I had run. I had leaned my head back against the seat, had stared out the window at the billowing blanket of clouds, picturing instead the park.

He had followed her, picking her up at King's Cross Station, perhaps knowing where she would go, but not yet having discovered where she was staying. He had stabbed her, cutting her throat open. Then Edwina Clarke and her dog Billy. So he had run, rucksack heavy on his back. Only he had never left the park. That patch of ground we had found, the blood, the footprint. He had stopped there, hidden by the copse of trees, and … what? Pulled his paramedic uniform from within the rucksack? No. Not just the uniform. He'd had a bag with him, full of his kit, or so I had assumed. But it hadn't been, had it? He had pulled on his paramedic uniform to cover up the bloody clothes from the slash to her throat, had tugged on a pair of gloves, disguising the fact that his hands were already soaked red. And the rucksack? That must have gone inside the kitbag, along with the envelope of evidence that Erin had collected. Because when we look at someone we see what we expect to see. I saw a uniform. Which meant I thought I knew what his bag contained.

I was wrong.

'What about the envelope?' I asked. 'Erin's collection of evidence.'

'I've flagged it up to the teams,' said the DI, 'but no sign so far. If it is what you think it is, he would want to keep it close.'

I had watched the sun dance across the boulders of clouds. He would have arrived at the fallen body of Erin Owens at a run, a paramedic determined to save her life. My stomach clenched, thinking of that moment, of her looking up and, for a second, seeing as I had seen. The uniform alone, thinking help was near. And then him drawing closer and the realisation sinking on her, that this was not help, rather the final nail in her coffin. And fighting him and fighting him. And then along comes this woman, this detective, and she will help. Only she takes hold of her hands and pins them down and now suddenly the fight is lost.

I had stared out at the limitless blue sky and had cried, silent tears. I helped get him what he wanted.

It was Naomi Flood's mother in the end. It was a hopeless call, as the sun had begun to sink below the sky-line, my voice hoarse with exhaustion, the knowledge already settling in, that in whatever game it was that we were playing, I had lost. But we all turn to our mothers, sooner or later. She had answered the phone with a cheery 'Hello', a rolling Welsh accent, sounded positively delighted to be speaking to me, a detective from London, well, isn't this lovely. I lied to her, this delightfully artless woman from the shimmering Welsh coast. Told her that I was working with Naomi on a story, that it was important I speak to her, that she had given me her mother's number in case of emergencies, because 'you always know where to find her'. You could hear it in her, the way those words puffed out her chest, tugging her into the heart of her daughter's important work. 'Well, do you know, she called me only this morning. They're up in the Peak District.'

It had stilled my blood, those words, the mention of my clambering hills, of my green fields, of my transcendent wildness. I thought of what Gabriel had said. It's you. He's fascinated with you. And so he had run, from London, straight into the arms of my home. It could not be a coincidence.

'Oh, lovely surprise it was for her. Chris came home from work, says pack your bags, love, we're taking the kids and we're heading off to a cottage for a bit, just the four of us. He's such a thoughtful boy, that one. Do you know him?'

'Yes,' I said, quietly, 'I know him. You know where exactly?'

'Oh, I'm sorry, love, but no. And they've got no signal of course. You know what it's like when you're out in the wilds. But I tell you what, when she calls me next, I'll ask her to ring you, is it?'

It was the moving of chess pieces. You take my rook, I'll take your bishop. My skin felt slick with it, this sense that he was infiltrating me, was working his way through every part of my life, so that at the end of it, nothing would be left but Wolf himself.

I stood up, my chair squealing hard against the floor. 'I'm going to the Peak District.'

The room had stilled then, everyone staring at me like perhaps I had lost my mind. Perhaps I had. It was hard to tell any more.

But it's pointless, said Poppy. You don't know where they are, said the DI. I don't have to come, do I? asked Harry.

Then Gabriel had stood, casual and easy. 'Let's go.'

I had grabbed the car keys. 'They are in a cottage in the Peak District. I need an address. Do everything you can. Rip apart their computers, their phone records, anything you can find, but get me an address.'

I should have been tired, should have been buffeted by jet lag. Yet the spiking adrenaline kept my eyes wide, fuelling me out of London, up past Northampton, Bletchley, Rugby.

'You can sleep if you want,' I said to Gabriel. 'I'll wake you when we get closer.'

He had shrugged, smiled. 'I'm fine. I'll just keep you company.'

I don't remember talking, although it seems now that we must have, that the journey would have stretched off endlessly into the horizon if we did not exchange a single word. Or perhaps we didn't. In the space of our week together, it seemed that we had developed a comfort together, such that easy silences were not worked at, rather pulled on like an old pair of slippers.

I told myself that this was responsible policing. That I needed to be there, to catch him, to prevent him from slipping through the fingers of another police force, one who did not understand the complexities of Wolf, could not possibly fathom just what he was capable of. Was it that? Possibly. Perhaps it would be permissible to give myself that much credit. But I am afraid that there was something else too, a certain inevitability to it. That he had tugged me into this game and that, whether I wanted to or not, I was bound to it. Tied in.

The call came in as we passed Matlock. 'Al? I found them.' Poppy's voice had come through the speaker, piano-wire taut. 'Naomi put a postcode in on her satnav. It's a rental property, just outside Bakewell. Noah is on to Derbyshire police. He's going to get a team to meet you there.'

My fingers curled tighter about the steering wheel. 'Tell them to hang back. We're fifteen minutes out. We'll set up a rendezvous point in the Morrisons car park in Bakewell. Unmarked cars only.'

I glanced across at Gabriel, could see his hand drifting unconscious to his hip, reaching for a missing weapon, felt my foot press down harder on the accelerator, speedometer creeping up.

We reached the supermarket moments before the

Derbyshire team, a couple of detectives; a tall, rangy man, a woman whose head barely reached my shoulder. I looked from one to the other. 'We need two more cars.' I twisted my phone towards them, showing them the map. 'Farm is accessed by a through road. We need a unit at either end in case he gets past us.'

The woman looked at me, unfairly maligned. 'He won't get past us,' she said, with the kind of confidence I might have had once. Before I met Wolf.

'I think we'd be better to be overcautious,' offered Gabriel, his quiet voice drawing them in closer to him. 'He's slipped through police fingers on more than one occasion.'

The woman stared at him for a moment, exchanged a glance with her partner, then shrugged. 'Fine,' she said, reaching for her airwave.

'Tell them that once we go in, no one gets past them. No matter what. They shouldn't assume they know what he looks like.'

We slipped out of the car park, twisting quickly through wooded country lanes.

'You know,' muttered Gabriel, 'I really wish I had my gun right about now.'

I slowed, taking the left-hand turning carefully, road narrow enough that branches squealed across the rolled-up windows. 'You know, I really wish you had your gun too.'

We plunged down a hill, could pick out the lights of a farmhouse in the settling twilight, make out the rough-edged shape of a barn behind it.

'There it is,' said Gabriel, pointing to a darkened square, a stone building that seemed to slip into the background, all but invisible in the failing light.

I nodded, adrenaline making my fingers cold. 'You see a car?'

Gabriel sat up taller in his seat, peering down into the valley. 'Can't see anything.'

I slowed, headlights coming towards us, the Derbyshire detectives slowing to allow us into the courtyard first. I pulled in, the second car stopping at the gate so that no one could squeeze their way out onto the road.

'Let's go,' muttered Gabriel.

Out into the bitter cold wind, still winter up here, spring only a distant thought. A misting wind swept its way across the field, soaking my face, and I pulled my asp out, racking it. Could sense Gabriel as he slipped into step beside me, his fists clenching, unclenching. Hurried towards the small cottage. There were no lights on, no suggestion of life inside. I gestured to the Derbyshire pair, calling them towards us, hand on the doorknob, a twist, and it gave beneath my fingers, the wooden door swinging open onto a darkened entryway. I stepped in, allowing Gabriel, the other detectives, to move past me, clearing a bathroom, a bedroom beyond that. Gabriel shook his head at me, gestured through the door to my left.

I eased it open.

Beyond lay a rectangle of a room, a clutch of sofas huddled around a wood-burning stove, ashy remnants still hanging in the air, a kitchen at its rear. I peered into

398

the darkness, my eyes adjusting slowly, features forming where there had only been shadow. Gabriel touched my elbow, pointing up a narrow, open-slat staircase.

A feeling settled into my stomach, of a move made too late, and I stepped carefully onto the wooden tread, keeping my weight close to the wall, and moved gingerly towards the top, path blocked by a wooden door. I hesitated, looked back at Gabriel, his face tense.

I confess that I thought only of the children then, of those that Erin had left behind. A fear had settled over me, the thought that running with children was so much harder than running without. And that surely, for a man like Wolf, at a certain point all connections become severable?

I gripped the handle, pulled in a breath and pushed the door open onto the darkened room.

It took moments for things to clear, for shapes to emerge from the darkness.

There a wardrobe.

There a desk.

There a bed.

And on the bed, a shape.

My breath caught in my throat, and I eased my way into the room, the floor creaking and groaning with the weight of me. Torchlight from behind, Gabriel shining the beam onto the sheet-covered mass. I reached for it, part of me not wanting to, afraid of what I would see. My fingers curled themselves round the sheet edge, carefully raising it up.

I didn't recognise Naomi. Not at first. Her hair tugged

back into a sleep-strewn knot, her face white-pale. And all breath escaped me, the thoughts cascading over me, that we were too late, that my move had been delivered once the game was already won.

Then something ... a change in the air, a movement small enough to be almost imperceptible.

'She's alive,' Gabriel breathed, voice rich with relief.

I dropped my asp then, reaching for the shoulders of Naomi Flood, turning her towards me, her body limp, heavy, yet the breath undeniable. 'Get an ambulance here!' I shouted it, voice deafening in the darkened room. 'She's been drugged. Naomi. Naomi?' Was I shaking her? I like to think not, but the truth of it is that seems all but inevitable. 'Where is he, Naomi? Where's Christian?' I felt my voice break. 'Where are the children?'

Epilogue – Seven Months Later

Alice Parr stood at the window, looking out over the never-ending whiteness of the rolling hills. The snow had stopped now, a brief intermission, the sky still weighted heavy with clouds, air thick with the inevitability of what was to come. A tumbling fire crackled in the stone-built heart, and Alice thought of a time where that had meant something different to her, where the whisper of flame had worked its way into every nightmare, the sound threatening to pull apart all that she had ever been.

'Holy hell, it's cold,' muttered Gabriel.

Alice pulled her gaze from the expanse of snow and grinned. 'Welcome to Wisconsin.'

Her throat felt roughened, weary from talking so much, her mind wearier still. But then, thought Alice, it was important that the girl knew the story. That she understood just what she was going to face.

A whistle of a kettle, a clatter and the bubbling of water into a pot, and Alice twisted to look at the young woman in the kitchen beyond them. She was younger than she looked, with her tumbled-down dark curls, her bright blue eyes. Alice watched as she arranged biscuits on a plate, long fingers carefully placing each individual one into the shape of a clock.

And Alice thought of Wolf and wondered if he had any idea at all of just where she stood now.

Rosa Fisher hefted the tray in her narrow arms and carried it carefully into the living room, stepping round the German shepherd that lay in the doorway, his nose buried beneath paws, eyes fixed on the visitors. 'Sorry,' she said. 'I'm rubbish at tea.' She waved them towards the sofas. 'Please,' she said, 'do sit down.'

Alice sank into one corner of it, and thought of Naomi. She had not seen her in a while. It had been, what? Six months now? Perhaps a little more. And then Naomi had been but a pale reflection of the woman she had once been.

How could I have fallen for it? How could I have been so taken in?

Little comfort that she had not been the first, that she was unlikely to be the last. Alice watched Rosa as she carefully set the tray down on the oak coffee table, and wondered if Naomi would recognise her, if she were here now. Would she see the lines of her nose, the depth of her eyes and find herself pulled backwards in time?

And Alice thought of that bedroom in that cottage in the Derbyshire wilds, of Naomi breaking the surface of sleep, slowly at first and then urgently, like a swimmer whose oxygen has run out. The realisation sweeping across her like a wave, of all she had lost and all that had never been. Naomi had looked up at Alice, her eyes wide and so like Erin's that Alice had thought her heart would break. I'm never going to see the children again, am I? And then she had cried, wrenching tears that had come from the core of her.

She had told her story through the tears, the words made dense by the weight of what she now knew. That she had suspected nothing. I thought that he loved me. That the children had become her own. At least until they were gone. And she talked of the tipping point, the day when it all changed. Of a park in North London and a whipping breeze, and a woman in a dark brown coat, with heavy glasses, her ebony hair cut into a severe bob, watching her children play with a look on her face that Naomi had not been able to identify. She could not remember how the conversation had begun, just that it had, and that the woman had struggled to keep her gaze on Naomi herself and away from the children who shrieked and whooped.

There had been an ice-cream van. The woman had laughed and said that ice cream always tasted better in the cold, and please, could she buy one for the children? Only Alfie, or Levi as he once was, he was lactose intolerant, so she had handed him instead a lollipop, with all the seriousness of one laying a crown upon the head of a monarch. Molly had accepted her cup of ice cream with its pink plastic spoon, had studied the woman, her four-year-old forehead creased up into a frown as if she was trying to recollect something that had happened long ago. But she was four and ice cream was, after all, ice cream, and she had soon eaten and forgotten what had preoccupied her so.

And when they had finished, the woman had collected the cup and the spoon, saying that she would take them home to recycle because, after all, wasn't the planet for our children. And she had looked at Molly and Alfie with an intensity that had stirred something primal in Naomi, finally shifting her into unease.

Yet it had seemed that that would be that. They had returned home and gone about their lives as this ordinary family of four, and it seemed that the incident in the park would remain locked in time, a discrete event without the fingers to stretch out and spill over into the moments that followed.

Then Naomi had told her husband.

She had said it with laughter in her voice, had joked of the children enjoying a free meal ticket, but the laughter had stilled when she had caught sight of his face, of the there-and-then-gone-again rictus of terror. Of course she had questioned – she was a reporter, after all, was built to question – but Chris, he had waved her away. He was tired. It had been a long day.

Had she noticed the change that followed? Perhaps, she had said. But only in a slight detachment in her husband, the faintest air of preoccupation. How could I ever imagine what he was really doing? she had asked. How could I have begun to suspect?

Alice watched Rosa as she lifted the round-bellied teapot, aiming a stream of dark liquid into a thin china cup.

'It's going to be okay, you know,' Alice said, softly. 'We're going to do all we can to help you.'

Rosa nodded slowly, not looking at her, but keeping

her gaze on the cup, on the flow of tea into it. 'I'm glad you're here. I thought … I thought I was going crazy. But now, with you here …'

'We're going to find him,' Alice said softly.

It had taken a matter of hours, after entering the farmhouse, after finding Naomi Flood, drugged and unaware, to trace the route of Wolf and his children. The rental car was found on ANPR, heading north. Another sixteen hours before it was finally located, in a residential street in Newcastle. And by that point the Wolf trail had grown cold. He could have gotten on a flight, or a ferry. Or he could have remained, holed up in some unknown quarter of that city. Although, for what it was worth, Alice's money was on flight. It was, after all, what he did best.

And so he was gone, vanished like the ghost that Alice had for so long suspected he was. Easy then, to let the case grow cold. To step away, move back into life that suddenly seemed potent with possibility.

But it seemed that, even for Wolf, this game was not one to be relinquished with ease. For in the back seat, carefully positioned in the gully between two children's car seats, there had been an envelope, large and tan, and inside had been the history of Erin's pursuit. The opening pages of the complaint letter from Adrienne Lee, all dense with tape in memory of its near destruction, the patient file and billing notice of Frederick Lee, and of many others besides, identification in the name of Ed Canning.

And scrawled across it in thick marker pen, a note – SEE YOU SOON, ALICE.

It seemed that in spite of everything, Wolf was not quite done with her yet. And yet all that would have amounted for nothing, to Alice, had it not been for one thing. That the information contained within the envelope, none of it had referenced the name of Jackson Wolf. That Erin had saved that nugget for Alice's ears only, a secret just for two.

He doesn't know we know, Alice had said.

And so Alice could not give up. In spite of all evidence to the contrary, it seemed that such was beyond her capacity as a person. Gabriel had shaken his head when she had told him that. Perhaps that was why Wolf was so fascinated by you. Because you are the only person who can stop him.

And Alice had thought of Naomi, of her tear-stained face, her eyes searching Alice's own, as if there she would find answers. You know he was asking me about you? Naomi had said. He was fascinated by your story, the fire, all that. He even got me to dig out that article I wrote about you. Said he'd never seen anything quite like it before. She'd shaken her head, large tears plopping onto her lap. I'm sorry, Alice. If I had only known ...

Alice leaned forward in the chair, her gaze fixed on Rosa. The younger woman looked up, startled by the sudden scrutiny, her hands playing with the knitted edge of her jumper.

'Rosa,' said Alice, 'I need to ask you, just what are you hoping to get from this?'

Rosa pulled in a deep breath, her hands folding into one another in a conscious stilling. 'I want ... I want to know what happened to me. I need to understand, I don't know, why it all changed, I guess. How we could go from what we were to ... that.' She reached forward, picking up the slip of newspaper, its edges wrinkled and furled with time, but the colours still standing true. Of red and of orange, a once-was barn, now an inferno.

The headline standing proud above it – 'Family Found Dead In Barn Fire.'

She smoothed at the edges of the paper. 'I want to know why. And, I guess, in spite of everything, I just want to find him. Ed Canning. Jacob Owens. Jackson Wolf. Whoever he is. I want to find my brother.'

Acknowledgements

It is a great privilege to write a book. But perhaps the greatest privilege of all comes at this point, when I have the opportunity to thank all those people who have made this incredible career of mine a possibility. *To Catch A Killer* is my first experience with writing a trilogy and venturing into this has been a wild ride of untrodden ground, of dipping confidence and of the limitless joy of telling a story on such a wide canvas.

Firstly, to my wonderful agent, Camilla Wray, to whom this book is dedicated. An agent is a cheerleader and a defender, but I am incredibly thankful to be able to say that mine is also my friend. In my moments of greatest doubt, it is your voice that I hear telling me not only that I can, but that I must. To the indomitable Sheila David, my television and film agent and one of the awesomest people I know. Combined, you both make this work of mine an absolute joy. And to everyone at the exceptional Darley Anderson Literary Agency. Thank you for all that you do for us.

To my editor, Fran Pathak, who has always just gotten me, even at times when I was struggling to get myself! Thank you for supporting me, for making me feel a part of a team, for making my book the best it can possibly be. I genuinely could not do this without you.

To the wonderful team at Orion. Joining you has felt like joining a family. Passionate, creative and insightful – you are all incredible!

To my author friends – by rights this should be a lonely job, yet I am surrounded by such a supportive, loving and often bonkers community of fellow writers. Thank you for being there for me when I need you, for making me laugh, for plying me with booze, and for all your general fabulousness. And to my other friends, the ones whose worlds do not revolve around the pages of a book, thank you for all the times you have rescued me from inside my own head.

To my dear family on both sides of the Atlantic, thank you so much for your constant support.

To my beautiful boys, Daniel and Joseph. I promise that one day I'll write that children's book for you.

And finally, to Matthew, my husband, first reader and favourite person. Your unswerving support is what makes this life of mine possible. Thank you for being my safe place to fall.